CANAAN FOUND

A NOVEL

O. MICHAEL DUTY

HIGH BRIDGE BOOKS
HOUSTON

We cannot attain the presence of God.
We're already totally in the presence of God.
What's missing is awareness.

—David Brenner

ONE

Rogers, Arkansas
Casper's Grill
Saturday, November 14, 2015
8:15 a.m.

Lonnie Rex Stanhope sat with his back to the wall in the corner of the back room at Casper's Grill. The back room was a regular hangout for Lonnie Rex because the management still allowed smoking. There weren't very many places that still allowed it, so he thought he would enjoy it while it lasted. Lonnie was always up early and made Casper's his first stop of the day. This morning was no exception. On any given morning, there was a group of "regulars" that frequented the grill for early morning coffee and lively banter with friends and "peculiars" spread about the main dining room. Questions or opinions would be spoken aloud and across the room to willing listeners. The subject matter was usually politics, local news, polite ribbing, or the weather. A visit to Casper's would keep anyone up to date on the goings-on in Rogers.

Lonnie Rex was from a long line of Stanhopes. They had called Rogers home since even before its founding in 1881 and subsequent naming after C.W. Rogers, a local railway officer. Lonnie's parents had passed on several years ago, leaving him with a stately home close to downtown. He was a very productive artist and well-known in the region. Marriage had been tried by Lonnie Rex, twice actually, but he had not found it to his liking.

8:15 was late for Lonnie Rex. He liked to start his morning at 5:30 a.m., but Casper's did not open until 6:00 a.m. Some time ago, he had prevailed on the owner to allow him a key so that he could arrive before opening time and make the coffee. He never turned on the neon sign over the door before the regular opening time, not wanting to encourage others to take such advantage and in so doing, interrupt his early morning solitude. When the staff did arrive, he surrendered to the start of the day and the steady inflow of the other regulars. Such was the opportunity afforded in a small town. By 8:15 on this particular morning, Lonnie Rex had consumed several cups of coffee along with his standard sausage and eggs along with biscuits and gravy, all topped off with a few cigarettes. Over two hours had gone by, during which he had enjoyed his breakfast, looked over the paper without really reading it, visited with some of the regulars, and played minor havoc with the men's room. He was ready for the day.

But this day was different. The routine was the same, but Lonnie Rex was to be joined by several others at 8:30 a.m. They wanted a morning meeting, and he had convinced most of the attendees that it should be held at Casper's Grill. It wasn't an easy sell, but there were more men than women on the committee, so Casper's it was. He thought that it was appropriate to meet at this little grill, which had maintained a regular presence in Rogers for decades. The official name of the committee was the "Rogers High School Class of 1976 40th Reunion Committee." Some form of this group had met every ten years. The players sometimes changed, but there were always those willing to serve. This year was the first time that Lonnie Rex had agreed to be on the committee.

Peter Mason was the first to arrive. He ran the local newspaper and would be valuable for his agreeing to advertise the reunion in the paper. Peter was glib and could talk it up in engaging ways. The news business had been his forte since college, having worked at his father's paper since graduation and then taken over ownership when the elder Mason had retired.

Misty Belle Masters followed Peter closely. She was the ever-so-organized chairperson of the committee. She had served three times before and saw herself as the "queen bee and keeper of the flame" when it came to reunions. No one criticized her handling of the position since they didn't want to do it themselves. Misty had been very popular in high school and was certainly aware of it. She had stayed in Rogers and married a local mortician. Her reputation as an organization freak served her well in any capacity. It was said that Misty had a file on most of the elderly people in town. Some would call it marketing.

Misty Belle claimed the head of the small table and greeted the others as she spread out her papers. She quickly asked, "Why on earth are we meeting here?"

Lonnie Rex considered her question and responded. "Well, first of all, we voted on it, but the best reason is that this place cooks using all the three main food groups; salt, sugar, and grease."

"Ugh, that's what I mean. Well, I won't be eating," she replied, then quickly summoned the waitress and asked for a chai tea.

"Sorry; we have regular coffee, decaf, regular tea, juice, and of course, sodas," the waitress informed Misty Belle.

"Well then, regular tea and a little milk will do."

"You should try the biscuits and gravy," Lonnie Rex added. "They'll stick to your ribs, and I could let you have a Marlboro to top it off. It don't get no better than that!"

"Oh stop! You'll be dead before the reunion," Misty Belle quipped.

"Well, if that happens, you'll be the first to know being as how your husband is the local undertaker. Maybe I should put him on a retainer!"

"He's not an 'undertaker.' He is a certified mortician and funeral director. He's very successful, you know."

"Calm yourself, Misty. I've known the 'formaldehyde king' for years."

"You're impossible, Lonnie Rex," said Misty Belle. "But the retainer might be a good idea," she mused.

Their banter was interrupted when the bell at the front door jingled and admitted Gina Houseman with Bobby Lane Driscoll following close behind. Gina was the ever-bubbly and outgoing former party girl. She now was a member of the school board and devoted to the sex education of Rogers' youth. Some felt that she was completely qualified but nevertheless needed to be held in check. Her presence was always appreciated because of her beauty, effervescence, and good humor. None of these attributes were lost on Bobby Lane. He and Gina had been an "item" on and off again over the years.

Bobby Lane had been a star football player in high school and had gone on to play division one ball in college, but his career had been cut short after he suffered a back injury. For some time after his football career ended, his life was a bit uneven and sprinkled with drug use. A brief stay in rehab had led to him settling down and focusing on an undiscovered entrepreneurial bent. That attribute had inspired him to open a local bar known as the Big-Wigs Lounge. It was a popular and rather "up-scale" stop on the evening circuit for those disposed in that direction. Rogers had been a dry community until a few years ago, but now the town rather celebrated the newfound freedom. Bobby enjoyed his role as respected native son and "success story." He and Gina were good friends who shared a healthy respect for their "fast lane" pasts.

"The party can now begin," quipped Gina with a glance at Misty Belle.

"Coffee, I need coffee," Bobby added. "It's too early to do this, but I agreed, so here I am. Gina, allow me," he said as he pulled out her chair.

"Thanks, and get me a coffee too, okay? Hi Lonnie, Peter, and Misty, how're you all doing?" Gina continued without waiting for a response. "This will be such fun. I'm looking forward to seeing so many friends from our class. Thanks for asking me to serve on the committee. It's my first time, and I will help however I can."

"We're sure you will be a great help, Gina. It's Lonnie Rex's first time too," Misty allowed. "It's always good to get new members on the committee and increase everyone's involvement."

"Lonnie Rex's first time too? Great! Gosh, I haven't seen much of you, Lonnie. What have you been doing?" asked Gina.

"Oh, living large and painting most days."

"I see some of your paintings at the Big-Wigs. You know, you are very good!"

"Thanks, Gina. It's a living."

Bobby returned with coffees for himself and Gina.

Misty got down to business. "Now let's try to get started. The purpose of this meeting is to get organized and make a few decisions and some assignments. We can bring in more help if needed, but we've done this quite successfully before.

"The 40th reunion of the class of 1976 will be held from June 2 through June 4 of next year. As you all know, there has been a regular schedule that we have followed in the past for the reunion activities. It can be changed, of course, but it has become a bit of a staple and has always been met with general approval. We've always enjoyed a good turnout—I guess we just have a good class, and we certainly do not want to disappoint. I have prepared an outline of past activities and schedule, possible new items, and some preliminary assignments for the committee," Misty explained.

"Can we have a cocktail party at the Big-Wigs?" Bobby asked. "This is the first time that the lounge has been open during a reunion, and it would be great to have something there."

"That would be great! The Big-Wigs is a pretty nice place; it's popular, and surely everyone would enjoy it," Gina offered.

"Okay by me," said Lonnie Rex, "I'll probably be there anyway."

Peter Mason spoke up. "You know many of our class members don't drink and might not feel too good about that. I mean, I'm fine with it in some form, but we should consider it carefully. Of course, I can see why Lonnie Rex would approve since he has a lot of his art on sale there."

"Which I think is great," Peter quickly added.

"That art is a bit of a draw. Everyone seems to like it, and we sell a few pieces for Lonnie Rex. It's really sort of classy. I love having it," offered Bobby. "It makes it more than just a bar; sort of a gathering place and social hang out. We definitely should hold something there."

"Let me give you the handouts I have prepared, and you will see I have indicated a proposed schedule. Then we can discuss venues and consider the Big-Wigs or anything else. Is that alright?" asked Misty Belle.

Misty was interrupted by the waitress bringing drinks and taking orders for food. While some ordered, they all looked over the proposed schedule.

"The most time consuming and important thing is to update the class roll and addresses for everyone. Our class had 194 graduates. We have always had a good turnout, in the order of 120 or so. We have a good list of people's addresses and statuses, but it must be updated. I have tried to keep things up to date, so hopefully it won't be too hard. There is the list of known attendees from last time, and the addresses can be confirmed. You will see two other lists. One is a listing of those who are deceased, and the other one is those who have never attended. For those who have never shown up, we should keep trying, but they probably won't start coming now. And those addresses might be the most difficult."

"I think this is a good schedule of events," Gina inserted. "The grand old 'Ozark Hotel' is always great. It is historical and has memories for about everyone."

"I bet it has some for you, huh?" asked Bobby, teasingly.

Gina replied, "You bet it does, and you were no stranger either. We had dance parties, one prom, and lots of other things. And, it has served well for each reunion. People probably expect it. I say let's do it."

"In addition, the hotel can serve as the central accommodation for those from out of town. I am sure that we can get a rate. We've done it before. They will also set us up for registration and general information," said Misty.

There followed a general murmur of consent.

"How about the picnic down at the lake at the group shelter? All okay with that?" asked Misty.

"That place is getting awfully crowded. Rogers has grown so much. Frequently the group shelter is in use on nice days," said Peter. "We would have to reserve it early and get set up."

"How about a Thursday night bonfire down there? And we could set up the shelter for the Friday picnic. Can you have fires?" asked Gina.

"Sure, you can. We did it once over by that big shelter, which is the place that we want anyway. We could have the bonfire and then free time afterward. On Friday following the picnic, we could have a mixer at the Big-Wigs—something for everyone that night," persisted Bobby.

"Yeah, both or either or," added Gina. "And music on Thursday night could be good. What do you think, Lonnie Rex?"

"Listen darlin', whatever suits you tickles me to death," Lonnie responded. "But remember, they won't allow any drinking at the lake, so if that is to occur, it would have to be at Big-Wigs or people's homes. There'll be some gatherings at private homes anyway. My house will probably be open. It was the last time."

Regaining control, Misty summarized, "This must be budgeted. We don't want the cost to get out of hand. Lots of people are tight, and we don't want to make it hard. That could be an issue with the music, especially if it is live, so we'll have to see. I can secure the hotel. Peter, would you investigate reserving the space at the park including the shelter, and Gina, could you research music for the bonfire night as well as the dinner and dance on Saturday?"

"Sure. It'll be fun. I think I know some guys that will play at the bonfire for very little money, and there are a couple of bands that would be good for Saturday," said Gina.

"Bobby, maybe the Big-Wigs is okay," said Misty. "Lay out a plan for review. You know how many you can hold, any specials you might want to have, maybe some non-alcoholic options, snacks, etcetera. We can publicize it with the packet. You can even mention Lonnie Rex's art and anything else you think of. But you must do it at your cost. Besides, you will make a good profit. Give the plan to me and we will confirm."

"What do you want me to do?" asked Lonnie Rex.

"It would be great if you would take on the list of those who have never attended and see what you can find out. I've already checked, and I don't have anything on any of them. Can you do that? One of your past wives may be able to help," needled Misty Belle.

"Which one, Jaws One or Jaws Two?" asked Lonnie.

"Oh, for God's sake, I don't know. Just do it, okay?"

"Sure. I think Jaws One would be the handiest," Lonnie Rex muttered. "Jaws Two can be a little unfocused!"

"Whatever you think," Misty said dismissively. "Now, we should get notices and advertisements out by next March. We can mail invitations and run ads in the paper. As you may know, there is a site on the internet for posting information. That will be very helpful, but we're not sure how many will make use of it. Any other ideas for marketing that you think of, we can use. Some will require calling for the best results. Maybe a calling team when we get close. For now, we will concentrate on the lists. After the holidays, we should get back together. I'll call and set up a meeting, but not here! Okay?"

"Yeah, but hasn't it been great while it lasted?" Lonnie Rex quipped.

TWO

Later that afternoon, Lonnie Rex sat on the front porch of his home on West Maple Street. The porch faced east and was the heavenly sweet spot of the stately old house. Good for morning coffee and protected from the west sun, the porch was a popular site for languid visits between Lonnie Rex and local friends. It was a welcome, "come any time" destination. If Lonnie was painting or napping, he would gladly interrupt his activities and amble to the porch for a "cig" and a visit. The large alabaster structure dated back over 50 years and had long been in his family. It afforded a substantial studio on the north side of the house with multiple windows overlooking the street, which also provided a steady light. Both of Lonnie's wives had enjoyed the charms and allure of the picturesque home for as long as they lasted.

There were no visitors yet today. Lonnie Rex pondered the list he held in his hand while rocking in one of the massive white rockers. The list held the names of the people who had never attended a reunion. Most were obscure to him. Only a few conjured up a recognition of a face or any other memories. Of those few he remembered, he was aware that he had no way of knowing where they were or of contacting them. There was one exception, however, who he knew very well, perhaps better than anyone from the class. Caleb Atwood was on the top of the list, having never attended. Lonnie Rex knew that to be true because Caleb was perhaps his best friend in life.

Lonnie Rex and Caleb had been close friends in high school, had dated some of the same girls, and had enjoyed each other's company in a host of activities. Taylor Atwood was Caleb's dad and was a moderately well-known country singer, at least locally. Taylor had a few recordings that had done well, and he was successful enough that it had been the family's primary source of income. Connie Atwood, Caleb's mom, was very close to Taylor and traveled with him on gigs or tours. Caleb's sister, Sarah, was a lot older and had married back when Caleb was in grade school. So, Caleb was alone much of the time, which suited him fine by all appearances, and certainly allowed a lot of freedom for any activities in which he and Lonnie Rex chose to indulge.

After high school, he and Caleb were separated by distance. Caleb went to the university in Fayetteville, and Lonnie Rex had left to study art on the west coast. Their paths would not cross again until years later.

Caleb had gone to law school at the University of Arkansas right after high school. His thoughts about being an attorney had lasted a little over two years until he lost interest in the law. Part of his lack of interest, Lonnie Rex knew, was based on Caleb's distrust of the obvious focus of the law. In Caleb's opinion, the study of law seemed to replace a sense of what was "right" with a sense of what was "legal." Lonnie Rex found substantial evidence in his own experience which supported that position. There was, however, another reason why Caleb had left college. His mother died while he was in the second year of law school, and Caleb's dad had simply come apart. When Caleb left school, he helped his dad through the loss, and soon thereafter his dad moved out west. Caleb went west with him, and no one saw him much anymore, except for his sister Sarah, who still lived in Rogers.

Lonnie Rex and Caleb began their friendship anew when Caleb had come back on one of his visits to see Sarah. Caleb and Lonnie had reunited, here on this very porch. Since then, they shared many adventures together. When Caleb came back to visit, they spent their time catching up, hashing out solutions to real and imagined problems, and comparing notes on all their friends in common. At those times, Lonnie Rex had learned about Caleb's love of horses and cowboying.

The other occasions in which they had been together had been when Lonnie Rex had traveled out to New Mexico and Colorado. Those times were spent together exploring the wilderness, fly fishing, and going on some extended trail rides. The wilderness and ranching were Caleb's life, which he was always anxious to share. Their renewed friendship had endured for the past thirty or more years, but Caleb had never attended a reunion.

Caleb had never married, and Lonnie Rex had neglected two wives, so women never got in the way of their adventures. Lonnie had last seen Caleb about three years ago on a road trip to Utah with a stop in Colorado to visit him at the ranch where he lived and worked. Since then, they had spoken regularly on the telephone. They shared an abiding love of many things, one of which was an unshakeable faith in the Lord.

Lonnie Rex knew that Caleb had recently inherited some property outside of Rogers. They had spoken of it briefly, and Caleb said that he would return to check it out before too long. That had been over a year ago, however, and they had not spoken about it since. It occurred to him that it might be possible to get Caleb back for a trip during the reunion since he needed to come anyway. Caleb had never shown much interest in prior reunions, but he had not spoken ill of them either. It just never seemed to work out for him. Lonnie Rex thought he would call Caleb and see what he thought about making the trip.

As Lonnie Rex pondered his past with Caleb, Bobby Driscoll pulled up to the curb in front. As he stepped up to the porch, Lonnie Rex greeted him with his old high school nickname.

"Stash, what's happening?"

"Going down to the bar to open up. Been busy lately," Bobby said as he flopped into the next chair. "I wanted to remind you that we could use some more art at the Big-Wigs. As you know, we have sold a couple of pieces, and with the plans for the reunion, I wanted to remind you to find some more. Plenty of time, so give it some thought."

"Sure, no problem. I've got several pieces that might do, and I will finish another one soon. That was good that they decided to have something at the bar. Could be fun."

"It will be great. Might keep out the church crowd, but that's to be expected."

"Careful now. There's nothing sinful with a little adult refreshment in the company of good friends," Lonnie retorted. "I'm a sinner and a believer. Don't reckon on any contradiction."

"Tell that to the church goers," Bobby allowed.

"I don't plan on telling anyone anything. Just speaking the truth."

"You got any coffee?"

"Yeah, it's on the kitchen counter. Help yourself."

Bobby returned to the porch with a fresh mug and told Lonnie, "I've been looking over the list; trying to see if there are any more dead people, and you know what?" asked Bobby. "I found out that Ricky Balen died several years ago. Remember him?"

"Sure. What happened?"

"Well, you know he was always a bit of a daredevil, always doing some weird stuff. Anyway, he was bungee jumping out west at some gorge. He had done it before and was very experienced. He got suited up with his harness and all, and climbed up on the platform, spread his arms, and did a perfect dive off into the canyon below. Trouble is, he forgot to attach the bungee cord to his leg brace and just kept on plummeting until he hit the rocks in the river."

"You're kidding!"

"Nope. Can you imagine? Probably didn't even realize it on the way down. Must have been one hell of a surprise!"

"Maybe it was suicide."

"Who knows, but it happened. I found out from his uncle who's a regular in the bar. I asked him about it when I was reviewing the list, and he was surprised that I didn't know. It's just a stunner, you know?"

There was a shared silence while each remembered Ricky.

"What you been up to?" Bobby asked, breaking the spell.

Lonnie thought for a minute then said, "You remember Caleb Atwood?"

"Yeah, haven't seen him in many years. I think it was at least 30 years ago. We were never close friends, but I remember him as a good guy. Aren't you good friends with him? What's his story?"

"I've known Caleb since high school, and we have done a lot together over the years. He has never come to a reunion, but I think I'll contact him and get him to come," said Lonnie.

"You know, he used to date Lori Beth Hightower. They were tight until senior year when she moved away. I used to admire her but never asked her out because they were together and seemed tight. She did come to the second reunion I think, without her husband. I think his last name was… Martin or something. Yeah, I think she is listed as Lori Martin."

"I remember. Caleb mentioned her a few times. Never said much. Reckon he got over her, but he never had anyone else or got married," said Lonnie Rex. "He can be kind of a loner. Loves the ranch, working cows, and everything about the wilderness. He's done a lot of guiding on elk hunts and extended camping trips. Taken me on some good trips over the years."

"Well, get him out here. Be good to see him. And don't forget that art. I gotta' scoot, and thanks for the cup," Bobby said as he rose to go.

"See ya, Stash. Come back by after the holidays. I'll round up some pieces."

Bobby headed down to his truck.

Lonnie finished his cigarette and thought about Caleb. He thought that he would call him soon, maybe dangle Lori as bait. No, that wouldn't be right, he thought. Besides, he didn't know if she was even coming.

THREE

Church Rock Ranch
North of La Veta, Colorado
Tuesday, April 5, 2016
11:30 a.m.

The grasslands were bathed in bright sun light, angling down just in front of dark clouds assembling in the east. Normally you could hear the prairie grasses swaying in the breeze from the approaching storm, but this morning all that could be heard was the bellowing of the calves as they were herded into the corral and the slamming of their bodies against the metal rails. Spring was still a little way off in the high country, but this morning held a promise for wildflowers to come. Normally a storm would build in the southwest and come down from the mountains, but this morning God had a different notion. Storms out of the east didn't carry as much water as those from over the mountains might, but they could still scatter showers over a broad section of the prairie.

Outside the corral, cowboys gathered up the herd and urged their horses into the melee of cattle to drive more of them into the corral. Once in, a cow could expect to be roped, headed, and healed, if need be, until it was subdued on the ground over by the branding fire. When brought down, the calf would be held by one cowboy at the horns as another one grabbed the rear legs while placing his boot into its flank to await the sizzle of hot iron on skin. The smoke from burning flesh surrounded the entire operation. The ears got tagged, and another cowboy inoculated the calf. The final injustice occurred when the calf was cut, and the bounty of his testicles were tossed into the sizzling grease in the handmade "cowboy wok." The wok was made by cutting the bottom off a large propane tank and welding horseshoe handles to the edges. Four feet in diameter and full of hot grease, and the cooking could begin. Hot dusty work with fresh mountain oysters as a reward! All the cowboys would grab some oysters fresh from the pan and continue work with grease dripping from their chins. This would be the only lunch that they would get today. Once the calf had endured all the unpleasantries and surrendered all he had to give, he was painted with disinfectant and released on wobbly legs to join his compadres.

Caleb Atwood was mounted on his horse, Cisco Bay, and circulated around the entire operation. Caleb was tall and muscular. He wore leather "chinks" in lieu of the more common chaps (pronounced "shaps"). A wool vest and a dusty "wild rag" adorned his upper body with a well-soiled silver belly hat atop his head of greying brown hair. As he worked Cisco back and forth in front of the nervous herd, you could hear the jingle of his spurs as they slapped against the stirrup skirt. Occasionally he would wave his coiled rope and push more cattle into the group while keeping his eye out for any "escapees." He oversaw all he witnessed and paid close attention to its progress. It was imperative to finish branding and cutting this lot before the storm arrived. They needed to finish in time to stow all the equipment in the corral shed and leave time for the six-mile ride back to headquarters. Caleb thought they could make it, and if they didn't, then a little wet never hurt anyone.

Clem Pierce was in the big corral managing the roping operation. It didn't need much management because most of the cowboys knew exactly what they were doing. But if any did need encouragement, Clem was the man to do it. Two roping teams were working the calves into the branding area as quickly as the branding and cutting teams could turn them out. At this rate, Caleb hoped to be finished within the next two hours. As the work proceeded, distant thunder could be heard in the east. This storm might be more than scattered showers, and that fact registered on all the cowboys as they picked up the pace.

When the final group of cattle was pushed into the corral, Caleb called for those cowboys that had been doing the pushing to begin breaking down some of the equipment and to prepare to complete the work. As the branding was finished, the propane stove along with the "cowboy wok" had to be cooled, sanded, and stored in the back of the ranch truck.

The operation was completed in advance of Caleb's expectation, and the equipment that was to remain at the corral was moved into the storage shed. The cattle milled about outside the corral and slowly began to move off to the west. They also sensed the approach of the storm. Once everything was cleaned up and stowed, all the hands got back in the saddle to begin the move back to headquarters. Two of the hands unsaddled their horses and let them trail with the cowboys riding back. This allowed them to bring the truck with all the gear to headquarters.

When Caleb was satisfied that everything was in order, he signaled it was time to move out, and a steady pace of cowhands headed south in a "high lope" toward the sanctuary of home. The wind increased from the east as the grasses and trees waved in submission to the oncoming storm. The smell of the approaching rain assaulted the nostrils of cowboys and horses alike. After covering about half the distance to the headquarters, it became clear that they were going to arrive with the storm as their companion. Slickers were broken out from saddle ties without breaking stride. Gates were opened by the front riders without dismounting, and the entire group passed through as one remained to close each gate.

When the rain finally hit, it came in a steady downpour, settling the dust while pounding the backs of the rider's slickers. The rain battered the hats and ran off the back brims onto the slickers and the saddle skirts. Some chattered with delight, for such was the welcome of a good soaking of the prairie. All was right with the world as the progression of cowboys was swallowed by the deluge that was upon them, and the cooling winds dissipated the warmth of the day. Those two who drove the truck had avoided the storm and missed out on a good spring soaking.

The entourage arrived at headquarters and collected under the roof connecting the hay shed and the tack room. As the rain turned the corrals to mud, the cowboys unsaddled their horses and stored their tack before turning their mounts into the corral. Brushing the horses would come later after the storm had completed its cleansing task.

Caleb was the last to move under the protection of the roof. He allowed some of the horses to be cleared out and then led Cisco Bay over to Clem, who was unsaddling his own horse.

With water dripping off his hat, Caleb said to Clem, "Let's gather at the barn after everything is stowed, and we can go over tomorrow's work. No sense in fighting this storm and mud. Let her pass by while we kick back."

"Will do, but I have a few repairs to complete in the tack room. Be right there."

"Sounds good," Caleb allowed, and raising his voice to be heard over the storm: "Okay boys, clean it all up, get it stowed, and we'll break off until supper. Gather up in the barn to go over tomorrow's doin's before you settle. Good job today."

After the brief meeting in the barn, all the hands ambled toward the bunk house porch. Caleb took his gear to a small cabin, which was separate from the bunk house. The cabin had been part of headquarters for a half-century. He had lived alone in the little house with its broad porch for many of the years he had worked on the ranch. It was his because of his seniority and the faith the ranch owner placed in Caleb. Without any clear title to denote his status, it was nevertheless clear to everyone that Caleb was the "top hand" and "cow boss" without question. Most of the cowboys could not remember a time when Caleb was not the man in charge.

The cabin had only two rooms, if you didn't count the bathroom. There was one large log room containing comfortable furniture in front of a large stone fireplace and a sturdy four-place wooden slab table, plus the L-shaped kitchen with a central worktable. The kitchen featured a large wood-burning cook stove against the log wall. The bedroom was more of an alcove off the living area rather than a real room, but it was sufficient to hold a double bed with assorted furniture. Even though the kitchen was well equipped, Caleb took most of his meals with the other hands when they gathered around the table set in the headquarters dining room. That was the domain of Leena Dawson, the tyrannical mistress of the ranch kitchen. Her cooking, if not her manner, was legendary for its quality and quantity. No one went hungry on this ranch.

As Caleb stepped into the cabin and shed his hat and vest, he noticed that a letter had been placed on the dining table. Caleb did not get mail with any regularity, so he quickly noted its presence and opened it out of curiosity. Inside there was an invitation to the Rogers High School reunion. The invitation announced that the 40th reunion of the class of 1976 was to be held in Rogers from June 2 through June 4 of this very summer. That was a little less than two months out. Lonnie Rex had called a couple of weeks ago and told him about the reunion, so it wasn't a surprise. He told Lonnie that he might consider coming this time since he had some other business anyway and since he hadn't seen his sister in a while.

Caleb had never attended any of the reunions. He understood from his friend Lonnie Rex that they had always been nice affairs. He had no lack of interest in the reunions; it just seemed that he never could attend in the past because of other things he was involved in. In fact, he was even unreachable for the first one because that was the time he was living in the wilderness. The other times were just not convenient, since early summer is such a busy time of year on the ranch. This was still true, but as he had told Lonnie, maybe he would come this time. He stopped and thought some more. It was still a busy season, but recent events were causing him to think about a trip to Rogers anyway. Maybe he could do both. He would have to give it careful consideration.

FOUR

The ranch had been Caleb's life for over twenty
years, with some breaks for walk-abouts or solo visits to the high
country. After dropping out of college when his mother died,
Caleb tried to be helpful to his father, Taylor, while they were
still in Arkansas. But Taylor wanted to make a change and decided to come west. They had ended up in Artesia, New Mexico,
where Taylor had stopped to visit Caleb's uncle Warren Atwood,
who worked for an oil company in the Permian basin. Taylor and
Caleb ended up staying. Taylor found work for the city administration, and Warren helped Caleb land a job in the oil fields.
The work paid well but did not inspire him relative to a future.
On a deep level, the oil business, while necessary, seemed to be
destructive of the land in a way he could not completely counte-
nance. Therefore, there wasn't much for Caleb in Artesia, so he
left his job and took some time to begin exploring further north
up the spine of the Rockies, all the way to Wyoming.

He found freedom and joy during those explorative days
like none he had known. His soul seemed to swell the further he
got away from throngs, or even large groups of people, and
deeper into the "wilderness." For Caleb, there was nothing
"wild" about it. The woods, fields, and waterways of nature
were the ultimate paradise. It had an order and an unflinching
integrity that could not be found elsewhere. Caleb was most at
home in the embrace of the mountains.

In the cities and towns of any size, and certainly at the university, the people who resided there each chose something to

chase. The chase focused them to be sure, but it just never seemed to have the ring of truth and harmony as Caleb imagined it. He was not critical of people as they pursued their goals of accumulation and success. Many seemed happy, but it wasn't for him. And in the "wilds" of the west, he wasn't chasing anything; he was simply "absorbed" into it. It felt right.

He frequently looked to the mountains towering in the west, all bathed in sun, yet buffeted by aggressive clouds, and recalled those times when he had lived completely there. For over two years, Caleb had lived alone with his horse and personal items in various stretches of natural forest and dedicated wilderness areas. Those two years had formed and defined his soul and allowed the presence of God to infuse his entire being. Each day became a walk with the Lord. And that walk continued throughout his life. He carried the Lord's presence with him every waking hour. He didn't try to push it on others, at least not when it seemed to be something that he was trying to "talk them into." If asked, he would gladly share his "walk" and how it was available to everyone to accept in all its simplicity. The opportunity to share his view of the Lord had presented itself on a few occasions, and all the cowboys knew of Caleb's dedication to his beliefs. Some had chosen to join him on such a walk while many others had listened respectfully without much comment.

On many occasions, Caleb had capitalized on his wilderness skills and his love of the land by leading people on extended pack trips into that wilderness. He was offered opportunities to guide hunting parties but had passed on that activity. However, taking people who were interested in discovering even a part of what he had learned about living in harmony with nature was of great importance to him. Many had gone on their "pilgrimage" with Caleb and emerged with a new respect for the land and for God's admonition to us to find harmony with the earth and to be protective of its bounty. In a very important way, it was Caleb's ministry. The living Caleb earned on the ranch had always been a perfect setting for Caleb to further this ministry and practice the presence of the Lord in everything he did. The ranch was an extension of the serenity he had found in the wilderness coupled with a dedication to accomplishing tasks he loved.

Caleb had been visited by only a few people while on the ranch. Lonnie Rex, or Lonnie, as Caleb usually called him, was one of those who came on occasion. Lonnie Rex had accompanied him into the wilderness on several of his pack trips and had grown to appreciate and to share Caleb's love of the land. In so doing, Lonnie Rex developed a shared walk with the Lord along with Caleb, and they spoke of God's presence in their lives often.

Caleb's sister, Sarah, with whom he was very close, had come for one visit and thoroughly enjoyed seeing Caleb's life and the grand sweep of the ranch, so different from the green hills of the Ozarks. She had come with her husband, Paxton Westridge. Paxton was less enamored with the ranch. He was more into real estate development and not inclined to be at home in a place sprinkled with cow shit. But Paxton had been a good husband to Sarah and had been successful in his real estate ventures. Caleb and Sarah spoke regularly on the phone, and he made a trip to visit her every few years. Paxton passed away in 2005, and thereafter Caleb's visits to Rogers had been slightly more frequent. Paxton had left Sarah in good financial shape, and she adjusted to life alone. Her life was a full one with her church activities, her social obligations, and her friends.

The only other visitor had been Caleb's uncle Warren. Recalling those visits brought back a flood of memories.

Taylor Atwood, Caleb's father, and Warren Atwood were always very close. They were the only Atwood boys. In Arkansas, Taylor had a career in country music. He managed a few hits and made a modest living traveling and playing. Connie, Caleb's mother, had traveled with him and supported his career in a loving way. Taylor had a bit of a drinking problem, but it always seemed in control until the loss of Connie. She died when Caleb was at the university. His father sort of fell apart at her loss, and that was when Caleb dropped out of the university to help his dad. After their move to Artesia, Taylor stopped drinking and settled into the job there. During that time, Caleb had become very close to his uncle Warren. They spent time together, and it became clear that Warren related to Caleb as the son he never had.

Taylor died in 1994 of a cerebral hemorrhage. Caleb and Sarah both went back for the funeral, after which Taylor's body was returned to Rogers to be buried there. Sarah had handled those arrangements while Caleb stayed in Artesia for an extended visit with Warren. Their relationship only grew. Caleb invited him to come to the ranch whenever he could get away, and Warren had made the trip two times after Taylor's death. It was during those visits that Warren and Caleb spoke in depth about the family history. It was on the first visit that Warren had revealed so much about how his life had transpired.

Right after high school, back in 1944, Warren left abruptly and joined the Army Air Corps. It was the end of the war, and rather than going overseas, Warren had been stationed at Alamogordo, New Mexico, where he became a crew chief on multiple airplanes. He got some engineering training during his service but left the military as soon as he could. Warren then signed on with an oil company and went to Saudi Arabia to work on oil pipelines. He remained in the Mideast for over 16 years, where he traveled to multiple countries before returning to the states in 1964. It was clear that Warren had many adventures while abroad. He had prepared a large scrapbook with pictures and souvenirs from all over that part of the globe. Warren was always pictured in kakis with rolled-up sleeves which prominently displayed his imposing strength. Most were scenes in various bars or at work sites in the desert. He was pictured in the company of oil field workers, local characters, and even some highly placed individuals. Warren went through the scrapbook with Caleb as he pointed out places of interest and related stories of his adventures.

Warren returned to the states, and after a brief visit to Rogers, he settled in Artesia, New Mexico, where he continued working in the oil industry. Warren's presence in Artesia was the reason for Taylor's visit and subsequent relocation there after Connie's death.

Warren opened his soul to Caleb and told of his adventures and of his regrets. It seems that Warren had returned with a sizeable fortune from the Mideast and only added to it with the work he did in the oil industry. He lived a simple life. He made no mention of how much money he had, only that he would be comfortable for many years to come.

His regrets were more pronounced. Warren admitted to killing or maiming more than one man. The first that he admitted to was when he got in a fight in a bar. The fellow had attacked Warren with a knife. He had defended himself in a raging manner, and it resulted in the death of the assailant. That was self-defense, and Warren was not punished.

The second event was also understandable. An oil field worker lived next door to Warren with his wife and baby. The man had a drinking problem and abused his wife when drunk. One night, the young wife knocked on Warren's door asking for protection. She knew that her husband would be home soon and be drunk and threaten her. Warren allowed her in, and they waited. When the pounding on the door occurred later that night, Warren opened the door to be confronted by the man holding a 45 automatic and demanding his wife and child back. Warren agreed and stepped out onto the porch. In one swift stroke, Warren hit the man in the face. He shattered his jaw in seven places with that one blow. The man had to be airlifted to Albuquerque to have facial surgery, but he did not die. In fact, Warren understood that the man had straightened up after his recuperation. Even so, Warren felt remorse that trouble always seemed to find him. He had alluded to another incident in his past but declined to elaborate.

On Warren's second and final visit to the ranch, he told Caleb that he was pulling up stakes and heading back to Arkansas. He thought he might get a small place and retire there in his "homeland."

Warren had said to Caleb, "Now listen, I'm going to live out my life back home. I don't know how long I will last, but whatever is left of what I own I will give to you after I am gone. If nothing is left, then so be it. I don't have anyone else. You are the son I never had, you were a loving son to Taylor, and I want you to get whatever is left. You have listened to my story and heard my confession—well, most of it—and it means a lot to me. Just know that you can come and visit."

With that pronouncement, Warren had left the next day for Rogers. That was in 1998. Warren purchased a small farmhouse and some land outside of Rogers. During each trip Caleb had made to Rogers since then, he had paid a visit to Warren's farm. Their time together was spent on the porch sharing stories and bringing each other up to date. Caleb shared openly with Warren his firm belief in the presence of the Lord in each of our lives. Warren always listened quietly and considered Caleb's witnessing with no argument nor any commitment.

Then in 2014, at the ripe old age of 89, Warren passed. Caleb was told of his passing by Sarah. She indicated that it appeared he had died quietly of natural causes sitting on the porch of the farm and that when the body was found, a few days had gone by, so they buried him quickly without a service. Caleb was deeply sorry to hear of his passing and regretted that he could not go back for a last farewell.

About two weeks after Caleb learned of Warren's passing, he received a registered letter informing him that Warren had arranged for the deed to his farm to be transferred directly to Caleb. The gift of the farm had been set up as a direct transfer of title and avoided any probate. The farm was free and clear without any debt, and it now belonged to Caleb. In addition, Warren explained in the letter that he had arranged for a large trunk to be delivered to Sarah for safekeeping until Caleb could retrieve it. It was locked, and Sarah was instructed not to open it until Caleb came back. He also said that the key to the trunk had been delivered to Nancy Matlock, an old family friend, for safekeeping and was only to be surrendered to Caleb upon his return. Both Sarah and Nancy had been instructed to remain silent on the issue until Caleb returned. Warren indicated that there was no rush on Caleb's opening of the trunk. Everything would keep.

Caleb knew the farm well since he had visited there. He had made a call to both Sarah and to Nancy that he knew about the trunk and would check it out the next time he came back. He figured that the trunk held some of Warren's memorabilia and personal items, which he would go through upon his return. He also instructed Nancy, who was a realtor, to visit the farm, be sure that everything was secure until he could return, and have any utilities transferred to his name. Nancy complied.

That had all been a little over a year ago. Caleb got some utility bills, which he paid. He was assured by Nancy that everything was secure at the farm and that she would check on it periodically. The only thing left for Caleb to do was to plan a trip to Rogers and decide what to do with everything Warren had left him.

As Caleb stepped down from the porch of his cabin to go to chow with the rest of the hands, the issue of a return to Rogers was uppermost in his mind. The time to return seemed to be at hand. A reunion might be a little fun while he was at it.

FIVE

"Who wants more Collards?" hollered Leena. "You know I don't make these too often, so get 'em while you can."

Both Caleb and "Digger" Wells waved their hand for more.

"These are good Leena. I grew up with these, and we don't get 'em out here so much. You've made a great batch," offered Caleb. "And for goodness sake, don't throw any out."

"You can feed them collards to the hogs as far as I'm concerned," mumbled Thumb Dickson. He was called Thumb because he only had one.

"We ain't got no hogs, stupid, and if we did, we might just feed you to 'em," came a rejoinder from down the table. Laughter rippled through the crowd of hands at the long ranch table.

Undeterred, Thumb said, "You know, hogs might be a good idea. They're smarter than horses, you don't have to round them up, they're good eating… and they live off'a slop,"

"After you boys finish a meal, there ain't nothing left to make slop," Leena pointed out.

"Who said that pigs are smarter than horses?" came a question from down the table.

"Years ago, I saw it on Johnny Carson. He had a dude on there who knew all about animals, and he said they were smarter."

"What does Johnny Carson know about pigs?" asked Hasty Mills.

"I said it was a guest on his show, not him," corrected Thumb.

Clem Pierce chimed in with, "Now boys, I happen to know that pigs are smarter than horses. No doubt about it, but I don't reckon that I would want to saddle a pig to work cattle."

A wave of laughter spread again.

"A saddle like that would have to be a special order, huh?" asked Possom.

A quiet settled for a moment while everyone considered Possom's question. No one wanted to make fun of him just because he was a greenhorn. In addition, the thought of a saddle for a pig had captured some of the hands' imagination.

"Reckon Mitch could make one. He can make about anything out of leather. And since he's a great horse trainer, I bet he could even train a pig," teased Thumb. "Could you make one, Mitch?"

"Gimme a pig, and I'll make a saddle for him," said Mitch Rawlings.

"How's about training one?"

"Gimme a pig, and I'll train him. Can't be harder than training you."

Most of the cowboys chuckled as they considered the truth in what Mitch said.

"Pass the gravy, Possum. Thinking on your question certainly gives a fellow an appetite," said Randy Skaggs. "And you know, I had me some pigs, once."

"Where did you have pigs?" wondered Possum.

"Back on our farm when I was young. I used to ride 'em around the barnyard. They'd let me get on 'em, but I didn't have no saddle."

"What'd you hang on to?" Possum fired back.

"Nothing. Just sort of balanced there. But if they got into a run, I usually fell off." explained Randy. "Except sometimes you could hold on to their ears. I tried making a bridle once, but the pig ate it!"

"Did you eat the pigs" asked Possum.

"Yeah, eventually. Mostly we smoked the meat. But there were always a few coming on or still wallowing around. I liked 'em. And, as I think on it, they did seem smarter than horses."

When Possum had run out of pig questions, Ricky "Flat Top" Blue asked Caleb, "Hey Caleb, you up for a little music session tonight?"

"Count me in. I'll get my fiddle and come down to the bunk house," Caleb said as he got up from the table. "We aren't too tired tonight so a session would do some good. Thanks, Leena, that was a fine meal. Especially the collards."

"Thanks, Caleb. My pleasure," said Leena.

As the cowboys finished eating, they each strode out of the dining hall and onto the porch for a smoke or a chew. There was a quiet satisfaction all around with their life and with each other. Clem and Mitch took a seat on the porch while the others wandered down to the barn to look to the horses' feed and water, after which they gravitated back up to the bunk house. A music night would be welcome fun. Music was an important part of life on the ranch, right after the steady work, the good food, and the companionship. Most would join in while Flat Top played the guitar, Digger Wells straddled the washtub bass, and Caleb led with the fiddle. Others would contribute their voices by singing favorite songs as well as many original tunes made up right there on the ranch.

After discussing the plans for the next day with Clem, Caleb walked across to the cabin, where he removed his spurs and boots out on the porch and stepped inside to get his moccasins and fiddle. Caleb had learned to play the violin both fiddle and concert style. He had learned from his father when he was young. Taylor was accomplished on many instruments and took the time to carefully nurture his son's progress on the violin. It was a difficult instrument to play well, but once learned, it allowed a great deal of energy and passion to be openly expressed. Caleb could make it "sing" with style.

They all gathered in the great room of the bunk house and waited as Caleb and Flat Top tuned to each other. When they were satisfied, they quickly started in on a spirited rendition of "Good Old Rocky Top." Most of the music they played was country and western with a few modern rock tunes thrown in. The resounding "thump" of the washtub bass kept the beat lively. The others joined in the singing of the tunes they knew. About halfway through, Caleb bowed some new tunes that he had been working on, followed by Flat Top's contribution of riffs and runs to complement. Beer was tossed about to those drinking, and remembered tunes were requested. The music and the comradery were seamless as everyone joined in the performance.

After a couple of hours of song and beer, some of the hands moved off to their beds, anxious to get a good rest before 5:00 a.m. came up on the following day, which would be a repeat of the one they had just finished. It was a dance that continued for six days a week with a solid break on Sunday. Some of the hands went to town to see friends on Sunday or do a little shopping. For those who stayed, they had cowboy church at the ranch followed by relaxing in front of televised sporting events. Caleb usually led the "church" services and shared any Bible verses that he knew and understood, and he told a few stories that seemed to apply or at least entertain. Sundays were good days.

As Caleb returned to his cabin after the singing, he became lost in thought about his need to leave for a time and attend to business back in Rogers. He would be missed, but Clem Pierce could handle the hands and get the work done. Clem would be the natural choice to fill in during Caleb's absence as cow boss and all-around top hand. Caleb would have to talk with Mason Stand, the owner of the ranch, and let him know about his plans once finalized. The ranch had been in Mason's family for over fifty years, and he had always managed it with care, competence, and good sense. These thoughts pestered Caleb's mind as he grappled with the knowledge that it was time to leave for an extended period. In his heart, he knew that it might even be permanent depending on what he found back in Arkansas.

SIX

The next day was spent at the headquarters for most of the hands. Caleb had two of the cowhands hitch up the long trailer and go pick up six new horses from another ranch outside of Pueblo. The horses had been purchased earlier in the week. When the men returned, the horses would be turned over to Mitch for settling in and training. Most of the rest of the men attended ranch chores at the headquarters and prepared to do a round-up the next day up in the far west pastures. It would be a continuation of the branding and cutting.

Inside the barn, Possum could be heard grumbling as he went about mucking out the stalls. It was his lot in life at the ranch to be given some of the less desirable jobs. Some of the hands thought that it was altogether fitting for Possum to remain on the bottom rung of ranch work. He wasn't the sharpest hand, and some never let him forget it.

Thumb checked on him and remarked, "Hey, Possum, you do good work. And you'll always have plenty of it if horses keep on delivering!"

"I've done wore out two pairs of gloves, and I cain't never get the smell off," moaned Possum.

"Shave off that peach fuzz on your upper lip, and the smell might go away," teased Thumb.

"Really?"

"Absolutely! I've never steered you wrong yet, have I? That's what you're smelling: your own lip fuzz!"

"Thumb, leave the lad be, or I'll have you pitch in. Go and run that sorrel in for reshoeing," Clem demanded.

"Just funnin'. I'll bring him up right away. Really Possum, you do mighty good work." Thumb teased in parting.

Caleb entered the barn and, having overheard the funnin' from Thumb, said to Possum, "Hey Possum, saddle up, will you? I'm going to get Cisco saddled. I want you to come and help me round up some more of those horses in the south pasture for re-shoeing. We got a good start, and I want to keep it up."

"You bet Caleb! Right away!" Possum said as he put his shovel in the rack.

"That okay with you, Clem?"

With a slight and knowing smile tossed Caleb's way, Clem allowed how that would be fine.

By early afternoon, Caleb had time to walk up to the main house. When he knocked on the door, the housekeeper answered. She smiled at Caleb and welcomed him in.

"Is Mason around?" Caleb asked.

"I think he is in the office, at least he was the last time I looked. Go on and find him. You want some coffee?"

"No ma'am, but I could sure use some cold tea if you have any. Unsweetened."

"Sure. I'll bring it in."

Caleb found Mason in his office working on the computer. Mason looked up and smiled. "Come in, Caleb. I'm glad you're here. I think I get bleary-eyed staring at this computer. You'll be a welcome relief." Mason greeted Caleb with unconcealed delight at his arrival.

"I want to come down and look over those new horses when they arrive. One of those, a big bay, caught my eye at the sale. Could be promising. Let me know when they arrive, will you?" asked Mason.

"Sure boss. I think they will be back by 4:00. I'll come and let you know."

"Great, so what's up?"

Caleb was interrupted by the housekeeper bringing him a glass of tea.

After thanking her for the tea, Caleb started out slow, "Well, you remember when I told you all about that farm that I inherited back in Arkansas?"

"Yes, I do. What's up with it?"

"Well sir, I'm thinking that I need to get back there and get things sorted out. It's been over a year. I'm sure the place is all okay, but some other things have come up, which make it a good time for me to go. I haven't given my sister a visit in some time, and there's a reunion this June. I've never attended one of my reunions, and it got me to thinking as how this might be a good time for a trip to check on things. It's all going fine here, and Clem can take over my responsibilities. He's a great hand, as you know."

"Well, I know how good he is, but this place won't be the same without you. When are you thinking of leaving, and how long do you plan to stay gone?" asked Mason.

"I don't need to pull out until mid-May. That's a little more than a month. It will be a busy time then, but I'll go over everything with Clem, and we should be all right. We have plenty of hands for everything that needs doing," Caleb said and then paused.

Continuing, he said, "The thing is, boss, there's a real possibility that I could find it necessary to stay a while, maybe even for good. I just don't know. I could sell the farm or maybe stay and improve it; I won't know until I get a feel for it. As you know, I haven't been to see my sister for almost three years. She's gettin' a little bristly on the subject. I need to spend some time with her for sure, and with the farm and all, I'm sort of feeling that this could be a real goodbye. Of course, I would like to be able to come back if it doesn't work out that way."

"Caleb, you know you always have a home here—no matter what. This ranch will not be the same without you. I don't want to see you go, but I know that you need the freedom to check this out completely. Take the time to be sure, and let me know your long-term plans as soon as you know them. What do you want me to do with your cabin while you're gone? Are you taking everything or coming back to load up if it's permanent?" asked Mason.

"I've thought that over, and I figure it this way. I can take everything I own in one trip. I have my trailer. It'll hold my horse and all my stuff. It's got the living quarters in the front, so I'll be fixed up on the road and at the farm, or whatever. If I decide that it's permanent, I'll let you know, and I won't have to make another trip for stuff left behind if I stay. As far as the cabin is concerned, I was thinking that you should give it to Clem when I leave. No sense in letting it sit empty. If I do need to come back, I'll fit in wherever. Work back up so to speak."

Mason thought for a minute. "You know that you have an ownership position in a lot of the cattle. We won't sell until fall, and then maybe not all of them. What do you want to do about that?"

"Boss, I figure you will do whatever is best. When you sell, some or all, just send me what you think is fair. As you know, I trust you completely. Oh, and one more thing. I have that filly that I got back in the fall. She's coming along nicely. Mitch and I have been working on her for some time, and she could make a good ropin' pony. I want you to have her. I'll just be taking Cisco Bay."

"God, Caleb, this isn't easy. You've been on this ranch for what... twenty years?"

"Yes sir, with a few breaks for frolic. It's not easy to leave. No sir, not easy at all."

"Have you told the boys?"

"No, not yet, and I don't plan on telling anyone but Clem 'till a little later. No sense facing any goodbyes 'till they're on us. If that's okay with you."

"That's fine, but I might not be able to hide my sorrow."

Mason stepped around the desk, and when Caleb offered his hand, Mason ignored it and embraced him completely. "Go with the God you love. We'll be here."

"Yessir, and thanks."

After dinner that evening, Caleb went to his cabin and settled in on the porch. The boys had gathered in the bunk house and started to slide off to bed in anticipation of a long day of branding and cutting the next day.

Caleb took off his boots and rubbed his feet in what was an evening ritual, fortified with a slight serving of Irish whiskey. Red Brest was his favorite label, and since it was expensive, he kept his own bottle handy for sipping at the cabin. Telling Mason about his plans was a difficult task to complete, but it had gone well, and as a result, Caleb was a bit more relaxed about his decision. As he looked out across the shadows in the valley below and sipped on his whiskey, he prayed,

"Lord, thank you for this day. You and I have been talking and thinking about this trip that I need to make back home. Well, I have finally decided to make it. I know that it is with your encouragement and blessing that I have made this decision. I know I've been a little slow in deciding, but, well that's the way I am, and I appreciate your patience. Help me as I finish up here and try to leave everything in good order. These men here are a good bunch, and I will miss them mightily. Help me as I travel and work toward planning my future. I'm feeling from You that this is the right thing to do. Help me do it well and allow my move to be a blessing to me and those around me, both here and back in Rogers. I ask that you continue to bless this ranch and everyone on it. It's been a fine home for me for so many years, as you well know. It

feels like the end of an era in my life, and the beginning of a new one. Can't help but wonder what will come. Well, I gotta get to bed; lots of whoopin' and spurrin' tomorrow. I'll talk to you in the morning. I speak to you in Jesus' name, Amen."

Caleb got up from his chair and walked over to the edge of the porch, where he again studied the valley below, thought of all the memories of his time in this beloved land and how the Ozarks might compare. He tossed the remaining ice cubes from his drink over the porch rail and went in to bed.

SEVEN

On the Road Along Highway 50
Outside of Dodge City, Kansas
Tuesday, May 17, 2016
4:30 p.m.

After loading his trailer, Caleb had said his good-byes to all the hands early that morning. It had been difficult to finally part with the ranch and his friends. The hands were very sorry to see him go. Caleb had trained most of them in ranching and all the aspects of cowboying. Clem and Mitch were experienced from other ranches, but neither could conceal their reluctance to have him leave. Everyone agreed that he should come back as soon as possible, but most sensed that this was likely the last they would see of him unless he came for a visit. They hoped he would and said so. Possum was especially distraught at Caleb's leaving, but Caleb had made it clear that Clem would be Possum's new mentor.

Mason Hand had given Caleb a few parting gifts consisting of memorabilia of Caleb's time on the ranch. He had assembled a scrapbook of pictures taken over the years. A special gift was a plaque with the ranch brand along with an inscription and brass plates with all the cowboy's names engraved thereon. In a bit of good-natured ribbing, he was given a brand-new mop and broom. Caleb wasn't noted for his house cleaning acumen, and they all hooted about how he would now be needing these things.

"Ain't no one to look after you now. Gotta cowboy up and get housebroke!" Thumb had yelled to general laughter. Caleb assented as to how that was true as he threw it all in the back of the truck and climbed into the cab. With a smooth start, Caleb waved goodbye as he pulled down the long drive to the highway.

He had made an early start across the Colorado plains and kept a due east heading through Kansas on Highway 50. Soon he would be close to Dodge City, where he thought he would find a spot to allow Cisco to stretch his legs, have some dinner, and settle in for the night. Everything he owned was in the trailer, some in the back with Cisco and the rest carefully stowed up front in the small living quarters. The trailer was fitted with twin beds, a small dining area with a small kitchen, and a bathroom. There was also a storage area for clothes and miscellaneous items. He pulled the trailer with his 2014 F350 diesel truck. With four doors in the cab and security boxes in the bed, he had a place for everything he might need during his move. Both the truck and trailer were a muted silver in color. Caleb enjoyed a sense of well-being and comfort knowing that everything he might need was self-contained and easily accessible within his rig.

Driving down the road in no apparent hurry had always appealed to Caleb. He enjoyed the expanse of the prairie as it spread out under the clouds, which cast their shadows in their wake as they moved across the land. May was a great month to travel, and he had no intention of hurrying through this part of the west. Soon he would be surrounded by trees, the sky would be reduced, and his joy would have to be discovered in all the green of the Ozarks. Until then, he just sat back and relaxed to the steady hum of the big diesel and the sing of the tires on the asphalt.

Caleb had called his sister, Sarah, about two weeks ago to tell her of his plans. She was very excited and wanted to immediately start doing anything she could to celebrate his arrival. He had instructed her to "calm herself" and simply wait for him to get there. He would go to her house and stay with her. There would be plenty of time to check out the farm that he now owned, and he wanted to relax with Sarah and catch up. He thought he might like to take Cisco out to his farm for grazing when it was ready, but in the meantime, they both would be happy at Sarah's little farm. She had a small barn and some decent grazing.

Sarah was the closest person alive to Caleb. As he drove, he found himself reliving all the times he had spent in Rogers and how big a role Sarah had played in his life. She was a good bit older than him and, since she had married early, had been gone from home. That left him alone with his dad and mother. But they all lived in Rogers and were together all the time. Those were good years comprised of fishing with his father, learning his music, and prospering in school. When Taylor and Connie had traveled together for music performances, Caleb had stayed with Sarah. She and her husband, Paxton, had always welcomed Caleb and took an active interest in everything he did. Paxton had been a good influence on Caleb, even though they were rather different. Paxton's hardcore work ethic was admirable, and he had provided for Sarah in meaningful ways. Now that he had passed, Sarah was able to maintain her small farm and house north of town without much difficulty.

After high school, Caleb thought that he might be interested in studying law and enrolled at the University of Arkansas to pursue a degree. The more he studied the law, the more he became drained of what interest it had originally held. He felt more and more empty with each passing month in school. It only took two years of studying law for any interest he ever had in being an attorney to slip completely away. He met a reprieve when his mother got sick and died. Caleb thought that he needed to help his dad through the tough time. He dropped out of the university and came home. Taylor always drank a little too much, but with Connie's death, it simply got out of hand. It seemed that Caleb was the only one who could get through to Taylor and help him deal with his grief. He never tried to get his dad to quit drinking, just control it. He even did a little drinking with him as a living illustration of his lack of any condemnation relative to Taylor's behavior. He just hung on and was always there for him. Sarah was a big help too but carried a resistance to drinking that occasionally expressed itself in negative ways. But they got through it. Of course, it meant the end of law school, but as only Caleb knew, it couldn't have come too soon.

During that time, he and Sarah had become even closer. He spent as much time with her as he could. She assumed that he would go back to school after Taylor steadied, and Caleb never told her any differently. He knew he would have to decide but wanted to delay it as long as possible. While he was in Rogers, he took a job on a local farm helping with all the work to be done. The owner of the farm owned several horses, but many had not been trained or "broken." It was there that Caleb first found his interest in horses. He learned to train them with patience and to gently prepare them to be ridden. It taught him a version of patience that would serve him well. While it was just fun at the time, Caleb had no idea that it would come back to him later as an active part of his life.

After about a year, Taylor got a handle on his drinking but needed to get away from the town where Connie had died. His music career had tanked, and his job at a local accounting office held little or no appeal. Caleb reckoned that his dad just needed a new start, and so he did nothing to dissuade him. In the fall of 1981, Taylor left and went west, leaving Caleb behind until it became clear what he was going to do. During that time, Caleb and Sarah continued to do things together.

Sarah was a devout Christian and felt strongly it was her charge in life to bring her little brother to the Lord. That was fine with him; he knew nothing of religion but felt no compunction to resist it. If it was good enough for Sarah, it might be good enough for him. Unfortunately, Caleb's first encounters with the Lord were to occur while sitting in the pews of Sarah's church along with her and Paxton. Sarah's steadfast "churchness" just didn't rub off on him. In fact, much of what he heard from the pulpit was a little judgmental for Caleb's taste and didn't really ring quite right with the teaching from scripture that Sarah enthusiastically provided at her home on the porch. It seemed to Caleb that scripture and "church" were in many ways at odds. This unease with church, once cemented, stayed with Caleb for the rest of his days. He had tried other churches for brief attempts to find the promises Sarah had outlined, but every such encounter was found wanting. He chalked it up to being a bit of a simpleton and could never escape his attitude about organized religion.

When Taylor had finally decided to settle, he chose Artesia, New Mexico. Soon thereafter he had called for Caleb to join him if he liked. Going west seemed like an adventure to Caleb, and he knew from talking to Taylor that he felt he needed him. With that in mind, Caleb had packed up and driven west. Taylor quickly demonstrated that the move was good for him. He landed a job with the city as a purchasing agent and settled down without the heavy remembrance of Connie that haunted him in Rogers. The primary reasons that Taylor had settled in Artesia were his stop to visit Warren and his discovery that he liked the town enough to stay. It was there that Caleb rekindled his relationship with Warren and began his long-running life in the west. After living in Artesia for a couple of years, Caleb struck out one summer to explore up and down the Rockies. He never went back. The mountains beckoned to him in such a strong way that Caleb simply lived in the natural surroundings of mountain meadows and timberland for over two years.

It wasn't until Caleb had lived in the wilderness and believed he had "experienced" the Lord that he began his long walk toward the joy that was subsequently revealed. His discovery of the presence of the Lord in his life had only deepened Caleb's respect for Sarah and her strength of faith. They openly shared their view and experience of the Lord in new and meaningful ways in regular visits on the phone. Caleb always listened to Sarah's guidance, but he still never found anything remotely appealing about church.

Caleb's reflections were interrupted by what he saw ahead. There was a turnout leading to a rest area. He didn't see anyone there, and there was plenty of room. The area was surrounded by a few trees with a grassy meadow to the south. He easily parked his rig next to one of the three picnic shelters. It wasn't an oasis, but it would do for Caleb and certainly for Cisco.

"Ready for a stop for the night, Cisco?" he hollered. Even though he didn't get any answer, he knew Cisco agreed. Tomorrow, with an early start, he could roll into Rogers in time for one of Sarah's dinners.

EIGHT

Caleb drove down Interstate 49 and turned onto
Highway 62 toward Rogers. It had been almost four years since
he had visited Rogers. It was amazing how it was growing. The
development on each side of the highway occupied what used to
be fields and farms in recent years. He reckoned it was the kind
of surprise anyone would feel when returning home after many
years, but this place seemed to be booming beyond reasonable
expectations. He wasn't sure that appealed to him, since the closest town to him for over 20 years had been the small village of La
Veta, Colorado. That historical little settlement wasn't changing,
other than a little deterioration nibbling at the edges of town. It
was quite different here.

Sarah lived north of Rogers on Highway 94, or North Second
Street, or the Pea Ridge highway, depending on what you
wanted to call it. All the same road by various names. Sarah and
Paxton had been there for at least 25 years. Paxton had purchased
it when it appeared on his real estate listings many years ago. As
a realtor and developer, he certainly knew what was good and
was priced right. That knowledge had served them well. In that
house, Sarah and Paxton had prospered until his death. They had
no children, so there were no little ones to enjoy the farm. After
Paxton died, Sarah stayed in the home she had come to love and
employed one or two local "hands" to help keep everything up.
It was a fine old home surrounded by oak trees and manicured
lawn. To the south, there was a small pasture of undisturbed
grassland. At the back of the house was a substantial shed full of

unending amounts of unnecessary items. None would ever be needed, but getting rid of "stuff" once you start keeping it is a task difficult for most people, and that was certainly true with Sarah. Caleb reckoned that he too had some "treasures" pushed back among the dusty boxes in the recesses of the shed, but nothing that he envisioned needing. Maybe he would give it a look this visit for a little entertainment. Or maybe not.

Caleb slowed and turned his rig onto the drive and up through the trees toward the house. He blew a couple of blasts on the air horn just for grins. As expected, Sarah bounded out the door and stopped on the porch while shading her eyes toward the big truck and trailer pulling up. He could feel her excitement even before setting the brake.

"Oh, I'm so glad you're here. I expected you might be here earlier this morning or even last night," Sarah exclaimed before Caleb could get down from the cab.

"I told you when I would be here, and I'm right on schedule, so why would you think otherwise?"

"Oh, you know, I'm just anxious!" she said as she moved up to give Caleb a big hug.

Hugging her back, Caleb said, "Well it's mighty good to be here. Been a while. You look good."

"Just stop. I'm pushing 68 and feeling every bit of it. You think I look good for a woman of my age?"

"I said I thought you looked good. And you do. What more is there to say?"

"Where did you spend the night? What did you do with your horse? You brought him, didn't you? Are you hungry? I've got a roast and a big salad. Does that sound good? Does…"

Interrupting, Caleb said, "Outside Dodge City; He got some exercise last night; Sure, I brought him; Yep, I'm hungry, and roast sounds very good. Did I miss anything? Oh yeah, salad is fine." After which he recharged his breath.

"Oh, I'm so glad you are here. Come on in, and let's have some tea. You want to sit on the porch? It's nice and cool now."

"Hold on a minute. I've got to pull the trailer around and unhook it. I'll let Cisco Bay out into the pasture. It's still fenced good, isn't it?"

"As far as I know. Yes, of course it is; the guys keep things up. You remember Dicky and Estes? They help me out and do a good job. Dicky is the...."

"Good," Caleb inserted to stem the flow. "I'll turn him out and bring my bag up to the house. I can unload anything I need later. I'll be up directly."

Caleb climbed back in the cab and fired up the diesel. Sarah followed behind telling him things that he didn't need to know. He pulled away and Sarah went back into the house.

After a substantial meal of roast beef with all the trimmings, Caleb pushed back from the table to savor the comfort he felt. Sarah's calling in life was feeding people. It was her gift to anyone at her table. She cooked very good food and delivered it in copious quantities.

"I'll take you up on that trip to the porch now, if you want," said Caleb.

"Oh good, let's take our iced tea out there. Gimme a minute to pee, and I'll bring it out."

When they settled on the porch, Sarah started to ask questions, but Caleb told her to allow him to tell the whole story. He began to tell of his recent times on the ranch and about the facts relative to his inheritance of Warren's farm. Sarah knew most of it since they talked frequently, but Caleb hadn't filled her in on his thinking. He informed her that he was considering making this move permanent depending on how things shook out. Caleb could tell by her reaction to his story that she was pleased with the thought that this could be permanent. He mentioned his plans to attend the upcoming reunion, to see old friends, and to go see Lonnie Rex as soon as possible. He told her that he had called Lonnie and related his plans.

After Caleb paused and there was a fleeting moment of silence, Sarah exclaimed, "I can't tell you how happy this makes me. I had always hoped that you would come back. I miss you so much and this just makes my day!"

"Well, I'm feeling pretty good about it too. It was powerfully hard to leave the ranch, but it just seemed that God was calling me back. In fact, it seems that He has been calling me for some time, but it took me a while to listen up and decide. Anyway, I'm here and ready to begin anew."

"Are you going to stay here? How long can you stay? The farm isn't ready, is it? You know I want you here as long as you want."

"Yes, I'll stay here and for as long as it takes, and no, I don't reckon the farm is ready."

Both Caleb and Sarah were quiet for a minute as they looked to the west and the setting sun. The shadows were very long, and a bit of the dying light made its way onto the porch. Sarah looked back and simply seemed to enjoy the view as Caleb did the same.

"Oh! We can look in that trunk that Warren left. It's been here so long. I have wondered about it but left it alone, just as Warren instructed. But I must admit to a strong curiosity. It's out in the shed."

"Then it's gone forever. Could be mulch by now," Caleb teased.

"No, no, I know right where it is."

"Just kidding, Sister. I'm sure we can find it and look at what's inside. I really don't expect much. Probably just some keepsakes or such. Warren told me everything else I think he wanted me to know when he visited and when he wrote the last letter I received. But we'll see. I must go over to Nancy's and let her know I'm here or get her to come out. We'll need the key."

"You want me to call her?"

"No, I think I'll go by and visit. It's been a long while," Caleb allowed as he remembered Nancy.

Nancy Matlock had been the oldest friend Caleb had. She was a little older than him, but both of their parents had been the best of friends. When they were young, Nancy and Caleb were constantly together when their parents partied, which was often. She was an outspoken person with great confidence in everything she did. That confidence had led her into a successful role in the community. Nancy loved Rogers and was active in many community affairs. She served on many boards, attended social gatherings, and was well respected locally. She had done very well in real estate and was the go-to realtor for fine properties. It was Nancy that had checked on the farm and had kept an eye on it during this last year. She could be a big help.

"You know what? Speaking of Nancy, she got me to join her on the Historical Preservation Board," Sarah inserted. "I didn't think I wanted to do it at first, but she talked me into it. What do I know about historical preservation? But it's fun, and I was surprised at how much history I knew about Rogers. I'm enjoying it."

"Great. You do know all about Rogers. All the way back to the old family farm and the local characters. You make a good board member."

"Okay, I've got your room ready. I'm going to tidy up the kitchen. We can just take it as it comes and enjoy every minute," said Sarah.

"My thoughts exactly. Now I am going to go down and feed Cisco Bay, make sure he is settled in. Grass looks good, so he should be fine. In fact, I don't think he has seen such grass in all his days. He'll be fat in no time if we're not careful. I'll be up soon, and I think I'll take a shower and turn in. It's been a long day."

NINE

Sarah arose the next morning at about eight o'clock and walked quietly down the hall so as not to disturb Caleb. Upon entering the kitchen, she noticed that the coffee had already been made and was about half gone. When she looked out the kitchen window, she saw Caleb riding Cisco Bay up from the draw east of the house. She wondered how long he had been up. Slipping on her robe and a pair of her boots, she went out to the fence line to greet them both.

Approaching them as they came through the gate, she asked, "How long have you been up?"

"Well, I slept in a bit and got up a little before six. When I was having my coffee, I saw Cisco staring at me over the fence, clearly wondering what we were going to do today. He thinks every day is a workday, so I saddled him up and we went for a little ride down through the draw. There's some new housing on the other side. It shortened our ride a little, but it was pleasant enough."

"Yes, it's building up everywhere, even this far out. Come on in, and I'll fix you some breakfast."

"Sounds great. I'll be right up."

Sarah returned to the house while Caleb unsaddled Cisco and gave him a good brush, after which he fed and watered him before turning him out to the pasture. He went up to the house and, after removing his vest and boots, settled at the table. "I think that the first thing I will do is go over and say hi to Lonnie

Rex. I want to catch up because it's been a while. Then I'll try to find Nancy and set something up with her. What're you up to?"

"I have a little luncheon with some of the ladies. We meet every Thursday for lunch, but I don't have to go. Do you need me?"

"Nope."

"After that, I'll go by the store, and I should be back by midafternoon. Are you sure you don't need me?"

"I'm sure. I'll get my visitin' done and be back later today. What's for dinner?" asked an interested Caleb.

"A big salad, and I thought I might get you to grill some steaks. That sound okay? Bring Lonnie Rex if you want."

"We'll see. I'll let you know."

Once breakfast was behind him, Caleb unloaded some of the gear that was in the truck and put it in the shed. As he stowed his stuff, he noticed a big trunk and thought to himself that must be it. Nancy and Sarah are probably anxious, he thought, but it could wait until the time was right. First things first.

Caleb pulled his truck to the curb in front of Lonnie Rex's house on West Maple. The house brought back memories of the good times had here during high school and on visits. The house had been in the Stanhope family for as long as he knew. Caleb went up on the porch and peered in through the screen door at the front. There on the couch was Lonnie Rex in full slumber. Caleb eased in the door quietly and went over to the recliner. While he waited for Lonnie's nap to conclude, he quickly succumbed to the power of suggestion and dozed off himself.

When he awoke, he was sure he hadn't slept too long, but his watch indicated that he had been out for more than forty-five minutes. Lonnie Rex was still passed out on the couch, so Caleb got up and went back out to the porch to stretch. He sat and studied the street for another twenty minutes when he heard the screen door slam. Lonnie Rex stepped past Caleb and plopped down into the other rocker.

"Howdy, pard. How're you doing?" asked Caleb.

"Been napping. When did you get here?" asked Lonnie.

"Oh, a little over an hour ago. Didn't reckon to wake you."

"You should have woken me up."

"Didn't need to. I went in and took a little nap myself. In the lazy boy."

"The hell you say!"

"That's what I said. Good little nap, too."

Lonnie Rex shook a cigarette out of his crumpled pack and lit it up. "When did you get in town?"

"Pulled in yesterday afternoon. I'm staying out at Sarah's"

"Figured you would. She doing okay?"

"Great as far as I can tell."

"I know you're here for the reunion and to check out the farm. How long are you going to stay?"

"Since I talked to you, I've done a little thinking. Nothing for sure yet, but I thought what with the farm, and my sister and everything else, I might look at staying permanent-like. Depends."

"Depends on what?" Lonnie queried.

"On the farm mostly. I gotta decide if I want to live there and give it a go. I went out to the farm back when Warren was alive, and it's a little ragged, but with a little work, it might suit. On top of that, Sarah might be needing me as time goes on, so there's that too. Plus, there's always you." Caleb said as he made a kissing noise toward Lonnie Rex.

"Well that sounds kinda good, except for the kissing part," Lonnie observed.

"Tell me about this reunion," directed Caleb.

"Just another reunion. You ain't never been to one, so that'll be different. I really enjoy these reunions, and I think you will too. I've been on the committee that plans the thing. Misty Belle's in charge, and there's a few of us helping."

"Misty Bell Glover?"

"Yea… well it's Masters now. She married the local undertaker. I've told you that."

"Undertaker! I don't remember that. But I bet she's got that guy organized and on the straight and narrow. She always seemed kind of firm in the spine."

"That's Misty, but she does a good job. Been doin' the reunion thing since the beginning."

"Who else is working on it?"

"Peter Mason, Bobby Lane Driscoll, and Gina Houseman— used to be Giles."

"Bobby Lane! He's back?"

"Oh yeah. 'Stash,' remember? He's doing good. He owns a local bar called the Big-Wigs. It's a nice place and very popular. He's straight now and holding his own. I've even got some art hanging there at the bar—well, he likes to call it a lounge—and I sell quite a few pieces there."

"About time you parted with some of your art. I always thought you were a little stingy about letting them go. They are so good. That's great."

"The art brings in some good money. I sure need it. Jaws One and Jaws Two sort of prevented me from getting too wealthy—still do in some ways. I don't owe them anything now, but they always seem to need some help and here I am. Regular money machine. Ah hell, the least I could do," admitted Lonnie.

"It's been a long time since I thought much about our old classmates. There were some good ones, though. Who all's coming?" asked Caleb.

Lonnie Rex got up from the rocker and headed toward the door. "Let me get the list."

When he returned, he tossed some pages in Caleb's lap. "Look it over, see who you remember, and I'll tell you what I know."

It was an alphabetical list of attendees. Caleb looked down at the pages and paused as he took in the names.

"Dumar Ashton! That guy went to the university with me. He was also studying law. Didn't get along with him too well. Is he a lawyer?"

Lonnie Rex smiled, "Remember his nickname? It was 'Dumb Ash!' Hasn't changed a bit. He is a lawyer but only practices a little real estate law. Mostly he's made his money doing real estate himself. He buys property and sells it after fixing it up some. Got involved in politics, mostly local. Some say that he has gotten some help from his political connections with the city, but I don't know of anything specific. All in all, he's respected in a grudging sort of way."

Caleb laughed, "I had forgotten that nickname. Wish I had remembered it at law school. Glad to hear he made it through."

Caleb looked some more and then frowned, "Eunice Biles. That sounds familiar, but I don't know why."

"It used to be Eunice Dimple. She married a fellow by the name of Dufus Biles from…"

"Dufus Biles! That's it. Now I remember. He was my roommate in my freshman year at the university. Real bloody smart, but no social graces at all. He was straight out of the mountains. Big hulk of a fellow. He got a scholarship and a full ride. He could just look at a book and know what was in it. But he couldn't resist his newfound freedom. He went and bought a pump shot gun with his first scholarship check, and in the second semester, he bought a Sears motor scooter. Lasted all of one year then went off to the Air Force, I think. And you know, I remember Eunice now. She was on the back of that scooter of his one afternoon before the semester ended."

"Well, he married Eunice. They came back here after he retired from the service. He owns and operates a Chicken Shack franchise out on West Walnut. Good chicken," Lonnie Rex said.

"I've got to go see him. After the first semester, everyone was changing roommates, but we stayed together. He's a good guy," said Caleb.

Looking through the list some more, Caleb said, "I remember Fletcher Cosgrove. That guy was super sharp, a great student, some scholarships, I think. Did he set the world on fire?"

"Oh yeah… you bet he did well! He went to Dallas and started a company that placed adult movies in hotels. All over several states in certain chains. Made a bundle. Fletcher the 'porno king!' But he's the nicest guy you would ever want to meet. Retired here now with his wife. He's become a good friend. So, don't mention the porno king thing. He's not sensitive, but his wife isn't too proud of it."

"Okay, I'll remember," Caleb said as he continued down the list. "Oh, here's Millicent Dupree. It says Riggs also. I remember her. She was gorgeous and very sweet. What's she doing?"

"That's her maiden name listed. She married Nelson Riggs. She was, and is, a very religious person—almost like a Mennonite or something. I don't know, but her husband Nelson is sort of a weird survivalist type. That guy lives in desperate hope of a major new world order event. While he waits, he runs a gun shop out toward Gentry called Shooters and Hooters. But he never comes to the reunions, just Millicent—she's got some close friends from our class, and they stick together. I don't think Nelson pays her much attention."

Caleb laughed heartily. "Shooters and Hooters! I don't know why I never came before. This is great, and I haven't even made it through the Ds!"

Recovering, Caleb continued. "Gina Houseman. You said that she's also on the committee. She was a bit of a tom cat as I recall. Fun loving but managed to keep out of trouble."

"Yeah, she skated the edges. She's okay, though. Bobbie Lane's kinda set on her, but they're just good friends. I like Gina a lot. She even bought a piece of my art from Big-Wigs."

Caleb had stopped responding. He held the list in his hand and was thoughtful. Finally, he asked, "Can I just keep this list to brush up?"

"Sure, but what's the matter?"

"Nothing, it's just…. Is this Lori Beth… Hightower? It says Martin."

"That's the one. Your old girlfriend."

"I lost track of her after she moved away. Haven't seen or heard from her since then. Just between you and me, she broke my heart when she left. But that's water under the bridge. Only, she didn't graduate from here, so why is she on the list?" queried Caleb.

"Well, I'm not sure I know. She came to one of the last reunions. All alone. She said that she just came to see old friends. She looked good, and I think she divorced her husband some time ago. Nobody ever knew him or anything about him, except that his last name was Martin. Now she's on the list again. Maybe she's looking for you," observed Lonnie Rex.

"Well, that's just peachy. Just when life gets simple, it starts getting complex," said Caleb.

"You'll be alright. Follow your heart, my friend."

"I followed it there before," Caleb lamented.

"Don't I know how that works! I'm still watching out for "Jaws Three," Lonnie claimed.

"Don't destroy another one, Lonnie!" advised Caleb.

"Leave that to me," Lonnie asserted. "But as far as Lori is concerned, I have no idea if she's coming to see you. After all, she came last time when you weren't here. She didn't know if you were attending or not."

"Everyone gets a list of who's coming, just like now, right?" asked Caleb.

"Sure."

Caleb pondered for a minute and told Lonnie Rex, "Actually I did sign up for the last one, but I didn't come. Too much was going on. And I guess I'm on this year's list, right?"

"So… the plot thickens!" Lonnie said through a controlled laugh.

"Well, it will be good to see her. It's been a long time. I guess I never put her out of my thoughts, but they are certainly buried deep," Caleb allowed.

Getting up from the chair, Caleb said, "I'll keep studying this list, but right now I need to go and make a stop or two. I'm going to find Nancy Matlock and see about the farm. You want to go out to the farm with me this afternoon?"

"Sure. Come back by, and we'll go. I'd like to see it."

"That's great, and we can make some plans. I want to hear more about how this reunion will play out," said Caleb.

"I'll be here, but just one more thing. They're putting together some music for down at the lake the Thursday night of the reunion week. Gina's putting it together. I let it slip that you might play your fiddle, solo or in a group. What do you think?"

"Music's the magic of the soul. I'll play anywhere I'm wanted," Caleb said.

"I'll let Gina know. You still don't have a cell phone, do you?"

"Nope. But I can be reached at Sarah's number."

"Why don't you get a damn phone?"

"It's just something that you carry so other people can make it ring whenever they want. One night a cowboy had one, and the stupid thing went off as the cattle were quiet. Almost caused a stampede!" exclaimed Caleb.

"Well, there won't be any stampedes back here, so get one."

"Yeah, maybe. We'll see."

Caleb stepped down from the porch and waved back over his shoulder as he headed to his truck. "Be back in a couple of hours."

"You got it," Lonnie Rex said as he waved.

TEN

It was only about six blocks from Lonnie Rex's house to Nancy's. She also lived in the home that had belonged to her parents. Caleb had many memories of times spent as a child playing with Nancy while their parents visited. Sometimes that took a long time spanning up to two meals, but he never tired of being there. Nancy was an only child, and her parents had seen to it that she did not want for anything. It was a joy to get to play with all of Nancy's toys and games. She had been through a couple of husbands in the ensuing years and had become a successful real estate broker in Rogers. Caleb knew that she was very professional, and that was why she was the first one he called about checking on the farm.

Today the house was dark. Caleb stopped on the side road by the back door and went up on the porch. He knocked on the door, but no one answered. While waiting, he felt a big grey cat rub against his pant leg.

"Are you the designated greeter today? Where's Nancy?" Caleb queried the cat.

With a resonant purr, the big cat rubbed some more and considered him through half-shut eyes. The cat gave no insight as to where Nancy was and only seemed to be looking for company. Caleb knew that Nancy loved cats. They weren't his favorite, but you had to love their independence. Give him a good dog any day.

Caleb knew that Nancy kept a small office downtown. It was on south Second Street, not far from the old Ozark Hotel. He figured that he might catch her there. She knew he was coming because Sarah said she had told her, but they didn't know exactly when he would arrive. Caleb realized that it was Thursday and still early enough that she might be at the office. Saying goodbye to the friendly cat with an ear rub, Caleb set off for downtown.

As he turned south on Second Street, he drove by a block of offices and stores that occupied a serious part of his memories. In the middle of the block was the old Viscount Theater where he had regularly attended movies with his father. Taylor loved to go to the movies and could be convinced to take Caleb with ease. Connie didn't go very often since she was always in a book, but it didn't hold the boys back. He could even remember some of the movies they had seen. Suddenly his memory was assaulted with the times that he had taken Lori to the Viscount on a Friday night. Those were good times, but he didn't think he could remember any of the movies he had seen with her. Perhaps she had provided a distraction that interfered with true movie recollection. The theater was closed in recent years, having been made obsolete by the multi-screen extravaganza at the new malls, where you had to pay a week's wages for popcorn. Some fancied this as progress, but Caleb held back on that a little. Now the Viscount was used as a community theater of sorts, although he had never been there for any event held there.

Caleb continued down Second Street, enjoying the song of the brick road under his tires. One of the distinctive characteristics of Rogers was the brick streets downtown. They had been red brick for as long as Caleb could remember, probably dating back to the thirties. He didn't think the city fathers would ever agree to pull them up, and that was fine with him. If it ain't broke, don't fix it.

The old Ozark Hotel loomed on the left in all its age-old splendor. It continued in service, having had some ups and downs, but the recent growth in Rogers coupled with a new and healthy respect for anything historical had contributed to its present prosperity. Memories of the junior prom with Lori bounced up from his deep regions almost instantly. Caleb wondered if he was now going to have to relive everything he and Lori did. Funny how the mind works — open a closed door and everything cascades out.

Nancy's office came up on the right, and Caleb pulled to the curb. At least he had never shared any time with Lori in a real estate office. A little mental peace was welcome. He could see that the office was open and thought Nancy might just be in. He stepped into the office and noticed a young lady at a desk to his left. She was young and blonde-headed with round, red-rimmed glasses perched on her nose. Looking up, she said, "Hi, can I help you?"

"I'm here to see Nancy Matlock. Is she in?"

"I'll let her know you're here. Who shall I say is calling?"

"Caleb Atwood."

"I'll get her, be just a moment. I think she is on the phone," she said as she walked toward the back.

The lobby had a couple of soft chairs and walls covered with pictures of properties for sale, all beckoning newcomers to make them their new homes. He looked closely and saw that some were whoppers! What was it about a house these days that they must be huge and all slathered with granite and tile and other fancy finishes? But they looked good even if Caleb could not imagine himself sitting in even one of the "great rooms" depicted. Well, maybe with a glass of Irish Whiskey — maybe.

"Caleb! There you are. I've been wondering when you would get here," exclaimed Nancy as she came out from an office in the rear.

"Yep, it's me. I went by your house, but you weren't there. Figured I'd find you here. How are you doing?" Caleb asked as he moved in for a hug.

"I'm fine and looking forward to your visit. Is this the first time that you have been to my office?"

"I think so. Usually, I come by your house, or we get to-gether with Sarah." Glancing at the young blonde, he continued, "How many people do you have working here?"

"Just myself and two others. Caleb, this is Naomi Henson. She's my office agent."

"How do you do? Nice to meet you," said Caleb.

Naomi displayed a sparkling smile and a nod of her head before returning to her desk. Caleb allowed her to resettle before returning his attention back to Nancy, who said, "Come on in the office, and we'll talk."

Caleb followed Nancy into her office in the rear. The office was small but brightly furnished with classic leather furniture. Nancy avoided her desk and beckoned Caleb to join her on the sofa.

"So, when did you get in?"

"Just yesterday afternoon late. Went to Sarah's and settled in first, then this morning I started my rounds."

"Bet you went directly to Lonnie Rex's," said Nancy.

"First stop this morning—then started looking for you."

"I guess you want to go out to the farm as soon as possible."

"Yes, that's on my mind. I thought I would run out this af-ternoon. Thanks for taking care of things and checking on it."

"I just want to get the key and then head out. You want to come?"

"Well, I'm available to go out anytime except today. I've got a showing in about an hour and two more this afternoon. Of course, you don't need to wait on me. I have the key in a lockbox on the front door."

"Lockbox?" Caleb asked.

"Yes, we use them for properties we have listed. We didn't list the farm, of course, but it makes it easy to just give the com-bination out on the lockbox to get the key. It's a lot better than putting it under a pot plant. It made it easy for me to have any service personnel to get in without my having to go out."

Nancy stepped over to the desk and looked at her calendar. "The combination is 61248. It will open, and the key is in there." She wrote down the numbers on a notepad and handed it to Caleb.

"Sounds good. So, bring me up to date," Caleb instructed as he pocketed the note.

"I've seen Sarah rather frequently lately. I got her on the historical board. We have meetings on the first Tuesday of each month. I think she is enjoying it. And sometimes we take in a movie. Just a couple of old gals out on the town."

"She mentioned that historical board thing. Said she was a little worried at first but was enjoying it."

"She almost always remembers something about properties that we discuss, you know—history and all. Sometimes it gets a little contentious on renovation cases, but generally people appreciate preserving our heritage," explained Nancy.

"Why don't you come out to Sarah's tomorrow for dinner? We can open that old trunk that Warren left. You've got the key that we need. Sarah's anxious to see what's in it, and me too, for that matter. I don't reckon it's anything much, just some old keepsakes."

"You're probably right, but Warren was a little weird what with giving me the key and giving the trunk to Sarah, and his instructions not to open until you got here. Sarah and I have been a little curious. Maybe he meant for just you to open it. Maybe it's something I shouldn't see."

"Whatever it is, it's okay, and if it's something weird, you'll get over it."

"You know, I can just give you the key. You don't need me," Nancy said.

"No, I think you should be there. It'll be fun."

"Dinner would be nice but wait a minute. Tomorrow is Friday. Sarah has Bible study on Friday evenings. She attends regularly. You better check with her first."

"Sure, I'll do that. I'll give you a call," said Caleb.

"Okay, and I'm available on Saturday if Friday doesn't work."

"Whenever it is, I'll pick you up."

"Why don't you? I'll show you my old house. You haven't been back in some time. I've made some changes."

"How many cats you got now?"

"Plenty—and don't start! Come a bit early, and I'll show you everything," said Nancy.

"Sounds good. I'll let you know."

Getting up from the couch, Caleb said, "I'm going to run out to the farm now. Lonnie Rex is coming along."

"It's good that you are here. It means so much to Sarah. She's been missing you. Your visit will be nice."

"This may be more than a visit. I'm leaning toward keeping the farm and staying here permanently if it feels right. I've been out west for a long time. This could be a new adventure."

"Really? I wondered what you would do with the farm, and I must admit that I hoped you could stay. I never realized that you might give up on the ranch. I know how you loved it out there."

"It seems as though I've been called. I'll just have to see," said Caleb.

He stepped out into the hall. As he passed Naomi's desk, he said that it was nice to meet her.

"Thank you, and nice to meet you too." Naomi's words trailed after Caleb.

With all the parting niceties over with, Caleb stepped out to the street, satisfied that he had started some balls rolling.

ELEVEN

Caleb drove north toward Pea Ridge with Lonnie Rex tugging on a cigarette in the passenger seat. They passed by Sarah's house on the way, but Caleb didn't stop. He knew that she was still running errands and grocery shopping. He would take her out to his farm later. Besides, you never wanted to interrupt grocery shopping. He and Lonnie would come back for dinner as Sarah had requested.

Once in the little town of Pea Ridge, Caleb turned right onto Lee Town Road toward the Pea Ridge National Military Park. The battlefield was the site of an early battle in the Civil War. Originally thought to be a minor skirmish, it was later learned through research and a concerted effort at unearthing the myriad of artifacts that this was a rather significant battle. A 16,000-man army of Confederates had moved north to the area surrounding the Elk Horn Tavern. There they were met by the Union forces, some 10,000 strong. On the first day, the South prevailed, but in a subsequent attack from the Union forces, the southerners were repelled and went into retreat. There were more than 3800 casualties in total. The route of the Confederate forces stopped their move into Missouri and gave the Union control of Missouri for the next two years. Caleb had walked all over the battlefield when he was young and had found a great many items scattered throughout the woods and fields illustrating where the fighting had been the most intense.

The farm was south of Lee Town Road and far back into the trees. It was about 45 acres, much of which was forested, but it also contained about 25 acres of pastureland. Caleb pulled up the drive through large oak trees, and in the clearing ahead stood the house. It was a simple home, not particularly large, but it had a long porch facing to the northeast. A high-pitched roof was covered in a metal roof, which looked fairly new. Caleb recalled that Warren was going to put on a new roof, and it looked like he got it done. There was a garage slightly apart from the house with two doors, one of which looked askew. Both the house and the garage had horizontal wood siding in a naturally weathered grey color.

"This place doesn't look too bad, Caleb," said Lonnie Rex. "Is that a barn in back?"

"Well, not much of a barn. I mean it's small but sound. There's room for a couple of stalls at most, and leave a little spot for tack, as I remember. The hay loft is good, but if I remember correctly one of the doors out to the pasture needs some work. It's been a while," Caleb said as he pulled to a stop.

Both got out of the truck and walked around the house together. In the back, there was another small porch that connected to the kitchen on the inside. Everything looked to be in reasonable shape. Caleb imagined he might move in right away. Then he thought it depended on how well the pasture was fenced for Cisco.

Coming back to the front, Caleb stepped up on the porch, which creaked a little under foot. As he crossed to the door, he pulled the note with the combination out of his pocket. The lock box was hanging on the door just as Nancy said. Once he entered the code, it snapped open and revealed the key inside. Caleb opened the door, noticing that there was no screen. Must fix that, he thought to himself.

The front door opened directly into the living room and dining room combined, which was a bit larger than Caleb remembered it. One end of the room had a large fireplace and wood box all constructed of river rock with a heavy timber mantel set in stone. There were windows opening out to the porch and looking out back toward the barn. The furnishings were very sparse and not very appealing, except for a large heavy and low "coffee table" in front of the fireplace. It was of hewn timbers and looked to be quite old. The entire room was a bit dark despite the windows and badly needed painting.

"Well, hell, I could live here," observed Lonnie Rex. "I guess."

"Yeah, it's not bad. Look at the kitchen, though."

Walking around a battered dining table with just three chairs, they entered the kitchen, which was at one end of the house. This was not at all appealing. The appliances were very old and set into cabinets that must have been there since the house was built. The island table in the kitchen was also on its last legs.

"Now this needs some work for sure. I'm not sure I can use anything—might need to start over," observed Caleb.

"Yeah, tear it all out. The floors are great though," Lonnie Rex said as he looked at the wide pine boards. "You don't see wood floors like that anymore."

"Let's go to the bedrooms. They're down the hall beside the fireplace."

The first bedroom was rather small but had large windows out to the south. Walking further down the hall, they passed a bathroom and then entered the larger of the two bedrooms. It was ample in size and had a large closet in the far wall but no separate bathroom. The floors were of the same wide board planks as was true throughout the house.

"You're not going to have much company, huh?" quipped Lonnie.

"Guess not, but I hadn't planned on any. I'll probably use that small bedroom as an office or music room or general storage room. Who knows?"

"This place doesn't have any central heat. All I see is those vertical heaters on the walls of each room. Must be propane," said Lonnie.

"The tank is out back next to the barn if I remember correctly. I was only here in the summer a couple of times, so I don't know how well they worked. And there's no air conditioning, just a couple of window units, the one in the large bedroom and that one in the living area. Might be a little hot, but it always seemed to be comfortable—good cross-ventilation."

"Let's go see the barn. I never spent any time out there, but I think I can fix it up. It's good storage though. I think it's dry."

After walking through the barn, Lonnie quipped, "Looks like moving in here will have to be delayed. There's a lot of work to do. You know that, if nothing else, you can stay with me. My house is huge."

"Thanks, but I'm good at Sarah's, and I have my trailer, which has living quarters in it. I can park it out here as a place to stay while I work on everything. I need to check the fence lines to be sure they are good for my horse."

"You brought a horse?" asked Lonnie.

"Of course. I don't go anywhere without Cisco Bay. He's my cutting horse. We go back a long way. I left a filly back at the ranch for the owner to keep, but Cisco is here."

Looking at the fence line, it was clear that there was quite a bit of repair to do before it would serve as Cisco's home. Caleb said, "That fence will be the first thing. We can't come out here until that is all good. But look at the grass! We don't have grass like that back on the ranch."

"What's the story on water? Good well?" asked Lonnie Rex.

"I have no idea. It served Warren, so it must be okay, but I'll have to get it checked out."

"The more I look, the more work I see," said Lonnie. "I'll be glad to help. I'm handy you know."

"I remember, and I expect I will call on you more than you might like."

"What's that little low building over there by the tree line?" asked Lonnie Rex.

"I don't know. I think Warren pointed it out one time and said it was an old still."

"Then I'm certainly going to help! You can pay me in moonshine."

Caleb laughed and, shaking his head, said, "I said at one time—long ago. We'll have to get by on store-bought."

"Speaking of which, don't you think it's time to get over to Sarah's for a little happy hour and some steaks?" Caleb wondered aloud. "I've got some Irish whisky in the trailer."

"Sounds good, and as you know, I ain't particular," Lonnie allowed.

"Let's go then. I'll come back out and do some more figuring on what all I'm going to do. I'm in no rush. A good long visit with Sarah is what's needed, and I think enjoying this reunion will be fun. I might not start anything for weeks."

Lonnie Rex sipped on his whisky as Caleb grilled the steaks. Sarah prepared other dishes to accompany the meat. While Caleb cooked, the talk turned to the reunion. Lonnie Rex outlined the events coming up in two weeks. The first "official" event was to be an evening bonfire with music to be held down at the lake, a few miles east of Rogers. Everyone would gather at the group shelter, which had been reserved for both Thursday and Friday. Lonnie expected that attendance would be approximately 50 people, maybe a few more. Gina had arranged for a local band to provide the music, a mix of country and western with a good sprinkling of rock music—all the stuff they grew up with. It was at this event that Lonnie Rex had indicated he wanted to get Caleb to play. Almost no one had ever heard Caleb play his violin, but Lonnie knew that his skill would fit in and be enjoyed.

Then on Friday would be a big picnic in the same group shelter. It would start at 11:00 a.m. with a barbecue served from 12:00 p.m. until 2:00 p.m. He expected that the gathering would last far into the afternoon. That night, starting at 6:00 p.m., there would be an "open house" at the Big-Wigs lounge. They had decided to call it an open house rather than a cocktail party, in the hope that more people would be inclined to attend. Lonnie said there would be an open bar but also soft drinks and selections of food, plus people could order from the bar menu. Nothing else was scheduled for that night on the understanding that there would be many small gatherings at people's homes. Lonnie Rex thought he would do one himself but didn't plan on doing any house cleaning in preparation. Whoever came over was welcome, but it would be after the Big-Wigs thing since Lonnie wanted to be at the lounge.

The following Saturday morning, there would be a sponsored breakfast in the ballroom of the Ozark Hotel. Casper's Grille was also available for the grease lovers who fancied that sort of a start to their day. The dinner and dance would be starting at 6:00 p.m. that night for cocktails, followed by a dinner at 7:00 p.m. and dancing until 11:00 p.m. Lonnie indicated that the hotel always did a very good job with the entire affair. The cost of the dinner/dance was $45 a head and the bar was a cash bar. The cost for everything else was $40, so the total cost was to be $85 per person.

"Sounds good to me," said Caleb. "When do we pay?"

"When you register—anytime from Thursday on. There'll be a desk at the hotel."

"Sounds like I may spend the night at your house, Lonnie. I'll bring my bedroll. That's the way we always did it at the ranches when we had a shindig."

"Whatever you want. Pick a room early! Just remember the next day starts at 6:00 a.m. at Casper's."

Sarah looked out from the kitchen and shouted, "Everything's ready. Are the steaks done?"

"Yours and mine maybe, but Lonnie needs it a little bit more brittle. Be a minute."

"Oh, let's go. It looks fine—I'm too hungry to be picky," said Lonnie Rex.

After dinner, everyone moved to the front porch. Caleb had some strong coffee along with some cookies Sarah had made. It took a while for Sarah to ask all the questions she could think up, many of which didn't even require answers. It was not often that she had company at dinner, and it was a welcome event. She had not seen Lonnie Rex for some time, and that alone required quite a bit of interrogation. Caleb occasionally attempted to interject things but without an all-out effort on his part, it just didn't stick. Lonnie Rex rose to the occasion and provided all the latest gossip of which he was aware.

There was a quiet spot in the conversation, and Caleb took the opportunity to change the subject. "Today I met with Nancy at her office. She was busy today but indicated she could come out tomorrow or Saturday so we could open the trunk."

Turning to Lonnie Rex, Caleb reminded him, "You remember I told you about that trunk that Warren left. We need to open it, and Nancy will need to be here too. You're welcome of course."

"You don't need me. If you like opening trunks, come to my house. I've got all kinds of crapola in the garage, some of it in trunks or boxes, all for your opening pleasure. I've even got stuff from Jaws Two—she left it and promised to get it later, but now she just uses me as a storage facility."

"No thanks, Lonnie. I shudder to think what you have out there," replied Caleb.

"Treasures, according to Jaws Two!"

Looking at Sarah, Caleb said, "Nancy thinks you have some sort of Bible study tomorrow night and the opening of the trunk might have to wait until Saturday."

"Yes, I do, but I'll skip it this week. Let's get on with it. I'm too curious to wait," said Sarah.

"Okay. I said I would pick her up in the afternoon. I'll call and let her know that we can do it Friday."

Putting her hand on Caleb's knee, Sarah said, "Now Caleb, I do want you to go with me to church this Sunday. Will you come? I know you're not a big fan of church, but you might like my little church. There's lots of good people whom I really love, and they would love to meet you. Would you come? I think it would be wonderful. I think you would like our preacher—he's retired from a bigger church in Little Rock, and he's been here for over four years. He and his wife. We just love him—well actually both; would you come?"

"Yes, okay, yes, and of course."

With that commitment from Caleb, the evening ended. Caleb took Lonnie Rex back to town. On the return trip, his thoughts returned to Lori. He remembered that she had an aunt still living here. That must be the real reason she comes back—it probably doesn't have anything to do with him. He was being stupid by getting stirred up by her name on the list. Those days were gone and would stay gone. He was sure.

TWELVE

When Friday came, Caleb picked up Nancy in the mid-afternoon. The sky was darkening, and a languid breeze blew steadily from the southwest. There was no escaping the conclusion that a bit of rain would be upon them before the evening was out. It wasn't like out west where you could see what was coming at you across the prairie. Here in the Ozarks, it just grew the darkness around you with no real warning as to when the sky would open up. You had to wait and wonder.

At Sarah's, they all gathered on the porch for a little catching up and a glass of tea. Caleb let the conversation run down and then said, "I'll bring the trunk up here to the porch. We can open it here."

"No, bring it into the living room. It could start to rain any time, and if it takes a long time to go through it, I want to be inside," said Sarah.

"No problem. It'll go into the living room."

"If it's too heavy holler, and we'll help," said Nancy.

"Shouldn't be a problem. Be right back."

As Sarah settled on the couch in the living room, Nancy got the key out of her purse and handed it to Sarah. "We've been wanting to do this for a long time, huh?" said Nancy.

"I was awfully curious at first. I mean, why the separate key thing, you know? But I learned to live with curiosity. After all, there's probably nothing significant in there. Warren lived a simple life in his last days and kept to himself. He wasn't involved in anything that I know of," allowed Sarah.

"I know. He had that diesel service station for a few years, but that's been over for what, four years? I guess he just leased it. And now they have torn it down and are starting some construction," Nancy reminded Sarah.

Both looked up when Caleb carried the trunk into the center of the living room. After he set it down, Sarah handed him the key, before pronouncing, "Hold it. I've got to go pee. Don't start without me."

Caleb paused, key in hand, and smiled at Nancy. "How about you?

Nancy only shook her head.

Both sat quietly for a minute.

"Okay, I'm back," Sarah said while entering the room adjusting her blouse.

Caleb inserted the key and removed the lock. Setting it aside, he carefully lifted the lid of the old trunk. The inside was full of various items, but taped to the underside of the lid there were two envelopes. Both were manilla, and the one on the left had OPEN THIS FIRST printed in bold letters. Taped next to it was another envelope marked DO NOT OPEN—EYES ONLY DALE BIVENS.

Caleb removed the tape on the first envelope and broke the seal. He pulled out a long letter from Warren. As if to emphasize the revealing of the letter, the storm broke with a peel of thunder and the pounding of heavy rain on the roof. Everyone paused and looked out. Proceeding, Caleb laid the letter on the coffee table between them, and they all read the following:

Dear Caleb:

Today's date is November 28, 2013.

If you are reading this letter, then you have opened the trunk. You will notice another sealed letter addressed to Mayor Dale Bivens. I want you to give him that letter once you understand the contents of this one.

It is my wish that when you deliver it to him, you stay and listen to its contents along with him—but only you two.

First, I need to tell you a little more history. I told you most of my life story when I visited you on the ranch the last time, but I didn't tell it all. You were very good to listen to me relate the things that have happened to me, and you know that there are many things that I'm not happy about. Remember I said that trouble always seemed to follow me? Well, there's more to tell.

When I was in high school, I got in several fights. I thought of myself as a tough guy and looked out for my little brother, Taylor. He didn't really need my help, but it was the way I felt. Taylor and I used to hang out down at the gas station owned by "Lippy" Bendix (I don't remember his given name). There were other men who came down also and on a regular basis. The attraction was that Lippy had turned one of the bays of the station into sort of a lounge with old couches and tables. The men used to hang out and gamble. And drink. Remember that Rogers was dry, gambling was illegal, and we were underage. This all appealed to Taylor and me, so we went often. We were young for that crowd, but for some reason Lippy let us hang around.

One Friday night I went to the station, but Taylor didn't come that night. Just me and about three other men, all older than me. Their names do not matter, and they're all dead anyway. Around 10:00 p.m. this deputy sheriff came to the station. His name was Hollis Bivens. He was the uncle of Dale Bivens, the current mayor of Rogers. Hollis was always a very bad guy. He liked to harass people and throw his weight around. He was proud of being a deputy and wanted everyone to know he was the boss. He drank quite a lot, and that Friday night was no exception. He threatened to run everyone in for drinking or gambling or whatever. He was in uniform but wasn't on duty. Anyway, he was drunk and loud. I think he had it in for Lippy, but I don't know why. The men calmed him down, and he backed off. But I said some things that made him angry. I was underage and more of a target than the rest. He left after telling me to watch my back. Later, about midnight, everyone had gone except me and Lippy. I was helping Lippy clean up around the station when this Hollis guy came back.

He pulled his pistol out and said I had to come with him. By now he was very unsteady, and I knew he wasn't going to arrest me; not in that condition, and I was fearful of what he had in mind. Lippy tried to intervene, but Hollis knocked him to the ground. Then Hollis came at me waving his gun and cursing. I tried to avoid him, but he hit me across the face with the gun. I went down, but when I came up, I was out of control, angry. I hit him as hard as I could, and I must say that it was damn hard. He fell backward and hit his head on the concrete under the gas pump. His gun slid out of his hand, and he was out. Then I went to see about Lippy. He came around but was woozy. I got him up and gave him some water and a towel. He seemed okay.

The next thing we did was check on Hollis. He was still down against the pump with his head at a bad angle. We checked, and he was dead. I think the fall broke his neck. We just sat there looking at him. Lippy said good riddance to the bastard, but I wasn't feeling too tough anymore. I had killed a cop. There was no way that anyone would believe that it was self-defense. An underage kid, drinking illegally and gambling illegally with older guys. I was in deep trouble and didn't know what to do.

Lippy told me to grab hold of the body and help him drag it behind the station. I know I just stared at him, but he demanded that I help him. I did. Behind the station, there was an excavation underway where they were installing a new underground tank. It was a big hole with a deep trench going between it and beside the station. It was deep because of it being gas and all. Lippy and I threw his body into a deep area away from the tank. We tossed in his gun, then filled dirt in on top of him. It took us till about three in the morning. I just shoveled and didn't really know what I was doing, but Lippy kept going and saying stuff. He said that the complete backfilling would be done the next day and that no one would ever find the body, and he damn sure would never tell. Lippy really disliked Hollis. I don't know their whole story. Lippy told me to just leave town. School was over and I could go without suspicion. He told me to join the marines or such. Just get out of town. This secret would be kept forever. He was so adamant that I believed him. I couldn't see what else to do. Taylor never knew any of this.

I hung around a few days trying to act normal but then went down to the recruiter and joined the Army; actually, it was the Army Air Corps. I didn't want to be a Marine. They took me, and I was sent to basic training and then to Alamogordo, NM, where I learned about crew chief duties on several types of planes. You know what came after that.

I learned that Hollis's body had never been found even though there had been a big search. Lippy was the only one there who knew about it, and I didn't think that he would ever tell. He didn't even seem to care in those two weeks I was still in town. So that's what happened to Hollis Bivens. Lippy died with his share of the secret, and I kept the secret until this letter, which is after I am gone.

There's more:

You remember that I said that I had plenty of money? Well, that is a bit of an understatement. I had money from several sources. First, I came back from the Mideast with a sizable amount. It's not important how I got it, but it wasn't illegal. There was a lot of money passing through many hands in the oil business in the desert. They did business when I was over there on a cash basis. That's what it took to get things done. I oversaw a lot of money, which I used to secure permits, approvals, laborers, and all sorts of stuff. Large sums of money came my way too, and it accumulated during 16 years of work. I also had a lot of gambling winnings (I never got over that little activity). And we all made good money working the pipelines. I accumulated a lot of cash. I began to wonder how I was going to get out with my money when an opportunity came along. They decided to close a big stretch of piping and send us all home. It had been 16 years for me. We could quit and stay in the Mideast, or we could hitch a ride back to the states on an oil company plane. That was how I got the money into the country—a duffel bag full of clothes and cash!

After getting a new job in Artesia, NM, still in the oil business, I began investing in the stock market. Nothing risky, just good stocks. I did it through a broker I had met. I did it a little at a time and hung on to everything without selling. It grew substantially. In addition, I had a good salary with the company and saved a lot. You know how simply

I lived. Long story short—when I moved back to Arkansas, I was rather wealthy. That was in 1999. I was 75 years old.

Once here, I bought the farm for cash. And transfer deeded it to you directly whenever I died. It's free and clear, and it is yours, which you know by now. In addition, when I found out Lippy's old station was still standing, I was amazed. It had not been a station for many years, and there had been some small insignificant businesses that had rented it, but nothing substantial. I found out that the local historical board would not let it be torn down, which I thought was stupid but must admit that I was happy about it. I think Hollis is still down there. Anyway, I found Lippy's son, Vernon. He is old but still alive at this writing. He couldn't ever sell the station for a good price since the city would not let it be torn down, but he needed money to cover his living expenses. So, I made him an offer he couldn't refuse. I didn't want my name on a deed, so I decided to rent it. I still had plenty of money and negotiated a lease deal that would give him significant income. The lease was until 2014 or his death or mine, whichever came first. At his death, if I was still alive, I could buy it for $50,000 from his estate, or walk away. He went for it. If I died first, who cared? It even made the city happy by my cleaning it up and operating it again as a sort of station. I never would sell any gas—I certainly didn't want them installing new tanks—and it made a great little shop for me to work on diesel equipment. It was something to do, and I made a little money.

I kept the station open as a diesel service center right up until I lost interest or couldn't do it anymore. That was in 2010. You know that I worked until I was nearly 85! I slowed down a lot when I did work, but I was good. When I quit working at the station, I paid up my rent through 2014, which was the end of the lease. I wanted that place untouched, and Vernon needed the money since he had moved into a rest home. We were both winners.

Healthwise, my life went downhill a little after I quit working. I just sat at the farm and made it through each subsequent day. I still had a good stash of money in cash on hand. When I first came back to Rogers, I opened an account and let a local accountant manage it. His name is Andrew Hastings, and his office is on 7th Street. There is a balance in *the account of around $65,000, and he has instructions to turn over any balance remaining to you. Just go see him, and he will take care of it. There is no will, as I'm doing everything directly.*

That takes care of all my assets except one. There remains some cash not in any account. My wishes for the dispensation of it are explained in the letter to Dale Bivens. When you and Dale read his letter, you will know the final task to be performed. I want you to do as it says in that letter. When you and he read it, you will understand. I checked with a local attorney about all of this. He is a man who brought his old Dodge truck to me to have the engine rebuilt. I didn't want to officially consult with any attorney, and I was pretty sure what I wanted to do was okay anyway, but I spoke to him. I only asked him if I could give money away as I saw fit, without any other consequences and he affirmed that I could, with the understanding that depending on the amount a person might receive, they might have to declare it on their taxes. Otherwise, it is mine to dispense with as I saw fit. He knows nothing about how much there is or where it is. All that I want done will be explained in the letter to Dale Bivens, which you must read with him.

The rest of the stuff in the trunk is just keepsakes, odds and ends, some books, and a bunch of photos. There is a pocket watch that belonged to your grandfather. He gave it to me, and you might like it. It still works. I also included copies of some documents in the manilla folder. There is a copy of the lease on the station, but it is over since I paid the rent in full and didn't choose to ever buy the station. Everything is just records for your information. Other than the letter to Dale, there is nothing for you to do. Enjoy the farm as you wish. By the way, the hot water heater needs to be replaced because it leaks a little, as you will see.

I don't know how long I will last. My health is clearly fading, and it's getting tough to get around. I'm not seeing any doctors or doing anything to prolong my life. I reckon I'll die here on the farm one day, and that suits me fine. I'm finished with everything in life now that this trunk has been delivered to Sarah, and you know everything or soon will.

Thanks for everything. I hope to see you in that place you promised,
Warren Atwood

In stunned silence, each one of them contemplated what they had just read.

THIRTEEN

Caleb spoke first. "Well I knew a lot of Warren's past, but this is certainly a surprise. He lived his entire life with this hanging over his head."

"When did all this happen?" asked Nancy.

"Warren was born in... what? Around 1924 or '25?" Caleb asked.

"That's right. Dad was born in 1927, so that means that Warren was born in 1925. He was two years older than dad. And that would mean high school would have ended for him in about 1943. So, this Hollis thing must have happened in late 1943 or early 1944," said Sarah.

"About right—toward the close of the war. Warren never went overseas with the military. By the time he finished basic, it was ending. And he went to Alamogordo. That's close to Artesia where he ended up," offered Caleb.

"Do you think this guy... Hollis is still buried down there?" Sarah wondered aloud.

"Warren said that he thought he was, at least while he owned and leased the station, but that ended in 2014 when the lease ran out. What's happened since then?" asked Caleb.

"Nothing really," said Sarah, "Except they've torn the old station down. They did some demolition earlier this year. I don't know what's going on though."

Nancy chimed in. "Don't you remember? The old station came before the Historical Preservation Board late in 2014. There was a request to have it torn down. The mayor, Dale Bivens, had indicated to the town council that he thought it should be torn down because it was a good location, and new development could benefit the town. Some of us didn't want to see it go, but we didn't have much ammunition. It was empty again, and there wasn't any indication that things were going to improve. It was a little piece of Rogers history, but we lost the vote, and the approval to remove it was granted. I think there were only two of us who voted to save it."

"That was before I got on the board," said Sarah.

"Yeah, you didn't come on until the first of this year," Nancy reminded her.

"Who wanted to tear it down?" asked Caleb.

"It was a corporate name, and I don't remember what it was, but the guy behind it was a local developer named Dumar Ashton," explained Nancy.

"Dumar!" exclaimed Caleb. "That guy graduated with me, and he was at the university when I was there—in law school. It's a small world for sure."

"Dumar Ashton doesn't have a great reputation locally. He's always buying depressed or tax-delinquent properties for a song, and then building something new. Nothing illegal, but some people have not appreciated how he's gone about it," inserted Nancy. "And now that I think about it, he has been associated with the mayor for some time. I think he ran his campaign in the last election and maybe the one before that. Anyway, they're tight."

Caleb started chuckling. When the girls looked at him, he waved his hand and said, "Oh, it's nothing. I was just remembering what Lonnie Rex said. He reminded me that Dumar's nickname in high school was 'Dumb Ash'—you know, Dumar Ashton...."

"Oh, that's horrible," said Sarah.

"But funny," responded Caleb. "I've known a lot of nicknames in my time, and many of them are not very complimentary. You should hear what some of the cowboys call each other."

"Anyway," continued Caleb, "It's got nothing to do with Warren's story. They can do what they want with the station. The only thing is if they dug up the body, it would be in the news. For that matter, we should do a little research into this story about Hollis. You know—check the news reports from back then, see what happened. Warren's story should be checked out. I reckon it's all true, but I wouldn't mind knowing more, especially since I must give this other letter to the mayor. I can't open it, but I would certainly like to know more about the history before I give it to him."

Sarah inserted, "This was all long before you two were born. And before me too. I was born in '46, a couple of years after it was supposed to have happened. I don't remember anyone talking about it when I grew up."

Thinking for a minute, Nancy offered, "Me neither, at least not about Hollis, but my dad was one of the ones who used to go down there to that station. The drinking and socializing continued for many years while Lippy owned it. Daddy died in 1989. I can remember him coming home from there back in the 70s. Mom used to get a little pissed at him. I don't think she minded his drinking, since she drank too, but she hated to miss out on any fun," said Nancy.

"I know what I can do," Caleb inserted. "I can call Peter Mason. He owns, or operates, the newspaper. I'll call him, and he can research it or let me come in and look at old newspaper accounts. He's on the reunion committee, and I knew him in high school."

"I know him. He's good and should be helpful. But you need to do it soon. When are you going to give the letter to the mayor?"

"You know, there's no rush, other than our curiosity. I will get the history and then see when to go. Probably next week."

Caleb turned his attention to the contents of the trunk. He found the things that Warren spoke of. The watch was a gold Elgin pocket model that seemed to work after he wound it. There were a great many photographs, which Caleb put aside to look through later. The files of documents were all there, and in the very bottom, Caleb found an old revolver. It was some sort of foreign make but looked to be in good condition. There was even a large sack full of coins from various countries. Quite a bunch of "treasures," Caleb thought.

"Let's eat," said Sarah. "I've got some French dip sandwiches and some potato salad. That sound good?"

"Sounds great to me," said Caleb, "and while you fix that, I think I'll call Peter at the paper. He may still be there, and it would be good if I can catch him before the weekend."

"I'll help you, Sarah. Do you have any sweet tea?" said Nancy.

The girls went into the kitchen while Caleb walked over to the phone. He looked up the number for the paper in the phone book. Caleb was surprised to find that they still used phone books in Rogers. It seemed that they were going out of style but was glad one was there. Then he noticed that it was quite old and scribbled on. 2011 it said on the cover. Still good for the newspaper, Caleb thought.

When the receptionist answered, Caleb asked, "Is Peter Mason available?"

"Hold on just one minute; I'll see if he is still here."

Peter came on the line after a few moments, "Peter here, how can I help you?"

"Peter, this is Caleb Atwood."

"Caleb? Heh, Caleb! I heard you were coming back for the reunion. Are you here?"

"Yes, I got in a couple of days ago. Looking forward to the reunion and to seeing everyone. How are you doing?"

"Great—still perking and printing stories of all the local goings-on. Full-time job, you know."

"I can imagine. It is in that regard that I called you. Can I ask for your help with a little research from history—you know, old articles from long ago?"

"Sure, what do you need?"

"I should tell you in person and explain what is involved. Would it be possible for me to come by and let you know what I need?"

"It's a little late for today and tomorrow's the weekend. Tell me what it is, and I can look through the files. They're all electronic now, and I can just pull them up. Otherwise, you can come by Monday."

"Monday's good, but I guess if you have the time, you could look it all up first. Whatever's easiest."

"Not hard. Tell me what it is," said Peter.

"I want to see any stories starting from say mid-1943 through 1944, about a sheriff's deputy who may have disappeared. His name is Hollis Bivens."

"That's quite a while ago. Some of those old files didn't get digitized, but I can look. Plan on coming by Monday before noon. I'll tell you what I find, and we can get some lunch. It'll be good to catch up."

"Sounds great. I'll be there."

When Caleb returned to the kitchen, Sarah asked, "Did you get him? Was he there?"

"Yeah, I talked to him."

"What is he going to do? Can he help? That's a long time ago, and it may take a lot of work to find information. Do you have to go down to the paper?"

"Uh, yes, he can help, but I don't have to go down until Monday. Most of the stories are in electronic format, and he can look them up and fill me in then."

"How much did you tell him?" asked Nancy.

"Just the year and the Hollis Bivens name. Nothing else. Nothing about Warren."

Sarah said, "Dinner is about ready. Take a seat, and we can eat. Sweet tea for Nancy, and what do you want, Caleb?"

"Unsweetened please."

"What are we going to do next?"

"Absolutely nothing. Not until Monday. I'm going to take a day to kick back. I need to work Cisco a little and do some laundry tomorrow. Otherwise, just look forward to each meal."

"That sounds perfect," said Sarah. "Then Church on Sunday."

"Oh, yeah… right," Caleb mumbled.

FOURTEEN

Sarah's church was located on West Poplar Street, a little south and west of downtown. The church was a stately edifice dating from the mid-1900s. It was originally known as the Shepherd's Baptist Church and had served its congregation faithfully until 1997 when it was renamed Pilgrim's Church. The little church was now non-denominational. The change had occurred many years before Sarah had begun attending. Her joy in the church was every bit a result of what it was today.

The church was clad in white wood and framed in front by four columns supporting a steeply pitched roof. Immediately soaring above was the bell tower, which culminated in a steep-sided spire. It was not unlike many small churches throughout the nation. It was a little bit "country" while having that old neighborhood appeal.

Sarah explained how much she enjoyed the church. It had become the center of her life in Rogers. The congregation was rather small, and while not presently growing, was very stable in its attendance and devotion to the Word. The parishioners were mostly middle-aged or older people steadfast in their shared worship. The church was scripture based and simple, as it searched for and shared the Gospel. Sarah could not contain her enthusiasm when talking of "her" church. She told Caleb everything about their preacher, Pastor Wendell Reid. He had come to the church a few years back just before she had begun attending and had fashioned a loving relationship with all in the congregation. In addition to Sarah's admiration of Pastor Wendell, she was especially thrilled by the church music. It was mostly traditional, but what set it apart in Sarah's mind was its quality. The church was fortunate in having several singers and musicians who brought strong talent and faith to every service.

Caleb was attentive to Sarah's joyful description of what was to come as they drove to church. He was very pleased with her enthusiasm and thought that was as it should be. He had never found such satisfaction in any church. To be sure, he had not attended many, and certainly not to an extent that he ever felt as though he belonged. He had been satisfied with his solitary walk with the Lord. He wasn't sure that could be improved upon. But Caleb also knew that Sarah, in her devotion, had led him in many ways to find the presence of God in everyday life. Well, with that one exception back in his college days, but that was certainly behind them, or at least he hoped so, and that it was not going to be repeated this morning.

As they turned onto West Poplar, Sarah drove slowly past the front of the church and pulled into the parking lot on the west. She waved at several people walking into church while she parked. Caleb tried to contain his laughter but was failing. Sarah looked at him with concern, and not wanting to give her the wrong impression, he simply stated, "Sarah, look at the sign out front."

"The sign? What about the sign?" she challenged.

"Just look at the sign."

As she got out of the car, she turned back toward the front and saw the sign. It read:

Today's Sermon
WHAT IS HELL?
Come early
and hear our choir practice

"What…. Oh, goodness!" She began laughing with Caleb. "Oh my, that won't do. I've got to tell Eddy. What was he thinking?"

"Probably wasn't," replied Caleb as he got out of her car, still chuckling.

"Come on in. I want you to meet people. Don't say anything about the sign. I'll find Eddy and let him know. Come on," she said as she reached for Caleb's arm.

"Don't worry about the sign. I'm excited about hearing the choir now — a lot more than when you merely told me how good they were." Caleb laughed again.

They stepped up on the porch and drew near to the man greeting at the door. Sarah tugged at Caleb and whispered, "Hush now." Continuing in full voice, she said, "Pastor Wendell, I would like you to meet my brother, Caleb. Caleb, this is Wendell Reid, our Pastor."

"Good morning, all." Looking at Caleb as they shook hands, he said, "So great to meet you and to have you with us this morning. Sarah has told us all so much about you. Sounds like you are a real cowboy and a lover of the Lord."

"Reckon that's true on both counts. Except maybe my cowboying days are coming to an end. Looks like I might become a farmer or some sort of local character. Time will tell. Whatever the Lord has in mind."

"Well, you are so very welcome. Sarah here is dear to all of us. She's always available to contribute her energy to anything we do. She's quite valuable to our congregation and dearly loved. We're so glad you are here, and I hope we get to visit more after the service."

"I got a kick out of your sign," said Caleb.

"The sign? What about the…" Wendell stole a quick glance. "Well, there you have it. We try to compose the sign so it imparts the essence of our morning in as few words as possible. Looks like we might have exceeded all expectations," he said as he joined in the laughter. "Maybe I should work the message into my sermon."

"Looking forward to it," said Caleb.

Moving inside, Sarah whispered, "I told you not to say anything."

"Yeah, but I did. Just couldn't help myself."

As she was laughing, Sarah was tapped on the shoulder by an elderly woman. Turning, she said, "Caleb, this is Ivey Furness. She plays the piano every morning. Ivey, meet Caleb."

"I'm glad to meet you, Caleb. I have so much I want to ask you, but now I've got to get up there. They want to start. Just had to say hi."

Ivey scurried to the front of the church as Sarah said, "Wait 'till you hear her play. She's so good! They all are—you'll see. Let's sit here. I always sit here."

Caleb looked around the sanctuary. It was about a fourth full, with people spread out alone or in small groups. Some talked over their shoulders or stretched toward a listener, while a few walked around and made greetings. There was a hum of visiting from every corner of the room. Just as Sarah and Caleb took their seats, everyone quieted in anticipation. The music began. The "band" consisted of a guitar, a bass guitar, a full upright bass, and of course, the piano. A couple of other instruments leaned in their racks. One man played the guitar introduction of the melody by smoothly picking out each note. It was Caleb's observation that the musician was very skillful. Then the piano embellished the tune into the familiar lilting melody. Immediately the choir began in unison and harmony to lead the congregation in "How Great Thou Art." It was a moving performance and quite a pleasant surprise to Caleb. This was a primary love of his: making real music with friends. He missed the ranch jam sessions instantly but quickly got lost in the gospel melodies sung and played by this little choir.

At the conclusion of a selection of several hymns, Pastor Wendell stepped to the pulpit and spoke to the congregation.

"Friends in Christ, welcome on this beautiful morning. I look out over you and see all the faces that grace my life and each of yours as we walk with the Lord."

"This morning, we have a guest, which I would like to introduce. Sarah's brother, Caleb, is with us today. Caleb, please stand so we can welcome you," intoned Wendell.

Caleb stood and looked around at the people seated around the sanctuary. "Thank you, I'm very glad to be here," he said to murmurs of welcome.

Pastor Wendell continued, "Sarah has told us all a good bit about you, and you are most welcome to join our worship services on this day. Everyone, please get to know Caleb after our services."

Continuing, he said, "Upon entering the church this morning, Caleb brought to my attention the unique message on our church sign. It appears that the message imparted about the quality of our choir as they rehearse is overshadowed by another interpretation—one that is rather humorous. It certainly was not the intent to plant the notion that listening to the choir would be hell." There was a ripple of laughter across the audience.

Looking at Eddy, Wendell said, "Eddy, don't be embarrassed. In fact, you can take full credit for what is to follow. I am going to skip my prepared sermon and take a new tact.

"I'll call this morning's sermon, 'Planting the Notion.'

"We 'plant a notion' in the eyes and ears of others with everything we do. When we act, speak, write, or just go about our daily business we leave a trail of impressions. As Christians, we are intently aware of the calling upon each of us to witness to all our belief and faith in the Lord. We imagine ourselves sitting over coffee and telling others about the Gospel and what it means in our lives. We live in hope that those who do not know the Lord will ask us important questions, such as 'Why do you believe?' or 'How do you know God,' or even 'Does God really exist?' Once asked, we can spring into action, if we're prepared, to tell the questioner all we know and believe. That is as it should be.

"However, we 'plant a notion' of the Presence of the Lord in everything we do—not just in response to a well-formed question, but because of how we live our lives. Every act or word can impart an impression of that which is important to us, intended or unintended. Anyone here could relate a strong impression of members of our congregation and of others we know. We can identify what is important to them and what they believe by the 'notions' we have received from them.

"We can and do follow our faith by our attendance at church, by our attention to the Word, and in our prayer life. These are the foundations of our practice as Christians. But does that impart a full picture of our walk with the Lord to those around us? Who watches us go to church? Who watches or listens to us pray? Who watches us read the Gospel? Of course, the primary answer is God. Absolutely. That is our communion with the Lord. But without watching us in our worship activities, how can others gain a 'notion' of how the Lord works in our lives? They gain that 'notion' from everything that they do witness—every act we perform, our response to the challenges of life, the words we speak, and any impression that we leave.

"We are painfully aware of the criticism voiced by non-believers in which they profess how they cannot understand how Christians could behave in manners that speak not at all to their beliefs.

"They see us when we tell untruths, when we harbor resentments, when we speak ill of others, when we fail to answer the call of others in need, and in a myriad of other ways. These actions are seen as a disconnect from our professions of faith. They watch our behavior, and what they see distances them from us and from the Lord. We all understand that we cannot avoid sinful behavior, for we are indeed sinners. But we have the power and the responsibility to address any sinful behavior by honestly acknowledging, avoiding, and repenting from such behavior. As we confront the sin in our lives, it does indeed 'plant a notion' in those around us. They see our humanity, our honesty, and our faith in our visible walk with the Lord. That is a 'notion' and a message that we should strive to implant.

"One may ask, 'How do we do this?' 'How do we display our faith?' Since we already worship, read the Word, and pray, isn't that the way? Isn't that enough? What is required for us to do to 'plant the notion' of the Lord in all we encounter?

"Therein lies the ultimate and truthful question. The answer is very simple to say. It's even simple to understand, and when understood and embraced, it is simple to do. To 'plant the notion' of the Lord, we must first allow Him to occupy a Presence in our daily lives. That Presence is to be constant—it colors our every interaction and decision. He speaks to us when we listen to Him. We listen to Him when we arise in the morning, we listen to Him when we make the coffee, we listen to Him as we pull weeds, we listen to Him when we shop, we listen to Him when we converse with others, and we listen to Him as we experience every joy and as we face every dilemma which confronts us. I said it was simple. He makes it simple by always being there. He makes it simple by fulfilling His promises to us. He makes it simple through His abundant understanding.

"When the Presence of the Lord is the true constant in our lives, then we will go forth and firmly 'plant the notion' of that Presence in all about us.

"Let us pray.

"Lord, hear the thoughts of your people today, and come peacefully into all our moments henceforth, so that we may enjoy your constant companionship in everything we say and do, Amen.

"Let's take the time made available by my relatively short sermon today to enjoy each other's company and go further along in our walk with the Lord, as we allow His Presence in every aspect of our lives. Go in peace."

FIFTEEN

The people of the church slowly rose from their seats and began to visit among themselves. Some gathered in the aisles and lingered in the aftermath of the sermon where they talked in quiet tones. Sarah and Caleb did not make it very far down the aisle before being inundated with visitors, quite intent on saying high to Sarah and meeting Caleb.

The first person to come up to them was Eddy Glover, who laughed and said, "Well, I guess I goofed on the sign this morning. I gotta go fix that thing right away and pay more attention. Wendell made it sound like he wasn't bothered by the sign, but I kinda think I'm going to get a chewing."

"It gave us all a good laugh and caused Pastor Wendell to go in a new direction. I think it was great what he said today," said Sarah. "Keep up the good work on the sign. You're cherished by all of us."

An elderly man nodded to Sarah and proclaimed, "I must check out the scriptures. I'm not sure just where in scripture it says the things that Wendell talked about today. Sometimes he gets a little off scripture. He didn't give us any passages. Not sure what to think of it."

"Caleb, this is Oscar Baxter. Oscar is quite the biblical scholar," Sarah intoned.

"Nice to meet you, Oscar. I found his words to be quite clear even without any scripture, and I must say, quite to my liking," Caleb responded.

"Still gotta check. Can't be too careful nowadays."

"Oscar, I can give you several verses that come to mind that directly address the things Wendell said in his sermon. Would you like me to send them to you?" asked Sarah.

"I'll let you know; gotta think about it first." Turning to Caleb, he said, "Glad you could come today. This is a welcoming church, and we hope to see more of you. Bye, Sarah."

Clarice Bouvier approached Sarah and Caleb. Clarice was a strong patron of the arts and active in community theater. She was rather dramatic for Sarah's tastes but nevertheless a strong proponent of the end times and of all prophesies, which fascinated both.

"Clarice, please meet Caleb." Turning to Caleb, Sarah said, "Clarice is a kindred spirit. She and I share our scriptural study regularly. Clarice brings a flamboyant reading to all the passages. We don't always agree but treasure each other's interpretations."

"Howdy miss Clarice. I'm pleased to meet you," offered Caleb.

"You're such a handsome man! Have you ever done any theater? The community theater is always looking for people to join in our performances. We could use you."

"Reckon I haven't done any of that, although I do find it interesting. Maybe I'll sign up. Do you have performances in the old Viscount Theater?"

"Yes, we do, mostly. There are some other venues, but that one is our favorite. They have done such a good job of renovating the theater and managing it quite professionally," responded Clarice.

"Let me know when you need a cowboy. Maybe I'll sign up."

With a twinkle in her eye and a squeeze of Caleb's arm, Clarice said, "Oh, we will. You may hear from us."

"Thank you, ma'am."

Several members of the choir made their way to Sarah's side. It gave Caleb an opportunity to meet them and to comment on how much he enjoyed the music and that it took him back to the ranch where the cowboys all joined in singing after work.

"Do you sing, Caleb?" asked Virginia Mackey. "Maybe you would like to join us."

"Well, I do a little singing, but my first love is the violin, or the fiddle as they say in my circles."

"You would be most welcome to join us. We don't have a violin player among the group. It would be a wonderful addition!"

"Might just do that, ma'am," Caleb responded.

"Oh, do! We practice on Wednesday just before services. Come and play with us."

"We'll see how it goes."

Turning to Sarah, Virginia said, "We're all going to the Fisherman's Grill out by the lake. Can you join us?"

Sarah looked at Caleb and, reading relaxation on his part, said, "Sure, that would be fine. Is that fine with you, Caleb?"

"Yep. Never pass up a meal with new friends."

"Okay, see you there," said Virginia.

Sarah and Caleb made it to the door where Pastor Wendell was saying his goodbyes to people as they filed out. "Enjoyed your sermon Pastor Wendell," Sarah said. "It was short but rather inspiring."

"That's welcome praise from you, my dear. Welcome indeed. It was a spur of the moment switch. I couldn't pass up such an opportunity to comment on the impressions we leave and how we leave them. I must congratulate Eddy for his "unintended" inspiration. And I also know that brevity is always appreciated." Turning, he continued, "Caleb, it was so good to have you today. Hope you can come again."

"I think I will be back. Your words may have been brief, but it doesn't take long to speak simple truths. I enjoyed what you said."

"Well, I can be long-winded when the need arises and would love to visit with you at length—get the story on your walk with God."

"I'm always ready for a little talk about the Lord. I've done my share of telling the Word to listeners when they're either willing or captive," Caleb said with a grin.

"Good. I look forward to having you back."

As Sarah and Caleb walked toward the car, Sarah asked, "What did you think of our little church?"

"Just fine, I do believe." Caleb summarized. "Now let's go get some catfish."

SIXTEEN

The bell on the door jingled as Caleb entered Casper's Grille at 7:15 a.m. on Monday morning. He looked around the dining area and saw various groups of men having their morning coffee and breakfast. He was immediately aware of the fact that their gaze was lingering on him a little longer than what must be normal. Caleb wrote it off to the fact that he was unknown and to how he was dressed. Caleb's entire "collection" of clothing was comprised of western wear. He had on high-top cowboy boots, wrangler jeans, a long-sleeve shirt with vest, and his slightly battered felt cowboy hat. He had avoided his spurs, chinks, and wild rag as being both unnecessary and irregular. That was as far as he could go to meet local standards until he made a trip to the store for some overalls and maybe a John Deere hat. Until then, his present "look" would have to do. As the stares dissipated, Caleb spotted Lonnie Rex sitting alone at a table in the back room. Lonnie had reminded Caleb of his morning ritual and asked him to join him as early as possible.

As Caleb approached the table, he noticed that it was covered with used plates, morning paper strewn about, cigarette buts in the ashtray, and a sketchbook. It gave all the signs that Lonnie Rex had been there for some time.

"'Bout time you got here," Lonnie allowed.

"Been up a while. I had to see to Cisco. We have been getting out early in the morning but we're going to have to do our rides another time of day if I keep to this schedule. I do like this morning routine here at Casper's, so I hope Cisco understands." Continuing, Caleb asked, "How come they let you smoke in here?"

"Long as you stay in the back room, they let you. It's the smoking section. It may not last, but while it does, I'm happy."

A waitress came to the table as Caleb sat down. "What can I get for you, darlin'?"

"Caleb, this is Shirly; Shirly this is Caleb Atwood. Do you remember him?" asked Lonnie.

"Oh, yeah. Been a while though. What brings you back to us?" she inquired.

"Just life, a serious hunger, and a tolerance for this pilgrim," Caleb responded as he pointed at Lonnie Rex. "Why don't you bring me coffee to start, then a large omelet with a bunch of vegetables in it—you choose. Oh, and some bacon on the side."

"Coming up. You want grits?"

"Please, and a little toast too."

Turning to Lonnie, Caleb asked, "So, what's up with you?"

"Nothing much. Just been working at home. I delivered a few more pieces of art to the Big-Wigs; getting ready for the reunion. How about you?"

"I went to church with Sarah yesterday, then worked with Cisco. After that, I went up to the farm and checked out the fencing."

"So, she got you to church, huh? How was that?"

"I enjoyed it. Good music. In fact, it was very good! I may go down there and play a little fiddle with them. I also liked the preacher—better than most."

"Sarah would love to get you corralled into her church, or any church for that matter."

The waitress brought Caleb's coffee and poured some more into Lonnie Rex's cup. Lonnie added some more cream and then turned back to Caleb. "Did you open that old trunk?"

"Yes, we did. On Friday night. It contained mostly some keepsakes as I thought, but it also included two letters of significant interest," Caleb said as he reached into his vest pocket. "There's two; one which I was allowed to open and one which I am to deliver to this, uh... Dale Bivens."

"You mean the mayor?"

"Yes. That's him. But I am not supposed to open his until I deliver it, and then he and I are supposed to read it together alone."

"That's strange. What was in the one you opened?"

"Here, read it for yourself," Caleb said as he handed Lonnie the letter.

Lonnie Rex opened the letter and began to read while Caleb accepted his breakfast plate from Shirly. He started eating while Lonnie slowly studied the letter.

"Damn, your uncle killed this guy, didn't he?"

"Appears so; just keep reading."

After some time, Lonnie Rex looked up as he knocked another cigarette out of the crumpled pack. After he got it going, he said to Caleb, "I remember when your uncle ran his diesel service out of that old station. He was good, and a lot of the farmers used him. He was a lot better than the dealerships or other garages. At least that's what I heard. That station has been around forever, but they started tearing it down recently. I heard that it is to be an office building."

"Don't know much about that, but Nancy told me about how it was removed from historical protection. Anyway, it finally got approved for removal, and that's been completed as a part of the new construction. She also said that Dumar Ashton is the one that's developing it."

"Really? I saw where they did some excavating at first. Did they find this guy's body?"

"I don't know. I called Peter Mason over at the paper and asked him to research the stories from back when. He didn't mention anybody being found recently. Maybe it's long gone—

who knows? Peter said he would look it up and see what the paper had and that I could come by today for lunch and he would fill me in. Want to come?"

"Yeah, maybe. But tell me more. Where is this money? Do you know?"

"I've got no idea. Warren mentioned all his other assets, including the account, but left me in the dark about any other money. Maybe it's explained in the other letter. I guess I'll find out soon."

"Have you called the mayor?"

"Not yet. I thought I would find out all I could before going in there. You know, the history behind the death of this Hollis character, and maybe some more about what is going on at the station site."

"It sounds like that lunch with Peter might be interesting. You sure you don't mind if I come along?"

"No, I want you to, but here's the deal: besides Sarah and Nancy, and me of course, no one knows anything about this. Now you know. I don't know what's in the other letter, and it occurs to me that Warren may not have intended all this to become common knowledge. So, let's keep everything confidential until we know more. I mean the death of Hollis was a long time ago and impossible to do anything about, I guess. I don't want to soil Warren's memory if it's not his intent. Come with me and find out what Peter has, but it will remain between us until we know more. Okay?"

"No problem," promised Lonnie Rex.

"Besides, you might be a big help if we need to look into this more. For instance, it might be interesting to find out who the attorney is who got his truck serviced at the station. Not sure why, but he clearly knows Warren's intent with the money. I mean I don't know where it is or how much it is or anything. I just want to find out as much as possible before I go to the mayor. It occurs to me that the most likely reason that Warren wants to tell the mayor something is to give some sort of confession. What else could it be?"

"Maybe he wants to tell the mayor just how bad a guy ol' Hollis was. I mean he's the mayor's uncle, according to this letter. Dale might need to hear the truth of what this guy was like. Of course, Warren can't tell that without confessing the killing..." Lonnie Rex trailed off.

"I know, I know. I've thought about it, and there doesn't seem to be any reason to write to the mayor unless he wants to divulge some, or all, of the truth. What's this Dale Bivens guy like?"

"He's an okay mayor, I guess. I don't follow it much. He's popular, I reckon, and he does have a hand in some development around here, but it's all straightforward stuff. Nothing I know about him that is critical, other than he's a politician," Lonnie said with a laugh.

"Nancy said that Dumar was involved with the mayor in political activities. She said something about his serving in the mayor's campaigns."

"I'm not familiar with that, but it sounds likely. Like I told you the other day, Dumar is into development, and his reputation is not great. He and the mayor know each other, and they belong to the same church. I have heard some say that Dumar has gotten lucky with the city when it comes to getting approvals for his stuff, but it's all rumor. I don't follow local politics much. I guess that it might be easy to find out more about his real estate ventures, if we wanted to."

"We can wait. Dumar might be irrelevant. No sense wasting any time if there is no real connection. The only thing Nancy said is that Dumar is the one behind the development at the old station site and that it was a little interesting that the board voted to allow it to be torn down. She even said that the mayor had lobbied some of the board members about allowing the removal. But he made a good argument about allowing good development to go ahead since it was a significant site and could be good for the city. That makes sense.... I mean the station was apparently a bit of an eyesore."

"That's true," allowed Lonnie, "But it had quite a history. It's been there a long time and was rumored to be quite a hangout for drinking and gambling. You remember the stories: the owner providing a place for the locals to drink and all, sort of a low-end men's club."

"Yeah, Nancy said her dad used to hang out there. He was a good friend of my dad's back in the day, but Taylor's been long gone from here since my college days, so I never kept up with anything. As far as I can remember from my visits, the station was there and had a turnover of other businesses trying the location. It wasn't important to me. My visits were always just to see Sarah and to porch sit with you."

"I think it stopped being a station around the early 80s, but I could be wrong. Lots of other things since that time. Mostly silly stuff." Lonnie continued in a pensive manner, "I even remember when it was a damn "juice bar" for a while—for the emaciated vegan crowd, except there wasn't even a crowd. Used to be a few though, and they liked the juice bar. They also hung out at the Earth Foods store, which is a place full of all sorts of interesting creatures. I went over there to check it out, and I didn't know whether to be amused or mad! There were oddities with tattoos, blue hair, and rings in their ears. I swear, one cashier had bass lures hanging out of her nose! They all had a hungry look in their eyes," claimed Lonnie.

"One time this big guy came into the store wearing a t-shirt with PETA written on the front, but printed underneath was People Eat Tasty Animals. I thought there might be a fight, but no such luck. Nobody said anything to him, so all of them vegans got to live to be hungry another day," Lonnie said with a laugh.

Thinking back, Caleb said, "I saw some of that when I went up to Denver on business. And occasionally there would be some in La Veta, but they didn't stick around. Maybe they got hungry and left. No way to survive the day on only leafy greens. I mean,

I love vegetables, but give me a steak to ground the affair," proclaimed Caleb.

"Yeah, but if the old characters who used to hang out and drink and gamble at the old station could see the patrons when it was a juice bar, I bet they did some rolling!" said Lonnie Rex.

Caleb laughed and shook his head. "Maybe we ought to go over to that Earth Foods store for lunch sometime. Might be fun to see them in their natural habitat."

"Speaking of lunch, where are we going to meet Peter?" asked Lonnie.

"At his office, then he'll tell us. We'll meet at the paper at noon."

Getting up from the table, Lonnie Rex threw down some bills. "This here breakfast is on me, but I won't get in the habit. See you at the paper at noon."

After Lonnie had left, Caleb finished his coffee deep in thought.

SEVENTEEN

Caleb sat in his truck in the parking lot at the newspaper. He waited until Lonnie pulled into the lot before stepping out of the cab and joining Lonnie in a walk toward the entrance. They entered the lobby and Caleb asked to see Peter Mason. He was told to wait just one minute and that Peter expected him.

Peter emerged from the hallway and greeted them. "Great to see you, Caleb. So glad you could make it back. Hey Lonnie," he said as Lonnie nodded back.

"Good to be here," said Caleb. "You look prosperous. How's the newspaper business?"

"The newspaper business has changed. Local interest mainly and advertisement. Internet news and ads make it hard on papers, but we adjust and find news angles. We're doing okay. You'll have to tell me all about yourself. I haven't seen you in a long time."

"I'll fill you in as we go. Are we going out or looking at stuff here?"

"Come on back. I'll show you what I've found, and then we can discuss more over lunch."

As they settled in Peter's office, Peter pulled up a file of copies of stories. "You know there was quite a lot on the disappearance of Hollis Bivens. Several articles and reports. I remembered a little about it from previous research I had done that cross-referenced it, but it took me doing some looking to fully recall the story. Do you want to read all this or have me summarize it?"

"Just tell us about it. If I can take copies, I can read it all later," said Caleb.

"Very well. Let's see, Hollis Bivens was a deputy sheriff for Benton County. He served from early 1940 up until his disappearance. That took place, or was first reported, on May 25, 1944. There was a lapse of two days from the time his family last saw him until they reported it. Apparently, it was not unusual for Hollis to be gone, sometimes for days, before returning home. He wasn't married. He lived alone, but near his parents. Anyway, it was reported by his father, Clayton Bivens, according to the earliest article I found."

"The sheriff's office didn't immediately spring into action. It seems that there was some initial lack of concern, but within a couple more days, and at the insistence of Hollis's parents, they began an all-out search. When the sheriff and police began looking into it, several reports came in about his activities. Not all of these "activities" reflected positively on Hollis. He was seen at the home of a local woman on the night of May 23, and that was the latest report submitted. That report wasn't very complimentary of Hollis. It seems that she came forth on the 24th claiming that Hollis had accosted her in some way at her home. This was before the disappearance was reported. She had no idea he was missing. She just wanted to get the police to keep him away from her. Nothing was done about her complaint since he turned up missing the next day. They had no way to investigate her allegations."

"Once Hollis was missing, and the sheriff took it seriously, the department notified the paper, put out information to other agencies, and the search began. Hollis's brother, Dennis, was especially insistent and active in the search. There is one article in which he was interviewed and claimed that Hollis had met with foul play. When questioned about any possible enemies Hollis might have, his brother was not forthcoming."

"The story of the search was in and out of the papers for about two weeks, but there was absolutely no trace uncovered.

Hollis had just vanished. His car was found at the home of the woman who had reported him for the abuse, or attack, or whatever it was, but that didn't lead to anything except to confirm that he had been there and that it was the last place he was seen. The woman became a suspect, but nothing was discovered which implicated her, and under the intense pressure of Hollis's brother, nothing was reported to the press about her complaint for over a month."

"Later, in an article written on July 8, the paper printed a story about the woman's complaint lodged at the start of the whole affair, with the implication that Hollis's behavior was potentially a cause of his disappearance. Speculation began that he might be guilty of something and was at large. But nothing was ever found, no evidence, no reports, and no contacts. The investigation, if it ever was one, ground to a halt. It tainted the family's reputation, and Dennis, Hollis's brother, was especially vocal about it. He was very critical of the sheriff's department for doing nothing and for allowing the negative reports to circulate. Of course, there was nothing to do. Hollis has been gone now for, what, 70-plus years? He was dead then or he is now. We'll never know."

"There's nothing else in the files except one reference on Hollis Bivens from 1996. In that instance, his name came up when Dale Bivens was appointed to the rank of captain on the Rogers City Police. Hollis was his uncle. The paper covered his appointment to captain with a short piece, and according to the story, Dale was quoted as making some remarks about his interest in discovering the truth behind Hollis's disappearance those many years ago. He said he had grown up with the Hollis story from family members, and it caused him to become dedicated to law enforcement. Nothing else ever got reported. That's it."

Looking up at Caleb, Peter asked, "Why are you interested in this story?"

Caleb and Lonnie Rex looked at each other for a moment before Caleb spoke.

"First off, I really appreciate your effort to get this stuff together. It's what I needed. Before I tell you more, can I ask some questions about Dale Bivens? He is now the mayor, I understand."

"Yes, he is. What do you want to know?"

"You know, just his recent history," said Caleb.

"He served on the police force for many years, rising to the rank of chief in 2006, I think. He served in that capacity until 2012, and he did a good job. Everyone seemed to like him. Anyway, he used his popularity as chief of police to run for mayor, and he was elected that year. He's been our mayor ever since and was re-elected to serve another four years. I like him, and it seems that he has been good for the community. I know him, of course, but I wouldn't say we're close. The paper reports on his administration and so far, the relationship has been good. I will say that he has gotten rather prosperous during his years of service, but most of that is in real estate. All up and up, if you know what I mean. That do it?"

"Yeah, I think so. Let's go to lunch, and I'll tell you what I can about my interest," said Caleb.

When they were all seated at a booth in the main dining room of the Ozark Hotel, Caleb remarked to Peter and Lonnie Rex that the old hotel looked good. "I can see why this will be the headquarters of the reunion. Should be fun."

"This will be your first reunion, won't it?" Peter asked Caleb.

"Yep. Meant to come last time, but something got in the way. I haven't seen our classmates for a very long time. Just Lonnie Rex and maybe one or two others during visits here. I'm really looking forward to it."

"When will you go back?" asked Peter.

"I don't think that I'll be going back. I now own a farm here, and I think that I might stay and make a go of it. If not farming, then something else. I don't see myself as a farmer, but it's a nice property and I'll find my way. My sister is here, as you may recall, and I want to be close to her, so that's the plan."

"No kidding! Where is the farm?"

"Up around Pea Ridge and a little closer to the battlefield."

"It's a nice place," inserted Lonnie, "Needs a little work but nice. Good piece of land too."

"When did you buy the farm?" queried Peter.

"Actually, I inherited it from my uncle. He died a little over a year ago and left the property to me. Free and clear. First home I have ever owned."

"That's good news. It will be good to have you back. Do you know what you are going to do?"

"Not a clue. Maybe I'll breed horses. That's a big love of mine. Or maybe I'll write short stories for the paper," teased Caleb.

"Do you write?"

"No, just seems like a good idea," Caleb said laughing. "I can tell folks all about the west and cowboying. Crazy adventures and such. You know that I'm just kidding; I have never written anything. Why, you got any openings?"

"Well, you write me a piece, and maybe I'll publish it. You know, local boy returns from the wild west—big hat and tall tales. Could be good," observed Peter.

Caleb paused while the waitress took their orders. As she left, Caleb was quiet for a minute and then began, "Peter, I'm trying to decide how to proceed here. I want to tell you the full story of why I am interested in this stuff. It has all come to light very recently, in fact, some of it just the other night. But I am also concerned about telling you everything. It is possible that there is a serious story here, all a part of Rogers history. However, I can't allow you to publish anything right away; it isn't a complete story yet. At least there is more to discover. There is nothing to hide, but there is the possibility that some may be hurt by the truth, and I want to get the whole story before anything gets out, if it ever does."

"I'm listening," said Peter.

"Okay, here's the deal. I can really use your help. You've already been a help. But there is probably more. If I let you know all that I know, you must promise to publish nothing until we know how it plays out. Later, if it is a story, you can publish it as you see fit. Will that work for you?"

"So, this is now 'off the record' as we say in the business, right?"

"Right."

"And I'll get the full story whatever it is, once we're done figuring it out?"

"That's the deal. Lonnie Rex knows all that I know up to this point, and he's willing to help on a confidential basis. But there's more to come. I don't even know the full story now, but I will hold nothing back from you if we go forward. I say this because I have nothing to hide and am only concerned that the story gets done properly so as not to hurt anyone unnecessarily. Can you help with that understanding?"

"I want to sell papers. The full story is better than just some, so I think I can commit to what you ask. I am rather good at research, so maybe I can help. Sure, count me in, but let me ask you: are you saying that you want the right to squash the story depending on how it comes out?"

"No, I'm not. I'm willing to trust you with your pledge to simply consider my thoughts as you write the story. There might be one exception, but I'll tell you about that after I give you more information. That's all I ask."

Caleb continued, "And one other thing—it's a minor point— I don't want anything published before or during the reunion. Don't want to talk about it while we're having fun. Later is okay. We probably won't have the full story for a while anyway."

"Alright, consider it done." Peter offered his hand to Caleb, and they shook.

"I'm glad we can work together. After we finish lunch, I will give you what I have. My uncle Warren left me a locked trunk, which only I was supposed to open. I did that last Friday night. In the trunk, I found several items including two letters. One letter was addressed to me. The other letter is addressed to Dale Bivens. I was only supposed to open the letter addressed to me, which I did, and I will give you a copy. The other letter is addressed to Dale Bivens, which I am to deliver to him, and it can only be opened by him, with the requirement that I am to be there when Bivens opens it. I don't know what that letter says. I have yet to deliver it."

"When you read the first letter, you will understand the story. At that point, you can ask whatever questions you have. There's some history concerning my relationship with Uncle Warren over the years. I can answer any questions you might have. Then after you look into it some more, we can meet and discuss how to proceed," explained Caleb.

"Also, Lonnie Rex is to be kept apprised of everything. I will take care of that," Caleb finished.

"Sounds good," said Peter. "When do you want to meet again?"

"Can we do it tomorrow?"

"Yes, tomorrow afternoon is probably good. I'll look at your stuff, do a little more research, and be ready. I'll give you a call to let you know when to come by the office," directed Peter.

"We'll be there. Okay, Lonnie?"

"Wouldn't miss it for the world!" replied Lonnie.

As the food arrived, they all fell to their plates, and each quietly considered where this was all going to lead.

EIGHTEEN

Tuesday afternoon, Caleb and Lonnie Rex sat across the desk from Peter in his office. That morning, Peter had called Lonnie Rex since Caleb had no cell phone. Lonnie had tried to get hold of Caleb at Sarah's, but he had been out. Finally, Caleb stopped by Lonnie Rex's house and found out about Peter's call. Lonnie told him about the afternoon meeting and suggested again that Caleb needed to get a cell phone as soon as possible.

That morning, prior to the meeting, Caleb had gone to find the accountant referenced in Warren's letter. His name was Andrew Hastings, as Warren had indicated. He was glad to see Caleb since he had been keeping the account Warren spoke of since his death. Mr. Hastings reported that the account had a balance of $67,259.00 in it. There had been no activity since Warren's death, except some interest, and he confirmed that his instructions were to turn it over upon Caleb's arrival. After signing a release, Caleb opened an account in the same bank and presented a check from Mr. Hastings, which effectively transferred the entire balance to Caleb's new account. Caleb was quick to note that so far everything was as outlined in Warren's letter. Caleb asked for copies of all the bank statements back to when the account was opened. Perhaps there would be some indications of payments that might have bearing on the current issues. Mr. Hastings indicated that he would have them printed out and that Caleb could swing by and pick them up.

Caleb wondered where he might get a cell phone but decided to wait. He was anxious to see what Peter thought about the letter and the entire affair.

Seated in Peter's office, Caleb and Lonnie looked on expectantly as Peter pulled up some notes and began. "This is quite a story huh? If it is true, then it solves a very old mystery, and it promises more to come when Dale Bivens sees what is in the second letter. When do you plan on giving the second letter to Mayor Bivens?"

"As soon as possible, but I want to know as much as I can before I deliver it. This morning, I confirmed the money in the account that Warren spoke of in his letter to me. The money was there, and I had it transferred to my new account without any difficulty. All as Warren said. The account contained slightly more than he mentioned, but close. It appears so far that everything is as he said it would be and is just as he wanted it. I can understand how this is a story with local interest, and as I said yesterday, I'll give it all to you. I mentioned one exception. If there is something in the letter to mayor Bivens that needs to be kept confidential, I may not have any control over that. You'll have to live with that understanding."

Peter reflected, then asked, "I understand, but before we go on, fill me in on Warren's history as you know it and how this all started."

Caleb recounted his past since leaving Rogers, his life on the ranch, and his relationship with Warren. He pointed out in as much detail as he could the timeline of how everything had transpired. He explained in detail Warren's story as it had been told to him during their times together.

After telling about the farm Warren had left him, he let Peter know of Nancy Matlock's involvement as a friend and caretaker of the farm until his return. He also made it clear that Nancy, along with Sarah, knew about the trunk and the letters and the history of Warren. In addition, he mentioned how it was Nancy who had told him some of the recent history of the station and the construction going on there.

When Caleb finished telling everything to Peter, he paused and thought some more about the question of when he should give the second letter to the mayor. Then he said to Peter, "Before I set a time to give the letter to the mayor, I want to know as much as possible, including the history of the station. It's the reported burial place of Hollis Bivens, according to Warren. I can't help but think that if he was dug up, we would know, wouldn't we?"

"Maybe, maybe not. He could be buried deep or away from the recent excavation," Peter reflected.

"There haven't been any reports of anything or anybody dug up?" asked Caleb.

"Nothing that I know of, and I guess I would know, since it would be a very exciting story," explained Peter.

"What about finding out who the owner is? Who is the contractor? That sort of thing. Nancy told us some of the information. She related how it got approval from the Historical Preservation Board for demolition and how there was a lot of discussion. She said that the owner was some corporation but that the listed person for the corporation was Dumar Ashton. He might know something," said Caleb.

"We can find all that out through public records. I can do that easily. I think there was even a short story about the approval from the Historical Preservation Board. I didn't think to look yet. The application should list the current owner, as well as the report of action taken. It would be interesting to know when the applicant bought it from the previous owner, or even if he did at the time of the approvals. It's not unusual for an applicant to only have an option or a contract on a parcel pending city approvals. If it had been bought at the time of the hearing, we will know. Of course, it had to have been purchased since then and prior to development, because you must own the property to proceed with construction. We'll find out everything including the previous owner. I remember that he's mentioned in

Warren's letter…" Peter paused as he pulled up the copy of the letter. "It says here that it is, or was, Vernon… what? Let me see… Bendix, yes, Vernon Bendix, Lippy's son. It sort of implies that he is still alive and in a rest home, or at least he was at the time the letter was written."

"I do remember Lippy, who was Vernon's father," continued Peter. "He owned and operated that station up until around the mid-80s. We were all nearly 30 when it closed, and since then many small businesses have tried to make a go of it at the location, but since they couldn't tear it down, it was limited in what could be done with it. I also know a little about Warren and his diesel service, which was more recent. It worked, I guess, and he had a good reputation. Anyway, I never knew Vernon. We can check on him, and if he is alive, he can tell us what he knows."

"Let me do that," said Caleb. "If he's alive in a rest home, he may be open to talking about it all since he apparently had a good relationship with Uncle Warren. Maybe that will extend to me. If he is mentally stable and willing to talk to me, the station deal shouldn't be too hard to figure out."

"If he's alive, I bet that geezer doesn't know anything about ol' dead Hollis," Lonnie Rex inserted. "Your uncle made it pretty clear that it was a kept secret."

"Or maybe that's the real reason he never sold the station," Peter speculated.

"Whatever is true, I would like to know. Look, if we think we know Hollis is still down there, then we have some sort of responsibility to notify someone before the building gets built. Don't you agree?" Caleb asked both.

"That's for sure. Which points to the urgency of giving the second letter to the mayor. It probably contains the final information on all this, and then the mayor will know. It'll be up to him to decide how to proceed," Peter said.

"What about Dumar Ashton? Maybe he has some information we need," inquired Caleb.

"You want my opinion, you leave Dumar out of this, or at least wait until last. He might be a little jumpy to learn that he's got a dead deputy on his hands. And he's not the easiest guy to deal with and certainly not the most honest. He can be a little goofy. That's my opinion," stated Lonnie Rex. "And remember, Dumar will be at the reunion, so if you want to keep this quiet, you should wait until we know more."

"Agreed. Peter, you finish your research, and I'll go about finding out if Vernon Bendix is still around and then visit him if possible. Lonnie, can you find out who the contractor is? You might know him. Then we can all meet again soon. I'm thinking we need to conclude our research and get the letter to the mayor. Get it all over with. Okay?"

"You going to get a damn phone?" asked Lonnie. "It might make it easier to talk to you. And wouldn't that be a hoot!"

"Okay, Okay, I'll get a phone. Will you show me where to go?"

"I'll show you. Just follow me. You're in for a real treat; twenty-first century and all. Even video games."

"Let it go, Lonnie. I said I would get one; don't spook me," instructed Caleb.

"Thanks, Peter. We'll talk tomorrow. Maybe I can get that letter to the mayor before the week's out," concluded Caleb.

Lonnie Rex and Caleb shuffled out with Lonnie extolling all the virtues of modern technology to Caleb's obvious indifference.

NINETEEN

Caleb followed Lonnie Rex to the local Verizon store. He reasoned that there was not any sense in putting this off. Lonnie was right. He had avoided the intrusion of such devices for as long as he could, and he thought that he needed one now.

When the two of them entered the store, Caleb was amazed at the number of phones on display. As he browsed and tried to make sense of what he was seeing, Lonnie Rex went directly to the salesperson and told her that his friend wanted a state-of-the-art phone with all the bells and whistles. Lonnie signaled to Caleb, and they followed the young lady as she led them to a display of smartphones. She told them that her name was Marcy, and she would take care of everything. As Caleb looked on, Marcy told of all the wonderful features of the phone and described all the activities that could be supported on the device.

"Wait a minute," said Caleb. "Do you have one which is just a phone? None of that other jazz—just gets calls—like, you know, a phone?"

"Look Caleb, you need one that does it all," said Lonnie Rex. "Sure, some of it you won't use, but just think of all you can do. You can get emails..."

"I don't have email."

"Okay, but you can get on the internet..."

"I don't get on the internet."

"Did you know that it has maps? Did you know that it has GPS? Did you know that you can get the weather? Did you know that it has messages? Did you know that it has a list of all your contacts? Did you know that it has a compass? Did you know tha—"

"Just stop," said Caleb. "Lonnie, no more words. I'll just get it. I trust you, and you can show me everything when I get it."

Turning to Marcy, Caleb said, "I'll take one."

"Great! Now all you need to do is pick a color, and we can open you an account and assign you a number."

"Black. Sign me up," Caleb said. "How much is it?"

"Well, it depends on what service features you want to have. For instance, if—"

"I tell you what. Lonnie, you pick it all out, set it up, and I'll carry it. See how it works out. Just as long as I can make calls. I can learn about the other stuff as I go."

Lonnie sat down with Marcy and told her what to include with a few interruptions to quiz Caleb about any preferences and information for his account. When they were complete, Marcy said the total would be $379.16 today and $29.99 per month with unlimited service, or it could be set up on a contract for $59.99 per month.

"You must be kidding me! For a phone?" exclaimed Caleb.

"Caleb, just pay for the damn thing. Do the $380 deal. It's like mine, and you'll love it," Lonnie demanded. "Did I tell you that it has a camera?"

"For $380, it better do my laundry!"

Marcy laughed but then insisted that he would learn to like it. She pointed out that most people keep coming back for the latest version and want all the features that this one will have.

"Do it, Caleb. Sarah will do your laundry!" Lonnie exclaimed.

With a look of resignation and defeat written across his face, Caleb said, "Sign me up, and let's go."

Turning to Marcy, Caleb nodded, "Thank you, ma'am, you've been very helpful. I'll be sure to tell all my friends."

As they exited the store, Lonnie draped his arm over Caleb's shoulder and said, "Good job, pard; now I'll take you over to see the Earth Foods store where we can get a drink, look at the goofy people, and learn all about your new phone."

Seated at a booth along the windows at Earth Foods, Lonnie Rex tried to fully explain the features of Caleb's new phone. It was a difficult task to hold Caleb's attention since he kept looking up at the people passing by on their way out of the store.

"I guess there are a few funny-looking people, but most of them seem fairly normal."

"It's not a busy time right now. Sometimes on the weekends, this place is crawling with interesting looks. Here comes one now—blue hair, torn jeans, and a tank top. Got some facial hardware too," said Lonnie Rex.

Caleb studied her as she passed. "You know, Lonnie, this is silly. You ought to see some of the wanna-be cowboys at a country western dance. Most of them have never been on a horse and certainly don't earn their living pushing cows. I've even seen some with spurs on. What do you do with spurs at a dance?" Caleb wondered. "On second thought, don't answer that."

Returning to the phone, Caleb said, "Okay Lonnie, enough of the show and tell. I see how to do stuff. Let's get out of here. I've got to look around for retirement homes and see if I can find Vernon." Looking around, Caleb queried, "I wonder if they have a phone book in here?"

"No, they don't, Caleb, but you do. It's right here."

Lonnie took Caleb's phone and punched in maps, then search, then typed rest homes in Rogers. Several popped up. Each one had a listing with a phone number. "Start with the best-looking ones and give them each a call. See if they have Vernon Bendix listed."

Caleb studied the phone and said, "Oh... yeah, I could do that."

"Start calling. I'm going to the bathroom, and from the way I'm feeling, it might be a while. If you haven't found him by the time I get back, I'll help. If I don't come back send for help for me."

Lonnie Rex shuffled away, leaving Caleb to the task of dialing and asking. It took four calls before he found Vernon. He was a resident of a retirement village a little south of Rogers toward Springdale. Caleb returned to people-watching while he waited for Lonnie to complete his task. Losing interest in people-watching, Caleb began exploring the phone by pushing what he learned were "icons" on the screen. He was ready to admit that he found a lot to explore.

Lonnie interrupted Caleb's focus on his new phone and slid into the booth. "Any luck?"

"Ah, you survived. You okay?"

"Never better. I think my pants even fit better."

"I found him. Only took four calls. This phone is nice. I might just get used to it."

"I told you. Now, what next?"

Caleb thought for a minute and said, "I'll go see Vernon alone; see what I can get. If you can, see what you can find out about the contractor and anything else you can think of. I'll come by your house to tell you what I found."

"I already know who the contractor is. The name is on the sign at the construction site. We can call him together when you get back. Meanwhile, I just might take a nap."

"You always rise to every occasion Lonnie, but we may hold off on calling the contractor until later—after the mayor gets his letter. We don't want to spook anyone until we know more."

"Come by anyway after you see Vernon. The porch is getting lonely," said Lonnie.

TWENTY

Two hours later, Caleb pulled up at Lonnie Rex's house. Lonnie wordlessly watched Caleb come up the walk to the porch and take a seat in the next rocker.

"Get a nap?" Caleb asked.

"Yep. Find Vernon?"

"I did."

"What'd he say?"

"The retirement home was nice. They took me back to his room. He's in a private room, and he seemed happy to have a visitor. Reckon not much happens there, so visitors must be a real event. Anyway, I introduced myself and told him about being Warren's nephew and how I was moving here into Warren's old farm. Just the basics. I didn't tell him about any of the things that are going on, just that I wanted to learn about the station and the deal they had."

"Did he seem curious as to why you wanted to know?" asked Lonnie Rex.

"Not really. He was anxious to tell the story, and it was clear that he liked Warren. He laid it all out for me. It seems that the station had been a problem for Vernon. He never liked the place much. His dad was always down there and not at home most of the time. When Lippy died, Vernon got the station, but he could never sell it right. Maybe he wanted too much money; I don't know, but he couldn't sell it. Mostly because of the historical problem. He said that he tried to get them to let him tear it down, but they wouldn't agree. So, he finally started leasing it out to various businesses. None were very successful, but it stayed leased much of the time. He said there was always someone wanting to take advantage of the location, but they couldn't do any serious improvements, and he wasn't going to sink any money into the place.

"That all worked until he retired. He was a truck driver, by the way. Anyway, when he stopped driving, his income fell off, and he was getting tight on money. That's when Warren approached him and asked a bunch of questions. He said Warren didn't want to buy it but would pay him a very good monthly lease amount. Enough to carry Vernon through. He was very pleased with the arrangement, and it was like Warren said in the letter—good rent with a right to purchase it from his estate for fifty grand. Vernon thought he got the best of the deal. The rent was great and would carry him along nicely. He said he sent everyone he knew to Warren for diesel service, and I guess he knew quite a few since he was a trucker himself.

"That all worked good for both of them. Warren came by to visit him frequently and to make payments. He always paid timely or even in advance if Vernon needed the money. Vernon enjoyed his visits, and they became good friends. Vernon didn't have anyone else, it seems.

"Everything was good until Warren made his final payment after 2012. Warren gave him a little "bonus" when he stopped paying the rent. It helped, but right after that, Vernon needed to move into assisted living. That was going to eat up his money a little quicker, and he became concerned about what he could do. He thought of borrowing some money on the property, but it was no good. Banks didn't want anything to do with a loan on property without an income to support it. So, Vernon just coasted and hoped he could last.

"Now here's where it gets interesting. Early in 2014, Vernon got a visit from none other than Dumar Ashton. Dumar asked a bunch of questions, and Vernon told him all about the lease he used to have with Warren. At that point, Dumar indicated that he would be happy to reinstate the lease terms that Warren had with the same buy out provision, but he wanted to make the buy-out an option to be exercised by the end of 2014. So, it meant that Vernon would go back to getting money monthly and get the fifty grand by the end of the year, assuming Dumar decided to close. It was great news to Vernon—he'd be back where he was with Warren and stood a good chance of getting the payout too. If Dumar didn't exercise the option, then he would at least get more of the good rental income. He was pleased with the offer and took it right away. Dumar drew up a lease and the payments began in April of 2014.

"Before the end of 2014 came around, Dumar exercised his option and closed on the property. Therefore, as of November of 2014, Dumar Ashton has owned the property. Vernon knows nothing about the property after that date. He thinks he came out good. I think that Dumar knew the property would be worth much more if he got it removed from its historical status, which he was able to pull off. It was a shrewd deal for Dumar, and he left Vernon happy. Two winners."

Lonnie Rex shook his head and observed, "Dumar lands on his feet again and leaves an old timer in his wake. That's his style."

"You must admit, Lonnie, that Dumar took some risk on whether he could get it removed from status, he paid out a size-able monthly rent, and he honored his deal with Vernon. That's about as good as it would have been if Warren had bought it," observed Caleb.

"Yeah, I know. But I bet Dumar didn't take much of a risk on getting the historical status removed. If we look into it, I bet we'll find that the skids were greased with the Historical Board."

"Nancy said something to that effect, but you have to recognize that a deal is a deal," Caleb pointed out.

"What was it you used to say about attorneys? They know what is legal, but not what is right?" challenged Lonnie Rex.

"Yes, I do remember."

"Well, we may be looking at it, pard."

TWENTY-ONE

Wednesday morning found Caleb in the kitchen at Sarah's house. He watched Sarah as she prepared the perfect veggie omelet, his favorite. With a little biscuit ham on the side, it would be the start to a very good day. He was certainly getting used to Sarah's touch in the kitchen. When she set the plate in front of him, he began to savor the delicacy.

While continuing to enjoy the flavors of the omelet, he brought Sarah up to date on all that he had learned. He planned to call Nancy and give her the information after breakfast. Lonnie Rex and Peter might have some new information later in the day, but right now it all seemed just as Warren had outlined, and there was every reason to believe that Hollis remained buried at the station site. Right now, it looked like he could get the letter to Mayor Bivens without delay.

"Are you going to give the mayor a call or just go in? He's not always there, and I don't know his hours. You should just call, don't you think?" observed Sarah. Continuing, she said, "You know, Paxton used to know Dale Bivens. I think they were in Rotary together. Dale's about eight years younger than us, which means that he is only a few years older than you. Did you ever meet him?" Sarah asked before pausing for a breath.

"No, I can't remember ever meeting him. During most of my visits here, he was a police officer, and since I never got arrested, I missed the pleasure," Caleb pointed out. "I plan to give him a call and get an appointment."

"Who's going to go with you? Will you want me or Lonnie Rex, or what?"

"I think I'll go alone. It's just he and I that are supposed to open the letter. I'll let you know when I get back, assuming the letter isn't supposed to remain confidential."

"Don't set anything up for tonight. I thought we might go to church. Remember they are playing music and then Bible study to follow. Didn't you want to play with them? That would be so great if you did!"

"Sure, that'll work."

"I've received several calls from the ladies in the church. Clarice is anxious for you to come, and so is Ivey—you know, the piano player—and Buster Biggs, who plays the guitar, and, of course, Carson—he plays the bass fiddle. I know they will all welcome you."

"Okay."

"You'll get to know some of the others too. Our Wednesday night turn-out is pretty good. It's just a special time."

"What time are we going?"

"It starts at five and goes to about seven. So, we leave here a little before five." Sarah smiled and exclaimed, "It's going to be so much fun!"

"Eat here afterward?"

"Hunh? Oh, yeah. I'll put something together," promised Sarah.

Caleb wanted to ask what was for dinner, but then he thought a surprise would be more fun. Remembering, he said, "Did I tell you I got a cell phone?" asked Caleb.

"You did? Where did you get it?"

"At the cell phone store. Lonnie Rex took me over." Caleb pulled the phone out of his pocket and showed it to Sarah. "Here it is."

"Do you have a number?"

"Nope, just the one."

"I mean, do you have a phone number?"

"Yep."

"Well, what is it?" Sarah inquired through her exasperation.

"I'll give it to you, but you must promise not to give it out to anyone, or at least, not till you check with me first. I don't want this outfit to start ringing all the time." Caleb wrote the number down and handed it to Sarah.

"I won't," she promised, then said, "You're going to give it to Nancy, aren't you? Can I give it to Ivey—she coordinates the music at the church—and maybe Pastor Wendell?"

"I'll give it to Nancy. But I don't want you... Oh, never mind. Sarah, you can give it to whoever you want. You probably will anyway, and they're all your friends. I don't see why they would want it, but it's up to you," said Caleb, knowing that the inevitable had just arrived. He thought that sometimes you could see a bus coming from a long way off, and no matter what you did, or how you moved, it was going to hit you.

Caleb pushed his empty plate across the bar and rose from the stool. "That was a fine breakfast, Sarah. I'm going to work with Cisco a bit, then I will call the mayor and set something up. Later I'm going to do some clean-up in my rig and maybe get a nap, but I'll be ready to go to church with you. We'll take my truck, okay?"

"That's fine, but you might have to help me get up in it."

"We'll get you in."

After a workout with Cisco, Caleb was able to get in touch with the mayor's office. He made an appointment for Friday afternoon. He was asked what it was concerning, and Caleb just said that he had some correspondence for the mayor and that he looked forward to meeting him. With that, everything was set for the final act required by Warren. Caleb would be glad to get it all over with and let the mayor worry about it.

It was fortunate that the meeting with the mayor was set for Friday because Lonnie Rex called after he had talked to the mayor's office and wanted to let him know that there was a final meeting with the reunion committee on Thursday morning. He thought that Caleb might want to go. Lonnie reminded him that they had to plan for Caleb to play next week at the picnic.

That call from Lonnie had been the inaugural ringing of Caleb's phone. It occurred while Caleb was brushing Cisco after their ride. The sudden harsh and unfamiliar ringing startled them both. Cisco's nostrils flared, and he pulled back on the halter with wide and frightened eyes. He circled and kicked against the stall in full flight intent. Caleb fumbled with the phone as he tried to hold fast to the halter, calm Cisco, and recall how to answer the phone. Between the gyrations of the horse and the jerking on the halter, Caleb found it almost impossible to silence the thing. He finally let go of Cisco, ran out of the barn, and placed the phone under a hay bale in the feeding trough. He realized that it might just ring again but couldn't care at this point.

Comfortable that the phone was secure, he returned and took some time calming Cisco and allowing the horse to regain his composure in this new world. Eventually, when Cisco was settled, Caleb retrieved the phone and discovered the number where the call came from. Just as he started to dial, the phone seemed to jump in his hand as it rang again. This time he was prepared and answered the phone. It was Lonnie Rex calling again with his reunion meeting information. Caleb hoped that this cell phone thing hadn't been a mistake.

Thinking again about Cisco, the need to have the fence repaired on his new farm came immediately to Caleb's mind. He had no idea when he might move out there but had to have everything ready for Cisco when that occurred. Remembering what Sarah had said about the men she used around her farm, he had talked to her and secured the services of Dickie and Estes to repair the fence. Sarah enthusiastically recommended their services, and a call to Dickie was all it required to arrange for their arrival the next Monday to begin work. If that went well, then maybe he could have them continue with all the other renovation activities that were bound to be necessary. It felt like progress. He had no idea when he might move out there, but it was not going to be until he figured out all he wanted to do with the place. With the money that Warren had left him and with his savings, he could easily afford to fix the farm up properly. He also remembered that there could be some significant money coming in on the cattle sale. With his resources applied to the task, it might mean there would be a lot of work to do before he could call it home. In Caleb's mind, there was no rush, especially when he considered Sarah's cooking.

Caleb planned to meet Dickie and Estes at the farm on Monday and let them look the job over. He would let them get the materials and get started. He would also see how much supervision might be required. With a little luck, these guys would be as good as Sarah claimed. Time would tell.

Sarah entered the barn and approached Caleb. "You know, I was thinking. Maybe Friday night after you meet with the mayor would be a good time to have a little dinner party. We could have Lonnie Rex and Nancy out and we could talk about everything. You'll need to let all of us know how it went with the mayor. Do you think that's a good idea? I could fix something special, and it would be fun. What do you think?"

Thinking for a minute, Caleb said, "That's fine. I might want to ask Peter also. It depends on what happens."

"That's not a problem. There will be plenty. Just let me know."

"What are you cooking?"

"I have no idea yet. I'll figure out something."

"I'm sure it will be wonderful. I'll tell Lonnie and Nancy."

"Let me tell Nancy. Maybe she can come out early and help me."

"Okay by me. I'll see Peter in the morning because there is a meeting of the reunion committee, and I reckon I'll go. He'll be there, and I'll let you know if he can come."

"All right. I'm going in and getting ready for church."

"I'll be along directly," said Caleb.

TWENTY-TWO

Caleb and Sarah pulled up to the church in Caleb's truck. They both checked the sign and discovered that it had been changed and now read:

Wednesday Night
Music and Bible Study
Experience the Joy of the Lord
through
Song and Verse

"Well, that looks better," quipped Sarah. "Maybe that will draw them in. We need to grow if we can."

"How many belong to the church?" asked Caleb.

"Not near enough. Probably about 75. I mean, it's better than a couple of years ago. It does grow, but not very fast, and I know that Wendell is concerned."

"Well, at least it's growing. The music is good, and word will spread, don't you think?"

"Maybe. I hope so. These people really love each other."

Caleb came around and helped Sarah alight from the truck cab. She was still mastering the use of the running step and hand-hold. She figured it out going in, and now she was applying herself to the coming out part.

"Why is this thing so big and so high?"

"It doesn't seem so big out on the ranch," explained Caleb.

Once he had her on the ground, he grabbed the violin case from the back seat and approached the front of the church following Sarah. The doors were open, and the sounds of instruments being tuned caught their ears.

Buster Biggs was the first to notice their arrival. Pushing the guitar to his back, he let out a friendly greeting and beckoned for them to come on down to the front. "We were hoping you would come. It's about time we had a fiddle," Buster said as he extended his hand to Caleb. "I'm Buster Biggs: guitar, banjo, and harmonica. You are most truly welcome!" Buster's biceps stretched his Walmart tee shirt to its limits as his stomach added its own pressure to the task.

The others joined in with warm greetings.

Ivey gushed with enthusiasm and invited Caleb to sit next to the bass player, who leaned forward and introduced himself as Carson Fines. Carson was a tall skeleton of a man with thinning hair and a crooked nose. He wore new overalls and smiled at Caleb through piercing blue eyes. No one would say he was good-looking, but no one could escape the joy in his face.

As Caleb stepped up on the platform, Sarah slid into the third row back, which Caleb remembered was exactly where they sat in church on Sunday. He wondered if the seats were assigned. More people filtered in and spread out as they had been in church. All of them gave vigorous greetings to each other. Some ventured forth to shake Caleb's hand and make it known how much he was welcomed.

Clarice Bouvier, the theater buff, came in and proceeded directly to the stage to welcome Caleb. She turned back and went to Sarah. They began chatting, and from the looks of their bobbing heads, they were both pleased with something.

As the band went back to preparing their instruments, an elderly couple entered the church. She was tall and rather eloquent, dressed very fashionably, and followed by what must be her husband. His face was etched in a perpetual smile with very prominent and white teeth. It appeared these very teeth were responsible for forcing his eyes almost to close and creating a fixed smile. Caleb wondered if he could close his mouth over the denture impediments. Could he ever frown was a question that was hard to escape. Neither person spoke as they took their seats, but it was hard to believe that they were anything but happy with the husband's perma-smile in place.

Pastor Wendell was seated at the front behind the lectern. Caleb had failed to notice him when they came in, but Wendell stood and approached Caleb after all the introductions subsided. "I'm so glad you are here. I talked to Sarah, and I knew you were coming. We welcome your fiddle to our sound," Pastor Wendell said. "I also play the guitar, although not as fine as Buster. I am sort of the lead singer, but we all chime in, in the fervent hope that true harmony won't elude us."

"Sounds mighty promising. I'll fit in wherever I can," said Caleb, as he rosined his bow and set his neck piece. "What are we going to play?"

"You know, we enjoy playing together so much that we go off on any number of tangents. It's not all church music, as you might assume. Some evenings we stray far and wide. But our first love is gospel, especially old-world country gospel. I'm sure we'll get around to that as the evening progresses."

"You get her started, and I'll fit in as we go."

"Perfect." With a quick nod toward Sarah, Pastor Wendell told Buster to lead them off.

Buster started a slow strum and then finger-picked a melody that Caleb quickly recognized as "Country Roads." Carson and Pastor Wendell immediately joined in with Ivey following on the piano. Caleb waited, and when they got to the chorus, he raised his violin and boldly drew his bow across the strings to produce the energetic melody of the song. He played concert style while laying on the vibrato to each measure. As they fell back to the second verse, Caleb lessened the volume and accompanied them as they began singing. He remained quiet until back to the chorus when he burst forth again. The other players played and sang the chorus, and then stopped playing as they let Caleb solo the final verse and chorus. After his violin brought the song to an end with the repetition of the last measure and fading tones, there was complete silence.

"My word, I believe Caleb might just fit in!" exclaimed Pastor Wendell. "Caleb, why don't you start one, and we'll follow?"

Caleb thought for a minute and decided to honor them with the song they had done on Sunday. He raised his violin and slowly drew out the lilting melody of "How Great Thou Art." They allowed him to play the first refrain, and when Caleb began the verse, Wendell sang forth with his deep baritone as everyone found their place in the song. Soon they were all harmonizing as the people in the church joined in. At the end, they paused for Ivey to do a piano solo to round out the song.

The energy among the players and all the congregation on that evening was the musical version of joy, expressed openly and without reserve as they went from song to song.

There was no Bible study that night. The entire two hours were devoted to the music.

TWENTY-THREE

On Thursday morning, Caleb sat with Lonnie Rex in the dining room at the Ozark Hotel. The meeting of the reunion committee was not scheduled until 8:30 a.m., but both decided to get an early start, having arrived a little after 7:00 a.m. Both Lonnie and Caleb were pushed back from the table after finishing their breakfast. Lonnie could not smoke in this establishment, so he graciously abstained with no visible effect.

The main dining room in the hotel was an elegant space with high coffered ceilings and bright patterned carpet. There were several diners, and most appeared to be businesspeople, either guests of the hotel or locals similarly starting their day. Caleb recalled times long ago when he had dined in this room. It had only occurred during community functions or special occasions. Caleb's father, Taylor, had performed here a few times by his memory. He could only remember attending one of his dad's appearances but knew that there had been several. He also recalled that he had brought Lori to this place on the night of the Junior-Senior prom. That had been just before the summer in which she had moved away. Her family had relocated to Nevada for her father to take a position with a major hotel in Las Vegas. Lori's leaving was a memory that rekindled a strong sadness in Caleb. He could never get past thinking about what could have been. The hurt of her departure was coming back from wherever he had filed it in his mind, and it seemed to have the same intensity even after all these years. Just unfinished business, Caleb reckoned.

Caleb's thoughts were interrupted by Lonnie Rex saying, "The breakfast here is not as good as Casper's. It's a might short on some special ingredients I need to maintain my youthful demeanor, and a little pricey for that matter."

"I found it tolerable, maybe even good. You can't just exist on grease."

"The hell you say!"

Caleb continued, "The omelet was good—not brown like some. I have never understood why a paid chef cannot understand that you shouldn't use a skillet that's too hot for eggs. You've got to let the heat sneak up on the eggs until they begin to get the picture and yellow up. Then flip 'em at the right time. Takes character, patience, and respect for the eggs."

"What are you, the uppity gourmet?"

"Just know what I like. Sort of like you, pard," said Caleb. "By the way, speaking of food, Sarah wants to have a little dinner party tomorrow night. She wants you and Nancy to come over; you know, all the conspirators in the Hollis affair. She thinks that we can compare notes and learn what might happen next."

"I'll be there if she's cooking. I might smell like paint if that's okay, or is this formal?"

"Very formal for you. Lose the clogs, clean your fingernails, and squeeze into a fresh Hawaiian shirt," Caleb instructed. "And you always smell like paint."

"I like Hawaiian shirts—harder to see the paint stains."

"Don't I know."

"What about Peter? He's a conspirator."

"I been thinking about that. I thought I would ask him over, but we would have to leave his wife out, or we will be spreading the story. And he seems sort of home bound and might not want to leave her behind on a Friday night."

"I see your point. They are close, and she likes to be involved. You can just tell him later."

"I'll do that. Don't mention the dinner to him today. I'll tell him that I'll call him on Saturday. That'll work better."

"Speak of the devil, here he comes now," Lonnie Rex said as he nodded his head toward the entrance.

Peter drew up to the table, and after spreading his greetings, he asked, "Any news to report on our story?"

"Just that I'm going to deliver the letter to the mayor tomorrow afternoon. I'll call you on Saturday to let you know what went down," said Caleb. "I'll be glad to get it over with. Then just focus on the farm and the reunion. Glad you guys included me in your meeting."

"Yeah, great. I understand that Lonnie has got you talked into playing at the bonfire next Thursday," Peter said.

"Don't take much talking to get Caleb to play his fiddle. He's a regular songster," allowed Lonnie. "You ever hear him play, Peter?"

"No. Is he any good?"

"Does Dolly Parton sleep on her back?" Lonnie challenged.

"I guess you're good then," Peter laughingly said to Caleb.

"I won't be tooting my own horn, but I do like to fiddle, and it will be fun if you want me," admitted Caleb.

"It was Gina's idea, but we all concurred. I think she has a small band lined up, and you can join in."

"Works for me, and it'll give me time to circulate with old acquaintances instead of playing all the time."

They all turned to see Misty Belle approach the group, burdened with her box of paperwork. She was fashionably dressed in a tailored business suit with a pink shirt sporting a frilly neckline. This was the first official "event" of the reunion, and she wanted to suitably impress. It worked on Caleb. He remembered her and her reputation as a studious yet attractive young lady with a leaning toward a regal bearing. It was more than an affectation; it was a lifestyle.

Misty sat down her box and looked first at Caleb. "Caleb! This is quite an honor. You finally attend one of these reunions! It is so good to see you!"

Caleb stood and addressed Misty. "I'm mighty glad to be here, ma'am. Heck, you haven't changed a bit! You look great," Caleb said in a gracious manner. "It's been a long time."

"We're all getting up there, but we can still party a bit, don't you think?" Misty asked.

Lonnie Rex quipped, "Yep, we may be too old to cut the mustard, but we can still lick the jar!"

At a loss for the appropriate words, Misty simply stared at Lonnie. Peter saved the moment by pointing out to the group, "Well, if not now, then it's coming."

Caleb lurched forward as Gina Houseman wrapped her arms around him from the back, nearly knocking his hat off. "Caleb! No one told me you would be here." She spun him around and exclaimed, "God, you are so gorgeous!"

"Hi Gina," Caleb managed to get out while he tried to stand.

Sparing Caleb any further dialog, Bobby Driscoll joined the group and reached his hand out to him. "Good to see you, man. It's been forever!"

"Yes, it has. Never made one of these before."

"Is this your hat?" Gina asked as she took his Stetson and placed it on her head. She turned left and right and said to Bobby, "How do I look?"

"You look great! Maybe you should get one."

Gina turned back to Caleb and asked, "Can I have this one?"

"Nope."

"Just kidding. I know you would never give up your hat. It looks so worn and broken in yet so perfect."

"Well, that's why I said no. Getting a hat like you want is a time-consuming job. That one's been around a good while. Been blooded some and used to hold everything from water to... well, never mind," Caleb said. "But you do look mighty good in it."

Caleb waited until Gina and Bobby had selected their seats, and then he sat back down. Misty nodded a final greeting to all and began unloading her box. She handed out a binder full of information to each person. She realized that she didn't have one for Caleb, and before she could utter any instructions, Gina said that she would share with Caleb, while flashing a conspiratorial smile. Misty continued and told everyone that first they would review the agenda for the weekend and look at who would oversee each of the scheduled activities. She mentioned that there were several volunteers outside the committee to help with all the different things, and there shouldn't be any difficulty in keeping everything running smoothly. She thanked everyone for the work they had done so far.

"Gina, the first item on the schedule is the bonfire and music on Thursday night. Is everything arranged?" inquired Misty.

"It is. I have put together a group who will play. They're not a band, as such, but have played together before. I've heard them play, and it should be good. I promised them each $100, which is well within the budget you mentioned. We were lucky to get them. Also, I've been hoping that Caleb would play," Gina said while turning to Caleb. "I didn't know you were already in town, or I would have found you earlier. Will you play?"

"Sure. If the band wants me."

"Yeah, they said they did. And we can get you the money too."

"That won't be necessary. You might make me a professional if you're not careful. But you can save me a dance."

"Oh, I will, cowboy!" said Gina.

"I just hope this musical group can keep up with Caleb," Lonnie Rex observed.

"Stop it, Lonnie!" Caleb admonished.

"Well, I'm sure we are all looking forward to the event. And it will be good to hear you play. You've been playing for a long time I believe. I think I remember you playing in high school," said Misty.

"That's right. My dad taught me several instruments, but I prefer the violin, or fiddle—all the same instrument, just playing style differences," said Caleb.

Continuing, Misty said, "The picnic is also at the lake in the group shelter. We'll need a few volunteers to clean up after Thursday night. I have three who have said they will be there and help. Anyone else can pitch in."

"I'll be glad to help," said Caleb. "And Lonnie too."

"I'll help, but there's going to be a get-together at my house afterward. Everyone's welcome. Party starts when you get there," explained Lonnie Rex.

"For the picnic on Friday, we're going to have barbeque. It's catered, self-service, and very informal," explained Misty. "It'll start at 11:00 a.m., we eat at about noon, and it can go on until whenever. For Thursday, we must remember that there is a 10:00 p.m. curfew at the lake, so keep that in mind. On Friday night, after the picnic, there is an open house at the Big-Wigs, courtesy of Bobby. I think most will come, but I'm also sure a few will do something else. We will have a sign-up sheet at registration for everything. You'll know then how many."

"Doesn't matter. Everyone's welcome. We can hold quite a few," said Bobby.

"Remember it is a cash bar—no money from the committee," Misty reminded.

"On Saturday morning, there is breakfast here at the hotel, with a tour of the high school scheduled for 11:30 a.m., and at 1:30 p.m., a tour of the museum downtown. Out-of-towners will probably focus on those, but who knows? Again, the sign-up will tell. The tour of the high school will be led by the current principal, Michael Davenport. He's not part of our class but happy to oblige. Lunch on Saturday is unplanned. Everyone is on their own."

"Finally, on Saturday night will be dinner and dancing here at the hotel. We have a different band for that event. The band is Dawn Rising. They play rock mostly, but I think they can play about anything. The cost of the bonfire, the picnic, and the Saturday night dinner-dance is covered in the reunion fee. Everything else is up to the individual. Most have prepaid, but those who haven't can pay at registration."

"The only thing that is unsure is who will be the Master of Ceremonies at the dinner. Fletcher Cosgrove has expressed an interest in doing it, and so has Franky Mango. I thought we would talk about that today and decide."

"Franky's a riot! He should be good," said Gina.

"Let's use them both. We don't want to leave anyone out. Fletcher is a good choice for the basics. He could handle the welcome and announcements. Franky would be great to do a stand-up. I mean, he was always the class clown and is very funny," proposed Peter.

"If everyone agrees, I'll let them know," said Misty Belle. "Anything else on the schedule?"

Peter spoke up again, "I'll have a photographer at most of the events. Then I can do a big story for the paper about the reunion. I might have interviews with a few folks to get some personal stories to include in any article. And it'll all be complimentary toward local businesses that participate. I thought I might even email copies of the articles to participants. We'll have a list, won't we?"

"Yes, we will Peter. I'll see that you get it afterward," promised Misty.

During the discussion, Caleb pulled Gina's binder closer and leafed through the pages until he found the list of attendees. He told himself that he wanted to see who was coming and to refresh his memory, but in truth, he was scanning the list looking for her name. On page three, about halfway down, was the name of Lori Beth (Hightower) Martin. She was marked as fully paid for all events.

The meeting droned on with more details and thanks from Misty for everyone's hard work. Caleb only half listened as he remembered that long ago time in this very room, which remained etched on his memory.

TWENTY-FOUR

Friday was the day of Caleb's meeting with the mayor, and after following his normal routine at Sarah's house, Caleb drove to City Hall. As he drove, he began to wonder just what could be in the letter to the mayor that told more than he already knew. About the only piece missing was Warren's reference to some other money, but Caleb could not understand what that had to do with the mayor, unless it was intended for him. He wondered who else would get the money. The mayor getting the money was the only conclusion that he could come to. But what was the point of that? Restitution? He realized that he would soon know, so he just let it go. At this point, Caleb was losing interest in the entire affair and just wanted to complete this final task for Warren.

It did occur to Caleb that whatever happened, it could make quite a story for the paper. Long ago mystery solved! There would be a lot of readership, and Peter would be in high cotton. Caleb realized that his role in all this would have to be included in any story, even if Peter tried to minimize it. He couldn't imagine a way for Peter to cover the story without referring to him in some way. He thought that he would have to be prepared to deal with it. At least Peter had agreed to hold off until after the reunion. Maybe by then he would be fully involved in renovating the farm and could just ignore any publicity. One could only hope.

Caleb's thoughts turned to seeing Lori's name on the roster yesterday. He had been quiet about it and just made it look like he was looking at everyone attending. Nobody had mentioned

Lori, so maybe she was just coming as she had before. He didn't know anything about her past other than she was now single. Her husband wasn't in the picture, according to Lonnie. Maybe she was divorced. He had never kept up with her and knew absolutely nothing. He wondered if she knew about his life. He had never heard from her, so it must all be nothing—just another reunion. If it was something, then she would have called or tried to connect with him, so it must be nothing. When he sees her, it will become clear, he assumed. He promised himself that he would be normal and not pry into her life or seem too concerned. Just a happy meeting. That's it.

Caleb pulled into the parking lot at city hall and proceeded directly into the lobby of the mayor's office. He informed the receptionist that he was here for an appointment and was instructed to have a seat. The receptionist returned and said that the mayor would be out shortly. His wait was longer than she indicated. After about thirty minutes had passed, she looked over and registered his presence. "The mayor will be out soon. He got tied up with some business," she said.

It seemed to Caleb that getting this letter to Mayor Bivens was becoming tedious. Maybe he should have told the secretary that he knew where old Hollis was buried. He thought that would put some hustle in everyone's step. The cattle-prod approach, he thought smilingly. His inner humor was interrupted by the receptionist announcing, "You can go in now." She pointed down the hall and told him it was the last door on the right.

The door was opened to reveal a rather large office, much bigger than Caleb had imagined. Mayor Bivens looked up from his desk and waved him in while he finished a phone call. As Caleb waited, he took note of the office. Behind the mayor were displayed numerous pictures of the mayor in various garbs. There was the mayor docked out in fishing attire holding up a large bass, pictures of him in a police uniform, and many pictures of him with some sort of celebrity. Not a man who lacks substance, the pictures said. The furnishings were plush with a large leather sofa and chairs and a conference table with leather swivel chairs. It all seemed grand for a city the size of Rogers, but what did he know? Trappings of office, he reasoned.

The mayor hung up the phone and apologized to Caleb. "I'm sorry. Sometimes it seems that you just can't get them to stop talking." Gesturing to the conference table, the mayor said, "Please, take a seat. I don't think we have met. I'm Dale Bivens." He offered his hand and inquired, "Can you tell me your name again? I don't seem to have it on my calendar."

"Caleb Atwood. I called Wednesday and made an appointment."

"Sure, sure. I had it penciled in but didn't get the name." Dale sat down across from Caleb and asked, "What can I do for you?"

"Well, let me start with a little background." Caleb proceeded to tell the mayor about the reunion and all about his recent move to Rogers as a result of inheriting the farm from his uncle.

The mayor broke in and said, "Oh yeah, the reunion. Big doings for some classes. Let's see, this is for the class of what... 1976?"

"Yes sir. That's the year. Forty years ago."

"Those are great fun. I always enjoy mine. I'm from the class of '74. So, I'm about two years older than you. You need some help with the reunion?"

"No, no, this is not about the reunion."

Realizing that he should just get to the point, Caleb asked the mayor if they could close the door. "I have a sealed letter for you to read. It's confidential and for your eyes only with me present."

The mayor considered the request and then rose and closed the door. "You have me curious, but I don't understand. Who is the letter from?"

Caleb pulled out both letters; the one addressed to him and the one addressed to the mayor.

"The letter to you is from my uncle, Warren Atwood. It is sealed and is confidential, as I said. This other letter is to me, also from my uncle, which I have read. Uncle Warren passed away recently but left me these letters. My letter contains his instructions, which I am following." Caleb placed the letters in the center of the table. He handed the opened one to the mayor. "I think if you read this one first, it will prepare you for the confidential one. You'll understand more when you digest the first one."

Mayor Bivens studied Caleb and then picked up the first letter. Caleb sat back and waited for the mayor to digest its contents. He knew this would take some time.

Just as the mayor got started, he looked up and asked, "What trunk?"

"Warren left me a trunk with things in it, including both letters. It was locked, and I only opened it last Friday. Keep reading, and it will become clear. Prepare yourself."

After a couple of moments, the mayor exclaimed, "Hollis! This is about Hollis?"

"Read on, please."

Stopping again, the mayor looked up and said, "This guy Warren, your uncle, claims he killed Hollis! He confesses!"

"That's right. Read on."

Stopping again, the mayor said, "I remember when the station was a diesel shop. And now I vaguely remember Warren. He came into city hall when he opened and applied for a business license."

"Read on."

Finishing the letter, Dale sat back and looked at his hands. He didn't speak at all. After some time, he looked up at Caleb and asked, "You didn't know anything about this until you saw this letter?"

"That's right."

"Why didn't you come in right away?"

"I wanted to, but I also thought that I should check on the other things that Warren said to verify they were true. It took three or four days to check them out, do a little research, and see if the facts seemed to hold up. Everything he claimed seems accurate. I have no way of knowing if Hollis is still down there, but it seems there is a very good chance. Then it took a couple of days to get an appointment with you."

"I never knew Hollis. He died, according to this, several years before I was born. I heard stories of his disappearance of course, but it was all old news, old unsolved news. It was a big deal to my dad. He had no information, nowhere to look, and no one to blame. This is incredible!"

"Your dad is not still alive, is he?"

"Oh, gosh no. He died in 1990. He was 66 years old."

Caleb studied the mayor, then said, "It's time to open your letter."

Dale looked back at the second letter like it was a bomb. He slowly picked it up and lamented, "I guess so."

Dale tore open the envelope and withdrew the folded letter. He pressed it out on the table, looked up at Caleb, and began to read aloud:

To: Dale Bivens
To be hand delivered by Caleb Atwood
For your eyes and Caleb Atwood's eyes only: please read together.

Dear Mr. Bivens,

My name is Warren Atwood. I do not think that we have met, but we have a connection, which I will address herein. This letter is personal to you and is not related to your role as mayor of Rogers, but for some of the provisions I outline herein, being mayor may come into play.

In the early summer of 1944, I had an unfortunate run-in with your uncle, Hollis Bivens. I was 18 at the time. On a Friday night, I was at the old gas station owned by Lippy Bendix (I've never known his given first name. Everyone called him Lippy). Several of us were drinking and gambling that night. During the evening, your uncle Hollis came by and harassed us, especially Lippy. Hollis had been drinking and was rather abusive. Lippy and Hollis were clearly not friends. I said some things that caused Hollis to ignore Lippy and to threaten me. He then left but came back later that night, around midnight. Lippy and I were the only two still there. Hollis was even more drunk, and he was in his uniform but clearly not on duty. He struck Lippy with his gun, and then advanced on me. He threatened to "take me in," but I didn't believe that was his true intent. Hollis then came at me and struck me in the head with his pistol, like he had done to Lippy. This only enraged me, and, to my regret, I was consumed with anger and came up and struck him in the face with all my might. It was a devastating blow. He fell back against the gas pump. When I tried to revive him, I realized that he was dead. I think he broke his neck and maybe cracked his skull. I don't know for sure, but I do know that he was dead. I was very distraught at having done such a thing.

It doesn't get any better. Lippy and I buried the body in the excavation underway in the back of the station where they had installed new gas tanks. We filled in around the body and left it to be completely covered when the gas company completed the work the next day. That's what occurred, and I assume that the body is still down there. I left town a few days after this event. I served in the armed services and worked abroad for much of my life. It is not important what I did with my life — this letter only concerns my telling the story of your uncle's demise at my hand. I won't insist on any innocence, even though I didn't mean to kill him. The fact is that I did. I was scared by his actions and at the time felt that I was defending myself from an unknown fate, but he did not deserve to die. Those are the facts.

Upon my recent return to Rogers, I discovered that the station was still standing, and I leased the place. I provided diesel repair services at the location. I sort of felt that I was looking over Hollis's resting place, both to prevent discovery as well as to protect the site. I have no good explanation, but that is what I did. If you are reading this letter, it means that I am deceased. Caleb Atwood is my nephew and is taking *care of this for me. Caleb knew nothing about this affair until I passed away, and then only after he reads this letter with you. With this letter, I wish to make an apology, ask for forgiveness, and make some sort of restitution. This confession will close the book on what happened to Hollis. I know that there was a long search for Hollis with no results, and it must have caused great concern to the family. Again, I am woefully sorry.*

As restitution, it is my wish that the city receives a donation to purchase the existing station, demolish it if possible, and construct a downtown park in that location. It is a prominent corner and can be a worthwhile addition to the city as a park. During the construction, the body can be exhumed and moved to a proper burial site. I think that there should be some sort of plaque or memorial in dedication to Hollis. Nothing needs to be said about any misbehavior on his part or any character flaw that might have existed. He did not deserve to die and should be remembered in some positive way. I will leave it up to you as to whether this is a good idea or not. Memorial or not, it will make a good park. If this plan is not possible for whatever reason, I release the donation to the city to use as you and the city fathers see fit.

I include herein directions regarding the substantial money I have left for this purpose. The amount I have left is a little over $325,000 and should be sufficient to achieve what I have requested. It is legal money earned by me over many years. The money is mine, properly earned and saved over a lifetime. At the bottom of this letter are directions to the exact location of the money in question. As you will see, it is in such a place to confirm the contents of this letter and in furtherance of my wishes. Caleb is at the reading of this letter to you to bear witness to this gift to the city.

I am sorry for the grief I have caused the family of Hollis Bivens, and I dedicate this money as my sole remaining asset in consideration of my role in officer Bivens's demise. It is my heartfelt hope that you can forgive this act I committed in the heat of anger so long ago.

Thank you,
Warren Atwood

Location of cash contribution:

The money is located on the site and is buried about three feet deep and directly above where Hollis is buried based on my recollection. For reference, the location is 71 feet west of the western property line, and 52 feet north of the south property line. It is in a four-foot-long metal box and is sealed against any moisture.

In the silence that followed Dale's reading of the letter, there was a knock on the door, and the receptionist stepped in. "You know that you have a staff meeting coming up. You about to finish up?"

"Please postpone the meeting if you don't mind. I've got to deal with something."

"Some of the staff want to leave early. How long do you want to postpone?"

"On second thought, just cancel. We'll get back to it on Monday," said the mayor.

"That won't disappoint them," she said and closed the door behind her.

Dale looked back at Caleb in a searching manner. Finally, he said, "This is a lot to digest. There's construction at the site. No one has reported finding anything. But if it's true, then it must be investigated soon."

"I understand; that is my concern, too." Caleb allowed.

"Does anyone know about this?"

"You and I are the only ones who know about the contents of your letter. That includes the information on the money. But the first letter was shared with four other people. My sister, my good friend Lonnie Rex Stanhope, Nancy Matlock, and Peter Mason."

"Peter Mason! My god, the news will be all over if the paper has a hold of it!"

"No sir. No one will speak up about this at this point. Peter Mason has agreed to hold off on the story until it is fully developed, and the facts are known. I promised to be forthcoming with him on the facts with the understanding that I would only share the contents of your letter if you allowed it. Right now, the money gift and location are only known to you and me. I will honor your wishes in the matter. In addition, Peter has promised to hold the story until after the reunion. That's kind of self-serving, but I didn't want to be answering questions when I should be dancing," Caleb responded light-heartedly.

"If that is true, then we have only a little over a week to get to the bottom of this. Please don't reveal any more to Peter Mason until I decide how to proceed. Get him to hold off. Of course, the story will break, but I want to see how to control it. I've got to think about this. Please, let's keep this between you and me until I can figure out what I want to do."

"I'm happy to do that, but I must remind you that what I know is fully contained in these letters. However, in addition, Peter and I have done some research into the disappearance of Hollis from newspaper accounts back in 1944. So that is a public record, and you can see it all without my help. But nevertheless, I'll help any way I can. Just let me know. I'll leave you my number."

The mayor seemed to be deep in thought and didn't respond to Caleb's offer of help. Finally, he turned to Caleb and said, "I am afraid that there is a bit more to this story. Recent stuff. I've got to think it over before we proceed."

"You mean about the construction? You know, it's not too far along. It should be easy to get in there and do the required digging," said Caleb. "Sooner the better, it seems."

"I know, it's just tha—oh, never mind, I'll set something up," promised Dale.

"You know, mayor, it seems to me that my uncle Warren just wanted to admit to all this, get it off his chest, and make some sort of restitution to the family and the city. It can finally be put to rest. It's that simple."

The mayor smiled weakly at Caleb and uttered, "It may not be that simple."

TWENTY-FIVE

Nancy placed the glasses around the table to complete the setting for four. Sarah had a fine collection of antique dinnerware, and she took pride in displaying it whenever she had an opportunity. Graceful dining at a table tastefully set and engaging in spirited dialog during a finely prepared meal was her first love. She loved to cook, and she loved to present a timeless ambience in a special meal. This was no exception. Nancy had arrived early and assisted her in the preparation of all that was before them.

Caleb and Lonnie looked on in anticipation of the event. As they waited, they enjoyed the antipasto platter and sips of the Merlot Sarah brought out. Of course, a sip of whiskey might be more normal to them, but for this occasion, they had forgone their usual inclinations and adopted the "high-road" approach to dining.

After everyone was seated and the blessing was delivered, Sarah served a cheese plate to each person to enjoy along with a handsome bruschetta plate. As they settled into their meal, Sarah intoned Caleb to tell them about the mayor. She had stifled any attempt to discuss these matters until all were seated. Now she was ready and wanted to know.

Caleb simply tried to summarize by saying, "We met after a short wait. It was busy, and it took about a half hour for me to get in. I was rather impressed with him. He seemed personable and interested in why I had come. I got right to the point by telling him a little history of just who I was and how I came to be in his office. I laid out both letters on the table and had him read the one to me first. That way he would have an immediate understanding of the issue."

"Was he surprised?" asked Sarah.

"First, he read the letter that Warren had prepared for me. When the mayor got to the part about Warren killing Hollis, he really tuned in. It was a total surprise to him. It seemed that he had not thought about the Hollis affair in a very long time. He even had to think a little to dredge up the Hollis history, which he proceeded to share with me. He mentioned that he remembered Warren and his diesel business. I think that he was in a bit of shock and just sort of mumbled his words as he processed the information. There was no anger or outward display. He had a few questions about when I found out about it all, and I told him."

"After a little pause, he took the letter addressed to him and opened it. He seemed both anxious and a little frightened of what it might contain. He read it aloud without stopping."

"Well, what was in it?" Lonnie Rex asked.

Continuing, Caleb said, "You know, there really was not much new about the killing. The new part was that Warren pledged or donated money to the city—some $325,000. Warren buried the money on the site in a steel box, directly over where Hollis' body was buried. He gave the specific location of the money so it could be easily found. Warren wanted to give the money to the city as some sort of restitution for what he had done. He also said in the letter that he wished for the city to use the money to establish a memorial to Hollis. Warren suggested a park at the site but said that the city could use the money however they wished.

Caleb paused while everyone thought this over. As he waited for questions, he went back to work on his cheese and bread. Lonnie also returned to his plate and refilled the wine glasses.

Sarah was the first to ask a question, "Did the mayor indicate that they had dug anything up yet, I mean, either the body or the money? It looks like you couldn't dig one up without finding the other. What did he say?"

"He said that no one had reported anything, and he understood that it would have to be dealt with soon, since construction was going on. The funny thing was that he became really focused on the publicity which might come of this. When I told him who knew about it and mentioned Peter, he got very concerned about the story getting out."

"But it's got to get out!" exclaimed Nancy.

"Sure, it does, but I told him that Peter had promised to hold the story until more was known and certainly until after the reunion. I mean the reunion doesn't matter, but I related how I didn't want to deal with it during the weekend of the reunion."

"Does Peter know about the money?" asked Lonnie Rex.

"Not yet, and that poses a small issue. I promised the mayor that I would hold the information in his letter until later and wouldn't tell Peter without his permission. I created a bit of a problem for myself. I don't see how the story can be written without knowledge of the gift to the city for the park or whatever. Peter must know at some time."

"But you have told us."

"That I have, and I will ask you to hold the information until I decide what to do. Let's give it some time to develop and then see."

Sarah got up and brought out plates served with veal scallopini, pasta, and asparagus. The letter was quite forgotten as everyone explored their plates and began to enjoy the food.

Nancy started in anew, "So what are you going to tell Peter?"

"I'm going to tell him the truth. I'm going to call him in the morning and tell him about the meeting and that I can't reveal the details of the letter to the mayor just yet, but that he will have to know soon to complete the story for the paper. I will tell him that the mayor said he will look into it immediately and let me know what he finds. Peter will just have to wait a bit."

"There's no reason that the mayor should try to cover up the story, is there?" asked Sarah.

"I don't see why he would do that. I think he just wants to be in control of it, like most politicians would."

"But he knows that all of us know about Hollis, so he can't really hide it even if he wanted to, and with Peter in the loop, there will be no way," offered Sarah.

"The mayor just wants to investigate it and try to have the information come out in the best light on the city and him, it seems to me," said Caleb.

Lonnie Rex looked up from his plate and said, "Or he might be trying to protect someone else."

"Who else is there to protect?"

"What if someone has already found the money and the body and didn't report it?" questioned Lonnie.

The table talk quieted as they considered this possibility. Nancy broke the silence and said, "If that is true, then the plot really thickens."

"You know what? Let's not speculate. The mayor has over a week to figure out what he is going to do, then we will see. Maybe they'll find it right away. I mean, they should—it's clear where it is. If he doesn't find it or if he tries to cover it up, then we can let Peter do the story. The mayor knows that, so he will probably want to get it all clear real fast and make a grand announcement."

"Dream on, pard," admonished Lonnie Rex. "What's for dessert, Sarah?"

"Not yet, Lonnie," answered Sarah. "The salad is last in true Italian fashion. It cleanses your palate after the main courses."

"Don't think I've ever had my palate cleansed. Does it hurt much?"

They all laughed, and Sarah added, "No, silly. You follow along, and everything will be fine."

Lonnie didn't want to give up on teasing, so he asked, "If we get our palates all cleaned up, can we still have dessert?"

"Yes, Lonnie Rex, you can still have dessert."

"Now we're back where we started. What's for dessert?"

TWENTY-SIX

Monday was Memorial Day, and Caleb pulled into the drive of his farm with the trailer containing Cisco in tow. He had to meet Dickie and Estes at 9:00 a.m. and thought that a turn around the farm on Cisco would be a good start for both of them. The grass was high and green with that pungent smell of an early spring morning with the dew just beginning to disappear to the demands of the day. Caleb stood in front of the house and looked at the farm anew. He had been so busy in his first days back in Rogers that he had neglected the task before him. His decision to stay here and make it his home had only become firmer in his mind. The farm was very different from the vast expanse of the ranch, but this land certainly had its own charms. For one thing, the grass here was infinitely richer than out west. On the ranches in the west, the grass determined how many acres were required for one cow or horse, while here it was how many of each could be sustained by one acre. Caleb caught the snorting of Cisco from the trailer. He smelled the very grass that Caleb was admiring.

Caleb had forgone the trip to Casper's with Lonnie Rex this morning. Not because it was the holiday, but he figured that Lonnie could get along without him. There was much to do today, starting with this ride about the farm. Then he would meet with Dickie and Estes and plan out some improvements for them to undertake during the week. He unloaded Cisco, who was already saddled and ready for a work-out. It felt good to step up into the saddle and begin a ride on his own land. First, he would ride the fence line in the near pasture and then could ride the entire perimeter of the property. He knew there was adjoining property, which he might also gain access to if he played his cards right.

When he returned to the house, he was pleased to see Dickie and Estes waiting by their battered truck. They had arrived on time and seemingly in the mood to get started. Caleb pulled Cisco up in front of them and dismounted. One looked to be about sixty years old and his buddy a few years younger. The older one was stout with broad shoulders and an amiable smile. He wore Carhart overalls and a well-worn denim shirt, along with a friendly and open smile. His buddy looked more serious as he stood there in blue jeans and a sleeveless shirt.

Overalls was the first to speak. "Howdy, you must be Caleb."

"That's me. Which one of you is Dickie?"

"Me. This here is Estes. He's my cousin," said overalls.

"I'm pleased to meet you. Sarah said you fellows are good hands and might be willing to help me put this farm in order."

Estes spoke for the first time, "Reckon we can do about anything, as long as it ain't illegal, immoral, or fattening."

Dickie added, "That's about the size of it. What 'cha got for us?"

"Well, now, first thing is to get the fencing on that pasture there straightened up to hold Cisco here. Then a few improvements at the barn. I want to have everything good for the horse for when we come out and work."

"Leave it to us. Do you have materials, or do we need to go to town?"

"I have a list here. I haven't bought anything yet. I have a few tools in my trailer, which I will leave, but generally we need to buy everything we need. If you look the list over and check out the needed repairs, I can give you a check for you to go get what you need."

Caleb handed Dickie the list, assuming he was the boss. "If I give you a check for, oh about $500, can you get started? Keep track and let me know when you need more money. I'll pay you for your time separately."

"That'll work," said Dickie. "Me and Estes work for Sarah for $15 an hour. That be okay?"

"Works for me. After we get into it with the fence and barn, I'll give you the plan for what I want to do in the house. I can pay you weekly or however you want."

"We're easy. We don't work on Sunday though. We go to a little church west of Pea Ridge, and Sundays are for all that there."

"Same here, it looks like," said Caleb. "I'm going to brush Cisco down and get him put up. We'll meet in a few minutes, after you have had a chance to look everything over, then I've got to take Cisco back and go into town myself. I'll give you a check before I leave. Alright?"

"You a cowboy?" asked Estes.

"Well, I used to be. Since the only real cowboy is someone who makes a living at it, I reckon I'm retired since I came here. I used to top hand on a cattle ranch in Colorado, but now it looks like I'm going to be a farmer or the world's smallest rancher. Maybe if I get me some cows, I can reclaim the title."

"You look like a cowboy," observed Dickie.

"It's kinda hard to shed the look, for sure. About all I got is cowboy gear. But I think I do have a couple of Hawaiian shirts just for grins."

"Needn't be breaking them out for us. We might not recognize you," laughed Dickie.

"Thank you, gentlemen, for showing up. Now let's get to it."

Caleb was pleased with these two and thought they would do just fine.

On his way back to Sarah's place, Caleb's phone rang. He fumbled for the phone as he focused on how to answer it. The thing was ringing and flashing a number. With newfound confidence, Caleb slid the button on the screen and said, "Hello."

Sarah's voice emanated weakly from the phone. Remembering what he had learned, Caleb pushed the speakerphone button and proudly said, "Can you hear me?"

"Yes, I can hear you. It's me, Sarah."

"Who?" teased Caleb.

"Sarah, your sister!"

"Calm yourself. I'm just kidding. I can hear you. What's up?"

"Where are you? Are you coming back here? Will you be here for lunch? What have you been doing?"

Let's see... I'm driving back to your place, and I'll be there in a few minutes. I won't turn down some lunch, and... what else? Oh! I've been out at the farm to meet Dickie and his cousin Estes."

"Good. Did you like them? Can they help you out? I really like those guys. They've been a big help to me. Did—"

"Wait. I'll tell you all about it when I get there. Should only be a few minutes, and after I put Cisco up, I'll be in."

"Oh, and Caleb, the real reason I called. You got a call here a little while ago. Lori something or other. Isn't that the girl you used to date back in high school? Is she here? What do you think she wants?"

Caleb was struck dumb for a moment. He was thinking that he might see her at the reunion, but this was a surprise. It was only Monday, and the reunion was a few days away. He was wondering what this meant and whether...

"Caleb?"

"Yeah, yeah, I'm here. I heard you. Did she leave a number?"

"Yeeessss. She did. She wants you to call her."

"Okay, I'll do it this afternoon. Be there directly."

As Caleb turned in to Sarah's drive, he was thinking about the call from Lori. Sarah didn't say whether she was in town or not. Maybe she was calling just to see if he was going to be there.

Or maybe she was here and just wanted to confirm that he was. He figured Sarah had confirmed his presence, so he wondered if he should call back. Of course, he should call back, he thought. That would be rude not to. He couldn't escape the feeling that things were fixin' to rachet up a bit.

While unloading Cisco, Caleb wondered what he would say. It had been forty years since he had seen her. What do you do in this situation? Just call her. Don't be stupid, he thought. Let the conversation go where it would. At least he won't have to wonder anymore. But he couldn't escape the feeling that he was a little boy fixing to confront something that he simply wasn't prepared for.

At least the mayor deal was quiet, for now anyway. Peter had agreed to wait on any publication until he knew what the mayor finds. He did say that he had some more information that he wanted Caleb to see, and he promised to write up a draft of the article for the paper to summarize everything we know. It could be revised before going to print. Caleb was supposed to drop by later today to pick up a copy. He was hoping that this business would soon be behind him. Looks like there was going to be plenty to concentrate on. And now Lori…

His thoughts were interrupted by Sarah hollering, "Caaal-lebb!" at the top of her lungs as she stood on the back porch. Why are people always hollering, Caleb wondered. Does it speed things up? Do they need to speed up?

Fighting the urge to ignore her, Caleb stepped to the barn door and, while looking at her, replied in a soft voice, "Yes?"

"Lunch is ready!" Another loud announcement echoed across the valley.

"Coming," Caleb muttered, as he heard the door slam. Well, even though everyone in the new subdivision to the east now knows they are having lunch, Caleb knew that it would be good. With a glance around, he proceeded to the kitchen.

Sarah sat at the table serving his plate for him. It was leftovers, but oh so wonderful leftovers! Caleb pulled up a chair and began to drain his iced tea. He didn't realize how thirsty he was.

"Well, tell me things," Sarah directed.

Stopping her before she could get on a roll, Caleb told her everything he had done since he had left earlier in the morning. He described what he had discovered at the farm, how much he and Cisco had enjoyed their ride, and all about Dickie and Estes getting started. He tried not to pause and leave an opening, but at one point he needed to breathe, and that's when Sarah asked, "What about this Lori girl?"

"I don't know. I'll call her after lunch. I knew..."

"Is she the old girlfriend that moved away back in high school?"

Recovering from the interruption, Caleb resumed, "I knew that she was coming but I'm a bit..."

"But is she the old girlfriend? I thought the name was familiar, but I wasn't sure. Is it her?"

Surrendering to the inevitable, Caleb resorted to simple answers that could be delivered quickly, "Yes, it is her."

"You're a bit what?" asked Sarah.

Caleb realized that he was getting dizzy, so he stopped and took a few breaths. "Let's see, oh yes, I'm a bit surprised to hear from her so early."

"Are you going to call her back? She must be here. Do you think?"

"I will call her back," said Caleb.

"Are you going to see her?"

Caleb was quiet.

"Well?"

"Well, what?"

"Are you going to see her? Do you want to?"

"I guess I will, at least at the reunion. I won't know anything until I call her. Let's just eat, and I'll let you know everything after I call and talk to her," proposed Caleb. "That okay?"

"Sure. I guess that it's none of my business. I don't need to get involved," said Sarah.

Caleb knew that was about as likely as a snowstorm after lunch, but it enabled them to finish eating in relative quiet, both in their own thoughts.

With the dishes cleared away, Caleb stepped out onto the front porch. The sun was high in the sky bringing early summer warmth, tempered by a gentle breeze hastening down the length of the veranda. It was the perfect time of day to make a call. Caleb settled into a large rocker and pulled out his phone. He quickly realized that Sarah had not given him the number that Lori had left. Stepping back into the house, and not wanting to yell, Caleb found Sarah in the den beginning to read her ever-present book.

"Sarah; what was the number Lori left?"

"Oh. Uh, I don't know. Try the counter by the phone."

Caleb uttered a thank you as he began looking. He could find nothing on the counter.

"What did you write it on?" asked Caleb.

"Something… Oh, I remember! I must have written it on my notepad where I do my list."

"Where's your notepad?"

"Isn't it there?"

"Where?"

"There. On the kitchen counter next to the phone."

"No, there's nothing. Okay, here's the deal. I'm going back out to the porch. Whenever the list or notepad or whatever presents itself, and I know the number, I will call Lori."

"You mean that you are going to wait?" hollered Sarah.

Caleb thought that if he was a crying man, this would be a good time.

"Yes, I'll wait until I find the number," said Caleb.

"Do you want me to find it?" asked Sarah.

"Would you mind?"

There was an extended silence in which the only thing Caleb could hear was the sound of the rocker rungs caressing the porch floor.

"Here it is!" shouted Sarah from the depths of the house.

She came out to the porch and handed the number to Caleb. It was written on a Walmart receipt. "I forgot. I took the call in the bedroom. That is all I had to write it on."

"Did you find your list?" asked Caleb.

"I wasn't looking for it. Is it missing?"

"No, I'm sure it's... never mind. I'll call now."

Caleb looked at the number. It had a local area code, so it appeared that she was here in town. He remembered that she had an aunt who lived here. Maybe that was where she was staying. Well, onward into the breech, he thought, and dialed the number.

"Hello," a scratchy voice came on the line.

"Is Lori in?" Caleb asked.

"Who's calling please?"

"Caleb Atwood."

"Hold on just a minute. Just hold on."

After a long wait, he heard, "Hello. Caleb?"

The sound of this familiar voice crashed down on him in a way he could not have imagined. It was like going back in time, or that no time had ever passed since she last had spoken a hello to him. For a split second, he wanted to hang up and start again, but then he said, "Yes, it's me. I got your message. Are you in town?" He managed to get the words out.

"Yes, I'm here. I came into town on Saturday night, and I'm staying with my aunt. She lives over toward Bentonville now."

"Lori, I can't tell you how incredible it is to hear your voice again. I was taken back for a moment. It's like time stood still."

"Time hasn't stood still, but I know exactly what you mean. It has been forty years though."

"No, I don't think so... seems like a few days at most, to me."

"Can we get together, Caleb? I don't want to wait until the reunion. Can we?"

"I'm totally free. I have moved back here... but there is too much to tell for the phone. We can talk and catch up when we meet. Can I take you to lunch or dinner or... you name it."

"I'm free also. How about lunch tomorrow?"

"How about dinner tonight?" blurted Caleb.

"Perfect. Where shall we meet?"

"I can pick you up if you want," offered Caleb.

"That would be good. I'll text you the address."

"Text?"

"Yes. Text. You know, on your phone. I have your number now."

"Oh, sure. Text it to me. It will be my first text. I only got a phone the other day."

"Caleb, some things never change, and I am so glad. What time?"

Caleb stared at his watch. He was ready but regained control of himself. "You name it. I just finished things here and... oh, how about six o'clock?"

"That will be wonderful. I'll see you then."

"Okay, six o'clock then. Goodbye."

As Caleb hung up the phone, he stared off into the distance, willing the sun to move deeper in the west. Four more hours until he would be caught in a new type of stampede, he thought.

TWENTY-SEVEN

Caleb stepped up onto Lonnie Rex's porch later that day. Walking into the house, he called out, "Lonnie, where are you?"

"In the studio. Come on back."

Talking as he walked toward Lonnie's voice, Caleb said, "How do you work this GPS thing? I gotta' find an address."

Lonnie emerged from the studio. He said to Caleb, "I thought you were coming over earlier. Where've you been?"

"I got busy. How do you find this address on the GPS thing?"

"Why didn't you ask Sarah? She knows."

"Because I didn't. She already thinks I'm a phone idiot. And I didn't have the time for questions. Now show me how to do it."

"What's the address?" Lonnie asked as he reached for Caleb's phone.

Caleb handed him the paper with the address.

"Look, it's right here. You go to the maps thing. Press it and you'll see the search window. That's where you type it in. Didn't I show you this the other day?"

"Yes, you did, but I did that and typed it in, and it showed Decatur, Illinois, and that ain't it. The address is in Bentonville."

"Did you type in Bentonville?"

"Uh, I guess not. I was coming by here anyway, so I knew you would show me. I am not going to Decatur!" Caleb said in frustration.

Lonnie completed the entry with "Bentonville, AR," and the location came up. "See here it is. If you want directions, you just hit directions. It shows you three ways to go. The shortest is 18 minutes."

"How does it know how long it'll take me to get there?"

"It just computes the time required to go there obeying the speed limit."

"How does it know the speed limit? I don't even know the speed limit. What if I drive slower?"

"Oh, Caleb. The damn thing just knows. All of it is programmed in. It'll even adjust if you go faster or slower, or if you make a wrong turn."

"That's weird. It knows all that?"

"Yep. Now come out to the porch and fill me in. What's going on?"

Once they were seated, Lonnie lit up a cigarette and leaned forward in anticipation. "So, what have you been so busy with?"

Caleb told him all about the farm and meeting the guys to work there, and about lunch with Sarah. He saved the bit about Lori until last. "Anyway, Lori called me at Sarah's while I was out at my farm, and I called her back after lunch. Her call was a surprise. I guess she got in this weekend. We talked a little bit, and we're going to have dinner together tonight. I said I would pick her up. At six."

"Well, don't that dill your pickle!" Lonnie commented.

"Yeah, well now I know how to get there. She's staying at her aunt's house."

"That sounds promising. Reckon she's durn sure here to see you after all."

"Maybe. I'll know more after I see her. Hey, I'm sorry I didn't get by sooner. I know you wanted me to help you get ready for the Thursday night party."

"No worries. It doesn't take much to get ready. But we do have to make a beer run and get some snacks or such. Maybe we should get some gluten-free birdseed and some tofu snacks for the granola crowd. There might be some of them, you just never know. Barbeque for the rest of us. What do you think?"

"You know that barbeque was invented so they could serve bad meat? At least in Texas, it was that way. Disguised the taste."

"The local barbeque is pretty good, and it isn't bad meat!" exclaimed Lonnie.

"I know, I was just giving you a little history."

Moving on, Lonnie Rex asked, "Anything more on Peter and the station? Did you talk to him?"

"Yes, I did. He's okay with waiting, but he did say he had some more information. I was going to go by and pick it up today, but I called him and said I would be by tomorrow."

"What new stuff does he have?"

"No idea. I'll let you see whatever he gives me. I just want this station business over. I have things to do."

"It sure sounds like you have things to do. This Lori business may just get you all fluffed and occupied."

"It is what it is. Do you have any iced tea?"

"I can make you some, but it's not a staple around here. How's about a Big Gulp from the 7-11? Got that."

"No thanks. Just some iced tea if you don't mind."

Lonnie Rex disappeared into the house while Caleb relaxed in the rocker. He only had about an hour until he picked Lori up for dinner, which reminded him of something else.

When Lonnie returned with a tall glass of tea, Caleb asked him, "Where's a good place to go for dinner?"

"What do you want?"

"Something nice, but not too fancy. I don't want to make it look like a big date or anything—just old friends having dinner. A steak house would be regular enough."

"Burl's chop house is good. It's over by Bentonville. Not too fancy, and the food is good. They have steaks, pork chops, some fish, and a very good salad bar. Also, a full bar. Does she drink?"

"Got me. I haven't seen her in forty years! She might be a vegetarian for all I know."

"Well let's hope not. That could be a deal killer," remarked Lonnie Rex.

After looking at his watch, Caleb downed the rest of his tea and said, "I gotta go. I should probably allow a little extra time in case I have trouble finding the place. Hey, I can use this GPS thing to find Burl's, huh?"

"That you can, my friend, that you can. You're coming right along. Remember your manners, say hi to Lori for me, and fill me in on how it goes."

"Will do. Don't wait up. I'll catch you tomorrow."

TWENTY-EIGHT

When Caleb finally found the house at the end of the address, he circled the block to take in the neighborhood. It was a nice area with new but small homes. It occurred to him that it might be a bit of a retirement area that would appeal to Lori's aunt. It looked that way.

He had a few minutes and didn't want to get there early. The GPS was right on. It took him 18 minutes just as shown. It still mystified him how that worked. He thought he could have used that on the ranch. Maybe the GPS knew how fast a horse could go over different terrain. Wouldn't that be a hoot? But then he thought that there were no addresses on the ranch, so that was silly. Now he had five more minutes to kill, so he pulled to the curb a block away from his destination, turned off the truck, and settled back. Then he started the truck back up and pulled out. He didn't want to be late either. Stop it! He thought. What difference does it make?

Caleb pulled to a stop in the driveway of the house. Just as he cut the engine and stepped out, Lori opened the door and came bounding down the steps. Her ash blond hair was in long ringlets that cascaded over her shoulder as she approached. She was in a light blue summer dress with tennis shoes on. Caleb barely had time to admire her before she leaped into his arms and hugged him tightly.

"Caleb! It's so good to see you!" she exclaimed as she hugged him deeper.

"And you too, Lori."

"God, I've missed you!" she said.

"You took a little while to tell me that."

"Well, I'm telling you now!"

Caleb realized that he was holding back and didn't want to, so he held her away and looked at her closely. "Lori, I just didn't know, 'till this moment, just how much I have missed you. You look great!" blurted Caleb.

Lori grabbed Caleb's hand and tugged him toward the porch. "Come in and meet my aunt. She wants to see you."

"Didn't I meet her back when?"

"Of course, but she doesn't remember. She doesn't even remember lunch. Come on."

Caleb followed her into the house and greeted the elderly lady sitting in the living room.

"Winnie, this is Caleb."

"I remember you," she said. "You and Lori used to go together back in high school. You came out to the house when I lived out by the cemetery."

"Well, what do they say about long-term versus short-term memory?" Lori said to Caleb. "That's right, Winnie. It's him. We haven't seen each other in a long time. We're going out to dinner."

"You better get on with it. We don't live forever you know."

"Oh Winnie, you're such a treasure!" said Lori. "We'll be back later, and I'll tell you all about it."

Caleb spoke up and said, "It's a pleasure to see you again, and so great to connect with Lori after all these years. Can we bring you anything?"

"No, dear. Just have fun. You've got a lot of time to make up for. I'll be fine."

Lori turned to Caleb and asked, "Where are we going?"

"Lonnie mentioned Burl's steakhouse. Is that good?"

"Lonnie Rex! How's he doing?"

"Same as always. Some things never change."

"I hope they haven't! He was always such a hoot," said Lori.

"He said to say hi for him. I saw him a little while ago," explained Caleb.

"Let's go. I'm so hungry. And Burl's is good. It's been a while since I've been there."

"I've never been there, but Lonnie said it was good."

Lori grabbed her purse and a sweater as she followed Caleb out the door. When they got to his truck, Caleb opened the door for her. Lori bounded up the step into the cab without even a hint of requiring assistance. Caleb circled around and joined her in the cab.

"I like your truck. I've got one too—well, it's a 150. This is a 350, isn't it?"

"Uh, yeah. Got to have a serious truck on the ranch. Things to haul, bad roads and all. Plus, I pull my fifth wheel trailer—Cisco's home—when we travel."

"Cisco?"

"Yes, Cisco's my horse. I couldn't leave him behind."

"Oh… I see. Gosh, there's so much to catch up on. We'll eat slowly and talk nonstop."

Caleb pulled into the parking lot at Burl's Steakhouse. It was a cabin-looking building with fake logs and a large front porch, which contained various memorabilia harking back to the farms and ranches of the past. It had a distinct western flavor, which, of course, was the idea.

When they entered the restaurant, the waiter led them to a booth. Lori slid into the booth, and Caleb sat across from her. He allowed himself to study her as he took in her beauty. The eyes were as he remembered, her hair was longer with the cascading waves, and her skin was a smooth buttery tan. He wanted to allow her to go first. Caleb's spell was interrupted when the waiter approached and asked if there was anything they wanted to drink.

"Just tea for me," said Lori, "unsweetened, please."

"Same here," Caleb said without lifting his gaze at Lori.

Lori looked at Caleb apologetically. She said, "I'm sorry, Caleb, if I bowled you over back at the house. It's just that I am so glad to see you. I didn't have any control at all!"

"No need to apologize, it was great. In fact, I couldn't have imagined a better start to our private reunion."

"Speaking of the reunion, this is the first one you have come to, isn't it? I mean, I thought you were coming to the last one, but I guess you didn't show. I didn't either. I came two reunions ago and signed up for the last one, then dropped out. I was alone then and not ready, I guess."

"Okay, let's get this show organized. There's so much to share. You want to go first, or do you want me to?" asked Caleb.

Lori thought and then said, "You know, it doesn't matter. I'll start."

She sat back and began, "Okay, from the top: I went to Las Vegas with my parents, as you know, right at the end of our junior year. It was very rough on me to leave. I missed you more than you can imagine. Plus, there were other friends and things I missed. But there I was—in Las Vegas. I mean, it was good in a lot of ways. My dad liked his position at the hotel, my mom enjoyed the town, and the school was nice. Las Vegas is a lot more than the strip, you know. Real clean and all. There's a lot of money for the town from the entertainment businesses.

"I finished high school and then went to college at the University of Nevada in Reno. I got a BS degree in veterinary medicine. After that, I got my doctorate in veterinary science from Stanford."

"You're a vet?" interrupted Caleb.

"I am indeed. And what's wrong with that?" challenged Lori laughingly.

"Nothing! Absolutely nothing! I guess I'm just surprised. That's great! Do you like it?"

"Sure. I have my own clinic in Vegas. Mostly small animals. You wouldn't believe the pampered little dogs that retired people have. They're a hoot! I do some large animals too, but it's not a big part of my practice."

"Please, continue. I'm sorry for the interruption," said Caleb.

Before Lori could continue, the waiter brought their drinks and asked if they would like to order. Neither Caleb nor Lori had even picked up the menu, so Caleb said, "Why don't you give us a few minutes? We're in no hurry and have a lot to catch up on."

"Of course. Why don't you just signal me when you're ready, and I'll step over. And also, if you want the salad bar, you can go up at any time, and order entrees later."

"Great. Thanks!" said Caleb, turning back to Lori, as she continued.

"After Stanford, I went back to Las Vegas and got a job in a small animal clinic. Let's see... that was in 1983. It was a good position and I jumped right in. I learned so much. It seems that college only teaches you the vocabulary — it's not until you work that you finally learn. The job was terrific, and I had no distractions. I got a nice apartment and began life as a professional. I really threw myself into my work. My folks were doing fine, and we got together frequently for dinners and such.

"As time went on, I began dating some, but nothing serious. I was just so focused on my work. It always seemed that guys wanted to go to the strip, which really didn't appeal to me much. There were some good shows, but it was all so garish! As time went on, I did meet a man who came into the clinic often. His name is Clifford Martin. Then one time, after I had treated his dog, he asked me out, so I said yes. For once, we didn't go to the strip — we just went to dinner, and it was fun.

"Clifford was very nice, and we got along. He was successful in what he did — mostly investments and some real estate. Vegas was booming then, and things were good. We dated for about a year and then we got married in 1985."

Lori paused for a moment. "I have a confession to make— nothing but the whole truth with you. I got pregnant. So, we had to get married. I mean, we were close, so it wasn't a mistake. We were probably going to get married anyway. I loved him you know, and he was good to me and for me.

"He had a large home in a gated community. We got along fine and began preparing for the baby. I think we were both excited. My daughter was born in late 1985. Her name is Gwen. Then we were a family, and it was a great time for all of us. I continued to work and spend as much time with Cliff and Gwen as my work would allow. Cliff traveled some, but generally was very attentive to the family.

"Gwen was a good kid. She was involved in just about everything, and during college, she met a man and got married. His name is Michael Esteban. That was in 2006. They live on a small ranch in northern Nevada. So, they are a little removed but not too bad. They have one child, a boy, born in 2008."

"So, you're a grandmother.

"That's how it works, you know. I love it. I don't get to see them as much as I would like. The clinic is very busy, and it takes much of my time—perhaps too much. The little guy is named Isaiah, and he's a dear. Eight years old now.

"But I'm getting ahead of myself. When Gwen was born, I continued to work at the clinic where I started and got more and more involved in the management and the work. I had a significant role in the clinic and enjoyed managing the entire operation. Things worked out well. But, as a result, my job got very demanding, and I took on a lot of responsibility. The truth is that I got so involved that I neglected my marriage a bit. Cliff traveled a lot, and we seemed to settle into our individual lives. It was okay but not great. I didn't neglect Gwen as she grew up or anything like that, but I know I neglected my husband. Things stumbled along like that until 1997. At that point, I was 39 years old, and I became pregnant again. It was quite a surprise to both of us. More than just a surprise—it was huge and not at all what we wanted. I was totally caught up in my career, and Cliff was sort of tuned out. It was a bad time. Clifford wanted me to get an abortion, but that was simply out of the question for me. So… I became a mom for the second time. My son Daniel was born that year. He's 19 now and…. You know, I'm famished. Let's get that salad and order something, then I can continue."

"Sounds great," said Caleb.

Both proceeded to the salad bar and served themselves. The plates were refrigerated, and the salad bar was extensive. Caleb even noted that they had anchovies, one of his favorites. Lori declined them despite Caleb's recommendation. After returning to their table, Caleb signaled the waiter, and they ordered the main course before starting on their salads.

Once they had set a good pace on the salads, Lori slowed enough to continue. "Where was I? Yeah, Daniel. After Daniel was born, things really went downhill. I was doing the mom basics and working very hard. Clifford just didn't seem to exist for me. Maybe by then I didn't even love him. One thing is for sure, his behavior changed. He was unfaithful. He openly admitted it and said that he wanted out. He never did step up to the plate with the reality of our having a second child and just seemed to want other things. One of those things was a young lady from his office. None of his affair matters here. What matters is that we got a divorce in 1999. Daniel was just two years old.

"The good thing was that the divorce was amicable. He knew he was at fault and wanted to take ownership of his guilt, so he left me in good shape—financially I mean. It really was not at all rancorous. Truth be told, I was also at fault for being so neglectful of him and so caught up in my work.

"Since the divorce, in 1999, I've been alone. That's 17 years. And I haven't disliked it, certainly not enough to go find another guy! If I ever had thoughts of another man, they always seemed to drift back to you. Don't be alarmed! I'm not here to snare you. I just mean that I had no image of someone new. You were the only man still lodged in my brain."

The waiter brought out their plates of food. Lori had ordered a filet, medium, along with all the fixings and Caleb had opted for the rack of lamb. Lori looked at his lamb, and said, "I thought you would be a steak man."

"I love steak, and it's certainly a staple on the ranch, but lamb is always a welcome option. I love mint jelly."

As Lori cut into her filet, she said, "Tell me about the ranch."

"Nope. We're still doing you. I'm going last remember?"

"That's right! I think I just need to eat. Let's take a chew break and then get back to it."

"I'm with you," said Caleb.

TWENTY-NINE

The arrival of their meals had allowed a respite from the telling of their stories. Both Caleb and Lori welcomed the interruption and savored the knowledge that they could return to the togetherness that each was experiencing. There was so much to tell and enjoy and neither wanted to rush through the details. Everything was to be savored.

Caleb sat back from his plate before Lori did. He signaled the waiter and requested black coffee. Lori nodded in agreement without looking up from her plate but did manage a late smile for the waiter. He asked if they wanted dessert, and Caleb answered that they probably would, but there was no rush. Caleb had no interest in any haste as they both intended to fully enjoy the evening.

When Lori finished her last bite, she looked up and said, "That was so good. I didn't realize how hungry I was. Maybe talking builds an appetite."

"I like watching you eat. And I love getting to talk. It takes me back. Remember when we just sat and talked forever? About everything?"

"I do. I always missed that with Clifford. He was always into entertainment, sports, all kinds of things, but we didn't just sit and talk. Maybe if we had…"

The coffee arrived. Lori added cream to hers and said, "I am going to want some dessert. I don't usually, but with you, I want everything…. I mean the dessert; you know what I'm saying. Oh, jeez!"

"I rather think I will have some too. Dessert and even everything if it arrives."

Both laughed and considered their coffee.

"I'm waiting for more," said Caleb.

"Yes, where was I? Yeah, the divorce. With my newfound independence, both personal and financial, I opened my own clinic. I ended up taking a couple of the people who I worked with from the other clinic. I was also able to take some of my clients and got some new ones in short order. Within a year, the new clinic was profitable and has been successful ever since. I now have two vets and three assistants on staff. It's been good.

"But I've continued to be a bit of a workaholic, and I'm afraid that I haven't been as good a mom to my son as I should have been. I mean, he's just fine but... well, I'll tell you more later. That's pretty much the summary for me. Lots more details I guess, but now I want to hear about you."

Caleb signaled for a refill on their coffee, then began, "What do you already know?"

"I know that you went to the University in Fayetteville for, what, two or three years?"

"Just two. I was in prelaw with every intention of becoming a lawyer, but that dog just wouldn't hunt. I lost interest in the law, and then my mom died, and I came home to help with dad."

"I heard some of this back during the second reunion. About you and your dad. And then you moved to New Mexico, and that's the last I ever heard about you. What happened after the move to New Mexico?"

Caleb began to tell his story in as much detail as she had offered about her life. He focused on the time traveling up and down the Rockies, his time in the wilderness, and the work on several ranches, including his position on the ranch in La Veta. He described all his friends on the ranch, and the work they did together. He mentioned his investment in cattle and how that may pay off later in the year.

Caleb was reluctant to explain too much about the affair with Warren, but it was so much a part of his recent story that it couldn't be neglected. He figured he would just be adding one more to the insider group. He told Lori about all the events that had brought him back to Rogers. He shared the story of his relationship with Warren and of his recent death. He enjoyed describing the farm Warren left him and that he had to get it fixed up so he could move in. Caleb fully related the details concerning Warren's description of the death of Hollis, including the station where Hollis was buried. He finished with the events of the last few days and how he was just waiting to see what would happen.

Lori was silent for a moment, then began with the questions. "Wow, that's quite a story. I remember that old station. It's been there forever! You mean this guy is buried there?"

"That's the way it appears. I guess we'll soon know. I've done all I can do and fulfilled Warren's wish, so that's it for me. I'll be glad when it's over," admitted Caleb.

"It will be interesting to find out what happens, but as you say, it's out of your hands."

Lorie drank her coffee, and continued, "You didn't mention anything about your love life. I guess you never married—you certainly would not have left that out! No women in your life?"

"None, really. I mean, I've known a few, but nothing serious."

"Nothing?"

"Look, I haven't exactly been celibate. There have been probably three or four women who have meant something to me or have occupied a spot in my life. There was a young lady in Artesia who was a great deal of fun. Those were sort of party days. I worked on the oil rigs four days on and three days off. The days off were spent with friends and with one particular girl. We got caught up in the bar scene. For me, it wasn't about drinking, because I don't drink much. I was playing some gigs with a country and western band in various locations, and she liked the scene. It was fun while it lasted."

"After I entered my exploratory phase up and down the Rocky Mountains, looking for I don't know what, women didn't figure in much. I couldn't find one that wanted to accompany me into the wilderness for months at a time. Go figure!"

"Besides, I had met and welcomed another companion into my life. It was during my 'wilderness phase' that I began to experience the presence of the Lord. He became my newfound friend. I don't mean that I 'got religion' exactly. It was more that I allowed Him to establish a presence within me and in my everyday activities. He became my constant companion and remains so to this day. With His presence, I just never felt alone. It's hard to explain.... No, it isn't! The Lord is with me constantly. I'm not saying that I am any sort of saint, just that He is with me and always inhabits my thoughts. He has always been present with very good guidance relative to any of my thoughts or actions. I reckon that may sound self-righteous, but that's not it. I believe he is there for all of us, always. It's just up to us to let him in.

"After that 'wilderness phase,' I followed the Lord's guidance in everything I did. He led me to fall in love with everything about the natural beauty of His creation. That appreciation led to my finding fulfillment in working on the land. I found the most joy in ranching. Every decision that I made seemed to lead to good results. I became a cowboy! I learned the trade and made my way nicely. It was work I dearly loved, and it was quite fulfilling. I met all those people I mentioned earlier. They all became important to me. I guess this is a long-winded way of saying that there didn't seem to be a vacancy in my heart for a love affair with any of the women I met. It has always felt like that spot is filled by the Lord." After a pause, Caleb continued, "But I must say that it is becoming clear that you have resided within me for all these years and apparently occupy much of that space. There just wasn't a spot for another woman. Seeing you here has been confirmation of that. I guess that's the reason that I never sought or found anyone. Could be all your fault!" Caleb laughingly admitted.

Lori was quiet for a moment and then shared, "Wow, this is all moving sort of fast, isn't it?"

"Maybe not. Could be that the stew has been simmering for a long time and we just lifted the lid and looked in," Caleb observed quietly.

"I think I want that dessert now," said Lori.

THIRTY

Caleb and Lori ordered dessert and finished it in relative silence. There was no "damper" on their conversation, it was just that each was absorbing what they had heard from the other and contemplating its meaning. While the presence they occupied in each other's lives had always been there, this was the first time that they had exposed it to each other and openly confronted it. What had always been held within each and in secret was now visible. They had indeed "opened the lid and looked at the stew" as Caleb had suggested.

"I've got to move around. When you're done, let's go for a walk or something. Anything to move around," said Caleb as he signaled for the check.

"Good idea, but you are not taking me home!"

"I have no intention of doing any such thing," said Caleb.

As they climbed into the truck, Lori said, "I know what. Let's go down to the lake. You know, where we always hung out."

"Sure. That's where they're going to have the music on Thursday night and the picnic on Friday. I'm going to play some Thursday with a group of musicians that Gina Houseman has put together. You remember her?"

"Yes, I think so. She was always bubbly and chasing the boys."

"Don't reckon that's changed much," agreed Caleb.

"After the music, Lonnie Rex is having people over to his house. I agreed to help."

"Sounds like fun. Does he still live in that big house downtown?"

"Yes, he does. Nothing has changed, not even the odor of paint."

Lori laughed openly. "I do remember. We went over there at the last reunion I came to. The whole place smelled like paint. Maybe that's what is responsible for Lonnie Rex's peculiar demeanor!"

"Could be. You know, Lonnie Rex and I have been close over the years. I didn't tell you about all the times we have been together. He made several trips out to Colorado, and I showed him around that part of the world. Lots of trail rides and such."

Continuing, Caleb said, "You know, I would like it if we could go together to the reunion events starting on Thursday night. You game?"

"Oh Caleb, you mean like a date?" Lori said teasingly.

"Whatever you want to call it, can I take you?"

"Thought you would never ask!"

After passing through town, Caleb turned and drove down the hill toward the lake. The area around the lake had always been a destination recreation area. In the past, there had been a huge swimming pool, skating rink, and restaurant. In recent years, the park had been developed and was widely used by the town's residents. Late on this Monday night, the park area was quiet. The weekends would find the park in use at all hours, but now Caleb and Lori had it to themselves. Caleb pulled the truck to a stop overlooking the lake and cut the engine. They both studied the moonlight shimmering across the water, lost in remembrance of times spent in this very spot so many years ago.

Caleb spoke first, "So where were we?"

"You were confessing your undying fixation on me, as I recall," Lori teased. "I'm not sure I want you to stop."

"Maybe I'll return to that theme, but I still want to know more. You mentioned your son and said you would tell me later. What's his story?"

"Daniel is 19 and has had sort of a difficult time. I told you about how I was so busy, but that's not all." Lori paused and gathered her thoughts. "Daniel does not have a good relationship with his dad. Clifford has never gotten along with him and has basically excluded him from his life. It has been hard on Daniel."

"Why would Clifford do that?"

"There are several reasons, I guess. I told you that Clifford never wanted Daniel. That led to our conflict and exposed how we had drifted apart. After the divorce and when Cliff had moved on with his new wife, he just never welcomed Daniel as a part of his life. Cliff had two children with her. She was younger and wanted children, so he was stuck. He didn't want Daniel, and that rejection carried over when they had the children. Fancy that—he didn't want Daniel, and then he ended up with two more. There just wasn't room in Cliff's new world for Daniel.

"He was never cruel to Daniel, but he has never welcomed him. Perhaps Cliff felt some guilt over the situation. He accepted his responsibility for the divorce, and Daniel was a reminder of his failure. I don't know, but it created a riff. Daniel has been conflicted because of it. I know that on some level, all he ever wanted was to earn his father's love or respect or something, but there has been nothing. Clifford can be a cold fish.

"And the two of them are very different. Cliff is hard-working and focused but rather rigid and set in his ways. I don't think of him as creative at all. He's rather dull and very inflexible. Daniel, on the other hand, is very creative and inquisitive. He has a variety of interests but never found any kind of support from his father.

"In addition, as I indicated, I didn't exactly step up to the plate. I was busy and just sort of hoped he would raise himself. I rather neglected him to pursue my own interests. So, Daniel is sort of isolated. I know he feels unappreciated and maybe a little unloved. I hope not.

"In that regard, and because he is rather close to my aunt Winnie, I had him come with me on this trip. Winnie loves unconditionally and has a special place in her heart for Daniel. He certainly responds to that, and Winnie loves it, so that is why he's here. He was out at the time you came to pick me up, and I figured I would introduce him to you when we got home or whenever. I love him dearly. I just need to allow him to see my support and acceptance. It's not easy.

"What's not easy, having acceptance or showing it?"

"Probably both."

Caleb rolled down the window to greet the night air. Turning to Lori, he said, "Well, I'll look forward to meeting him."

"Good. He needs involvement with people as he develops his interests. I think that, in many ways, he is very mature, but he also can seem vulnerable. Without a father figure in his life, he may be a little naïve and unguarded. He's going to college soon and I am concerned about how he may do. Maybe I'm just being a mother."

"Daniel is very interested in design and is very talented in that regard. He loves creating things and building almost anything. He's very artistic yet pragmatic. Right now, he's planning on pursuing a career in building design. Maybe architecture or engineering, although math isn't his strong suit. He is set to start school in August at UC Berkeley."

"UC Berkeley! That's a big ouch!" exclaimed Caleb. "Oh… erase that. You didn't ask my opinion."

"No, that's okay. I know what you mean. Berkeley has a good program and all, but it's so big and has such a reputation! I worry if it's right for him. Perhaps a smaller school would be better, but that's where we are. He seems to be okay with it, but I don't sense that he is very excited," replied Lori.

"What are his other interests?" asked Caleb.

"He's sort of outdoorsy. He reads a lot and seems to focus on nature. I think he finds inspiration from nature as it relates to his design. He used to like to go with me when I treated large animals, but he fell short of wanting to be a vet. Whatever his interests are, his father never took an interest or provided any encouragement," said Lori.

Thinking for a minute, Caleb continued, "You know, I might have a summer project for him. That farm I inherited needs a total rehab. I have no real idea what to do with it, but it's a great structure, and if he's interested, he could design me something, and we'll build it."

"You're kidding! He would love that!" exclaimed Lori. "Well, you'll have to ask him, but I think that it would be great. I've seen his work, and he does have a good sense of design, and he is also down to earth."

"How long is he going to be here?"

"That's undecided. He wanted to stay here with Winnie for a while, but nothing has been finalized. If you really wanted him and he agrees, it would be possible for him to stay a while. But it would be totally up to you. Whatever you want to do."

"Speaking of that, when are you planning to go back to Vegas?"

"I must return to run the clinic. On the other hand," Lori thought for a minute. "I do have some flexibility. I have a good staff and could arrange some absences if needed. I'll have to think about it, but I will need to go back next week in any event. Daniel can stay if he wants, and I could come back if I'm wanted or needed. Winnie would be ecstatic if Daniel gets to stay."

Caleb thought it over. "I'll talk to Daniel if it's okay with you, take him out to the farm if he is interested, and go from there. As far as your schedule, I hope that you can keep your bags packed."

"That sounds like a plan," said Lori. "Let's go have you meet Daniel."

As Caleb and Lori pulled up into the drive at Winnie's residence, the lights were still on in the house. Lori placed her hand on Caleb's arm to restrain him from exiting the cab. Caleb stopped and settled back. When the lights of the truck finally went out, Lori gave Caleb's arm a squeeze and looked at him for a long moment.

"Caleb, tonight has been unbelievable! I never knew what to expect when we finally got to meet again. I had imagined all sorts of things from the cold shoulder to feigned interest. I didn't even know how I would react. When I saw you, I just blew apart with excitement. Please forgive me if it was too much. From the moment of that first hug, it seems like we started exactly where we left off all those years ago. How can that be? That's what I keep asking myself. Maybe it's just the magic of the moment, but whatever happens, I want you to know how much I treasure you and always have."

Caleb searched for the right words. He too was surprised at how the evening had unfolded. He knew, as did Lori, that something had transpired which would not go away.

Finally, he said, "You know, Lori, you have always been my soul mate. I have learned that I can live without you if it is necessary, but I can never deny your presence in my heart. You will always be here," Caleb said as he lifted her hand to touch his chest. "If we are meant to be together, the Lord will provide that outcome. We shall follow His lead in all things."

Lori began to cry. She uttered quietly, "Thanks. Let's do this together."

At that moment, Daniel stepped out the front door, and from the porch, he shouted, "You two coming in?"

THIRTY-ONE

Caleb arrived late at Casper's the next morning. Lonnie Rex looked a little put out as Caleb crossed the dining room to where Lonnie occupied his usual table in the back.

"What's up, pard? You're getting in the habit of being late or completely absent. Was it something I said?" Lonnie asked whimsically.

"Give me a break. I need some coffee," Caleb said as he pulled out his chair.

"Didn't you get some earlier or take Cisco out?"

"Nope."

"So, where have you been? Oh, don't tell me—you spent the night with Lori?"

"No! I've been asleep! Now let me get configured here with a little coffee. I need breakfast too," Caleb said as he looked over at the waitress.

As she approached, Caleb said, "Uh, let's see… first some coffee black, then three poached eggs, some grits, toast… and bacon… no, make it sausage today… please."

When the coffee arrived, Caleb drank it slowly and silently as he fully awakened. When he felt ready, he looked at Lonnie, who was patiently waiting for him to embrace the day and fill him in on his dinner with Lori.

With most of the liquid fortification consumed, Caleb began. "Last night, Lori and I went out to eat. We went to Burl's, as you suggested, and had a very fine meal. We got all caught up in the past and had a great time."

"That's it?!" quizzed Lonnie.

"That's it for now! There's a lot more, and I'll fill you in on a need-to-know basis!"

Lonnie Rex laughed. "Looks like you either fell in love all over again or went down in flames," he observed. "Haven't seen you behave quite so peculiar."

"I'll get you caught up. Give me time."

Unwilling to wait, Lonnie continued. "Reckon you fell in love again. If you had been shot down, you would be all composed and stoic like nothing ever matters, but you're as nervous as a cat in a room full of rockers."

"I am not nervous; just got a lot on my mind and a lot to do. Now shut up and follow my lead," instructed Caleb. The waitress arrived with his breakfast, and he said to Lonnie, "Let me eat, and then I'll fill you in. Tell me something interesting while I eat."

"Okay…. Yesterday afternoon, they started digging some over at the station," Lonnie informed Caleb.

"Really? Well, that's good. Glad they got started. If they get it all dug up, we can put it behind us. That reminds me. I've got to go by and see Peter and see what he has. He'll be chomping at the bit to do a story."

"Are you coming by my place today?" asked Lonnie Rex. "Still got to make that beer run. Thursday night's coming up."

"Not immediately. I need to tell you more. Last night I met Lori's son. His name is Daniel."

"He came with her? What's his story?"

"Daniel is 19 and likes to visit here. He's close to Lori's aunt. He's going to go to college in the fall, where he's going to study architecture or interior design. Lori said that he was talented, so, I asked him to take a look at my farm and give me some ideas. I'm going to pick him up this morning to go out there."

"What do you want him to do?"

"Look at the house and see if he has any ideas on how to renovate it. I'm open, and it sort of gets the ball rolling," said Caleb.

"Lori going with you?"

"I don't know. She can if she wants to," Caleb said as he finished eating.

"Lori, you, her son, and your new farm. Could be getting ahead of the herd, but it sounds like you better watch out or she could become your own Jaws One!"

"Yes, you are getting way ahead of things. I just want to give Daniel a chance to do something real before he goes off to the head cases at college."

"Where's he going?"

"Berkeley."

"The hell you say! That's the capital of indoctrination hell! No one can survive that place and come out sane. Just tie him up 'till the holidays. That ought to do it," said Lonnie Rex.

"The thought has occurred to me, but it's not my business. Lori is a little worried about him, though. Maybe I will tie him up, if he doesn't squeal too much," Caleb laughed as he spoke.

Caleb got up from the table and threw some money down. "This one's on me—you got the last one. I'm going over to see Peter before I go out to get Daniel. Want to come to Peter's?"

"Naw. I better get on with getting ready for the party. It's clear that you're going to be useless in that endeavor. I'll go it alone."

"Sorry man; gotta follow my nose. I'll stop by after the farm."

"Bring Lori by if she's with you. I'd like to see her."

"Maybe," Caleb said as he started for the door.

Peter had Caleb follow him into his office. Standing by his desk, he picked up a file folder and handed it to Caleb. "Here's some notes on what I have found out. There's also a draft of the story that we can publish in the paper. It's just a draft. We'll know some more soon, and it will have to be updated. However, it gives you the flavor of the approach I want to take, and you can see if you like it."

Caleb opened the file and said, "Give me the highlights. Anything earth shaking?"

"As far as Warren's story, no, but after doing some research I'm thinking that the mayor has been involved in this station deal in ways that maybe he shouldn't have."

"What do you mean?" asked Caleb.

"I talked to one of the members of the Historical Board, and he told me that the mayor had contacted two of the more, how shall we say, 'conservative members' on the board. At any rate, the mayor seriously twisted their arms to get them to vote to allow the station to be torn down."

"So what? Maybe it needed to come down."

"Hang on. There is some indication that the mayor is financially involved in the development at the station site. If that is the case, then the mayor should not be using his influence in decisions that could benefit him financially. This whole thing could prove embarrassing to him, depending on how it comes out."

"Are you saying that the mayor is the developer?"

"No, he is not. But he has been an investor with the developer in the past, and it looks like maybe this time too," explained Peter.

"Let me guess," said Caleb. "It's Dumar Ashton."

"Bingo!"

Caleb continued, "He's the one that bought the station, according to Vernon, and Nancy mentioned him as being the name behind the entity that submitted for approval to demolish. It all fits. But so what? Anyone could have been the one to purchase and develop. I mean, I understand about the mayor, but that doesn't mean that Dumar is guilty of anything, does it?"

"Look at the big picture Caleb. Dumar develops regularly with investment from the mayor, he gets the mayor to clear the way with the board, then he buys the station at a reduced price, and then he develops. He and the mayor make a neat profit. That's collusion."

"I see." Caleb thought for a moment before continuing. "Peter, remember when I called you on Saturday to tell you about the meeting with the mayor?"

"Sure. You want me to wait until the mayor investigates it. That's not a problem, but it sure makes me anxious to find out how he handles it. When they dig up the body, it'll be a story and we'll print it. Our reporting will have to include the mayor's involvement in the deal. I can't suppress that. If they find nothing, it is still a story. The confession of Warren's and his claim about Hollis's death is certainly newsworthy. Even without a body, it's still a story. Maybe if they don't find the body, the mayor's involvement could be kept quiet—I don't know. I'm not anxious to accuse him of anything without reason. But even the slightest indication of a coverup, and I'll want to print it."

Caleb thought to himself about how to handle his pledge to the mayor. Peter didn't know about the money yet. If they dug up the money and the body, then Peter would have the whole story. On the other hand, if they tried to cover anything up, especially the money, then he would have to tell Peter everything. Either way, Peter will know, he thought, but it did nothing to ease his concern about his pledge to the mayor. However, if the mayor's involvement is unethical, withholding this information could make Caleb sort of an accessory. He couldn't allow that to happen.

Turning to face Peter, Caleb said, "Look Peter, I have some additional information on this deal. It comes directly from the letter to the mayor. I can't reveal it just yet. If the mayor gets everything dug up, then you will know everything I know—any of the collusion stuff is up to you to decide how to handle. If I am not satisfied that all the information from the letters has come to light, I will tell you then, because at that point it will be significant. In any event, you will have the entire story before printing anything, just as I told you. Let's wait a bit longer and see what the mayor does."

"You've got me curious," said Peter.

"That's probably why you are a good journalist," commented Caleb.

THIRTY-TWO

On the way to get Daniel, Caleb was mulling over what Daniel might do in designing the renovations at his farm. Last night when Caleb had met Daniel, he was rather impressed with him. Daniel was tall and handsome with close-cropped hair and firm in his handshake. His appearance was almost military looking. He spoke easily and was relaxed toward his mother going out with Caleb. He even seemed happy about it. When they spoke about his farm and Caleb's offer to enlist his help in the renovation efforts, Daniel was genuinely interested and pleased to be asked. Caleb offered to pay him, but Daniel said that he wanted to wait to see how much work was involved. Waiting was agreeable to Caleb, but he made it clear that he wanted to pay Daniel for his work. He was glad that Daniel had acted so professionally as he accepted the invitation to help.

Caleb had not given a lot of thought toward the farm renovation and wasn't sure exactly how to proceed. He wasn't ready to tell Daniel what he wanted to do because he simply didn't know. He told himself to give Daniel free reign and see what he came up with. All he had to do was give Daniel some sense of what he liked in a home, how he lived, and then stand back. That should work, but he still couldn't shake the feeling that he might have invited a problem into his life. What if Daniel came up with things that he didn't like, and Caleb had to reject it. Would that create a problem with Lori? Surely not—Lori would trust them to get it done and would appreciate the opportunity Caleb had given him. That must be true, he hoped.

When Caleb pulled up to Winnie's house, Lori was sitting on the porch. She stood up and leaned across the porch rail as Caleb got out and approached. This time she had on well-worn Levi's with a white and loose-fitting linen shirt. Her sleeves were rolled up, and she was simply beautiful. Her hair hung loosely about her shoulders. Her attire signaled she was ready to go to work. Caleb wondered if she was coming along. That would suit him fine, but he also wanted to scope out Daniel without any other agendas.

"Afternoon, ma'am," Caleb said in greeting.

"Ma'am?"

"Afternoon, Lori," Caleb corrected as he wondered if he was off to a bad start.

Lori smiled radiantly. "I like ma'am. Don't hear it much."

"Reckon it's a habit, but I think I'll just stick to Lori if it's okay."

"Absolutely, and good afternoon to you, Caleb. Daniel is ready." Lori turned to the house and called Daniel's name.

"Are you planning on going with us?" asked Caleb.

"I can, if you want, but I thought I would do a little shopping instead. I've got a date Thursday night."

"You do?" Caleb responded before he thought. "Oh, yeah, right, with me." Caleb knew that he had just become an idiot.

"Yes, with you, silly. I'm looking forward to it."

"Me too," said Caleb sheepishly.

Daniel stepped out onto the porch at that moment. He was carrying a camera and a small briefcase: all very professional. With a quick hug from his mother, he turned to Caleb and said, "All ready to go."

"Then let's go. We're burning daylight."

"You two have a good time. When will you be back?" asked Lori.

"We'll be back in time for dinner," said Caleb. "Maybe the three of us can grab a bite, and we'll let you know how it went," offered Caleb.

"I'm cooking for Winnie tonight, but you can join us."

"Well, if it's no bother, I could do that," said Caleb.

"No bother. In fact, Winnie wanted me to ask you."

"Sounds good. See you then."

"Bye, Mom," Daniel said as he got into the truck.

On the way out to the farm, Caleb told Daniel about how he had inherited his farm from his uncle when he had passed away and a little about their past relationship. He didn't go into the story about the station and what was buried there. He just wanted to leave that all alone for now. Besides, Daniel didn't need to know about what was going on and thereby increase the number of confidants. Caleb described the farm briefly but waited for any real conversation about the renovation until Daniel had seen it. The night before, Daniel had spoken of his intent to go to design school and fully informed Caleb of his interests. He had also demonstrated a clear willingness to be helpful with Caleb's project. There was nothing left to ask as they rode, so Caleb drove in silence.

When they drove up to the front of the farm, Daniel suggested that he would first like to just look the farm over, go through the house, and gain his own impressions while taking pictures. Afterward he wanted Caleb to tell him what he thought he needed or wanted in any renovation. That was fine with Caleb. They walked all around the house, looked at the barn, and then toured the entire house. Finally, Daniel sat down at the table and got out a tablet, as well as a laptop computer from his briefcase. He then proceeded to ask Caleb how he wanted to proceed and what he wanted to accomplish. Caleb decided to follow Daniel's lead in the conversation.

"The truth be told, I haven't thought too much about it," began Caleb. "The last house I lived in was a cabin on the ranch. It was small with one bedroom and suited me well. My lifestyle then was rather simple. I worked on the ranch mostly and only came to the cabin to relax or sleep. I had always taken my meals at the headquarters and didn't even cook much."

"Now this farm may be different," allowed Caleb. "I'm actually a pretty good cook, so the kitchen needs to be fully functional. It's bad right now and needs a complete overhaul, maybe even a modified layout. The living and dining combination is fine as far as the room goes, but I will completely refurnish it. So, furniture layout is part of the deal.

"The place only has two bedrooms. One is small, and the other is only average. And the one bath. I could get by with it like it is, but I really prefer to make it nice—you know, a master bath and better closets. The second bedroom will probably become an office of sorts or a music room—I don't know. My needs are rather basic, but I do want to consider making it substantially nicer. I never had much company at the ranch cabin, but I might have some here, so we must think about that.

"There's not much storage. I'll need a good pantry close to the kitchen, better closets, as I said, and some general storage. I have a small collection of instruments. Two violins, a guitar, a twelve string, and a mandolin. They all need to be stored properly, maybe even displayed. In addition, I will need a place for a gun safe. Nothing huge."

"What kind of guns do you have?" asked Daniel.

"Not many. I have my Colt 45 pistol plus four long guns: a Winchester 45-70, a twenty-two, a shotgun, and a Sharps 45-100."

"Wow, the Sharps is very special. That's a big load," remarked Daniel.

"I don't use it much, but out west sometimes you need to bring something big down and sometimes at a longer range. It's no fun to have to shoot a bear, unless he's so close that you can smell his breath. Then there are elk and a few bison. It's nice to be able to drop them from a distance. You know about guns?"

"I've been more interested in the historic ones—you know, in the early days out west. My dad has a few, but he would never let me even look at them. But yeah, I like to learn about guns, and the Sharps is kind of special. I've read about it," said Daniel.

Caleb continued, "I had it modified for the bigger load by a gunsmith in Colorado. It's quite a weapon and very accurate. Maybe we can shoot a few rounds one day out here."

"That would be great.... So, a medium-size safe. Do you want it close to the bedroom?"

"No. Anywhere out of view would be fine. I don't want it in the garage though, just somewhere in the house."

After thinking for a minute, Caleb started again. "The windows need to be replaced. Most are single pane and should be upgraded. I like wood rather than aluminum. The heating and air conditioning need to be completely redone. It's hot here—not like in the mountains. Out there, we could get by with a wood stove and operable windows, maybe a fan or two. But here, I know it will be different. This needs to be done right.

"Also, we must keep in mind that I might end up selling it. Probably not—I intend to stay, but if I do, it should be ready to go and easy to sell."

Caleb paused and waited for a response from Daniel, who was busy typing away on his laptop.

"Well, what do you think?" asked Caleb.

"What kind of a budget do you have?" Daniel inquired.

Caleb thought it was a very good question and showed that maybe Daniel was going to be attentive to the important details. After thinking a moment, Caleb said, "Daniel, I am financially able to do what is required to make it right. I don't want to waste money on anything frivolous but would really like to make it nice. I could see my way clear to spend up to about $200,000 if warranted by the results. I would like to look at a basic, minimum-cost approach and maybe a more aggressive one and compare the two. Don't forget that I also need to spend some on the barn. I've got one horse now and may get another one or two."

"You've got a horse?"

"Yes, I do. His name is Cisco, and we're best friends. He's over at my sister's farm, and we ride nearly every morning. Cisco is a trained cutting horse, but he's got good stamina and has never failed me. He might want some company, and I thought about training some new ones, maybe train and sell, or train for others. Anyway, some of the budget will have to go toward improvements in the barn. Now that's a place where I know what I want to do. You don't have to worry about it. I'll tell you later what I want done out there."

"Sometimes my mom goes on a call to treat a horse. I've gone with her, and it was a lot of fun. I haven't ridden much, but certainly would like to," said Daniel.

"Well, there you go. Guns and horses. All a man needs to know. I can teach you all about them if you want, assuming you're here long enough. By the way, when do you go to school?"

"Not until mid-August. I'm not too excited about it. Mom signed me up for Berkeley because it has a good program, she thinks, but I'm not so sure it's for me. I mean, I like California and all, but it's a big school. I'm not sure how it will turn out."

"You know, my father used to say that things may not turn out the way we think, but they will sure turn out. Sort gives you a tear, doesn't it?" kidded Caleb.

Daniel laughed. "I reckon, as you would say."

Getting back to work, Daniel asked, "Do you entertain?"

"Gosh no. I mean I never have. But, sure, out here I might do some. My sister will come out. We might have some dinner get-togethers or such. My friend Lonnie Rex will be out, and I might even have some visitors from the ranch. As I think about it, I might have some jam sessions with musicians if I meet some. I love to play music," Caleb declared. Continuing to think, Caleb said, "I don't know where they would sleep, though. That small room should be an office of sorts, so that would limit overnighters. Could be an issue."

"Is there a woman in your life?" asked Daniel. "You know that they can have a big impact on all this."

Caleb was flummoxed by the thought. In all his years he had never lived with a woman. Considering such an event was new territory. He gave his only answer, "There's no woman. I've always been a bachelor. A woman is a new situation and one that would require some serious thought."

Daniel went right to the point. "What if you hook up with mom? I mean, I know that it's way too early to consider such a thing, but as an example, it illustrates that it isn't impossible. What would you do if you did meet someone?"

Caleb answered with confidence. "Even though I've never lived with a woman, I have a lot of experience studying female critters in the wild, and based on those observations, I would say that I would get out of the way and let her decide. She can call me when it's done."

Daniel laughed and said, "This is going to be fun!"

Looking for a change in the subject, Caleb asked, "How do you want to proceed?"

Daniel entered some more in the laptop before responding. When done, he asked, "Do you have any plans of the existing house?"

"Nope."

"I'll need to develop some plans to proceed. Once I have those, I'll do some simple sketches of whatever I come up with. Nothing too elaborate, but enough for us to talk over the different approaches and focus on a direction. Can I come out and do some measurements to get a start?"

"Sure, I'll give you the key."

"You know, this construction might take a while, whatever you decide. Will you continue to live with your sister?"

"Yes, probably. We have a good time together, and there's no need to miss any of her meals. She's a good cook. But when work starts, I can pull my trailer out here and live in it if required."

"Then, if it's okay, I can come out tomorrow and start. I might need some help measuring the place up. You or mom could help—it wouldn't take very long. Then, I think that by next week, I could have some things for you to look at."

"Sounds good to me. Bring Lori out to help. Maybe she will have some input."

"Be careful what you ask for," admonished Daniel as he packed up his computer and pad.

Caleb was picturing Lori looking the place over. Would she like it? How could it matter—she lives in Las Vegas, right? As he continued to think about a visit from Lori, he said, "Yeah, bring her out."

THIRTY-THREE

Wednesday morning found Caleb sitting at breakfast with Sarah. He had already told her about his dinner with Lori—the highlights at least, on the previous day. However, they hadn't had much time to talk, since Sarah had been busy with errands. Now there was time to go over it all again and to also tell her about the trip to the farm with Daniel. Caleb thought that he had been rather thorough in relating the facts, but Sarah had an endless stream of questions. As he ate, she started in.

"Okay, back to your dinner with Lori; how did you feel about being with her again? You told me about the dinner and all, but I didn't hear how you felt. Was it good? I mean really good?" quizzed Sarah.

"Yes, it was wonderful, I…"

"You didn't tell me how she looked. Or what she was wearing. Can you give me the details? Was she happy to see you?"

"Yes, Sarah. I would say that she was very happy to see me. In fact, she leaped into my arms and almost knocked me over. It was as if—"

"Oh, I knew it! This is exciting. Go on."

"Well… let's see… she was wearing a dress and, uh, tennis shoes I think. She looked very good—in fact, quite beautiful. We spent the entire time going over each other's past lives. It seemed like just yesterday that we were last together. It was eerie even. After dinner, down by the lake, she told me even more and included the story of her son, Daniel. He was anxious to help with the farm, and we had a good session out there talking about what I want to do with it."

"What are you planning? Was Daniel helpful? Did Lori go?"

"Uh, no, Lori didn't go. She had to do some shopping. Daniel and I went, and he was very professional, it seemed to me. Lots of questions about what I wanted. It was good."

"What's Daniel like? You just said that he was tall and good-looking. I mean, what was he really like?"

"Daniel was great. I liked him and am glad I got him involved. He was very interested in my needs and seemed to focus on the relevant issues. He's going out again today to take some measurements and should have some ideas by next week. I'm looking forward to meeting with him again."

"Did you like him?"

"Sure."

"How was dinner with them?"

"Fine."

"Just fine?"

"Yeah, it was fine. Lori cooked enchiladas. I haven't had those in a while. She did a good job and must have had all the right ingredients. It wasn't like what passes for Mexican food around here. It had some kick, and I liked it."

"When will you see Lori again?"

"I guess not until tomorrow night when I pick her up for the bonfire get together," said Caleb.

"What are you going to do today?" asked Sarah.

"I'm going to go over to Lonnie Rex's house and help him get ready for the party he's having after the bonfire. I can't imagine what he will do to "get ready"—probably nothing except empty the ash trays, but we'll see what there is to do. I know he wants me to go with him to get some stuff. Probably just some beer."

"What time will you be finished? Tonight is church. They'll sing again and then have a service. Can you go? Do you want to?"

"I'm planning on it. Your church is nice. It's not just the music. I don't recall being attracted to any other church before, but this little church just seems to suit. The music had a strong pull on me, of course, but I also liked what I heard and witnessed among the congregation. There was an absence of pretense coupled with such a warm and welcoming atmosphere. I want to go back."

"I'm so glad you like it. It is wonderful and fills my life, but I'm worried about the church. I love it, as do all, but we aren't growing much, and I know that it is tough on Pastor Wendell. He's a great preacher, but he doesn't seem to do too well with outreach—nor does anyone else, for that matter. We would like to grow and share our experience. I try to help, but I'm not sure what to do."

Caleb thought for a minute and then said, "You know, I think that the future of the church lies in its hands and those of God's. What you offer will be received. You know it, and I know it."

"I know, but I worry. We'll just have to wait and see. Anyway, we need to be there around five o'clock."

"That'll do. I'll come back after Lonnie's and pick you up. I think I'll take my twelve-string tonight in addition to my fiddle. The twelve might add a lot to the instrument volume and depth."

"Okay then. I'll be ready. What else?"

"Nothing," said Caleb, but then continued with, "Except I didn't tell you about my meeting with Peter. He says that he has information on how the mayor pressured the Historical Board to approve the demolition of the station. And Peter knows that the mayor has been involved in developments with Dumar Ashton who bought the station. So, Peter thinks that this might be collusion of some sort, as well as the mayor using his influence for personal gain. You know, the mayor uses his position with the board to grant approval on the station that he is potentially part of as an investor. And Dumar bought the station for a low price knowing that the mayor would get the necessary approvals.

Once the approvals were in place, he closed on the purchase. Peter thinks that it stinks."

"I've only been to three meetings of the Historical Board since I got appointed. I haven't seen or heard anything about the station. That's old business. But what you describe does stink. Does Nancy know what you found out? Or Lonnie Rex?"

"Not yet. I'll tell them later," said Caleb.

"What about the buried money? Did you tell Peter about that?"

"Nope. I'm going to wait and allow the mayor to do the right thing. If he does, then it's all good."

"What if he doesn't?"

"Then it's not all good," stated Caleb.

"Caleb, I just had a thought. What if this Dumar, what's his name… Ashton knew about the money and bought the land because of it?"

Caleb pondered the thought. After thinking it over, he said, "I think that's impossible. After all, he bought the station last year, and the information about the money was in the mayor's letter which we just opened last week. I don't see how it was possible for him to have known."

"I guess. It was just a thought," Sarah reflected.

THIRTY-FOUR

After having lunch in town, Caleb went to Lonnie Rex's house to help with any preparations. All was quiet as Caleb came up the steps. Looking around, he found Lonnie Rex asleep in a large hammock at the end of the side porch, languidly swinging in the shade provided. A slight breeze carried his reverberating snores out to the south lawn. Caleb considered tossing him out but decided on delivering a simple thump to his forehead. Immediately following the hollow sound of the thump, Lonnie Rex's eyes fluttered open. Seeing Caleb, Lonnie said, "Howdy pard. Been waitin' for you."

"I can see."

Reaching out a hand, Lonnie instructed Caleb, "Help me out of this thing."

Lonnie Rex made it out of the hammock with a little assistance from Caleb and over to his favorite rocker. Lonnie settled in and lit a cigarette pulled from his ever-crumpled pack. Caleb went into the house and looked around. Returning to the porch, he said, "Looks okay for the party. What else is there to do?"

"Else? I haven't done anything. Jaws Two came by to get some money, so I had her tidy up a bit. She was always a good housekeeper and knows how important it is to me to have a clean house," Lonnie said while rolling his eyes. "Now, we just have the beer run. You can help with that big truck of yours."

Caleb glanced at his truck. "Just how much beer do you need?"

"Plenty. It might have to last the whole weekend."

"How much did you consume at past reunion parties?" Caleb asked.

"Not much. Took me the better part of six months to get it all down."

Caleb plopped down into the other rocker. "Well, whatever you want. I'm ready when you are."

"I'm ready," Lonnie Rex said without moving.

After a moment of silent inactivity, Lonnie Rex turned to Caleb and said, "You remember that I said that I would check out that contractor on the station?"

"Yeah. What about it?"

"I found the general contractor, but he had subcontracted out the excavation work to a local outfit that did the actual digging and backfilling in the beginning. I followed up and found the subcontractor and asked him if he uncovered anything. He asked me which time I was talking about. This confused me, and I told him I didn't know there had been other digs. Then he continued to tell me that before he did the actual excavation for the building, he had provided borings and some digging to get clearance of any contamination from the old tanks. They had to get samples and approval before proceeding."

"Really? Two digs? When was the first one done?"

"He didn't say, but it was certainly after Dumar cut the deal with Vernon, and before the Historical Board approval. Probably early in 2015, maybe a little later. It takes a while to get the release from the environmental agency, so that's why they dig early. The actual excavation for the building started in late 2015. It was well underway when you came out. Anyway, back to the first dig. They didn't uncover anything, but they hit refusal on their rig in a couple of spots."

"Refusal?"

"Yeah, that's where the boring sample equipment hits something and can't go deeper. They just pull up and move over a bit. So, they didn't dig anything up but hit something down there, and not very deep," explained Lonnie.

"That could have been rocks or anything."

"Yep… or the box containing the money."

"I don't guess we have any way of finding out, huh?" speculated Caleb.

"No, we don't. But there was something else he told me. He has a lot of illegals working for him as laborers. After they finished with the borings and the digs for environmental and collected all the samples, the owner asked the subcontractor if he could use one of the laborers for some work that weekend. The subcontractor said that it was okay with him. None of the illegals were on payroll, so they could work for anyone. These illegals are mostly Mexican, and they come and go, but the guy that went to help the owner that weekend had been working for the subcontractor for some time. Then the next Monday, the guy didn't show up for work, and he hasn't seen him since."

"What happened to him?"

"He doesn't know. The missing guy is the brother of one of the subcontractor's other workers, also a steady hire, and that guy won't tell him what happened. The subcontractor thinks that he knows where he is, but he still appears worried. The subcontractor doesn't speak Spanish and can't get the whole story. The other Spanish speakers won't talk about it either—they just indicate that they don't know anything."

"I speak Spanish, you know," offered Caleb.

"You do?"

"Sure. You knew that. Remember when you used to come out west? Some of the hands spoke only Spanish. I've learned."

"Do you really speak it fluently?"

"Well, I guess so. I mean I can carry on a conversation with anyone."

"I'll be! I completely forgot. We should get you to go talk to the missing guy's brother."

"I would be glad to, but why do we care? I mean, I'm glad to help, but it doesn't have anything to do with us, does it?"

"Probably not, but think about it. This guy disappears after working for the owner for just one day. Remember that the owner in this case is our friend and classmate, Dumar. What did Dumar have him doing? Does Dumar know where he is? We might want to find out."

"We can ask Dumar. He speaks English," proposed Caleb.

"Sure, but I think it would be good to get the brother's story first," said Lonnie.

"Set something up, and we can go over and talk to him. Whenever you want."

Lonnie nodded his agreement, then asked, "What did you find out from Peter yesterday?"

"Oh, yeah. I met with him before going out to get Daniel. He gave me a draft copy of the article he might run. He said that it could be revised after we see what the mayor does. I've got a copy I'll give you, but there's nothing that you don't already know in the article. What's not in the article yet is a result of Peter's digging. He outlined how the mayor had prevailed on the Historical Board to approve the demolition of the station and that the mayor was potentially involved in investing in the new construction at the station site. He thought this because it is common knowledge that the mayor invests in many of Dumar's projects. If true, that's applying his influence for personal gain. In addition, Dumar only closed on the purchase of the station after the board approval for demolition. If he was working with the mayor to get that done, then it is collusion. He bought the station for much less than it might be worth with the demolition approval in place. Sort of screwed Vernon out of his property's value. You said yourself that you had suspicions about Dumar."

"Sounds just like him. I wouldn't be surprised if it's all true," Lonnie Rex pronounced, but continued, "Does Peter know about the money?"

"Sarah asked me the same thing. No, Peter doesn't know. I'll keep my word to the mayor until I see how he handles it. If the mayor doesn't make it all public, I can give it to Peter then. That's my thinking. Let them prove themselves or hang themselves."

"You've gone and set yourself a crooked politician and developer trap. I like it."

"It's not a trap. Whatever it is, they created it, not me. All Warren did was try to make restitution by his confession and contribution. Perhaps a bit late, but honest," said Caleb. Continuing, he reflected, "It's funny how honesty exposes a lie, eventually."

"Well, I honestly want to go get some beer. Are you ready? You've been putting me off for two days," Lonnie complained.

"Get in the truck," ordered Caleb.

"Yeah, and on the way, you can give me the details about you and Lori. You're in love, aren't you?"

"Just get in the truck."

"I knew it! You are in love!"

THIRTY-FIVE

Sarah and Caleb arrived at the church a little early.
Caleb wanted to take his instruments in and get set up. As he
suspected, and as Sarah had promised, the choir and band members were very happy to welcome him back. It seemed that he
was now an official member of the group. That's the way it is
with music, thought Caleb. He recalled all the times that he had
played with the ranch hands and at bars, big and small. There
was always such a unity inspired by making music. It brought
people of all kinds together as they swayed to the rhythm and
beat. He had seen a lilting melody bring a dusty cowboy to tears.
Of course, there were occasional fights, but they never broke out
during the tune. That was the gift of musical gatherings. It was
natural that it should also occur at church. If only everyone could
experience its power!

Caleb searched the faces as they filtered in for the service.
There was an expectancy of what was to come on every face. It
was so different during the other, although few, services he had
attended in his life: people all dressed up and uncomfortable, just
wanting to get it over with. At least that was what he had seen
on so many occasions. Now here he was watching folks hug and
greet as they settled in for the service. It was the music, but not
just any music. It was this gospel music that vibrated from a
shared faith; it anchored everything about the service and stirred
those in attendance to rise to a sought-for release. If these people
want to grow in number, then they simply need to take the light
of their music out from under the basket and let it shine!

Caleb watched Sarah as she made her rounds greeting old friends and new ones. They were all checking on one another as they shared the burdens and joys of life. Of course, they wanted the church to grow, but it wasn't to fill the plate; it was to share this feeling and this unity with all who might come. It wasn't to lecture one another about certain scripture but merely to be one with each other and therefore with the Lord. It was to reach out and sweep others into this circle of love. Now that's church, thought Caleb.

His attention was brought back to their role as the makers of music when the piano started in with a prelude. Ivey made the piano whisper an invitation to get ready. Everyone moved to their seats with parting hugs as they settled in for what was to come. The band members took their instruments up and stood in preparation. Soon they all joined in a spirited instrumental as they followed the lead provided by the piano. Caleb started out with his twelve-string guitar and provided a rhythm with both volume and depth to the melody.

Tonight, the group concentrated on gospel music. The old pieces of gospel were particularly resounding. Caleb found some of the songs to be unfamiliar, but he was able to play along and augment any piece. At one point, he picked up his fiddle and allowed the instrument to find the melody. He enjoyed playing the faster tunes because it was there that the violin seemed to make its most strident contribution, and then, in counterpoint, slowed it down and drew long languid notes out into the spaces left by the other instruments.

Pastor Wendell led the voices into each composition with a full expression of the harmony. His voice was the anchor for the group. It was full and could slide from booming to soft and sensitive. Wendell had some help this night from a new addition to the choir. MaeBelle Jackson had recently begun coming to services and had been welcomed into their ranks. She was a robust black lady with a clear love of the Lord as evidenced by her solo treatments of many of the gospel tunes. Caleb had rarely been involved in such a full and expressive performance as was occurring at this little church. At the conclusion of the selections, Pastor Wendell stepped to the pulpit and invited everyone to join him in prayer.

"Our Father in Heaven, bless this time of worship as we share Your spirit openly in everything we say and do. Thank You for Your blessing of the expression of our love for You through our music and praise. We seek to always walk with You, and we use this time of togetherness to underline our devotion to that very walk.

"We worship here in thankfulness for the opportunity You have afforded to each of us to find ourselves within Your presence. It is through that presence that we seek to see the world and find our rightful place in it. We openly acknowledge sin in our lives and ask for Your support as we seek deliverance from it. May we seek to devote ourselves to the inward and outward practice of loving actions toward each other and all mankind. Join us now as we turn our attention to scripture and guide us in our understanding of Your word. Amen."

Pastor Wendell delivered a heartfelt sermon to the congregation. He provided scripture quotes in support of a message centered on our free will, as allowed by God, and how the exercise of that free will always have consequences, both temporal and eternal. It was a sermon with application to the lives of each person, delivered without judgement but with encouragement to understand how our choices manifest themselves in events both in the here and now and in our salvation.

At the completion of the sermon, the band members returned to the stage and performed a selection of songs, all of which pointed to our personal relationship with our God. In closing, MaeBelle Jackson led a performance of "Amazing Grace" with a vocal strength that rang throughout the sanctuary.

As people began to move about and engage in quiet talk, Caleb sat still for a few moments before beginning to put his instruments up. He was still in the moment of the service and had no intent of rushing his exit. He acknowledged the pats on the back from others with a quiet head nodding thanks. He watched as Sarah completed her visit with her close friends and wondered if he had that kind of relationship with others. While he believed that his walk with God was complete, he also wondered if he had only lived a singular life when it came to those whom he loved or might love.

While driving Sarah home, Caleb was quiet.

Sarah sensed his solitude but finally asked, "Did you enjoy the service?"

Caleb turned to Sarah and said, "Yes, I did."

THIRTY-SIX

Thursday morning began very early for Caleb. He had Cisco saddled by 5:30 a.m., knowing that he owed a good ride to the big guy. He had neglected Cisco for two days and could tell that this was not acceptable to his dear friend. He planned to ride until about 7:00, at which time he could leave Cisco a good bit happier and then get on with the day.

This was the first day of reunion activities, starting with the bonfire. Caleb planned on picking Lori up for an early dinner and then going to the lake. However, Lonnie Rex had called last night to tell him that he had arranged for them to go over and talk to the subcontractor's hired hand about the disappearance of his brother. Lonnie wanted to do it later this morning. Caleb wasn't very motivated toward this issue and thought that it could wait for a few days, but Lonnie insisted that there's no time like the present. Caleb questioned himself as to when Lonnie Rex had gotten so motivated. But he had agreed to meet Lonnie at Casper's and, after having breakfast, to go from there to see the subcontractor.

Lonnie Rex was waiting for Caleb at his usual table and in his usual demeanor. He had been fortified with several cups of coffee, a grease-laden breakfast, and a few cigarettes as the topper. Caleb had to quickly order his breakfast to stay with Lonnie's proposed schedule.

"What's the rush on this visit with the illegal?" asked Caleb after ordering. "Do we have to go today?"

"It's either today or wait until next week. The subcontractor said that today was good since the work schedule was slow. He told me that anytime this morning would be fine but starting tomorrow they were working out of town, and the guys would be busy. I said we would come over this morning," Lonnie informed Caleb.

"I sort of wanted to start the day out slow and taper off," lamented Caleb. "I'm not sure that this missing guy has anything to do with us, but, if you want to go over, it's alright with me, I guess."

"Good. Come by the house and pick me up after we finish eating. I'll leave my car and ride with you. I hope your Spanish is good."

The two of them pulled into the construction yard at the subcontractor's office. The yard contained various types of equipment for earthwork all parked in a row against the fence line. When they got out of the truck, a man in work overalls emerged from the office. He met Caleb and Lonnie Rex in the center of the yard and introduced himself.

"Howdy, I'm Jersey. Jersey Stone. I'm the foreman here. The boss tells me that you're here to talk to Javier Montoya. He's the one with the missing brother."

"If you think we can help," said Caleb.

"What's your interest in doing this?" questioned Jersey.

"None really; it's just that I am good with Spanish, and I guess your boss thought that we might be helpful in finding out what happened to the missing guy," explained Caleb.

"Yeah, well, the missing guy is a good hand and we've missed him, but his brother seems reluctant to tell us what happened, if anything. The missing man's name is Onofre Montoya, and he's the brother of Javier Montoya. They have both worked for us off and on, mostly on, for a couple of years. The boss thinks there is something wrong with the whole deal and wants to get Javier to tell us. Sometimes these guys are tight-lipped. If Onofre met with a difficulty, then the boss wants to know. Frankly, I think that Onofre has moved to a better job but doesn't want to tell anyone or lose out on this one if he comes back."

"How long has Onofre been gone?" asked Lonnie Rex.

Jersey thought for a minute and then said, "About seven months. I mean, that's a long time. We stopped being concerned, but then recently Javier asked if Onofre could come back. Javier's English is so bad that we couldn't get any information as to why Onofre had left and weren't sure what was going on. If you can help, have at it."

"Where is he?" asked Caleb.

Jersey led them both deeper into the yard. There they found two men servicing one of the backhoes. The front bucket was being replaced with a new one. As they approached, Jersey motioned for one of the men to come over. As the man approached, Jersey said, "This is Javier."

Caleb stepped forward and greeted Javier. *"Buenos dias, señor. Me llamo Caleb."* (My name is Caleb.)

"Buenos dias," said Javier.

"Hemos venido a aprender sobre tu hermano," (We have come to learn about your brother.) said Caleb. *"Sabes donde esta?"* (Do you know where he is?)

"Si." (Yes.)

"Donde esta?" (Where is he?)

"Onofre esta en Branson." (Onofre is in Branson.)

"Quiere volver al trabajo?" (Does he want to come back to work?)

"Si." (Yes.)

"Por que se fue?" (Why did he leave?) asked Caleb.

"Le dijeron que se fuera," (He was told to leave.) said Javier.

"Quien le dijo que se fuera?" (Who told him to leave?)

"El hombre para el que trabajo," (The man that he worked for.) said Javier.

"Como se llamaba el hombre?" (What was the man's name?)

"No se." (I don't know.)

"Por que no volvio?" (Why didn't he just come back?)

"Tenia miedo," (He was scared.) explained Javier.

"A que le tenia miedo?" (What was he scared of?)

"Tiene miedo del hombre para el que trabaja. Dice que no es un buen hombre," (He is scared of the man he worked for. He says he is not a good man.) explained Javier.

Turning to Jersey and Lonnie Rex, Caleb explained that Onofre was in Branson, Missouri, and that he left out of fear of some man he worked for. Also that Onofre wanted to come back to work at this time.

"So, tell him to get Onofre to come back. He's welcome, and we've got work," said Jersey.

"Dile a tu hermano que vuelva al trabajo; es bienvenido," (Tell your brother to come back to work; he's welcome.) translated Caleb.

"Si. Se lo dire y puede venir si no tiene demasiado miedo," (Yes. I will tell him, and he can come if he's not too scared.)

"Okay, he'll tell him, and Onofre will come back, he says. But only if he is not too scared," said Caleb to Jersey.

"What's he scared of?" asked Jersey.

"He really doesn't say except that it has something to do with the man he worked for."

"You mean us?"

"No. No—some other man he worked for. Javier doesn't know who."

Lonnie Rex interjected, "Ask Javier if we can talk to his brother when he returns."

Caleb turned back to Javier. *"Javier, podemos hablar con tu hermano cuando regrese?"* (Can we talk to your brother when he returns?)

"Si señor. Si viene." (Yes sir. If he comes.)

"*Gracias, Javier. Cuando Onofre vuelva, hablaremos con el.*" (Thank you, Javier. When Onofre comes back, we will talk to him.)

"*Si señor. Gracias,*" (Yes sir. Thank you.) Javier replied as he bowed slightly.

As Javier walked off, Caleb told Jersey that they would like to talk to Onofre if he returns, if that is okay. Jersey told them that Caleb should call next week, and if Onofre is here, then it would be fine if Caleb wanted to return. Caleb and Lonnie thanked Jersey and headed for their truck.

"So, he's scared of this guy that he says is no good. That right?" asked Lonnie.

"Yep."

"Sounds like it could be Dumar. Apparently, he's the one who Onofre worked for, based on what they told me when I called," said Lonnie.

"Yeah, maybe. We'll have to wait and see," stated Caleb. "In the meantime, I'm going to get rid of you and go back to Sarah's. I've got to get ready for tonight."

When Caleb returned to Lonnie's house, they saw Bobby Lane and Gina sitting on the front porch. Caleb went up onto the porch with Lonnie and greeted them both. Caleb had not seen them since the reunion planning meeting but wanted to say hi.

Gina spoke first. "Hi, guys. We wanted to see if you could come early tonight and help us get set up. Can you come early, about five o'clock?"

"I can come," said Lonnie Rex. "But what are we going to do? It's just a fire, and all you gotta do is light it!"

"Oh, nay nay! We have to haul and unload the firewood, simpleton," teased Bobby Lane.

"Well, okay then! I'll be there. But Caleb here has a date," explained Lonnie as he turned and smiled at Caleb.

"Who's your date?" asked Gina. "I was hoping to claim you for myself."

Lonnie quickly interjected, "Now Gina, calm yourself. Caleb's working his own angle tonight."

"Shut up you guys. I'm picking Lori up for dinner, and then we'll be over about 7:00."

"Lori! Well, you don't waste any time, do you champ?" kidded Bobby Lane. Then turning to Gina, he said, "Guess you're stuck with me sweety!"

"I could do worse," Gina said adoringly.

"How about me?" asked Lonnie Rex.

"Like I said, I could do worse."

THIRTY-SEVEN

Caleb had never had such a case of flutters. He was on his way to pick up Lori when all the things that were happening in his life started to clutter his mind. He didn't feel this way the other night when he and Lori went out. That must have been because the entire time the focus was on the past and catching up. Now, with Lori and Daniel in his present life, and with Daniel working on the farm, and with Lori being so great, and with all the station intrigue, and with tonight's appearance at the reunion with Lori, and finally with the fact that he didn't know if he could even remember anyone's name at the bonfire since it's been forty years… it was just a bit too much! Oh well, he thought, they'll all get name tags, wouldn't they? And the farm is off to a good start; and whatever happens to the station, did it really matter? And it was sure nice to be going with Lori! There. Things are fine!

All the flutters evaporated when both Daniel and Lori welcomed him from the porch. Both were smiling as if something good was happening.

"Hello all! Lori, you look mighty nice. Daniel, how are you?"

They both spoke at once, "Good… Thanks!"

Lori took control, "We had a good day. Yesterday I went out to the farm with Daniel and helped with the measuring. That place has some real potential! Daniel has been working on it today. I'm staying out of it. You don't need my two bits."

"Well, you never know," said Caleb. "You might just have a good thought. I mean anything is possible," he teased.

"When do you want to meet next?" asked Daniel.

"Not 'till next week. I want to concentrate on the events this weekend and especially on your mom. Come Monday, just tell me when you are ready."

"Okay, I'll let you know."

Caleb and Lori drove down the hill to the lake. They had gone for a quick hamburger prior to setting out for the bonfire. As they neared the recreation area, they saw that the parking area was already half full of vehicles. Several people were milling around at the large shelter with a few more stacking wood and preparing to start the burn. There was a concrete area outside the shelter where a group of musicians were setting up some microphones, speakers, and other equipment. It looked like it would be possible to dance to the music. Caleb parked as close as he could get to the shelter but decided to wait to unload any of his instruments until things got started.

They walked toward the shelter searching for familiar faces. It was Caleb's first reunion out of four, and he felt some trepidation that he would be unable to recognize anyone. Lonnie Rex had told him not to worry, that the former large ones would be skinny, the ugly ones would look good, and all of them would look old! Lonnie had backed up his observation on the nature of human change with the information that one of their classmates was a man that was a terrible student in high school and now was a state senator. Lonnie also had said that no one really changes, and identities would all come back to him. Caleb thought the information to be contradictory but then again, ignoring Lonnie's advice came as second nature. Caleb would see for himself.

It was a slightly different story for Lori. In the first place, she had not graduated with this class and could easily be forgiven for not remembering someone. But she had several friends in the group from when she lived here that she wanted to see. Of course, the truth was that her only real interest had been Caleb. She was infinitely pleased to be on his arm at this moment.

The shelter tables were covered with a variety of coolers and picnic baskets. There was no catered food—that would be tomorrow—but many had brought snacks and drinks. There was no alcohol allowed, but Caleb was sure some would find a way to cheat on that rule. It would be interesting to see how.

Gina was helping the band members get set up when she turned and saw Caleb with Lori. She came over to them and exclaimed, "Here you are! Caleb and Lori—shades of the distant past. My, you two look good!" She gave both a hug with an especially affectionate one for Caleb.

Others gathered around and began introductions. Caleb was struggling to keep up with the introductions but felt more at ease when the memories of the people came back to him. He recognized Fletcher Cosgrove immediately. Lonnie Rex had spoken of Fletcher's success with the pay-to-view films for hotels and his subsequent return to Rogers. Caleb stifled a grin as he remembered Fletcher's acumen as a student only to be followed with achievements in the video business. Fletcher's interest turned immediately to Lori.

"Lori Martin! Or is it Hightower? You were Martin last time we saw you."

"Martin still. Name stuck, but Mr. Martin didn't."

"And here you are with Caleb. Some things never change! So good to see you!" panted Fletcher. Turning to Caleb, he continued, "This is your first reunion, isn't it Caleb?"

"Yep. Finally made one."

Everyone's attention was diverted when Lonnie Rex yelled out, "Hey, listen up! We're going to get things started with a bang. In a few minutes, when the mortar goes off, the party will officially begin."

"Mortar?" asked Lori.

"That's what he said," stated Caleb. "I don't know what he is talking about."

Lonnie looked around and saw Caleb. "Caleb, could you help me for a minute?"

"Yeah, I guess. What do you want me to do?"

"Just follow me down to that big tarp in the field. Let Lori mingle. It'll just take a few minutes."

Caleb left Lori to visit with classmates and followed Lonnie Rex. They approached a canvass tarp draped over a large unidentifiable item. Lonnie Rex pulled the tarp back and said with great pride, "This here is my homemade mortar!"

Caleb studied the black steel monolith. It was a giant tube pointed up with large, welded steel legs. "What is this?" he asked in amazement.

"This is my mortar. It's an oxygen tank cut to the right length and welded upright. There's a base plate you see, with a fuse hole at the base. You dump powder in, stuff in some wadding of cloth like these, then load and fire."

"What do you load it with? I mean what do you shoot?" asked Caleb.

"Bowling balls, of course. See that large tub over there?"

Caleb searched in the direction Lonnie was pointing and, finding the item, said, "Yeah. I see it."

"Ok, It's full of bowling balls on dry ice. When I'm ready…."

"Wait! Did you say 'bowling balls on dry ice?'"

"Sure. Dry ice. It cools the bowling balls to just the right diameter. At room temperature, the bowling balls are just a tad too big, but freeze 'em a little bit, and they fit perfectly!" explained Lonnie.

A few others wandered over to listen in. As they gathered, Lonnie gave out instructions. "In order to fire this baby, first you put one and one-half large dixie cups of powder from the keg over there. Just one and one-half cups, not more. Then you stuff a piece of this cloth down with the broom handle, then when I call for 'ammo,' someone grabs one chilled bowling ball from the tub over there and runs over here with it. We drop it in, I place the fuse, everyone scatters a bit, and I light it. If things go well, the ball should land out in the lake," he said as he pointed out over the water. "I'll do the first one, then others can shoot."

Caleb had witnessed Lonnie's "inventions" in the past, and asked, "How do you know this will work and not just blow up?"

"Because I tried it. Earlier this afternoon before everyone got here. Stash was here and helped."

Bobby Lane, nicknamed Stash for his colorful history, chimed in, "Yeah, we did it. It works. Shoots a long way too!"

Caleb saw that Lori had walked over. He looked at her, rolled his eyes, and silently mouthed the words, "Stand back."

Lonnie began the final preparations. He put on a pair of massive welder's gloves and said, "Okay, now for the fire team. Caleb, if you could get the powder, please. Remember, just one and one-half cups. Stash, get ready with the wadding. Everyone get back, except someone be ready to bring me a ball when I yell AMMO! Got it?"

Without much hesitation everyone began to scatter except the "fire team." Caleb strolled over to the keg of powder and inspected the cups sitting there. He measured out the required amount and returned it to Lonnie Rex. After the powder was poured in, Stash did his job and plunged the wadding down. Lonnie yelled for the ammo, and a little guy in suspenders came running carrying a bowling ball. "That's cold!" suspenders complained as he handed it to Lonnie.

"'Course it's cold. It's gotta be. Now everyone, get back."

Caleb found Lori and walked over to her. When he wrapped his arm around her, she said, "He's an idiot!"

"Yeah, well, every village needs one."

Just as Caleb turned, a massive boom echoed across the park and over the lake. As flame and smoke erupted from the "mortar," the bowling ball sailed to a great height. It made a rhythmic whoosing sound as it finally fell into the center of the lake with a great splash.

As a cheer erupted, Lonnie Rex yelled, "Next!"

As a few tentatively approached, Misty Belle hurried over and, with great agitation, asked Caleb, "What in the world is he doing?"

"Shooting off his mortar, I should say."

"He can't do that!"

"He did it, and it appears he's going to do it again," Caleb informed Misty. "Go on down if you want a turn."

"He's going to get this entire party closed down!"

"Maybe not. He's only got a few bowling balls. If you want a turn, you better hurry."

Lori leaned into Caleb's shoulder to conceal a laugh.

Misty started toward Lonnie and yelled, "Stop thi—" Just as another booming explosion propelled the next bowling ball into the bosom of the lake.

"Next!" yelled Lonnie Rex.

As several more moved toward the mortar, Misty pushed her way forward. She was able to make Lonnie Rex pause and acknowledge her presence.

"Stop this insanity!" Misty implored.

Lonnie Rex patiently waited for her to spew forth her concern that this could ruin the party. After being reminded that he was on the committee and must demonstrate proper decorum, Lonnie finally acquiesced while grumbling, "I figured I would only shoot three anyway. Two's not so bad. Maybe a few at the end of the party, what do you think?"

Misty glared at Lonnie, then turned and stormed back up to the shelter as Lonnie yelled, "That concludes the introductory show. The party can now begin!"

As things returned to normal, the crowd began to gather around the shelter. Misty stood and addressed the group. "I want to welcome all of you to the 40-year reunion of our class of 1976. Tonight is the inaugural event of the weekend. The display you just witnessed was not a planned part of the festivities, and we will continue in the hope that the police were not alerted.

Shortly we will have live music and dancing to be followed by the bonfire once the evening darkens. So, everyone can mingle and renew old friendships as the band sets up. Thanks for coming—let's have fun!"

Caleb and Lori returned to the crowd and began to make introductions with the attendees. Lori quickly reunited with Angela Dawes, who was a childhood friend. As they visited, Caleb went to meet with the band members. It was decided that Caleb would play his violin and guitar during the country-western selections. That suited Caleb as he wanted to circulate and enjoy Lori much more than he sought the opportunity to play.

Peter Mason walked across the lawn with his wife at his side. He stopped and said hello to Misty Belle. From her gestures toward the "mortar," it was clear that she was informing Peter about the serious infraction that had occurred. Caleb walked over and overheard Peter say that he was sorry that they had missed it. Both Peter and his wife were laughing, but it did nothing to ease Misty's concern.

Turning to Caleb, Peter said, "Hey Caleb, how are you? This is my wife, Shirley."

"Hi Shirley. Lori is around here somewhere," he said as he looked back toward where he had left her.

"You came with Lori?" asked Peter.

"Yeah, we hooked up last Monday night and thought we would come together."

"That's great! I'm anxious to see her." Continuing, Peter asked, "Anything new on the station story front?"

"Nothing that I know of. What about you. Has anything happened on the mayor's end?"

"Nope. All quiet. I said that I would leave it alone until after the reunion, and that's what I'm doing."

Everyone paused as the band started up. They launched right into some rock and roll tunes. No one responded by dancing, but all seemed to enjoy the music. Caleb excused himself and returned to Lori.

"Are you going to play?" asked Lori.

"Maybe later. I'm not sure if they need me or know what to do with a fiddle player. I think I'll just play with you for now. Let's circulate and see some more people."

Lori followed Caleb as they mingled with the crowd and started the process of trying to place everyone and touch their shared pasts.

The bonfire was a hit. By the time darkness fell, some of the attendees had engaged in a little dancing, but mostly it was a time for visiting. Caleb had indeed played a few tunes with the band and led them into some classic western music, which was clearly not as popular as the old rock tunes they had grown up with. The crowd regarded Caleb with a combination of curiosity and reverence. It had been a long time since they had seen him. His appearance, his music, and his arrival with Lori created a curiosity that could only be satisfied with multiple interrogations. By the time that the bonfire started, Caleb was ready to recede into the darkness and watch. Lori seemed to be of the same mind. They both stood on the outer periphery but could feel the heat even from that vantage point.

Lonnie Rex drifted over to Caleb and asked him, "Did you see who is not here?"

"What do you mean?"

"I mean, who is missing?"

"Oh, about half the class. It's only Thursday night. Most will start coming tomorrow, I reckon," answered Caleb.

"The guy we been talking about is not here. Dumar."

"Yeah, that's right. But so, what? It's not like we were going to confront him tonight."

"I know, but I can't get over the feeling that he's at the center of all this," pronounced Lonnie.

"Just leave it alone. I'll check with the mayor on Monday and see what he says. Let's stay away from Dumar, okay?"

"If you say so. Now for subject number two: can you help me haul my mortar back to the house? I better not shoot it anymore or Misty will hemorrhage and self-destruct."

"Sure, but how did you get it here?"

"That's the problem. Bobby Lane helped me. He has a pickup, but it's kind of small. It's a Ford Ranger, and that makes it the training-bra of pickups. It won't haul much. We barely made it over here with the mortar. Besides, Bobby and Gina have disappeared."

"We can load it in my truck. How many does it take to lift it?"

"I'll round up three or four. That should do it. I want to get it loaded and go on over to the house. People might start arriving before long. The word is out!"

"You going to shoot it off at your house?"

"Hell no! The police might come."

Caleb laughed and then turned to Lori and asked, "What do you think? Wanna' go to Lonnie's house now?

"I'm with you, cowboy. I wouldn't mind plopping down in a big easy chair. You got one of those, Lonnie?"

"Do I look like I have a big easy chair?"

THIRTY-EIGHT

Caleb started out slow on Friday morning. The party at Lonnie Rex's house lasted until past midnight. That wasn't the reason that he was slow this morning. Lonnie's party was a success with many in attendance and happily indulging in the abundant supply of beer. Misty Belle even showed up with her undertaker husband in tow. Apparently, the mortar event was all forgiven.

Caleb and Lori had left Lonnie's party after about an hour and had returned to her aunt's house. They collapsed in the living room and sat up talking about the people whom they had seen during the evening. Daniel had joined them and listened to their stories, showing special interest in Lonnie's mortar—its construction as well as its performance. He had openly wondered how an adult could get away with doing such a thing, but it didn't damper his enthusiasm for the story. He remained engaged until he had enough and went off to bed. Caleb and Lori continued to talk until quite late, after which Caleb returned home to Sarah's.

Caleb was preparing the coffee as Sarah joined him in the kitchen. This day's events would include the official catered picnic and then the gathering at the Big-Wigs lounge for a mixer. Lori had some things to do this morning and had agreed to meet him at the picnic. She indicated that she wanted Caleb to pick her up for the mixer that evening. Caleb thought he would check in with Lonnie Rex later this morning, and then they could go over to the picnic. He would prevail on Lonnie to leave his mortar behind.

After their morning greetings and the coffee was poured, Sarah began to ask about the details of the previous evening. Caleb obliged her willingly. He realized that the reunion was as much an event for her as it was for him. When he related the part about Lonnie Rex's mortar, Sarah laughed openly and expressed sorrow that she had not been there to see that. It caused a flood of recollections of all the things she and Paxton had done during their high school days and afterward. Their marriage had been long and fruitful, but it had yielded no children to afford them the joy of watching them grow. In many ways, Caleb was as much a son to her as he was a brother. It was increasingly clear to Caleb how happy Sarah was to have him back, and indeed how happy he was to be back. They had so much to share and so much time apart to make up for. For Sarah and Caleb, this reunion was much more than a high school event—it was a rebirth of their family.

Caleb told Sarah how much he was enjoying his return. He expressed his growing sense of returning to his roots and the important part of his life that Sarah occupies, even during all the years they were apart. Now he was here and very glad about it. He and Sarah could now be inseparable. He felt grounded and completely at home.

As he talked to her, he realized how very important it was to include her in everything he did. She could be a big part of the building of his new farm. He knew that she would willingly have him live with her, but both knew that it was not the time for that. They would simply be here for each other and share in their lives. An unexpected bonus was Sarah's church. Attending there with her stirred a desire in him to find a church home. This was not something he had ever felt before. Part of his joy, to be sure, was seeing how much Sarah enjoyed having him join her in this church she so loved.

Since Lori had shown up, his attention had been diverted from these thoughts. He was completely immersed in his reclamation of the past that he and Lori shared. This was much the same as that which he was experiencing with Sarah. It was all part of the big transition that was happening. Caleb had a strong urge to now unite the events and allow Sarah into what he was experiencing with Lori, whatever it turned out to be. He felt he had to bring it all together. He wanted Lori to see the relationship he and Sarah had, and he wanted to include Sarah in everything he did.

Caleb said to Sarah, "I was thinking. Lori is leaving on Monday. I don't know when on Monday, but she said as much. With all the reunion events, things have been busy. I want to have Lori and Daniel out here to meet you and for all of us to have some time together. Do you think we could have them out on Sunday for a late lunch or dinner?"

"That would be just wonderful!" exclaimed Sarah. "Either would be fine with me. You pick."

"I think a late lunch would be best, don't you? She may be busy Sunday night preparing to return, and the afternoon just seems more relaxed to me."

"You're right. After church, you guys can all come out. I'll fix something light, and we can eat on the porch, and we can talk, and relax, and… oh, it'll be so much fun! What do you want to have?"

"You're the cook. I know it'll be great. I haven't asked Lori yet, but I'm sure she would like it, especially if we include Daniel. She has hopes for Daniel and me to get along and for this summer to be good for him."

"I'd like to meet him. Will you go to church with me or not? Is there something else happening on Sunday?"

"No, nothing else. Let me see, uh… Saturday will be late, I guess, because there is a dance at the hotel. I don't know what will happen early Sunday; nothing, I guess," Caleb reflected. "I know—why don't I ask Lori and Daniel to come to church with us. Make a day of it."

"Oh, my goodness! Sure, that would be fine, if they would like to. After church, we could come straight back here. I would really love that."

"Then I'll ask them and let you know. Both about church and lunch," said Caleb.

"So, what will you do today?" asked Sarah.

"Well first, I'm going to take Cisco out for a good workout. Afterward, I will go to Lonnie's and then to the picnic. I'll give Lori a call about Sunday, and then we will go to the reception at the Big-Wigs. I guess we'll get something to eat before—we'll see. I reckon I'll be late again."

"If it's not too late and I'm still up, fill me in when you get home, okay?"

"You bet."

THIRTY-NINE

Lonnie Rex was back in the hammock on his porch and snoring like a freight train. The mortar was turned over in the front yard, and the tub full of the remaining bowling balls rested alongside. The dry ice had long since evaporated, so the balls had long ago given up their chill and returned to normal size. The front porch had a large trash bin full of empty beer and soda cans. By all appearances, it had been a successful party.

Caleb let Lonnie sleep and went into the house to see if there were any other victims strewn about. Seeing nothing except more evidence of a good time event, Caleb returned to the porch and settled into a rocker as he watched Lonnie sway gently in the breeze. Caleb wasn't sure whether the breeze or the snoring propelled Lonnie. He thought about waking him but noticed the remains of an egg yolk smeared down his shirt front, which meant he had succeeded in obtaining breakfast. Casper's Grille again, for sure. Perhaps a good sleep was in order. Caleb decided not to wake him.

Letting Lonnie continue in his repose, Caleb moved over to the other chair away from Lonnie and dialed Lori's number.

It was Daniel who answered. When Lori came to the phone, Caleb confirmed their plans for the day. He would see her at the picnic and then pick her up at 7:00 p.m. for the visit to the Big-Wigs. "Also," said Caleb, "I would like you guys to come out to Sarah's house for lunch on Sunday."

"Well, I told Winnie that we would go out on Sunday, so that's a conflict," said Lori.

"If you want, you can bring Winnie too. I should have mentioned that. I originally thought you and Daniel, but it would be great if Winnie wants to come."

"She would like that. She doesn't get out much, and I've been busy with you and the activities. If you think it is okay with your sister, then sure."

"I know Sarah would like that. Let's say about 1:00 p.m. She and I are going to church, and I would like to invite you to go with us—whoever wants to," said Caleb clumsily.

"What church?"

"Sarah's church. It's called Pilgrim's Church. Funny name, but I guess we're all pilgrims. The church is small, and Sarah is very involved. I have gone a couple of times and have been playing with the choir or band or whatever you want to call it. The music is very good, and so far, I've enjoyed everything about it."

"Gosh, Caleb, I haven't been to church in many years. They might not let me in. I mean, I consider myself a Christian but apparently not a very good one," explained Lori.

"If you are measuring it all by church attendance, then I haven't been a good Christian either, but that's not how it's measured. Come and you will see. They'll let you in."

"Daniel too? Winnie won't come—she watches a certain preacher on TV. It might be nice if I don't have to sit through that again."

"Of course. Bring Daniel. We can go and pick up Winnie afterwards on our way to the farm."

"Okay. No, wait a minute—I'll have to drive Winnie in her little van. We'll never get her loaded in your truck. Daniel and I will meet you at church and then come back here to get Winnie after. Would that be alright?" Lori asked.

"Yes, that'll be fine. The church is over on West Poplar."

"I'll find it. I think I know where it is. It used to have a different name, didn't it?"

"Yeah, it was Shepherd's Baptist Church. It was named that back when we lived here. It's been here a long time. It's quite an old building," explained Caleb.

"Alright. I'll confirm that Daniel wants to come to church, and let you know when I see you at the picnic. Then later we'll go to Big-Wigs. What should I wear?"

"Look, you can't ask me that. You always look great. For me, it's got to be boots and jeans 'cause that's about all I have. It's a bar, I reckon, and certainly casual."

"Oh golly! Look at the time. I've got to get ready for the picnic. See you there, sweetheart!"

"Uh… okay, bye."

Sweetheart! She had called him sweetheart. What had he called her? "Uh, okay bye." Was that it? Smooth, Caleb, he thought. Real smooth! Another wrinkle in the universe, but this one did make him feel a bit special.

"Lonnie!" yelled Caleb toward the swinging hammock. "Wake up!"

Lonnie groaned, opened one eye, and searching for the source of the noise, asked, "Why?"

"Cause it's time to go—almost."

"Well can't you see that I'm almost ready? I'll let you know when I finish up," he said as he went back to sleep. Unfortunately, Lonnie tried to roll over, which was a movement the hammock did not easily accommodate. The shift of his weight suddenly dumped him out onto to porch floor.

"Now are you ready?" asked Caleb.

"Yeah, that about did it," Lonnie said as he tried to get up. "Just a cig and we can… where is it we're going?"

"To the picnic. Did you get drunk last night?"

"Of course not! I don't get drunk! But I got a little happy. Other people got a little bit happy. Even Misty's husband the undertaker got a little bit happy. Most everybody got happy."

Lonnie Rex lit a cigarette and belched at the same time—a difficult feat to complete in Caleb's estimation.

"You better change shirts, at least," said Caleb. "You've got breakfast down the front of the one you've got on."

"Yep." Looking down, Lonnie observed, "It was eggs for sure. Casper's did it again. Where were you?"

"I stayed at Sarah's this morning. Took it easy. I'm going to the picnic with you. Lori will come on her own."

"You guys have a spat?" asked Lonnie.

"No, no. We're going together tonight to Big-Wigs. Everything is fine."

"Well, alright then. I'll get me another shirt, and we can go. What are we having for food today?"

"I thought they said barbeque. It's catered."

"I guess I better pick a brown shirt, huh?"

FORTY

The picnic was better attended than the bonfire had been. Caleb and Lonnie arrived a little late and had to park far away from the shelter. Throngs of classmates congregated in groups amid a constant hum of conversation and laughter. The caterer had not begun to serve the food, but most people gathered close to the food tables.

Caleb and Lonnie tried to bypass the larger groups but were soon pulled into conversation with old classmates. Caleb saw Eunice Biles standing apart with her husband Dufus. Caleb hurried over to greet Dufus. He had been meaning to go by and see him ever since he had discovered that he was now living here. Dufus had been Caleb's roommate in college for the first year before he married Eunice and dropped out of school. Caleb had understood that he had joined the Air Force.

Caleb walked up to Dufus, and holding out his hand said, "Dufus! It's really you. I can't believe that you live here!"

Dufus stared at Caleb and then broke into a broad grin. "Caleb! I didn't recognize you for a moment. It's been so long since the university. Where have you been?"

"Mostly living in Colorado. It's a long story, but I moved back here a few weeks ago, just in time for this reunion. I look back on our days at the university with fond recollections. I understand that you went into the Air Force."

"Yeah, that's right. Went my twenty years and retired. Eunice and I came back here, and I opened a chicken restaurant out on West Walnut. Damn! It's good to see you. Did you finish up and become a lawyer? You don't look like no lawyer."

"No, the law wasn't for me. Lasted two-plus years and then moved on. Ended up on a ranch doing cowboying. It was a good life, but now I'm starting a new one here."

"Yeah, you sure look more like a cowboy than a lawyer for sure, especially with that hat."

Caleb turned to Eunice, "You remember me, Eunice?"

"Yes, but barely. When I came to the university to see Dufus, it was usually just him and me, but we met once or twice when you guys lived in that little house during the second semester."

"Oh, what a dump that place was. You had to chain yourself to the bed to keep the cockroaches from carrying you away!" exclaimed Caleb.

"No kidding," said Dufus, "It reminded me of home back in Eldorado."

Caleb received a tap on his shoulder and turned to see Lori smiling up at him.

"Dufus, Eunice, this is Lori. She and I go way back. This is my first...."

"Oh, I remember you!" claimed Dufus as he appraised Lori. "I mean, we never met, but Caleb told me about you. Back when. I told him that he should go find you, and I guess he took my advice."

Lori smiled at Caleb as she responded, "Yes, he did, but it took a lot of years until he pulled it off. Or I should say, we pulled it off. Too much history, but here we are."

"I guess it could be said that I move rather slow. But steady!" allowed Caleb.

Lori and Caleb moved off with Caleb, making a promise to come by the chicken restaurant for a meal and a good long visit.

They angled over to where Lonnie Rex had settled in with some admirers of his art. Caleb overheard Lonnie remind them that his art would be on display at the Big-Wigs lounge during tonight's mixer. Selling some art would not hurt Lonnie's feelings.

Lonnie turned and greeted Lori. "You missed most of the party last night. What did you guys do?" asked Lonnie.

"That's none of your business," Lori teased.

"Oh yes, it is. I'm Caleb's spirit guide. I need to be kept abreast of all developments."

"Lonnie, you'll be the first to know if there are any developments," promised Lori.

"I sure hope so. I've got a lot of experience with this man-woman thing. Been through a few, and I'm looking out for the both of you."

"How many times have you been married?" asked Lori.

"You know that. Twice. First to Jaws One, and then Jaws Two. Love em' both!"

"You two quit ignoring me," said Caleb. "Lonnie, you stay out of my business. And you are not my spirit guide; you're just a best friend."

"Well, as your best friend, let me call your attention to who just arrived," Lonnie Rex said as he nodded toward the parking lot. "Ol' Dumar himself!"

"What's with him?" asked Lori.

Caleb interjected, "I haven't told you, but he may be somewhat involved in the story of the station I mentioned the other night."

Lonnie Rex nodded and asked Caleb, "You see what he's driving? It's an old Dodge power wagon. Looks restored. What's that remind you of?"

"What about it? I mean, it looks good—those are something else. But what... wait a minute. I know what you're getting at. Warren mentioned a lawyer who he rebuilt a diesel engine for. You think it was him?"

"Got me, but I do wonder," said Lonnie. "Maybe we should go find out. Might explain a few things."

"I don't think we should let on we know anything just yet. Let him approach us if he wants to and see what he says. He doesn't know what we know. Play dumb, Lonnie. That should be easy," said Caleb."

"Sounds like a plan. But if he corners me, I'm gonna tell him we know all about his shenanigans, and we're gonna squeal!"

"Stop it, Lonnie!"

"Will someone tell me what's going on?" pleaded Lori.

Caleb took her aside and said, "We think he might be guilty of some sort of collusion with the mayor on the development of the old station. We're waiting to hear from the mayor if they find anything. Dumar's involved as the owner of the development. Lots more, too, but... Here he comes. And you, Lonnie... where'd he go?"

"He wandered off," said Lori.

Dumar approached and said, "Caleb! Long time no see. Last time was at school. Did you ever make it in the law?"

"Howdy, Dumar. No, I never made it. It wasn't for me, after all," explained Caleb.

"Who's this pretty little lady?" Dumar asked as he leered at Lori.

"Dumar, this is Lori Martin. Lori, meet Dumar Ashton. He and I were in law school for a while until I dropped out. Lori used to—"

"I don't think I can remember seeing you around before, darling. You Caleb's guest or are you a hired floater?"

Lori responded, "I don't remember seeing you around before either. Are you naturally that crude or did you learn it at law school?"

"Whoa! Back off little lady. My apologies. You got yourself a feisty one here, Caleb. Where did you find her?"

"Dumar, this is a good time for you to get out of my sight. I'm going to turn around, and when I look back, if you are still here, I'm going to put you on your ass!"

"Cool off, man. Just having a little fun," Dumar said as he walked off.

Lori stared at Caleb and uttered, "Hummmh…"

"I know, I know," said Caleb. "Not good."

"You don't know," said Lori as she squeezed his arm. "It was very good. I would have helped you put him down, but I don't think you would have needed my help. Come on now, let's mingle and find some nice people."

The caterer rang the bell, calling people to the barbeque.

"Saved by the bell!" proclaimed Caleb. "Let's eat."

Making their way to the food line took longer than they expected. Lori's friend Angela Dawes joined them in the line. She was accompanied by a tall, slender man who was nicely dressed and had a confident bearing. Angela said hello to Lori and then introduced the man at her side.

"I would like you to meet my husband, Henry Dawes. Henry, this is Lori and Caleb. I graduated with Caleb, but Lori has been my friend since childhood," said Angela.

"Yes, Angela spoke of you, Lori. It's nice to meet you. And you too, Caleb. We've never met, and I never saw you at previous reunions. This your first?" asked Henry.

"My first one! Took forty years to get here, but I finally made it."

"I was hoping to meet you. Your name has come up down at the city. The mayor told me about the issue relative to the construction at the old station site."

"Really? What do you have to do with the city?"

Angela chimed in, "Henry is the district attorney."

"Oh, I see," said Caleb. "I haven't spoken to the mayor since our first meeting. I expect to meet with him after the reunion and see what he found. It's all rather interesting."

"I'll say! Quite the story. I'm sure the mayor will be contacting you this next week."

"Did he mention if he found anything?" asked Caleb.

"He's been sort of closed mouth about it all. I know what he said he was looking for, but he hasn't revealed the results, at least to me. I guess we'll find out together. I'm not sure how I will be involved, if at all, but if he finds what he was looking for, there may be some legal issues. I just don't know yet."

"Well, I'm sure you can be of help to him if needed," offered Caleb. "How long have you been the DA?"

"A little over eight years. Angela and I met in Boston after I finished law school. She wanted to come back home, and I wanted to start a practice in a reasonably sized town. I had my fill of the big city, and Rogers looked good, so we moved here. I practiced with a local firm until I got the appointment as district attorney."

"I tried law school, but it didn't stick, so I ended up out west, but now I have returned. Just a couple of weeks ago," explained Caleb. "Just in time to find Lori!"

"Henry, Caleb and Lori go way back. Old friends from high school," said Angela.

"And Angela and I go even farther back," Lori said as she gave Angela a hug.

Angela brightened, "We should get together. I mean after the reunion. Lots to catch up on."

"I'll be going back to Las Vegas on Monday, unfortunately. I've got to get back to my practice. But I know that I will be coming back soon, so that would be nice," said Lori looking up at Caleb for confirmation.

"You bet! I'll be here. Got a lot of work to do on my farm."

The line was moving nicely, and they each grabbed their plate and made their selection of the barbeque offerings. They joined a group comprised of Gina, Bobby, and Lonnie Rex. After a few introductions for Henry's sake, the topic turned to food. "These guys do a great job of catering, and their barbeque is my favorite," said Henry.

"Caleb thinks barbeque was invented to disguise bad meat," observed Lonnie Rex without looking up from his plate. "Ain't that right, Caleb?"

"Now Lonnie, you know that there is some truth to that. Long ago it was hard to preserve the meat like we can today. Sometimes it got a little randy, so they cooked it into oblivion and drowned it in hot sauce, and "barbeque" is what you got. Don't mean it's still true today. This is great!"

"It always agreed with me," said Lonnie as he wiped his hand on his sleeve.

Gina observed, "Lonnie Rex, anything would agree with you if you can eat it."

"One of my virtues, Gina, one of my virtues. Anyone got an extra napkin?"

"You don't need any Lonnie, you just need a new shirt," teased Gina.

Turning to Lori, Gina said, "I saw you two talking to Dumar. He seemed a little stricken afterward. He was kind of quiet—not like him, but welcome for sure. What did you do to him?"

"It was nothing, Gina," said Lori. "Dumar was just a little rude, and Caleb, uh… offered to uh… well, sort of sit him down."

"Oh, I would have liked to have seen that!" exclaimed Gina. "What did you say, Caleb?"

"I can't abide rude behavior. Enough said."

"Don't piss off old Caleb. It's a rarity, but I've seen it a few times myself," said Lonnie Rex without pausing in the middle of a short rib.

Henry looked at Caleb as he considered what he was learning about Caleb Atwood.

FORTY-ONE

Caleb and Lonnie Rex were back on Lonnie's porch after the picnic. Lori had gone home, and Caleb would pick her up for the mixer. Lonnie was attempting to stay awake as he gently rocked to the sound the rocker made on the porch floor. Caleb was similarly disposed and not very talkative. It's funny how complete quiet between friends is the most ideal form of communication.

The afternoon promised light showers, and it was that moment when the breeze subsided as a welcome to whatever the sky wanted to bring. Lonnie Rex and Caleb waited in anticipation. As it started to sprinkle ever so lightly, Lonnie sat forth and spat over the porch railing. He reached for a cigarette and, after getting it lit, he asked, "So what went on with Dumar?"

"Nothing really. He just made some thoughtless remarks to Lori, and… well, it didn't sit right. I allowed as how he might want to walk away," explained Caleb. "I think Lori was as ready as I was to… uh, well… diminish his presence."

"He didn't say anything about the station?"

"Nope. I didn't give him much of a chance. His demeanor presented itself right up front. Didn't get any further."

"Yeah, I talked to him too. He didn't say anything to me either, except that he thought you had a short fuse. I told him your fuse wasn't short, but that his flame might be a little big."

Caleb said, "You know, I was quickly reminded why I didn't like him back at school. It is sort of weird. It seems that it is easy to find something you like about each person you meet and if you relate to that, then it is good. Even when it is hard to find good things, if you look, you generally can find something you like. But with a few, like Dumar, it just seems that it is impossible to find anything to relate to. You just need to walk away."

"Sounds like he's the one who walked away."

"That's right, but he needed a little encouragement."

Lonnie changed the subject, "I didn't know that Henry Dawes was married to Angela. He's been the district attorney for a while. He comes to breakfast at Casper's Grille occasionally, mostly in the winter. He seems to be a good guy, but I've only talked to him a few times."

"He knew about the station. Said he had talked to the mayor but didn't know what he had found at the site. He seems to think that the mayor may need him for legalities. I don't know what that means. Maybe there are some legal loopholes to jump through when there is a donation to the city."

Lonnie considered his words for a moment. "It seems to me that if Dumar had uncovered the body and the money, he would have been open about it. I mean, it is a windfall for the city, and it doesn't necessarily mean anything negative for his project. Warren allowed that the city could use the money anywhere. It wouldn't shut down the construction. He should have been open about it if he had found anything. It's an interesting story, you know. The fact that he was quiet and even a little hostile bothers me."

"I know what you mean. I think we should check back in with Javier and Onofre as soon as we can. We need to get the rest of the story if there is any. Can you set something up for Monday? I want to know everything I can before I talk to the mayor. I'm getting a bad feeling."

"I'll call him first thing and see if Onofre is coming back. We'll call him from Casper's."

"I might have to take Lori out to the airport. Don't know yet, but it won't interfere with Casper's. If we do it early. I should be there," said Caleb.

"Oh, we're gonna do it early!"

Caleb got up from his chair and moved toward the steps. "I'm going to go find Nancy. I haven't told her about the things that have happened. I need to, and I also want to ask her more about the approvals the board gave for the demolition—who was involved and so forth. I never cared much before, but now I'm interested."

"Sounds good. Think I'll give the hammock a chance to redeem itself. Dumps me again and I'm going to kill it."

"How do you kill a hammock?" Caleb wondered aloud.

"Don't worry, I'll find a way."

Caleb stepped down the steps and turned. "I'll see you at Big-Wigs after I pick up Lori. Do they serve anything to eat there?"

"Yeah, bar food, sandwiches, snacks, and tapas."

"Big-Wigs is topless?"

"No! It's not topless! I said tapas."

"Oh. Well, good. What's a tapas?"

"You speak Spanish. Figure it out. I'm sleepy."

Caleb found Nancy at her office. She was pouring over some real estate contract and looked up as he entered. "Hey, Caleb. How's the reunion going?"

"Good—all good. It's nice to see old friends. Kind of sorry I never came to the earlier ones."

"I know. I always enjoy mine. I love seeing how people look and what they are doing. The surprises are what make it so much fun. What surprises did you encounter?"

"Oh, I don't know. Maybe a few. I saw my old roommate from the university. Been forty years. He married a gal from Rogers and ended up back here. Small world." Caleb paused and reluctantly continued, "I even hooked up with my old girlfriend.

Lori Hightower. We've been going to all the events together. It's been nice."

"Well, that sounds promising. You never did have another person in your life, did you?"

"Nope. Been a few adventures, but nothing that led to my boots being under anyone else's bed, at least for any length of time," Caleb admitted sheepishly. He had known Nancy for too long to feel the need to hold anything back. Continuing, he said, "The truth is that I have always been taken with Lori, and it seems, after this week, that she feels the same. Don't know where we will go with it, but it is sure great to get back together."

"I hope something good works out for you guys. It's been a long time for you."

"Funny how time doesn't seem to matter much, you know? I mean, what is time? You find old feelings that are there just as you left them, no matter how much water has gone under the bridge. And not just with Lori. I had a run-in with Dumar Ashton at the picnic, and all my old feelings of dislike surfaced almost instantly. He made some rude remarks to Lori, and I almost misbehaved. Threatened him a bit—it wasn't called for, but those feelings of dislike came rushing back instantly."

"Well, I've never liked him. What do you think his involvement in the station is? Is it what we talked about the other night?"

"I don't know for sure, but some things are piling up. Lonnie Rex and I went out to talk to the contractor who did the construction site work for the new building. He had some illegals working for him. One of them disappeared recently because he was scared off by the owner. Lonnie thinks that it must be Dumar, based on what the contractor told him, and that Dumar is the one responsible for the worker's disappearance. But now the worker wants to come back, and we hope to see him next week. Maybe we can find out what happened.

"Also—and this is a little tenuous—Dumar came to the picnic driving a big diesel truck that had been totally refurbished. You may remember that Warren had mentioned in the letter that he had talked to an attorney who had done some work for re-building an engine. What if it was Dumar? Then that would mean that he knew that Warren had some money stashed away. Maybe Dumar knew more about Warren than we realize. I don't know what it means, but we want to find out as much as we can before I talk to the mayor again."

Nancy thought for a minute. "If Dumar knew about War-ren's situation, it might explain how he got involved in the sta-tion. I don't know, but there could be a connection."

"I know what you mean. After Warren's death was when Dumar made his deal with Vernon to buy the station and then worked to get the station declassified as historical in order to get to tear it down. He got it for a song, then created real value. Kind of left Vernon with little to show for it. Also, it seems that he got the mayor involved in the process. We don't know for sure, but it does start to smell."

"Dumar has a history of buying property after someone passes, when it goes into probate, or if it has tax liabilities. He's done it before. All legal, but that's what he has done. I've learned about some of his real estate dealings through my experience on commercial property. In addition, the downtown is in sort of a renaissance. Old buildings and sites are being developed. The downtown is being reborn. That's great, of course—I love that it's happening. This is the center of Rogers and holds a lot of memories. And now it holds increased value. There's new res-taurants and shops and improvements along the rail line. The old hotel is doing good, and it all has a good feeling. Being on the Historical Board gives me a chance to be involved in its happen-ing," explained Nancy. "And I know that Sarah is enjoying being on the Board. She's been sort of isolated in the past but has so much knowledge of the town's history. Anyway, returning to the subject, Dumar knows all about the value of downtown prop-erty."

"If possible, look into the historical approvals in more detail. See what can be determined about the process. See if we can determine how the mayor is involved. I mean, was it only his intent to influence the Board because it represented a good move for the city, or was he financially involved and therefore conflicted?" Caleb requested.

"Sure, I'll do that. I'll look through the submission to the Board."

Caleb stood up to leave. "I've got to go. I just wanted to bring you up to date. After the reunion is over, we'll find out more, and we can let Peter loose with his article in the paper. I'm sure he's chomping at the bit."

As they stepped out into the lobby, they were interrupted by Naomi sitting at the same desk that she occupied on Caleb's last visit. "I couldn't help overhearing your conversation. I wanted to tell you that when we were keeping the keys to Warren Atwood's farm for you Caleb, I got a call from a real estate agent who wanted to see the place. The person who called was Dottie Boothe. I told her that it wasn't for sale, but she insisted that their office was only interested in the general area and just wanted to look."

"Did you let her go out there?" asked Nancy.

"Yes, I did—I mean, I gave her the combination to the lockbox. I knew her from the local real estate meetings. She was legitimate, and I thought it would be okay. But it turns out that it wasn't her that went out. She was working at the time for Mr. Ashton, who you were talking about. Later she told me that it was him who wanted to see the place. When I heard you mention his name, I remembered the event. Did I do wrong?"

"No, I don't think that at all. You could only assume that her interest was normal. Did she say anything else?"

"No, nothing. She quit working for that Ashton character, though. She is now with another agency. She didn't really say outright, but I got the impression that she didn't like Ashton at all."

Caleb and Nancy looked at each other for a moment. Nancy broke the silence with, "Thank you, Naomi for telling us. That's a good catch."

"Is there a problem?" asked Naomi.

Caleb interrupted, "No, we don't think so. So, he looked. That's okay, but it just seems he keeps coming up in everything we do."

"Everything was in order when I visited the place. I went out several times during that period up until you got back. I never saw anything disturbed," said Nancy.

"Makes you wonder just what he was looking for now doesn't it?" asked Caleb.

FORTY-TWO

Big-Wigs Lounge was at the center of the renaissance of downtown Rogers. Bobby had combined the leases on
two adjacent retail buildings along First Street. They were in desperate need of repair, and, as a result, he was able to get the
owner to spring for serious rehab with a long lease and a pledge
of a share of the profits. The inside was opened substantially by
large timber framed openings in the common wall. There was a
spacious grandeur to the place, yet intimacy was achieved by
carefully arranged seating groups and low-level lighting. The bar
itself was situated in the center of the back of the lounge, allowing plenty of social space for patrons and for various events.
Thankfully there were no big TVs on the walls blasting various
images to the crowd. That was a current "style" Bobby Lane had
resisted. Everything about the establishment spoke of sophisti-
cated relaxation.

Big-Wigs enjoyed a significant role in the resurgence of the
Rogers downtown. With a selection of tapas, light fare, and some
standard pub selections, it had become a gathering place for diverse groups. At lunch, it catered to the business crowd, while at
night, it became a popular destination for relaxed social dis-
course. It was indeed a classy place and much more than a bar.

Bobby had chosen Lonnie Rex's art to showcase at Big-Wigs.
Lonnie was the only artist who was allowed to hang works of art.
Some said it wasn't fair, to which Bobby usually replied, "I
know." But the truth was that Lonnie Rex's work had a unique
quality. An astute observer of Lonnie's work would pick up the

subtle but constant change in subject matter. In the early days, there were a lot of classical still-life and landscapes, all painted in great detail. As his work progressed, there was a strong shift to portraiture in timeless settings, delivered with sensitive brush strokes. Western art was strongly featured along with a slight shift to impressionistic landscapes. In recent years, there was more and more impressionism. If you asked Lonnie Rex about it, he would simply tell you that the phases were in response to his wives. Jaws One was very classy, Jaws Two was outdoorsy and moody, and Jaws Three hadn't made an appearance so he only had an "impression" of what she would be like. It was all a silly story but made as much sense as anything else Lonnie might conjure up. And it seemed to satisfy the occasional local who inquired with knitted brow as he studied Lonnie Rex's art. The one thing that was true, however, was that it sold! Big-Wigs was becoming known as the only place on earth where you could see the celebrated work of Lonnie Rex Stanhope and enjoy the social atmosphere while you were at it.

On this reunion evening, the full glory of the place was being appreciated by a full house with spillage out to the sidewalk. It was Friday night, and the action at Big-Wigs only added to the robust atmosphere along First Street. Inside there was a loud hum of voices all mingling in tones of laughter and questions. It was difficult for Caleb and Lori to make their way through the crowd.

"I thought this might be well attended, but I imagined nothing like this!" exclaimed Caleb.

"Looks like everyone in Rogers is here!" added Lori.

Caleb saw Lonnie sitting on a large leather couch in a seating area against the old brick wall where much of his art was on display. He was joined there by two young and extremely attractive young ladies whom Caleb didn't recognize—one on each side of Lonnie. Also in the group were Fletcher, Bobby, and Peter, all of whom seemed to be paying rapt attention to the conversation or, more likely, the ladies.

As Caleb and Lori finally pushed themselves through the crowd and got close enough to hear what was being said, they could hear Lonnie speaking to Bobby. "I didn't say that I 'found them'—I said that I 'invited' them to join us here tonight."

Lonnie turned to the ladies and began the introductions, "This is Chandelle, who is from... where did you say?"

"Memphis," she said with a twinkle.

"Right, Memphis.... and this is Mira, who came over with Chandelle. They are travelling across the country. I saw them going into the sushi place, so I quickly rescued them and brought them over here. No one should die like that!"

"Well, you are welcome tonight as guests of the class of '76, and, of course as my special guest since I own the place," said Bobby proudly.

Fletcher and Peter both seemed to nod their enthusiastic agreement. Peter added that he also didn't trust sushi, but it seemed to fall on deaf ears.

Lonnie looked up and saw Caleb for the first time. "'Bout time you got here. See what happens when I am left alone. These beautiful ladies have adopted me, and I have become incapacitated. As a result, I am unable to perform my duties to the class of '76 as the host for the art lovers among us. Plus, I need to sell some art."

Turning to the girls, Lonnie said, "This is my best friend Caleb, who is accompanied by the lovely Lori Martin. They will assist me as I try to refocus on my responsibilities. I will leave you in the good hands of Bobby here, who will, I am sure, attend to your every need."

"Thanks, Lonnie," said Chandelle. "You're a sweety, and this is such a friendly place! You have made our visit memorable." Mira nodded in agreement.

Lonnie took Lori's arm and pulled her toward the bar area. "Food. I need food. Come along with us Caleb. We will now fortify ourselves, and you will learn what tapas are."

"Are you going to leave your girlfriends behind?" asked Caleb.

"They're not keepers—didn't even put up a good fight! No, I need food."

As they made their way around the food table filling their plate with a variety of fares, Misty Belle approached in the company of Franky Mango. The reunion committee had agreed to have Franky share the master of ceremonies job with Fletcher Cosgrove at the Saturday night dinner and dance. Misty said to Caleb, "Look who's here. Do you remember Franky?"

"Sure, I do. It would be hard to forget your antics, Franky. You live back east, don't you?" said Caleb.

"Yes indeed. I'm in the Boston area. I do market research but dabble in stand-up for events."

"Franky, this is Lori, who you should remember. She left during our junior year but comes to these when she can," added Caleb.

"Oh, I remember you, Lori. You and Caleb were very close as I recall. Is this your first time getting together with Caleb since high school?" Franky asked.

"That's right. This is our own personal reunion," Lori said with sincerity.

Lonnie Rex inserted, "Franky! Nice to see you. I understand that you're going to entertain us tomorrow night."

"That's my intent. And in that regard, I am looking for ammunition." Franky turned back to Caleb and said, "So, Caleb, tell me more. What have you been doing? It's been forty years. There must be some juicy stuff there for me to kid about."

"You can do what you want. I'm an open book. Just been a cowboy for all these years—plenty of cowboy jokes."

"But it gets more interesting with Lori here. Are you guys a new item? Is this a 'pick up where you left off' sort of a deal?"

Lori took control of the conversation. "Now Franky, you need to be careful. I'll just say that we have indeed picked up where we left off, but we're not ready to come out of the closet."

"So, you've been to the closet, have you? That's news right there! This looks promising!" exclaimed Franky.

"You won't get anywhere trying to discourage him, Lori," said Caleb. "He'll do what he wants. The best thing is to not give him any ammo. He can twist anything into humor."

Franky shifted gears and said to Caleb, "I heard that you had a run-in with Dumar at the picnic. Old issues that needed settling?"

"Nope. No old issues. Just a little rude behavior on his part. Nothing more. Man, news travels fast. Do me a favor and stay away from that, okay?" Caleb delivered the request with a certain clarity which made Franky pause.

"Sure, no problem. He's not very funny anyway."

"I guess you could make fun of my fiddle playing if you want to. Or, better yet, look at Lonnie Rex here. Now, he is a subject worth studying."

"I ain't funny—I'm real! Huh, Franky?" Lonnie said in a manner that implied shared experiences, most of which should remain private.

"No, Lonnie, you are funny, and you're damn sure real. But I may have to dredge up some old stories just for the joy of the telling," reminisced Franky.

"Okay, I release you," said Lonnie with a smile, "But be gentle. I'm sensitive."

Caleb nearly spewed out his drink at this remark. "Lonnie, you ain't sensitive! You're like a rock in a mud hole!"

"A rock in a mud hole?" questioned Lori.

"Well, that's what came to mind. It fits, doesn't it?" pleaded Caleb.

"While you guys debate that, I'm going to circulate and sell some art," declared Lonnie.

"Let's circulate a bit ourselves," Caleb said to Lori. "I've had all the tapas I can stand."

For the next two hours, they greeted old friends and made a few new ones. The atmosphere was cordial and relaxed, and both

Caleb and Lori enjoyed themselves. There was no sign of Dumar, so at least they didn't have to deal with him.

Toward the end of the evening, Peter Mason made his way over to Caleb and inquired if there had been any new developments. Caleb informed him that there would be some news on Monday, but for now, all was quiet. He reiterated his desire to let it go until next week.

Peter persisted and said that he had heard about Caleb's run-in with Dumar. "What was that all about?" he asked.

"Nothing to do with the station stuff. He was just a little rude, and I didn't appreciate it. No big deal. Listen, we're going to head out. We'll see you tomorrow night."

"Okay, looking forward to your fiddle playing. Be sure and let me get a few pictures for the article on the reunion. You're becoming a bit of a celebrity what with your fiddle playing and your hook-up with Lori, not to mention that this is your first reunion," said Peter.

"Will do," Caleb promised as he and Lori moved toward the exit.

Lonnie Rex was sitting on a bench on the sidewalk having a smoke when they exited.

"Guess how much art I sold tonight," challenged Lonnie.

"Couldn't possibly know. How much?"

"Three pieces for sure, with a couple more probable. Good haul, but hot, sweaty work. I need the porch," lamented Lonnie. "How'd you like the tapas?"

"They were okay, but I was disappointed that they didn't have any mountain oysters," replied Caleb.

"Dream on, pard, dream on."

"Mountain oysters?" Lori asked.

"Never mind. Let's go."

FORTY-THREE

Saturday morning was to start with breakfast at the Ozark Hotel to be followed by a tour of the High School. Lori suggested that they skip all of that and go out to Caleb's farm. She had only been out with Daniel that one time to do measurements. This suited Caleb fine. He needed to check on the progress of the fencing anyway, and now would be a good time. He suggested that after a workout with Cisco, he would pick her up, and they could go out together. Maybe lunch afterward.

The drive to Pea Ridge was quiet. It was a beautiful summer morning with a promise of slight rain later in the day. Lori looked out across the landscape as they drove.

"You know, this place is quite beautiful. I don't think I appreciated it enough when I lived here."

"I know what you mean. I've seen some beautiful country in the high mountains and the vast prairies of the west, but coming here does seem like home to me. I guess you can't completely escape your roots."

"Las Vegas isn't very appealing. I mean it's clean and vibrant, but it doesn't seem to have the sense of place like this does. And it's all rather new. It wasn't even there until the casinos came back in the late fifties. And they're just gaudy and loud. There's no history there. Here there is history. I like it."

As they passed through Pea Ridge and drove east toward the Pea Ridge Battlefield, they passed a nice veterinary clinic set back from the road. Lori looked it over as they passed. "That looks like a good setup. Almost as big as mine."

"How's the clinic doing in your absence?"

"I guess I'm sorry to report that it is doing quite well, according to the staff. They don't seem to need me much. I don't know whether to be pleased or insulted," observed Lori.

"Just be pleased. Joy always works, especially when it is deserved."

"That's good advice. You know, I'm sorry if you wanted to go to the breakfast and all. It's just that the only thing we do is the reunion stuff. I want to make the best use of my remaining time with you and with your farm and, you know... everything else."

"No, I'm glad you suggested skipping. At this point, the only person I really want to see at this reunion is you, so why keep wading in a batch of people? We got our own reunion going, don't we?" declared Caleb.

"That was my thinking," admitted Lori. "I've enjoyed the events, of course, especially last night. That was a good gathering.... Hey, I know what I meant to ask you—what are mountain oysters? You didn't say."

"Oh. Well, when we brand and castrate calves, we fry the..."

"Say no more," interrupted Lori. "I got it. I always heard them called calf fries. Now I understand. Do they taste good?"

"Oh, perhaps it's an acquired taste, but yeah, I like them," Caleb admitted. "Speaking of acquired tastes, that reminds me of a story a cowboy used to tell. He was from North Dakota, up there near the Canadian border. Anyway, he told us about Lutefisk. It's dried fish, aged, salted, and cured in lye. He said that it tasted like a mixture of lighter fluid and dirty socks."

Lori laughed as Caleb continued, "You know the difference between Lutefisk and snot? The little children won't eat the Lutefisk!"

They both laughed heartily, Lori because of the comparison, and Caleb with a fond memory of his cowboy friend who had passed on. This brought back a flood of memories of the west and of what he had left behind. He hadn't reflected much since coming back to Arkansas. So much seemed to be happening, and in only a few weeks. To Caleb's surprise, his recollections were not made of a longing to return but were just a part of what seemed a past phase of life. It strengthened his sense that this move to Rogers was what God had in mind for him.

Glancing over at Lori, Caleb said, "I'm looking forward to tomorrow. Church and then dinner at Sarah's. She's very excited. And the fact that Winnie has agreed to come will be special."

"Oh, I know. She's mentioned it several times. She doesn't go out much, so it will be special for her, and Daniel too. You know, he's been bent over some sketches on the farm and is looking forward to getting together this week."

"Yeah, me too. Which reminds me. What time is your flight on Monday?"

"Oh, I didn't tell you. I pushed it back to Wednesday afternoon. I want to be here when you get together with Daniel to see what he has done. The staff had no problem with the delay," said Lori.

"That's great! I wanted you to be here when Daniel and I met, but I wasn't sure we could pull it off. Ask Daniel if Tuesday morning would be good. Monday may be a little busy."

"What's happening Monday?"

"I'm going to go with Lonnie to talk to that contractor after breakfast, if we can arrange it, and then I may want to go see the mayor. Maybe even Peter. I don't know yet, but it could be a full day. You can come with me if you like, or we could meet for dinner. Whatever you want. That's just great that you're staying a little longer."

"I'll pass on the day, unless you think you need me, but dinner will work. Anyway, I'll tell Daniel about Tuesday morning. Should be fun."

They had turned onto a dirt road and were approaching the farm. The gate was open, and as they approached the house,

Caleb could tell that Dickie and Estes had indeed been busy. Materials were stacked up by the barn. Much of the fence had been rebuilt and a new gate to the pasture was hung.

"When do you plan on moving in here?" asked Lori.

"There's no rush, and it all depends on what I decide to do. It'll probably take a while, and Sarah is happy to have me. So, no plans."

They both went into the house and quietly gave it a good look. Caleb was mindful that Dumar had been out, so he looked carefully to see if anything seemed amiss that he didn't notice during his other visits. He didn't share his concern with Lori because it wasn't necessary and was probably nothing.

Lori called Caleb from the larger bedroom. "Caleb, it may be none of my business, and I know you are a guy, but this place needs a great deal of work. I don't see how this is going to be quick or simple."

"That's because it's not. I've been mulling it over the last few days, and I hope Daniel gets something together that will be aggressive. It's got to have a new master bedroom and bath, the kitchen needs to be totally redone, it needs to have a guest room and much more. I want to be happy to have people out for dinner and get-togethers. I will occasionally have overnight company. This is going to be a rather big project," Caleb admitted. "Plus, I want a lot more in the way of porches, maybe covered and screened in. I'll spend most of my time outdoors, weather permitting. Maybe a fireplace out on a back porch—give me year-round porch sitting."

"Closets, Caleb. There are very few closets. You've got to have more. And a proper laundry room. That washer in the kitchen won't do."

Caleb had some mixed emotions. On the one hand, he agreed with Lori completely and had been thinking along the same lines. But he also was getting a glimpse of what it would be like to have someone else placing demands on him or telling him what to do. He reckoned that this would take some thought to fully come to terms with it. Forty years of living alone had molded him in ways that might take a little time to reshape. But he wondered, what was he thinking? He would still live alone, just in a nicer place. At that moment he had to confront the fact that he was envisioning Lori there with him. It was a wake-up call. His gut was hollering at him, and he was just starting to listen.

"Caleb, did you hear me?"

"Yes, I did. More closets. Absolutely. 'Course if I do that, I'll have to buy more clothes to fill 'em up," Caleb said jokingly.

"Men!"

"That's me."

Caleb rushed to change the subject. "Let's give the barn and outbuildings a good look."

He led the way to the barn. He had seen it but wanted to look again since the news about Dumar. He couldn't quite imagine where Dumar would have looked. Where would Warren have hidden money if Warren had hidden money? Did he really ask himself that? Was that what Dumar believed? It could have been anywhere, but Caleb knew it wasn't here, so why bother? Then he remembered the shed. That's where money could be hidden if it had been hidden... so he would look there. He stopped on the way out the door of the barn. This was ridiculous. Even if he found evidence of someone looking, it meant nothing. It was like beating your head against the wall—it feels good when you stop. So, he stopped.

He turned around quickly and bumped into Lori trying to keep up with him. He grabbed her in his arms to prevent a fall and found that he hung on to her for a long time.

"Oops. Sorry. You okay?" Caleb asked without relinquishing his hold.

"Caleb, if you want to kiss me, just do it. We don't have to play bumper cars."

Caleb pushed her back a bit and said, "That was just to keep you from falling. This is for a kiss," he uttered as he pulled her close again and kissed her deeply.

They stood there in each other's embrace, enjoying the moment of intimacy. Then he turned her with his arm over her shoulder and started back up toward the house. When they got close, Lori said, "Caleb?"

"Yes."

"Does the bathroom work? I've gotta pee."

"I think so. Let's find out, then we will go and get some lunch."

"Good plan."

Lori was slow to let go of his hand as she turned to go down the hall.

FORTY-FOUR

The dinner and dance on Saturday night were shaping up to be a big affair. Caleb and Lori had arrived a little early to help if required and to allow Caleb to check out the band. Lonnie Rex and Misty Belle were sitting at the check-in table taking late registrations and handing out keepsakes along with information about classmates.

After their time at the farm in Pea Ridge, Caleb had stopped by Sarah's house to get his violin and to change clothes. That wasn't a significant event. All he had was clean blue jeans and a fresh shirt. He spruced up a bit by draping a silk bandana around his neck and added a light leather vest. He brushed his hat and told himself that it would have to do. He stepped into cream-colored high-top cowboy boots which were his "dress-up" boots and hoped it would all serve. Lori inspected his efforts and seemed to approve, so all was well.

A trip to Lori's house was the next event of the afternoon. Caleb waited patiently while Lori disappeared into the bedroom to prepare. She was gone quite a while, and Caleb joined in conversation with Winnie and Daniel. He and Daniel had agreed on Tuesday morning to review the plans, and Daniel said that he would be ready. Winnie chatted on with numerous questions about Caleb's farm and what he was going to do now that he was moving back to Rogers. Since he hadn't given much thought to the issue, it was a good introduction to the need to make some plans. Caleb knew that he would have to make a living, as they say, so the issue grew in his mind. He shared with Winnie his interest in horse training, cattle raising, farming, fiddle playing, and anything that might serve. Truth is, he had no idea. He figured that it would come to him in time. After all, he did have a good amount of money saved up, and inherited, and soon should see some significant income from the cattle he had in Colorado. Winnie seemed satisfied with his answers. He wasn't sure that he was satisfied, however. How would he make a living?

Caleb's thoughts came to a halt when Lori emerged from the back of the house. She was stunning! She had mimicked Caleb's "look" with fitted jeans and a silk shirt with a large scarf as decoration. Her hair was bouncy-fresh, and she was simply beautiful. To complete the ensemble, she also wore colorful boots. It was a dance, after all, and she was clearly ready. Properly prepared, they had headed off to greet the evening.

Lonnie and Misty Belle looked them over when they stepped up to the table.

"You two look grand!" said Misty. "A touch of the west, I should say!"

"About the only choice for me, I reckon, but Lori here does it proud."

"Dang, Caleb, I didn't know you had any good jeans," quipped Lonnie. "You clean up just fine. And you, Lori, well…. What can I say? It don't get no better than that!"

"Thanks all around. We're prepared for some dancing," responded Lori.

"Anything we can do to help? We came a little early in case," offered Caleb.

"Heck yeah," Lonnie said as he got up. "I'm gonna get a smoke outside. You can sit here and do name tags and pretend that you know what Misty is talking about. She never really says."

"Lonnie, just take your break. You have been most helpful, but I'm sure we can manage without your assistance for a little while," said Misty Belle. "Lori, why don't you sit down and help me. Caleb needs to go see the band, don't you Caleb?"

"Uh… yeah, that's right. Do they really want me to play?"

"Ask them. They know about you, and I think they want to fit you in."

Caleb angled off toward the stage, leaving Lori and Misty to conspire in whatever way they chose.

"You guys are together all the time," observed Misty. "Is it serious?"

"Well, we seriously care for each other—always have. And we're having a seriously good time."

Misty reflected, "You know, there was a time when I wanted Caleb to ask me out, back when we were seniors. He never did. I tried almost everything to let him know of my interest, and he was always very nice but never called. I think he was still only thinking of you."

"Must have been thinking of something, because you would be a fine catch, Misty."

"Maybe, but he wasn't fishing," Misty mumbled as she watched Caleb approach the stage.

Turning back to Lori, Misty said, "Well, that was forty years ago. We've all moved on with our lives. Has it been good for you in Las Vegas?"

"Sure. It's been good. Got two great children, one grandchild, and a successful clinic to run. I've been alone since the divorce, but it's all good. Cliff moved on, and I have enjoyed my independence."

"Me too," added Misty. "I mean, not independence. I'm happily married and have been for thirty-five years. However, I must say that being the wife of a mortician has its dull moments. But we've done well."

"I understand that you have managed the reunion committee since the beginning," said Lori.

"That's right. I do take it seriously and just can't seem to let go. I always worry that someone like Lonnie Rex might take over. Then what?" Misty said without laughing.

"Oh, it would be different for sure!" laughed Lori, "But fun."

"Maybe, but he is the most exasperating man!" pronounced Misty.

Several people came in the door and approached the table. Misty registered each guest, and Lori made out their name tags. She found that this was a great way to get to know people better. Writing down their names established them in her mind.

Fletcher Cosgrove came in with his wife. As he approached Misty Belle, he asked, "What do you want me to do? What is the schedule of events?"

"At about six thirty, after cocktail hour, you can announce dinner. When people take their seats is when you can welcome everyone. I would like you to introduce the reunion committee, mention the hard work we did, and anything else you plan to say. Then, we can have a blessing and eat. We have a reverend, as you know—Richard Myers. He will give the invocation. Right after dinner, Franky Mango is going to give out some awards— mostly silly stuff—and then say a few entertaining words. When he finishes, the band will start the dance, say about 8:00 or when-ever Franky finishes," Misty instructed. "Here is a note with eve-rything."

As Misty finished, Lonnie Rex returned.

"Don't I get to say anything funny?" Fletcher asked Misty.

"Fletcher, you well know that anything you might say is bound to be funny," inserted Lonnie. "You want me to give you a few quips or quotes?"

Fletcher paused to think, "Uh, no. I don't think that will be necessary. I'm good."

"Good idea. Let Franky make an idiot of himself. You stay strong," added Lonnie.

"Lonnie, shut up. Fletcher, you can say anything you want, just be sure to cover all the stuff I told you about," instructed Misty.

Lori rose from her seat and moved around the table. "I think I will go find Caleb and have a drink. Lonnie, thanks for allowing me to assist you, but Misty was hoping you would return soon. I think she needs you. Here's your chair back."

Lonnie smiled at Misty and gave her a wink. "I knew it, I just knew it!"

The dinner went well, with Fletcher's opening remarks failing to inspire either laughter or criticism from the audience. The tinkling of silverware and the hum of conversation, with regular open laughter, filled the room as everyone attacked the food. The fare for the evening was grilled chicken displayed atop mashed potatoes surrounded with asparagus squizzled with some type of sauce. It was all in keeping with the latest presentation trends for assembly line food. Not good enough to make the meal worth the trip, but perfectly suitable as a backdrop to the continuation of friendly banter.

Lori sought out her friend Angela and her husband, Henry Dawes. Caleb joined them at the seats they had chosen, and they renewed their conversation with others around the table. Henry did not mention anything else about his role as district attorney or anything more about the mayor. Caleb had no desire to speak of it, so they joined in the lively discussion involving memories and shared experiences.

At the end of the dinner, Franky Mango stepped up on the stage. He gave out some very dubious awards for nonsensical things, such as who came the farthest, who looked the youngest, who married above themselves, and so forth. He followed the awards with a rousingly funny tale of his life as a marketer and entertainer at events. He was self-deprecating and worked in his love of Rogers. His capability was on display, and everyone appreciated the well-placed humor. Franky made no mention of Caleb and Lori until the very end, at which time he reminded everyone that Caleb would play his fiddle in true western style along with the band and when finished, Caleb and Lori would take the dance floor as the "love story" of the reunion. They would proceed to show everyone how dancing should be done in real western style.

As the music started, Lori looked at Caleb and asked, "Can you still dance."

"Yep."

"I haven't danced in a long time," said Lori.

"You'll do fine."

"I hope so. Everyone will be looking."

"I reckon everyone will be looking at you even if you aren't dancing."

After a few numbers of country-rock numbers, the band summoned Caleb up to the stage, with the observation that he needed no introduction. After Caleb got his violin, he stepped up the microphone and announced, "Now for some classical country—stuff my daddy used to sing right here in this room. Songs I have enjoyed for all these years. You'll remember these tunes, and if you don't, then it's time you learned 'em. Boys... follow me!"

Caleb led into the music, and the band joined in. They played many songs from the past as the audience crowded the dance floor in fond memories of old moves to the lively beat. When the oldies finished, and everyone thought Caleb was done, he asked to borrow one of the electric guitars. He announced that he wasn't entirely mired in the country music of the past. With a flourish on the guitar, Caleb started into a rendition of "Panama" by Van Halen. The band was taken by surprise, but only for a moment, at which point they joined in as the beat and the decibel level increased. Hard rock had arrived at the reunion!

After his set with the band, Caleb returned to the table to join Lori and the others.

Angela said to Caleb, "I guess you are a man of many surprises."

"I rather think that he might be a man of many talents," beamed Lori.

"Now ladies, let me hydrate a little, and then we can dance."

Lori and Angela excused themselves for a trip to the lady's room, and for a short period, Caleb was left to himself. He sat back and enjoyed the music. He hoped that he might escape without having to dance the way Franky had promised, but such was not the case. When Lori and Angela returned, they sat through another number along with Caleb. The band had the dance floor full of happy people all waiting for the next number to start. The band leader stepped to the microphone and said, "Now for that dance Franky promised. Caleb and Lori, come up here and show us how it's done. You want rock and roll or two-stepping country?"

"Country, of course. I don't like rock!" Caleb said to a response of loud laughter and catcalls. "How's about 'El Paso?'" Caleb shouted over the din.

Caleb took Lori out on the floor, where people stepped back to give them some room. He said to Lori, "This here is a waltz. Let's show them a little class!"

As the music started, Caleb led Lori around the floor in expressive swirls to the music. He knew very well that she knew how to dance. It had been their favorite activity when they were young. The crowd let them swirl and then joined in to complete the number. There was rousing applause at the end, both for the band's ability and for the couple who led the dance.

FORTY-FIVE

On Sunday morning, Caleb waited on the front porch of Sarah's church for Lori and Daniel to appear. After all the activity last night at the dance, it was a bit difficult to get started this morning. He was glad that he and Lori didn't drink, to speak of, or the morning could be worse. Sarah had gone into the church to visit before the service, and Caleb had told Sarah to tell the band that he was going to sit this morning out and join Sarah, Lori, and Daniel in the pews.

As the last of the congregation arrived, Lori came down West Poplar Street and turned into the church parking lot. She had Daniel with her, and they were hurrying to get parked. Caleb was anxious to see Lori even though the time since he last saw her could be measured in hours.

Lori and Daniel briskly came up the walk and spotted Caleb waiting. Lori was a bit dressed up from Caleb's point of view, but of course, everyone was dressed up from his vantage point. Perhaps Lori's church-going harked back to the time when people all looked nice. Daniel was casually attired and even had on socks, so that was apparently still acceptable. Both seemed enthusiastic to be arriving.

Lori smiled at Caleb and gave him a kiss on the cheek as they turned to go into the church.

"Last night was fantastic!" Lori whispered to Caleb.

"To be followed by another fantastic day today," responded Caleb.

"You guys be quiet: we're in church," admonished Daniel as forcefully as the silence would allow.

Caleb guided them to where Sarah was sitting, and they all joined her in the pew. Lori went in first and Daniel followed with Caleb at the end. Sarah beamed at Lori as she greeted her quietly.

The service began with the band performing several numbers and everyone singing along. A few of the congregation looked over toward Caleb, obviously wondering why he wasn't up there playing his violin. Establish any sort of pattern, and everyone wonders when it changes. It was the same the world over, he reckoned. He noticed that nearly everyone was seated in the same seats they occupied before and probably since the beginning of time. Interesting.

After the opening prayer, Pastor Wendell stepped to the lectern and greeted everyone. He mentioned that Caleb was not playing this morning because he wanted to share this time with his guests and that everyone should give them a warm welcome. All the heads turned toward them, accompanied by enthusiastic nods, waves, and whispered welcomes. At least now they knew why he wasn't playing and would realize that everything is going to be okay. He smiled back. Lori acknowledged their welcome with a similar smile and nod. Daniel, on the other hand, looked like a doe in the headlights of a Peterbilt. Perhaps it was the first time he had ever been called out in church.

Pastor Wendell proceeded to tell everyone that this was a special morning. He said that the sermon today would be delivered by a distinguished visitor. He explained that in today's changing world, there are multiple avenues available to bring the Word to light and to inspire each of us as we explore our own walk with the Lord. He explained that today's guest speaker was Dr. John Clinton Isaacs, who is a theologian and author of many Christian books. Today's sermon by Dr. Isaacs would specifically address the new evangelistic movements and their reliance on personal engagement among Christians.

Dr. Issacs stepped up to the lectern and thanked everyone for having him. He spoke briefly of his writings and of how his personal call to serve the Lord had come about. His sermon was captivating in the way it engaged each member of the audience in recognizing their own gifts and how they could become instruments of inspiration to those who we encounter, even within the simplicity of our daily routines. He encouraged all of God's people to understand the history of church leadership, how it had evolved over the ages, and the role it currently played in our daily worship. As explained by Dr. Isaacs, there is a renewed focus on the wonderful opportunities to share the truth of the Word through our personal engagement with others. Our lives are His as He is ours. At the conclusion of Dr. Isaac's remarks, he invited everyone to come to the front of the church and in a group to join him in a prayer of engagement. All joined in crowding together beneath the lectern as Dr. Isaacs prayed. At the conclusion of the prayer, the band began to softly play the gospel song "He Lives."

There was an increased quiet in the sanctuary as the congregation moved toward the door. Pastor Wendell and Dr. Isaacs stepped to the porch and greeted everyone as they came out into the light. Many lingered in the front and shared their joy of the service.

After some exchanges with what seemed like newfound friends, Sarah and her group strolled to Lori's van. Sarah was unusually quiet. Caleb thought that she was waiting to hear from him or from Lori about the service.

It was Daniel who spoke up. "Wow, that was intense. I mean, not bad, but intense in a good way. Mom, how come we don't go to a church like that?"

"You really liked it?"

"I did. It sure made you think. I don't remember church making me think. Anyway, I liked it."

Unable to contain herself any longer, Sarah injected, "I thought it was wonderful! Pastor Wendell told me that he was going to bring in some other speakers, but I didn't know that I liked that idea. After today, I think I might give it more of a chance."

"Looks to me like you should give it a chance," offered Caleb.

Caleb stepped over, opened the door for Lori, and said, "So, if you get Winnie and come out, how long do you think it will take?"

"Oh, not long. I told her to be ready by noon. We should be there soon; 1:00 at the latest."

"Mom, I think I would like to ride out with Caleb while you get Winnie." said Daniel. "I have some questions for him on the design stuff."

"Sure," said Lori as she looked at Caleb for confirmation.

"Fine by me. Daniel and I can talk and then help Sarah with lunch," said Caleb.

"Great. We'll be along soon."

━━━━━━━━━━━━━━━━━━━━━━━━━━━━━━━

When Lori and Winnie pulled into the drive to Sarah's house, they saw that Daniel was mounted on Cisco and riding down the hill toward the creek. Caleb was leaning against the fence watching them go.

"How did you get him on a horse?" Lori said to Caleb as she pulled to a stop and stepped out of the van.

"What do you mean? He wanted to ride. It's okay, isn't it?"

"Yeah, it's okay. I'm just surprised, that's all. I never thought that he liked horses."

"He likes 'em enough to ride 'em!"

"Yeah, I can see that. What got him interested?"

"When we got out of the truck, Cisco hung his head across the fence and requested some attention. Daniel went over and stroked his nose, then asked if he could ride him. I said yes. That's the whole story."

"Will he be okay?"

"Yep."

They both watched Daniel and Cisco disappear into the woods. Just as they lost sight of him, Winne hollered from the van, "Well, are you going to let me sit here, or are you going to help me in?"

"Sorry, Winnie. Let's go. We'll walk up to the back door. There are only two steps."

Caleb helped Lori walk Winnie into the house. As they stepped through the door, Sarah hurried to greet them. "I'm so glad you've come! Let's sit on the front porch and visit. The dinner will be ready shortly. You want some iced tea? Do you want sweetened or unsweetened?"

Winnie studied Sarah. "We're glad to be here. The front porch sounds just fine. Iced tea would be nice, and sweetened please. Let's see, was that all?"

Sarah laughed. "Caleb says I ask multiple questions. I just can't help it. My mind goes rather fast, and I just let it all out."

"That appears to be the case. But I can keep up. Keep 'em coming—I bet I won't falter," claimed Winnie.

"Lori and I will have some unsweetened tea too. Thanks, Sarah," said Caleb.

"Where's Daniel? Is he in the barn? Did you show him Cisco?"

"Actually, we watched him ride off on Cisco," said Lori. "Caleb assures me he will be alright."

"Cisco will take good care of him," promised Caleb.

Everyone gathered on the porch and settled in the chairs. Winnie took what appeared to be the biggest and softest. Lori sat next to Caleb on the couch. As Sarah returned to the kitchen for the drinks, Winnie spoke up. "Oh, this porch is nice. It's so cool and comfortable. And the front yard is so spacious and green. I think I just might stay a while."

Sarah returned with the tea, and before she could launch into any questions, Winnie asked her, "What smells so good?"

"I've made rack of lamb with mint and chutney sauce. There are potatoes au gratin, along with asparagus and, of course, a tossed salad. Oh, and some French bread."

"Mercy! Not my usual Sunday frozen entrée. I might get used to this. Caleb, why don't you marry Lori so we can do this some more?"

There was a stunned silence for a moment, and then Winnie continued, "You know you two have wasted forty years at this point. Don't waste any more time. I'm old enough to appreciate each day. If you two get married now, you can still have a good run. I remember every day of my life with Joshua, and such a blessing it was! Quit piddlin' around and grab on to each other. There, I've said my piece."

Lori spoke up tentatively, "Well, you know, Winnie, we've only been reunited for less than two weeks. Maybe you're pushing it a little."

"If you think that I'm pushing it, it's because that is exactly what I'm doing. Been thinking about it since Caleb came to town. I've watched you two—every day. Posh! You guys belong together and always have. Been waiting 'till a good time to tell you, and this is it, especially since I smelled that dinner! Now you two figure it out," directed Winnie. "When do we eat?"

Sarah interjected, "Uh... well, uh... it's all ready and we can—"

Caleb interrupted Sarah, and looking at Winnie, he said, "You know, Winnie, you are a very wise lady. Can't say that I disagree with you one bit. As you say, we'll have to figure it out."

"Caleb! Are you asking me to marry you?"

"Nope, just saying that we will figure it out, like Winnie suggested. Let's start figuring it out the first chance we get. What do you say?"

Tears came to Lori's eyes, and she nodded her agreement. "Okay, I'll be ready."

"Now that's the ticket! Sieze the day!" exclaimed Winnie.

"Well, if it's time for dinner, I'll go get Daniel to come back up and unsaddle Cisco. I told him to make it a short ride because everything was about ready. He should be back by now."

Caleb moved out the back door as Sarah and Lori helped Winnie into the dining room. Sarah asked Lori to help her in the kitchen after Winnie was comfortably seated. As they got into the kitchen, Sarah leaned against the counter and looked at Lori. "Your aunt is a hoot!"

"Oh, that she is! However, I just might find myself agreeing with Caleb about her wisdom. But there's a lot to think about, and of course, he hasn't even asked me. Wow! This is getting real interesting real fast!"

"Yes, it is. So, let's put the dinner onto the table. I hesitate to keep Winnie waiting," said Sarah, "I don't know what she might do."

Lori laughed. "Good idea."

When Caleb and Daniel returned and they were all seated, Sarah asked if Caleb would deliver the blessing.

As they reached out and held hands, Caleb began, "Lord, our Father in heaven, we welcome Your presence at this, our table. You have watched over each of us with steadfast love and brought us to this moment together. We thank You for the blessings that we receive, and we ask that You should always help us to recognize those blessings each and every day of our lives. We ask for Your continued guidance and blessing in everything we say and do. We ask for Your loving presence as we make those decisions that will shape our future. Thank You for our experience of You this very morning. Bless everyone at this table, with a special nod toward Winnie and her life fully lived and for her wisdom lovingly shared. And bless Sarah for the preparation of the feast before us, and bless it to the betterment of our bodies. We pray in Jesus' name, Amen."

Winnie quickly added, "And a thank you from this old lady who, with Your help, tries to find the right way forward and who is anxious to have some of Sarah's cooking. Amen again."

"We were mighty windy. Hope the food didn't get cold," said Winnie. "Pass the bread, please."

When dinner was completed, they once again gathered on the porch. It had cooled considerably, and a breeze swept across the gathering. Daniel had gone back out to the barn to unsaddle Cisco, who they had left tied up before dinner. He had listened to Caleb tell him about what to do with the saddle and where the brush was. Caleb was confident that he could get it done in good fashion.

When Daniel returned, the talk turned to the church service that they had attended that morning. Lori had been quiet after the service but now found her voice. "I was quiet after we got out of the service. It was so different from what I expected that it set me back a little. I haven't been a churchgoer for a long time. Cliff, my husband, was not religious at all. I took Daniel for a time, back when Gwen was still at home, but it was not particularly engaging to any of us. We all felt we were being lectured rather than loved. We talked about it and decided to try a different church, but it was the same thing. It just never felt right, and certainly didn't lead any of us to feel closer to the Lord."

"Mom, I felt the same way. I mean we only went this morning, the one time, but I got sort of revved up listening. And the music was spontaneous and great," explained Daniel.

"Winnie, I'm sorry we didn't take you. I knew that you liked to listen to your preacher on TV, but I think you would have liked it if you had come. I wish I had brought you."

"Oh, that guy on TV is okay, but mostly I just prefer my chair. And if I dose off or snore, no one pokes me in the ribs. Besides, I am what I am, Lord knows. I hope and believe He will understand and cut me the slack I need," Winnie explained. "Maybe I will go with you if you go again. But you must promise not to poke me."

Sarah interjected, "I'm so pleased that you and Daniel liked it, Lori. The church is rather small, and sometimes we worry about how to grow. Wendell is concerned, and in addition, he doesn't know how much longer he can keep it up. I know he worries about who might succeed him and whether the congregation will respond to a new minister."

Caleb seemed rather distant during the discussion and remained silent. Finally, Sarah looked at him and tried to draw him out. "Caleb, tell us. What do you think?"

"Sarah, I've gone to church with you now, what, three or four times? Not much to be sure, but during those visits, it has become sort of special to me. I mean, I like the music and participating in it to be sure. But it's a lot more than that. Like Lori, I visited churches throughout the years—big ones in the city and little ones in the small towns. The big ones were sort of corporate, with lots of dressed-up people all fitting into a role. I never felt completely welcome, even after several visits. And the small ones were better regarding friendliness but seemed to be a closed society. All of them seemed to be doing what Daniel said, lecturing me. I'm aware that on occasions maybe I needed a little lecturing, but all in all, it just didn't suit me.

"There is love in your church, Sarah, love for each other and love of the Lord. His presence is constant, and that presence affects the music, the sermons, and the people who gather in His name. That is as it should be. I also think that the Lord will not allow it to die. Pastor Wendell is not going anywhere, in my estimation. He just speaks of that out of his concern for the future. He'll stay as long as he has a voice. And his bringing in other speakers is excellent. In many ways, that is what a church should be—a place where anyone and everyone can listen to the Word, witness, be fed, and feed others. In short, to gather in His name, like it says in the Bible. Your church will be fine, and I hope to be a part of it," said Caleb. "There, used up my words for the day."

After a thoughtful quiet, Sarah said, "I'm so pleased that you all enjoyed it. It means so much to me; you just don't know."

Winnie let out a simple little snore, and everyone realized that her afternoon nap had begun.

"Oh dear, maybe it's time to be taking her home," observed Lori.

"And interrupt that nap—I don't think so. Let her be. She'll let us know when it's time for the next event. Meanwhile, Lori, could you come with me to the barn while I check on things?" Turning to Sarah, Caleb said, "We'll be back directly, everyone."

"I've got some dessert and some coffee. Come back when you're ready, and I'll get it out."

"Okay, but wait for Winnie," Caleb instructed.

Caleb led Lori to the barn. Before entering, He turned and sat down on some bales of hay and patted on the unoccupied portion of hay next to him. Lori hesitated for a minute and then joined him. "What are we doing?" she asked.

Caleb looked at her and said, "Lori, I've been thinking; will you marry me?"

Lori stared at Caleb for a long moment. "Yes, I will," she stated.

"There you go. See, we got it figured out," Caleb said as he leaned in to receive a kiss.

Sarah hollered from the back porch, "Hey you guys, Winnie's up and wants dessert."

"Good thing we didn't need long," observed Caleb, as he arose from the hay bale.

"I know! But let's keep our engagement between us until we work things out, okay?"

"You're right. We certainly can't tell Sarah yet, or she will start cooking!"

"Well, Winnie might like that," observed Lori, as they approached the house.

FORTY-SIX

As Caleb drove to Casper's Grill on Monday morning, he had a lot on his mind. He was engaged! The significance of Lori's quick affirmative response to his proposal of marriage was not lost on him. It was stunning how it transpired so simply. He loved her, and he knew she loved him. That was real, and it was right here and now. Forty years of having a void in his soul that was now suddenly filled.

With all his happiness at the engagement, he was, nevertheless, full of questions. What would Daniel think? When should they tell people? When could they get married? Where would they live? How soon could he get a ring? It was making him dizzy. He knew in his heart and in his faith that all these things would be worked out, but in his mind, there was a tornado spinning.

Caleb contemplated perhaps the biggest issue—that of where they should live. Could he move to Las Vegas? Well, of course he could, but was that the right thing? Could Lori move here and give up her practice? How would she feel about that? Or should they go somewhere new? Too many questions. Leave it to the Lord and base it on Lori's desires. He could cope with anything the two of them came up with. So there! Then another question struck him. Does he continue with the renovations at the farm, and if so, in what direction? Daniel would have to know immediately, wouldn't he? Should he sell it as is, or fix it up first? Oh, jeez, what would Sarah think if he up and left after the happiness she expressed at having him home?

Caleb pulled off the road for a minute. Get a grip, he told himself. When you have a lot to do or a lot to decide, do it one thing at a time. That's what he always told the ranch hands. He would start by listening. To Lori and to the Lord. Even if it takes a while for them to figure it out. He would wait. He could go in about any direction if he could be with Lori and if she was happy. The rest would fall in place. Wouldn't it?

He told himself to just do it one day at a time. He had to meet Lonnie Rex and get on with their plans to see the contractor and get the station stuff over with. Caleb pulled on his ear to signify flushing his mind. Ka-whoosh! There, my brain is back on task. He proceeded to Casper's.

Lonnie Rex was leaning back against the wall in his usual seat in the back room where the smokers go. His head was chin down on his chest, and he was asleep. Caleb approached all stealthy-like and said, "Mornin' pard."

Lonnie didn't even move, and then after a long double second, he raised his head slightly and looked at Caleb. "Not yet it ain't a good morning. Where've you been?"

"Following my own schedule. Just like you do all the time. And I'm hungry."

"You didn't have to interrupt my nap to tell me that. Just order and eat. We have things to do. I'll be ready when you are."

Caleb sat down across from Lonnie. "I'm gettin' married!"

Lonnie looked up. "Well, ain't that a whack on the head! Done it twice myself. It's good fun. Now, pray tell, who are you marrying?" asked Lonnie.

"Don't act dumb, Lonnie. 'Course with you, it isn't all an act," reflected Caleb. "I'm engaged to Lori, dimwit. Asked her yesterday afternoon, and she said yes." At that point Caleb remembered that they had agreed to keep it quiet, and here he was telling it to the first person he saw. Maybe Lonnie didn't count. "Now that's confidential, Lonnie. You're the only one knows, and I want to keep it that way, agreed?"

Lonnie held up his hands in surrender. "I'll keep it. Now eat and let's go."

"Don't you want to know more?"

"I thought you said it was a secret. You going to keep talking about it?"

"It's you, Lonnie. I'm telling you. Just keep quiet, that's all."

Lonnie Rex stared at Caleb with a vacant look on his face. "This is me keeping quiet."

"Okay, nothing's been worked out yet, so I guess there isn't much to tell, but it's true."

"Then it's true. Got it. Tell me more when it ain't a secret. You're getting married. Simple secret. Save the details 'till you got 'em. Details might slip out. Now eat."

Caleb ordered his breakfast. "Are we going to call the contractor and go over?"

"Already did. I talked to him last night. He said to come early this morning, just like last time. They'll be off to a job mid-morning after getting all set," said Lonnie. "That Onofre character is back at work."

Caleb and Lonnie arrived at the contractor's yard by 9:00. There was a lot of activity as the workers loaded up some machinery and gathered tools. The office door opened, and Jersey Stone stepped out to greet them. This time he was accompanied by the owner, Dennis Chiles. Dennis introduced himself and asked what this was all about.

Lonnie Rex nodded toward Caleb.

"There's a simple version of the story and a detailed version. Which do you want?" asked Caleb.

"Let's go with simple first. Then we'll see," replied Dennis.

Caleb began. "Last week, we came out and talked to Javier. I speak Spanish. He told us about his brother Onofre being scared and leaving town. We're back to talk to Onofre and get the story. We're just trying to help," summarized Caleb.

As Dennis thought it over, Caleb thought that he appeared a bit wary of his story. Finally, Dennis said, "Yeah, well okay, maybe you can find out what's bothering Onofre. Those guys are tight-lipped, and it isn't just the language barrier. I guess it's okay."

Jersey took Caleb and Lonnie out to meet the brothers while Dennis returned to the office. Upon seeing them come, Javier brightened and spoke to another man with him. They greeted Javier and were introduced to Onofre. *"Este es mi hermano, Onofre."* (This is my brother, Onofre.)

"Buenos dias, Onofre. Soy Caleb." (Good morning, Onofre. I am Caleb.) *"Este es mi amigo, Lonnie,"* (This is my friend, Lonnie.) said Caleb.

"Si señor, buenos dias," (Yes sir, good morning.) replied Onofre.

Caleb turned to Jersey and asked, "Is there somewhere we can sit down? I think we should be comfortable as we talk. I don't want him to feel threatened."

"Sure. There's a picnic table over there under the shed roof. It's where the guys take breaks and have lunch."

Jersey led them over to the table, and they all sat down on the bench seats. Caleb resumed talking to Onofre. *"Javier dijo que tenias miedo de alguien,"* (Javier said that you were frightened of someone.) said Caleb.

"Si, señor. Es um hombre malo," (Yes sir. He is a bad man.) explained Onofre.

"Quien es este hombre?" (Who is this man?) asked Caleb.

"Su nombre es el Sr. Ashton. El es el dueno del edificio donde trabajamos." (His name is Mr. Ashton. He is the owner of the building where we worked.)

"Que trabajo hiciste por el?" (What work did you do for him?)

"Me pidio que le ayudara a desenterrar algo." (He had me help him dig something up.)

"Que has desenterrado?" (What did you dig up?)

"Era una caja de metal." (It was a metal box.)

"Que habia en la caja?" (What was in the box?)

"No vi el interior. Miro pero no me lo mostro.) (I didn't see inside. He looked but wouldn't show me.)

"Has quitado la caja del suelo?" (Did you remove the box from the ground?)

"Si. Lo pusimos en la parte trasera de su camion." (Yes. We put it in the back of his truck.)

"Has desenterado algo mas?" (Did you dig anything else up?)

"No. Solo la caja." (No, just the box.)

"Por que tienes miedo?" (Why are you frightened?)

Onofre appeared to form his thoughts, then proceeded, *"Me dio dinero. Mucho dinero. Al principio estaba contento, pero luego me dijo que tenia que irme de la ciudad. Dijo que me denunciaria a inmigracion si me volvia a ver, y que me enviarian. Me dijo que no se lo dijera a nadie."* (He gave me money. A lot of money. At first, I was pleased, but then he told me I had to leave town. He said that he would report me to immigration if he saw me again, and I would be sent away. He told me not to tell anyone.)

"Cuanto dinero te dio?" (How much money did he give you?)

"Mucho dolares. Casi 5000." (Many dollars. Almost 5,000.)

"De donde sacaba el dinero?" (Where did he get the money?)

"Creo que lo metia de la caja." (I think he got it out of the box.)

"Que hiciste a continuacion?" (What did you do next?)

"Me fui a casa. Luego sali de la ciudad y no hable con nadie." (I went home. Then I left town and didn't talk to anyone.)

"A donde fuiste?" (Where did you go?)

"A Branson. Hay trabajo alli, pero no es un buen trabajo." (To Branson. There is work there, but not good work.)

"Como supiste Javier donde estabas?" (How did Javier know where you were?)

"Despues de dos meses, lo llame. Dije que no se lo dijera a nadie. Pregunte si todavia trabajabamos para el Sr. Ashton." (After two

months, I called him. I said not to tell anyone. I asked if we still worked for Mr. Ashton.)

Caleb stopped and related the complete story to Lonnie Rex and Jersey.

Turning back to Onofre, Caleb continued the questioning. *"Que te dijo Javier?"* (What did Javier tell you?)

"Dijo que ya no trabajabamos alli y que me ocultaria. Penso que deberia volver." (He said that we no longer worked there, and that he would hide me. He thought I should come back.)

"Nos alegramos de que hayas vuelto. Veremos que no te pasa nada." (We are glad you came back. We will see that nothing happens to you.)

Turning to Javier, Caleb asked, *"Puedes ocultar a Onofre?"* (Can you hide Onofre?)

"Si. Vivimos en un remolque fuera de la ciudad. Creo que estamos a salvo." (Yes. We live in a trailer out of town. I think we are safe.)

"Bien. Ayudaremos." (Good. We will help.)

Javier paused and seemed to be unsure whether to continue. Finally, he said, *"Señor, hay mas en la historia."* (Sir, there is more to tell.)

"Que quieres decir?" (What do you mean?) asked Caleb.

"Preguntaste si Onofre desenterro algo mas?" (You asked if Onofre dug anything else up?)

"Si." (Yes.)

"Onofre no lo hizo. Pero cuando volvimos a trabajar en el sitio, desenterramos un cuerpo. Era muy viejo y estaba enterrado profunda mente." (Onofre did not. But when we went back to work at the site, we dug up a body. It was very old and buried deep.)

"Cuando?" (When?)

"Despues de que Onofre se fuera. Un par de semanas." (After Onofre left. A couple of weeks.)

"Lo sabe el jefe?" (Does the boss know?)

"Si, el lo sabe. Dijo que era muy viejo y que debia eliminarse." (Yes, he knows. He said it was old and must be disposed of.)

"Como lo hiciste?" (How did you do that?)

"*Lo cargamos en un camion y el jefe se lo llevo.*" (We loaded it into a truck, and the boss took it away.)

"*Te refieres a Dennis Chiles?*" (You mean Dennis Chiles?)

"*Si. El jefe.*" (Yes, the boss.)

"*A donde lo llevo?*" (Where did he take it?)

"*No se.*" (I don't know.)

"*Lo sabia el Sr. Ashton?*" (Did Mr. Ashton know?)

"*Creo que si. Los vi hablando. Dijeron que estaba bien. Dijeron que era solo un viejo cuerpo indio. Pero no lo creas.*" (I think so. I saw them talking. They said it was okay. They said it was just an old Indian body. But I don't think so.)

"*Por que no lo pensaste?*" (Why do you not think so?)

"*Dejame ensenartelo,*" (Let me show you.) said Javier. He got up and went over to his truck. While he was gone, Caleb told of what he had learned to Jersey and Lonnie. Both Jersey and Lonnie began to ask questions but were cut off by Javier's return. He was carrying some items wrapped in a roll of soiled paper towels. He placed the roll on the table and unwrapped it for all to see. The roll contained a tarnished sheriff's badge and a rusted pistol.

Jersey spoke up, "Are you crazy?! That wasn't no Indian! Why didn't you tell us?"

Javier was immediately frightened and withdrew the items.

Caleb turned to Jersey and said, "Stop. You're frightening him. We want the whole story."

"*Javier, no pasa nada. No estas en problemas. Donde los encontraste?*" (Javier, it's okay. You are not in trouble. Where did you find these?) asked Caleb.

"*Debajo del cuerpo cuando lo quitamos,*" (Under the body when we removed it.) explained Javier.

"*Se los mostraste a alguien?*" (Did you show these to anyone?)

"*No, nadie.*" (No, no one.)

"*Por que no?*" (Why not?)

"*Tenia miedo. Creo que el Sr. Ashton estaba enfadado con el jefe. Pense que podria hacerme algo si supiera que los tenia.*" (I was scared.

I think Mister Ashton was mad at the boss. I thought he might do something to me if he knew that I had them.)

"*Encontraste algo mas?*" (Did you find anything else?)

"*No. Pero me hice una foto con mi telefono.*" (No. But I did take a photo with my telephone.)

"*Donde esta la foto?*" (Where is the photo?)

"*En mi telefono. Te lo puedo ensenar,*" (On my phone. I can show you.) said Javier.

Javier took his phone out of his overalls and fumbled with it. Shortly he brought up a photograph of the body lying at the bottom of the dig. The body was significantly deteriorated, but the skeleton was intact. There were only a few vestiges of rotted cloth in various spots. The body lay face down, and it was possible to see that the skull had been cracked at the back of the head.

"*Javier, hiciste algo bueno. Estos son muy importantes,*" (Javier, you did a good thing. These are very important.) explained Caleb.

"*Siento no ha decirselo a nadie. Perdere mi trabajo?*" (I am sorry I didn't tell anyone. Will I lose my job?) asked Javier.

"*No, Javier. No dejaremos que te despidan. Pero tenemos que tomar todo esto y hacer una copia de la foto. No estaras en problemas.*" (No, Javier. We will not let them fire you. But we need to take all of this and make a copy of the photo. You will not be in trouble.)

"*Bien. No los quiero. Son de un hombre muerto.*" (Good. I don't want them. They are from a dead man)

Javier continued, "*Onofre no sabia nada de esto. Solo yo.*" (Onofre didn't know about this. Only me.)

"*Lo entendemos. Gracias, Javier,*" (We understand. Thank you, Javier.) said Caleb.

Caleb translated the latest exchange for the others. He emphasized that Javier should not be punished in any way. Finally, after looking at his watch, Caleb said, "It's time we all went to talk to Mr. Chiles."

FORTY-SEVEN

Before going into the office, Caleb and Lonnie conferred with Jersey Stone. He said that he wasn't even at the project site and knew nothing about any of the excavations at the site or the body or its removal. Jersey indicated that Onofre had worked "off the clock" for Dumar Ashton on a weekend and that the first excavation they mentioned didn't involve the company. They found Jersey believable and indicated that they needed to document the information that Javier had related and record the items recovered, including the gun, the badge, and the photograph. They instructed Jersey that this could be important evidence and must be documented. Jersey understood and agreed to help.

Caleb described what was needed. "Jersey, what we will do is prepare a letter listing what we learned today from Javier and what he and Onofre found. We will just include the facts and ask for your signature as a witness. Okay?"

"Yeah, sure."

"We can keep the gun, badge and phone, or let you keep them, but they must be safe," said Caleb.

Jersey thought for a minute. "Uh, why would you want to keep them? You're just translating. Isn't this company business or legal business?"

Caleb explained, "That's a very reasonable question. There are two reasons for us to keep the stuff. First, it is possible that Dennis has committed a bit of an illegality in removing the body. It's not much of a crime, and indications are that he didn't know about the badge or the gun, but it could still pose a difficulty for him, and we wouldn't want him to be tempted to mess with the evidence. With me so far?"

"Yeah, I guess, but there's been other times when we have uncovered bodies, so I'm not sure he would consider it wrong or illegal," said Jersey.

Caleb continued, "I understand, but there is another reason. This one is a long story, but let me summarize by saying that my uncle notified the city of an incident long ago that led to the death of the man uncovered at the site. In addition, he bequeathed a large amount of money to the city as part of his restitution for the incident. It is therefore the city's money. He also gave specific instructions as to where the money and the body could be found. It was at the construction site in the exact place where they were found, according to the Montoya brothers. It appears that the owner of the project, this Dumar Ashton, has behaved wrongly, maybe illegally, when he interfered with the recovery of both the money and the body. This story told by Javier and Onofre makes Ashton's activities suspect, and the badge and photo confirm it. If Ashton learns of this, I will feel better if the evidence is safe. We will turn it all over to the police."

"If you are turning it over to the police, then I guess it is okay. But I don't want it to be used to hurt the boss unnecessarily. I'm not sure he did anything wrong."

"Well, let's go in and talk to him, and give him all the facts. We can see what he says. We're not out to get him in trouble, but we must preserve this stuff properly," said Caleb. "What do you think, Lonnie Rex?"

"I'm with you. All out in the open. Sooner we get it to the police, the better. Dumar has committed a big no-no, and he should get no wiggle room."

"Jersey, we will type up a report or such and bring it by for your signature, and ours, Onofre's, Javier's, and maybe Dennis's if he agrees. That report will go to the police along with the badge. Fair enough?" asked Caleb.

"Yes, that sounds right. Although, I can type something up here. Wouldn't that be better?"

Caleb thought for a minute. "That's even better. Let's do that. Right after we talk to Dennis."

The three of them walked into the office lobby. Jersey stepped back to Dennis's office to tell him of the need to talk. Caleb and Lonnie could hear some muffled discussion between the two, and then Dennis stepped out in the hall and motioned to the small conference room. Jersey went into the room first, followed by Caleb and Lonnie Rex.

"Okay, what's this all about?" asked Dennis when all were settled.

"You got any coffee?" asked Lonnie. "I'm parched."

"Uh... sure," Dennis said irritably. "Sonia! Can you bring in some coffee? Maybe the pot. Please," he shouted to the secretary. Turning to the others, he said, "But let's get started. I've got a busy day. This about them illegals?"

Jersey jumped in first, "No, not exactly. It appears that Onofre did some work outside the company that led to his issues. It also appears that Javier Montoya has some information that is important to these gentlemen. Caleb, you tell him."

"Let me get the entire story out first, so you will have all the facts we have. I think that will save the most time and will lead to your understanding of what's involved."

"Alright, let's go," Dennis said impatiently. "Try to make it brief."

Ignoring Dennis's attitude, Caleb began to tell the story, beginning with his interview with Javier last week and then his interview with both Javier and Onofre this morning. He stuck to the facts and made no conjecture. In the process, he showed Dennis the rusted gun and the badge. In addition, he showed the photo on Javier's phone. After relating the recent events, Caleb summarized the history of the issue beginning with Warren's bequest to the city in the form of the money. Caleb left out the details of Warren's previous life, but he told all the facts since his arrival in Rogers.

As he talked, Dennis remained quiet. His stern and impatient demeanor at the beginning changed to an appearance of anger, then modified again to that of thoughtful concern. Finally, as Caleb finished, he had a resigned look on his face. There was silence in the room.

Caleb began again. "If you have questions or observations, we want to hear them. If not, I have a few questions I would like to ask."

Dennis looked up. "No, go ahead. I'm getting the picture."

"Have you worked with Dumar Ashton before?" asked Caleb.

"A few times. Each time, I swear it will be my last. The guy is difficult. But he pays his bills. With this story, however, it will be the last time I work with him."

"Why did you remove the body?" asked Caleb.

"A mixed bag. Finding old bones can slow down a project. So, we try to get rid of them if possible. They are only significant if they're historical in some way. If they are historical, which they rarely are, it can hold you up quite a while. The other reason is that Dumar pitched a fit. He threatened me. He said if we shut down because of some 'stupid dead Indian,' as he put it, then it would be the last project I did for him. He maintained I had no reason to think it was anything important and I should get it out of the way. In fact, he demanded it."

"Isn't there a process you are required to follow if you find something like this?" asked Caleb.

"Yes, there is. But sometimes we try to avoid it if we think it is nothing. I had no way of knowing what you are now telling me. My guys said it was some bones. I was beginning to look into it when Dumar showed up and made his stink. He didn't even want me to examine the bones, just get rid of them. He was very anxious and threatening. He said he would take full responsibility."

"What's the penalty for failing to report a discovery like this?"

"Generally, it's a fine. Small fine if it's what I thought this was. If it is a part of criminal intent, then the penalty could be more severe. Loss of your license all the way up to legal action. But I didn't know any of this. I just knew that we found some bones. I could be fined when this comes out, but based on my information at the time, a small fine is probably all."

"How about Dumar? Does he have liability?"

"Well, yes, he does. He is the owner of record. If he knew nothing about it, then probably no liability on his part. But if he knows, which he did here, then he could be liable for fines or more like I mentioned."

"Where did you dispose of the body?"

"I drove the truck out to the big landfill and dumped it. I watched it get buried by the dozer."

Pretty poor burial ground, thought Caleb.

"Was the body really that of a deputy sheriff?" asked Dennis.

"There's a lot more to the story, but yes, it appears that is true. There will be a full recounting of the story in the paper soon. There you can read all about it, or if you want, I will be happy to sit down with you and tell it all in more detail."

"Oh jeez, will this get into the paper? That's not going to look good."

"Yes, it will, in some form. I don't control that, but I will be giving many details to the paper, and I will try to be clear about the limits of your involvement. There are bigger fish in this pond of activity, and I don't think you will be focused on much. In fact, I fully believe your story, but you may get a visit from the police. I'll back you up on the facts," said Caleb.

"Thanks... I guess," responded Dennis.

Caleb continued, "Dennis, I promised Javier and Onofre that they would not be penalized in any way. They were doing what they were told by people they considered their boss. You're not thinking of firing them or anything are you?"

"That's the first thought I had earlier, but with the information I have been given, I won't do anything to penalize them. Maybe I should give them a raise to reassure them," admitted Dennis.

"I think that's a very good idea," said Caleb.

Dennis looked up at Caleb. "What are you going to do with this information and this stuff?"

"Jersey has offered to type up a report on everything that has happened here this morning, including what has been said and what has been found. He will do it now, we will all sign it, then I will take it, along with the gun, the badge and the photo, to the police. I don't think it will take long. Can I ask your secretary to print the photo off Javier's phone?"

"Sure. I'm on board. Jersey, take the time you need."

FORTY-EIGHT

Caleb and Lonnie Rex pulled out of the construction yard a little after noon. Jersey had worked hard on preparing a proper report on what they had found. Lonnie had suggested that they should put it all in the form of an affidavit to be signed by all. That had caused a lively dispute between Lonnie and Jersey on just how to spell affidavit. Each had a notion, but both were wrong. Before Caleb could speak up, Sonia, Dennis's secretary, intervened in the debate and instructed them on the proper spelling and format. When it was finally completed, all had signed it, and all the evidence was inserted, along with the affidavit, into a sealed box.

Lonnie asked Caleb, "Are we going to take this to the police right now?"

Caleb pondered the question. "I think we should do it soon, but I would sort of like to go see Peter and let him know the latest developments. I told him that this week I would tell him the latest, including the letter to the mayor. I was reluctant to violate the confidence relative to the letter to the mayor, but now I don't retain any of that reluctance. Let's go see Peter and then afterward, we'll get this stuff to the police."

"All this investigative activity has created a serious hunger on my part. It's well past noon, and I need some sustenance," declared Lonnie. "You want to eat?"

"That's a good idea. You got any food at your house?"

"You bet. We can raid the 'fridge and feed our faces in the embrace of the porch."

"Got any iced tea?"

"Of course not, but we can make some."

"You got tea bags?"

"Nope."

"I'll pull into the grocery store, and we'll get some. I've gotta have some tea."

As Caleb arrived at the grocery store, Lonnie said, "I'll wait here in the truck and have a smoke. If you're going in, go ahead and get some lunch meat and bread, and maybe some chips and maybe some pickles. Also, they have some good potato salad. Get that too."

"I thought you said you had something to eat at the house," challenged Caleb.

"I said we could raid the 'fridge, but I have no idea what's in there. Jaws Two shops for me occasionally, but she's been sort of tardy lately. Pays to be safe."

"Oh, for… okay, I'll get the stuff. You sure you don't want dessert?"

"That's a good idea. They have some cherry pies that are pretty good. And maybe a large bottle of Dr. Pepper," said Lonnie Rex. "Also, get some toilet paper. I'm about out."

"Just wait here and roll the window down if you're going to smoke," Caleb said in exasperation.

"You got it. Hurry up, I'm getting mighty hungry."

━━

Once Lonnie and Caleb had prepared their plates in Lonnie's kitchen, they moved to the porch and relaxed while they ate. Both were lost in thought at what they had discovered that morning. Lonnie finished off another pickle and then belched as a preamble to his next words. He looked at Caleb and said, "You know, we got the goods on ol' Dumar. That guy is one slimy dude. I wonder what he did with the money. What do you think?"

"I have no idea. Coulda hid it or deposited it. I guess he would have to deposit it in order to use it. But, you know, that's not my worry. I say let the police unravel the whys and wherefores. I just want it off my plate. I got other things to do."

"Oh, yeah. You're getting married. How's that going to play out?"

"Nicely, I hope, but I need to talk to Lori and work it all out. I won't see her until tomorrow. That's when we're going to meet and let Daniel tell us what he has done with the farm renovation. That'll be interesting, for sure."

"Just fix it up nice. If you stay here, you're fixed, and if you move and sell it, you'll probably get a good price. Of course, I hope you stay here," Lonnie admitted.

"We'll see. I'll let you know as it unravels. First thing I gotta do is buy a ring. I didn't plan the proposal and wasn't properly prepared. I should go look for one today and give it to her tomorrow. Of course, it would be nice to know whether Daniel approves. I don't know—too much to think about."

Changing the subject, Lonnie asked, "When you going to call Peter?"

"Right after we eat. In fact, I can do it now."

Caleb went to the truck and retrieved his phone out of the console. As he came back on to the porch, he looked at his phone and realized that he had a message from Sarah. As he sat down, he told Lonnie about Sarah's call and dialed her number. Caleb let it ring to no avail. That was no surprise. Sarah spent a good part of the day on the phone with her various lady friends. He imagined her in deep analysis of some urgent worry about something neither Sarah nor her caller knew anything about. She would call back once they had settled the troubling issue.

To his surprise, his phone rang immediately. When he answered, Sarah began right in, "I was on the phone but hung up immediately to call you. Where are you?"

"I'm at Lonnie's house. Just had lunch. What's up?"

"Well, the chief of police called this morning. He wanted to talk to you. He said it was urgent. I told him that you were out but I would call you and have you call him. He seemed insistent that he get in touch with you. What's that all about? What do you think he wants?"

"Sarah, I haven't called him yet. You just told me. I'll call him and let you know, okay?"

"He seemed quite anxious. He's waiting for your call. Are you going to call him now?"

"Yep."

"Good. Let me know," instructed Sarah.

"Sarah."

"Yeah."

"Did he leave a number?"

"Yes, don't you have it?"

"No, I do not."

"Here it is," she said as she related the number. "Give him a call."

"Will do. Bye. Talk to you later," said Caleb as he hung up.

Caleb turned to Lonnie and told him what Sarah had said. Then he returned to his phone and dialed the number Sarah had supplied. It turned out to be a direct line to the chief, as Caleb discovered when the call was answered immediately with, "Chief Blaylock speaking."

"Chief, this is Caleb Atwood returning your call. What can I do for you?"

"Caleb. Yes, I need to speak with you soon. Is it possible for us to meet this afternoon?"

"Sure. I can come by in a little while. What time is good for you?"

"Can you make it by 3:00 p.m.?"

Caleb consulted his watch as he contemplated his answer. He quickly decided to hear what the chief wanted before speaking of what he and Lonnie had found. "Yes sir. 3:00 p.m. is fine. I'll be there."

Caleb turned to Lonnie and said, "Looks like Peter will have to wait. The chief of police wants to see me at 3:00 p.m."

"Well, you want to see him too. Do you want me to go?"

"No. I've got a funny feeling. He seemed very insistent. Something is up. If the mayor had called to tell me what had or had not been found, that would have been what I would have expected. But if the mayor has involved the police, then I don't know what to think. I intend to be quiet and hang on to everything until I know what is going on. Probably best if you stay here."

"What if it's about the bowling ball caper?" asked Lonnie Rex.

Caleb just stared at Lonnie, then laughed. "I sorta doubt that, but if it is, I'll give you a call. I won't take the fall for that."

"You'll squeal on me, won't you?"

"In an instant!"

"I smell a nap. Call me if you need reinforcements," declared Lonnie Rex.

FORTY-NINE

Caleb walked into the office of the chief of police a few minutes before 3:00 p.m. It appeared to be a quiet Monday. There were no handcuffed criminals waiting for interrogation or other distractions. In fact, the entire atmosphere was serene and professional. The receptionist, or dispatcher or whatever you called her, looked up at Caleb with an inquiring smile. "Can I help you?"

"Yes ma'am. I'm here to see Chief Blaylock. We have a 3:00 p.m. meeting. My name is Caleb Atwood," he informed her.

"Wait here, please."

Caleb was becoming rather anxious to find out what this was all about. There didn't seem to be any urgency in the demeanor of the receptionist. She didn't even know who he was, it appeared. He wondered what the chief knew—if he even knew about the station or the letter to the mayor. But he must, Caleb reasoned, otherwise why get involved? He took a seat and decided that he would find out soon enough. As he sat, his mind wandered back to Lori. Tomorrow they would be together, and it would be a good time to give her a ring. Make it official. He would have to take the time to go shopping, then he thought that maybe he should take her with him and let her pick it out. That was a good idea. Break the news to Daniel first and then proceed. Let Lori take control. That should work.

His thoughts were interrupted when the receptionist returned and asked Caleb to follow her. She led him down a corridor to the chief's office. The chief was sitting at his desk and rose to greet Caleb in a friendly way.

"Thanks for coming in, Mr. Atwood," the chief said. "My name is Chief Blaylock, Delvin Blaylock. Won't you have a seat?" He gestured at a chair opposite his desk. After shutting the door, the chief returned to his desk where he sat down and looked steadily at Caleb.

"What's up, chief?"

"Mr. Atwood, there has been a complaint lodged against you. As such, I must investigate the matter and decide on a course of action. In that regard, I would like to schedule a formal meeting during which we can get to the bottom of the complaint."

Caleb was taken aback. "What sort of complaint?"

"It has to do with the recent letter you gave to the mayor. I think it was from your uncle, Warren Atwood."

"That's right. I delivered the letter last week, as Warren requested. It was delivered to the mayor in confidence. I assume the mayor has shown you the letter," responded Caleb.

"Yes, he has. The complaint has to do with the information in the letter and the subsequent efforts on the city's part to confirm the contents."

"Why is there a complaint? I merely delivered a letter."

"The city expended considerable resources following up on the letter and, in so doing, we have caused some hardship and costs to be experienced by persons involved."

"Who are these 'persons involved' if I may ask?"

"That's not for me to reveal currently. I simply want to collect all the facts concerning what has transpired and ultimately find out if we think the complaint has merit."

"I'll be happy to assist you in any way I can. How do you want to proceed?"

"I suggest that a meeting be held with the participants, at which time we can get all our questions answered. We should meet here at the station, at which time you will be instructed about the nature of the complaint, and you can respond to our inquiries. I must inform you that the complaint, if true, is potentially serious and could involve fraudulent or criminal behavior on your part. You must treat this as a serious matter."

"I see. That's fine. I will answer any questions or supply any information I have at that time," promised Caleb.

"It's important that we do this sooner rather than later. I understand that you recently came back to Rogers and have no current residence."

"That's not true. There were two letters. Have you also seen the first one—the one addressed to me?"

"Yes, I have."

"Then you undoubtedly know that I inherited a farm in Pea Ridge. That is now my legal residence. I am currently staying with my sister, Sarah Westridge, until I get the farm renovated with some much-needed repairs."

"Is it your intent to remain in Rogers?"

"Yes, that was and is my intent. However, I recently have become engaged. The lady I am engaged to lives in another city, and we have yet to discuss where we will permanently locate. I will certainly remain here until things are worked out and probably until I complete the work at the farm. So, I should be here for a good while, if not permanently."

"So, congratulations. Is it your first marriage?"

"Yes, it is."

"Then it is in everyone's interest to get this cleared up as soon as possible. We would like to schedule the meeting, I think perhaps it is more like a hearing, for later this week. When are you available?"

"Let me ask a few questions if I may. I have no problem with the meeting or hearing or whatever, however I will want to bring all the information I have to the meeting. That will be allowed, right?"

"Of course. Bring whatever you have that can shed any light on your activities."

"Good, but in order to know what to bring, I should know the nature of the complaint, don't you think?"

The chief thought for a minute. "It is our procedure to do the questioning before revealing the nature of the complaint. However, I can tell you something about it if that helps you prepare."

"Alright. I'm listening."

"It is being alleged that your activities and the letters you delivered have caused damage to the city and certain individuals. There is an allegation that you have undertaken to make fraudulent claims to the city for reasons unknown, and that those claims have caused the damage experienced."

"Who makes these claims?"

"The city for one. The mayor feels that the letters contained false information."

"Just the city?"

"There is also a private party involved who joins in the complaint."

"Will these, how do you say, complainants be present at the meeting or hearing?"

"Yes. That is our intent. I will allow them to supply the information they have as it relates to their complaints."

"Thank you for explaining that. And in that regard, I can prepare accordingly. Will I be allowed to supply all the information I have at my disposal?"

"Of course. I already said so. We expect that."

"And if that information includes witnesses on my behalf, will that be allowed?"

"Well, perhaps. I mean I didn't think that you would have witnesses, but if it helps clear it up, then of course."

"In that case, I would like to have until next week to prepare. I think I know what I need, and it will take a little while to get it together. Can I suggest Tuesday of next week?"

"That's a little longer than I had in mind. What takes so long?"

"Are you prepared to charge me with a crime?"

"Not at this point. I'm just investigating."

"And I'm just cooperating. But I need to do it in a manner which will resolve the issue quickly. That will take me until next Tuesday."

The chief considered the timing. Finally, he said, "Alright. Next Tuesday, June 14, will work, I think. I will check with the complainants, and if there are no problems, then we will meet on that day. Let's say 2:00 p.m., here at the station in the conference room. Please be here and be prepared to respond to all the allegations. We have your number if there are any changes."

"That will work for me," said Caleb.

"I now must request that you not leave the vicinity. You must remain available as we have discussed. Do you understand?"

"Absolutely. I'm not going anywhere."

"There is one other matter. It has come to the attention of the mayor that this story has been leaked to the newspaper. Is that true?"

"I don't know whether 'leaked' is the proper term. But yes, the paper is aware of some of the story—the background at least—but is not aware of the letter to the mayor or its contents. The paper has done its own research into the story based on the history of the issue, that is all. For instance, it has been determined through research that, in fact, one Hollis Bivens did disappear back when, just as my uncle alleged. Everything that Warren Atwood asserted to me has checked out based on what I know. I have no reason to doubt what he claimed. The paper has supplied some of the research I have relied on in order to be firm in my beliefs. I have only requested that the paper hold on the story until all the facts are in."

"It would be a good idea for the hold on the story to remain in place. If the complaints are with merit, news reports, especially uninformed ones, might exacerbate the potential damages."

"I can understand. However, I have no control over the news as reported by the paper. I can reinforce my request of the paper to hold on any publication since there may be more to the story. And I will suggest the paper should do so to avoid any unwarranted damage. I'm sure the paper would agree and not want to print falsehoods."

"Then you have been informed, and we are agreed."

"Can I make one further request?"

"What is it?"

"I would like to have the district attorney present at the meeting. Henry Dawes."

"I will see that his presence is required."

"Thank you. I'll see you Tuesday," said Caleb as he rose to leave.

Caleb left the police department offices and got in his truck. When he got in, he opened the console and took out his phone. First, he placed a call to Peter, and when he got through, he said, "Peter, how are you?"

"I'm fine, Caleb. What's up?"

"It's time to bring you into the loop. There have been some developments, and I want to get all the information to you. Don't print anything until we meet. When would be a good time?"

"Oh, about any time. I'm not going to print anything. I want the whole story. How soon can we get together?"

"Tomorrow I am busy in the morning. Can you come over to Lonnie Rex's house in the late afternoon, say about 5:00 p.m.?"

"Uh, yeah, I guess. Why can't we do it here at my office?"

"I just want to be very careful and meet at Lonnie's. Keep it very private. Alright?"

"I'll be there. Do I need to bring anything?"

"Nope. Just your brain," concluded Caleb. "See you then."

After hanging up, he called Lonnie. The phone rang a few times before Lonnie answered. "Hello, this better be good!"

"I don't know about good, but it's sure interesting," said Caleb.

"What's up?"

"I met with the chief of police. He says there has been a complaint lodged against me. They want to have a meeting to get answers. I agreed to next Tuesday."

"What kind of a complaint?"

"I'll tell you all about it, but for now I just want to have a meeting with Peter. I said we should meet at your house tomorrow at 5:00 p.m. Does that work for you?"

"Oh, I think I can fit you into my busy schedule. Is it just us and Peter?"

"Yes, that's all. Just us."

"Sounds good. If that's it, I'm going to finish my nap."

"Have at it. If we meet for breakfast, I'll fill you in before I meet Lori and Daniel."

"Casper's it is. I'll be in my usual spot."

"Good. I'll see you then."

Caleb started his truck and headed for Sarah's. He would have a lot of questions to answer, so he might as well get started.

FIFTY

Over breakfast the next morning, Caleb related the story of his meeting with the chief of police to Lonnie Rex. He explained it in detail and added that he assumed that Dumar was the other "private" complainant. He could see how stopping the project and doing the search on site for the buried remains of Hollis and the buried money would take time and cost a bit to complete. Obviously, if they had found what Claude predicted, then the cost of the search would be small by comparison. And, therefore, no complaint. Since he and Lonnie now knew that the items had been removed by Dumar, then that meant that Dumar had lied to the city by not informing them of the find. Therefore, Dumar's "complaint" was a subterfuge to disguise the fraud. What is it they say, "a good offense is the best defense," or is it the reverse? One thing was clear. Caleb and Lonnie had the proof that Dumar was lying.

Caleb told Lonnie that he was less sure about the mayor. One possibility was that the mayor believed Dumar knew nothing and concluded that there was no money or body. In that instance, joining a complaint against Caleb would make sense. In addition, the mayor could also be motivated by avoiding any publicity that might expose his investment in the project and his subsequent "collusion" on getting the project approved. However, if the mayor knew Dumar was lying and participated in the lie, then he would be in real legal jeopardy. In that case, the mayor would also go along with a complaint and certainly an effort to keep it out of the papers. So, a complaint by the mayor was not a conclusive indication of the level of the mayor's guilt, if any. It was baffling.

After listening to Caleb's explanation, Lonnie asked, "So, what do we do with the stuff we found?"

"There are two possibilities. One is that we go ahead and turn it over to the Chief and let him do his investigation. It will show Dumar's guilt, probably expose the exact role of the mayor, and clear the complaint against me."

"And number two?" asked Lonnie.

"We keep the stuff and only expose it when we have the meeting or hearing. That should also get me off the hook, and then the chief can do what he will with Dumar and the mayor."

"Either way, you get free of the complaint, right?"

"Right."

"Which way do you want to go?" asked Lonnie.

"Legally, I think we should give it over now, and let law enforcement handle it. But that leaves me with a big concern. What if the city, along with the mayor and the chief and even Dumar all conspire to cover it up? They could let me off the hook and not prosecute the case while putting pressure on the paper to not run any story exposing what we know. All in exchange for me, and us, keeping quiet."

"Personally, I think that's a strong possibility. It's hard to trust the law when they might be part of the crime," observed Lonnie.

"I know. We see so much of that nowadays with government at all levels. When they control the story, anything can happen. Dumar has influence with the mayor, the mayor invested and colluded at the very least, and the chief owes his job to the mayor. They could spin the story in any number of ways to protect themselves," claimed Caleb.

Lonnie thought as he lit another cigarette. "It doesn't seem right to risk letting Dumar get away unscathed. We know that he has the money, right? That's like, what, $300,000 or more? And we know that he pressured the contractor, and we know that he extorted Onofre. In addition, it appears that he cheated Vernon out of the real value of the property. He's a real crook. He could walk away, and if the mayor is in on it all the way, then he's corrupted too."

"That settles it. I can't let them get control. I'm not going to turn in the evidence yet. I must keep some kind of control and get cleared in the process."

"I'm with you," said Lonnie.

Caleb reflected for a moment. "There's one other issue. I had the chief promise to have the DA in the meeting. You know, Henry Dawes. I asked for him to be there because I wanted someone in the meeting that wasn't part of any conspiracy, if there is one. I don't really know him, but he seems like an okay guy. On top of that, he is the DA and would have some say if there is any prosecution of Dumar, maybe even the mayor. He should see the evidence at the same time as the chief and others. No deniability."

"Like I said before, I don't really know him, but he seems straight. Angela, his wife, is Lori's friend. Maybe you should ask what she knows," suggested Lonnie.

"I don't want to get Lori involved, and it's a done deal anyway. The DA's in," explained Caleb.

"You wouldn't be getting her involved. Just tell her you liked him and ask what she thinks."

"Maybe, but if I talk to her about this, it will only be with the total truth," said Caleb. "Besides, she may not want to marry me if I go to jail!" Caleb laughed.

"If you go to jail, then I'll marry her. She should be done with me by the time you get out. None of them seem to last very long."

"Real funny, Lonnie, real funny. Sometimes your friendship is questionable."

"Hey, I'm just saying—I'm here for you!" claimed Lonnie.

Caleb looked at his watch. "I've got to pick Lori up at 8:00 a.m. If we get done with the farm, I might want to take her to look for a ring. Where should I go?"

"Tiffany's in New York?"

"No, really."

"You're asking the wrong hombre. I don't think I ever shopped for jewelry. It's kind of against everything in my nature."

"Didn't you buy rings for your wives?"

"Not me. They went, picked it out, and I paid for it. I stayed on the porch. Walaa!"

"Quite the romantic, aren't you?"

"Hey, they shopped all over. I didn't go, and I didn't interfere. Just paid for it. You should see some of the crapola they bought," pleaded Lonnie. "They were happy!"

"Thanks for the input. Now I'm going. I'll meet you and Peter at 5:00 p.m. at your house. We can talk it over and see what he thinks. No one else is to be involved; just us," instructed Caleb.

"Don't forget, I've got iced tea. I'll brew some up. Where did you put it?" Lonnie asked.

"Somewhere in the kitchen. Just look for it, okay?"

"Will do. See you at five. I'll be in the hammock."

FIFTY-ONE

Caleb arrived at Winnie's house on time. Lori was sitting on the porch waiting for him. As he got out of the truck, Lori came down to him and halted his progress by giving him a big hug. When she released Caleb from her hug, she held onto his arms and said, "I must tell you before we go in. I told Daniel about us getting married."

"You did?" Caleb asked with only a small level of surprise in his voice.

"Yes. I know we said we would keep it a secret for now, but he needs to know, and I needed to know how he feels."

"Well, sure. I understand that. And I must admit that I told Lonnie Rex," Caleb admitted.

"You did?" Lori responded with her own surprise.

"I had breakfast with him, but I made him promise not to tell."

"Have you told anyone else?" Lori asked.

"Uh, well, as a matter of fact, I was talking to Sarah last night and she was asking so many questions, and you know how that makes me get disoriented, and I guess I let it slip. But she won't tell."

"You seriously believe that Sarah won't tell her friends? How could she resist? She could be worse than Winnie!"

"You told Winnie too?"

"She pried it out of me. She seemed to know anyway."

Caleb paused for a moment. "Alright, let me get this straight—we told each other that we wouldn't tell anyone until we were ready, but each of us has told every human being we have encountered since last night. Is that right?" Caleb said and laughed.

"Yeah. That's about it."

"Neither of us could resist, huh?" Caleb observed.

I guess not, but I just had to tell Daniel. I really needed his approval and, on top of that, how can we have a discussion with him this morning about the farm unless we let our plans factor in?"

"I can't argue with that. I had the same question in my mind," admitted Caleb. "What did he think?"

"He just studied me for a moment and then said that he thought it was great. I could tell his wheels were spinning in his head, so I pressed him. It turns out that he has plans of his own and our getting married was a positive. He was happy!" said Lori.

"That's wonderful! What about Gwen?"

"Oh, yeah. I called her too," Lori said sheepishly.

"So now, Nevada knows."

"Well, some of it."

"Clearly neither of us should ever work for the CIA," said Caleb.

Daniel stepped out on the porch and asked, "Are we ready to go? I've got my stuff."

Caleb and Lori both looked up at Daniel. "We sure are ready. I'm looking forward to what you have developed," Caleb told him. "Let's look at it out at the farm, okay?"

"Let me get my sweater. I'll be right out," Lori said as she disappeared into the house.

After she went in, Winnie appeared at the door. She haltingly opened the door and took a few measured steps out to the porch rail. She looked appraisingly at Caleb, and said, "It looks like you two didn't waste any time in heeding my words. It's always wonderful to see people so blessed with intelligence! Now stay smart as you work this all out. Obviously, you have my blessing!"

"Thanks, Winnie. We might have gotten it done without you, but your pronouncements had a great ring of truth."

"I know, I know, now get on with it. You're burning daylight, as Joshua used to say." With that parting comment, Winnie shuffled back inside.

Caleb went to get into the truck and noted that Daniel climbed in the back, preserving the front seat for Lori. It seemed like it was Daniel's endorsement of them as a couple. And it felt good.

While they waited for Lori, Daniel said to Caleb, "I think it's great about you and mom."

"Thanks, Daniel. She seems happy. I know I am."

As they drove out to the farm, Caleb wanted to know more about what Lori had said about Daniel's new plans. This was a new item to be added to the list of questions in his mind. He really hadn't had much time to talk with Daniel about his future, and now that there were wedding plans in the making for him and Lori, he couldn't resist the urge to find out more about what Daniel was thinking about doing.

"So, Daniel. Lori mentioned that you had some new plans. What are you thinking?"

"Only one thing for sure. I'm not going to Berkeley in the fall. I don't find myself looking forward to any of that. I was never sure. This summer has given me a chance to think a lot, and I have made up my mind."

"So, what are you thinking of doing?"

"It's up in the air at this point. There are a few things that I know for sure, and they should figure into what I decide. In the first place, I do not want to go to a big city. That holds no appeal. I like the less crowded areas and the small-town atmosphere

here. I'm sure it's like that many places, but it just appeals to me. I also have realized how much I like building—construction and design. I've always liked it, and working on your farm, even though it's a small project, has been very revealing to me. I could see myself involved in construction in some form. I know how much I love to draw, and I think that I would also like the actual building. I don't think that you and mom getting married really figures in, but it feels good to think that you both will be together and maybe here."

"Your mom and I haven't even talked about where we will go. We might end up in Las Vegas just as likely. Your mom's got a successful business there, and that might be hard to leave. We haven't decided anything."

"Oh, I know. Wherever you guys end up is fine by me. I can go anywhere I want. The money I have for Berkeley will serve me at any school if I choose to do that."

Lori chimed in, "What do you mean 'if I choose to do that?' You're still planning on college, aren't you?"

"Yes, I am. But I might work a year or so and then go, or if I can decide now, I can just go in the fall. I should tell you that I have contacted the University of Arkansas about this fall. I can get in without any problem, and I understand that they have a good architectural school. Maybe that is of interest. I need to look into it further."

Continuing, Daniel said to Caleb, "You went to the University of Arkansas, didn't you Caleb?"

"Yes, I did. Only for two years, and then I dropped out of school and of the law. I decided I didn't like the law, regardless of the school. But I did like the University of Arkansas. It's not as large as so many of those state schools, and Fayetteville was fun. Of course, this was my home area, so it's not surprising that I liked it. The law just wasn't for me," said Caleb without getting into the details of his mother's illness and his father's needs.

"What was the architecture school like?" asked Daniel.

"Well, I was there in '77 and '78. I remember that the architecture school was in the old library in the center of campus. The university had built a new library a few years before that, and the old one went to the architects. It's right in the center of campus. They're still in there as far as I know. A couple of my friends were in architecture at the time, and they seemed to think the program was great. But I don't know about nowadays," replied Caleb. "It would be easy to go visit the school and check it out."

"Would you mind taking me down there? We flew out, and I don't have my car. I'm reluctant to borrow Winnie's van. She gets worried about stuff and would just sit there and vibrate if I drove away in it."

"That's no problem. Might be kind of fun to go back and look around."

Daniel touched Lori on the shoulder and asked, "Actually mom, it might be a good idea for me to fly back with you and get my car and come back. Once you leave, I'll be sort of stranded. I didn't realize how worried Winnie gets about her van."

"I understand. We never thought when we came out here that you would be staying longer. I can get you a ticket and we can go together. But I'm leaving tomorrow. Will that work?"

"Sure. The sooner the better. That will make it possible to get things done."

"You mean you're both going to abandon me?" Caleb lamented.

Lori reached over and squeezed Caleb's arm. "Just for a little while."

Dickie and Estes were hard at work when they arrived at the farm. Caleb noted they were moving down the fence line replacing as they went. The pasture could be ready for Cisco soon, and that meant that he could come out and work on the house and give Cisco a frequent workout. He was also aware that they had done some demolition of the old kitchen cabinets. They were indeed making good progress. He would need to decide on the full extent of the renovation to stay ahead of them and make full use of their time. Well, that was what he was here for.

Daniel spread out his drawings and notes on the old table as Caleb and Lori moved over some chairs. Caleb noted that there were a great many sketches and some various plan views of different approaches. He decided to be quiet and let Daniel go through everything fully. Lori was obviously of the same opinion as she waited expectantly.

Daniel looked at both of them, then began, "When Caleb and I first talked about this, I thought that I should look at maybe two approaches. One would be minimalist, just a simple renovation to provide for Caleb's basic lifestyle, and another would explore how to expand the house in a way that would appeal well into the future. Caleb gave me a budget and even the expanded plans take that into account."

"Now, as we look at these plans, we must recognize a new twist. When you two get married and decide where to live, it will affect what we do here. For a plan to be good, it must take into account your needs. If you decide to live here, then the expanded plan may be more in the direction you want to go. You're building your home. If you plan to live elsewhere but keep this farm, then maybe it is more minimal and accommodating for short visits only. Sort of a get-away. And if you decide to sell the farm, then the only decision to make is how much you do to put it on the market. It becomes a speculative venture to obtain the best sale price.

"Let me explain the plans so far, and then we can determine the direction you want to go. I think it best to let me give a complete overview first, and then we can discuss the options."

Daniel selected a plan and some sketches of his "minimalist" approach.

"In this scheme you will see that I have basically cleaned up or rebuilt what is here. There is a small expansion of the house to the rear next to the master bedroom. It contains a very small office area next to the master bedroom with some expanded storage including new closets. Getting the old closets out of the bedroom makes more room. The other bedroom remains as is but refurbished. In this approach, there is still just one bathroom with new fixtures. The kitchen is completely redone with all new cabinets and appliances. The laundry stays where it is but utilizes an over-and-under washer and dryer, which gives more storage. There is a small porch added to the back, and the front porch is kept like it is with paint and cleanup. I'm thinking all new windows throughout. And of course, the heating and air conditioning systems need to be redone."

Caleb and Lori remained quiet as they studied the plans. Daniel shuffled the drawings on the table to display the other scheme.

"Now in this plan, I have tried to take every advantage suggested by the existing house and make it much more of a complete residence. You will note here how I have proposed two major additions to the house. It makes a basic "U" shape that embraces a completely new back porch, all covered and screened in. There are two new wings, one small and one large. The large wing provides a new master bedroom and bath with plenty of closets and storage. The existing large bedroom is planned as a combination music room and sitting room off the new master bedroom. The existing bathroom is retained but fixed up, and the existing small bedroom becomes an office. Now, to provide for guests, there is the other wing at the other end of the house next to the kitchen with access to the main dining and living area. This wing contains a bedroom and bathroom suite with closets and provides a small laundry room. That gets the laundry out of the kitchen and makes for a better kitchen, which is refurbished like in the other scheme. Also note that the back porch between the two new wings is rather large and allows for a lot of outdoor living. The front porch is fixed up with new railings and steps."

"That's the two approaches. The floor is now open for discussion," declared Daniel.

Caleb spoke first. "Daniel, this is really a good start. It is clear that we must make some decisions before we go much further. I like both schemes for their intended application. From my view, the minimal scheme is only good for a sale or if we want to keep this place as a part-time residence. I can't see us living in it permanently. The "grand" scheme is great! I can see us living in that one full-time. About anybody could. What do you think Lori?"

"Okay. This has been a time of fast-moving changes and big decisions. Not what I expected when I simply came to a reunion. But I came to find you, Caleb, and I did. Now we are already down the road. The wind is whistling in our hair as we speed along. I can't find the inclination to apply the brakes. So, this is what I think."

Lori paused and continued, "We are getting married. We are going to live together. We should not live in Las Vegas—I don't like it, you won't like it, and Daniel is moving on. We should live here, where we have roots, where we have a farm, and where we like it. In addition, Cisco won't like Las Vegas, and he certainly will like it here. That's what I think."

"What about your veterinarian practice?"

"I'll go back and continue the practice. As I do, I will plan on how to sell it. Even if we never got back together, I would be selling it before long. I'll retire or do something out here. Sick animals are everywhere. I'm excited, hopeful, and confident all rolled into one. That's what I think."

"Wow, we sure are having trouble making decisions, aren't we?" Caleb teased.

"They're being made for us, are they not?" smiled Lori.

"I think so."

"Now before you get the wrong idea, I am going to have plenty to say about this plan that Daniel has developed. I can see a lot of things that I want to consider. Daniel, you have only be-gun to work."

"Alright, alright, alright!" said Daniel.

FIFTY-TWO

As expected, Lonnie Rex was asleep in the hammock when Caleb arrived for their meeting with Peter. It was a bit before 5:00 p.m., so Caleb thought to wake Lonnie and get him alert. He had formed a rough plan in his mind and wanted to get Lonnie's and Peter's input. Especially Peter. Caleb wasn't quite sure how to proceed and thought Peter could supply some needed advice.

Caleb had taken Lori and Daniel home just after a late lunch. Lori had talked almost nonstop while they ate. She had many suggestions for Daniel to consider as he proceeded to develop the plans for the farm. Caleb had listened intently and was very pleased at all the details that Lori brought to the effort. His greatest joy was how quickly and completely Lori had made her decision. It had answered the questions he had been pondering, and he knew that her commitment was total. She was a wonder.

Caleb had to remind them that they were going back to Las Vegas tomorrow and she needed to get Daniel a ticket. He also made the point that work on the farm would not progress until Daniel returned. Lori and Daniel considered that fact but returned to their discussions, nevertheless. Lori felt that they might even get a little work done while they were in Las Vegas. She wanted to show Daniel what furniture or major items would eventually make their way to the farm and had to be considered in the development of any new plans. Lori did stop long enough to make a call and get a ticket for Daniel for the return trip.

Lori's take control attitude toward the farm renovations might make most men feel a little loss of control, but it didn't affect Caleb that way. Not at all. He was pleased to follow along and share their pleasure with their new project. As he listened, he never heard anything that would give him any concern. Perhaps it was because having a full home like this was a first for him, but he also knew just how adaptable he was. If Lori got it the way she wanted, he could fit in fine. Nothing that had been said gave him concern about the budget either. It was probably going a little over what he and Daniel had originally talked about, but he knew he could provide the additional funds required.

Caleb's only concern was relative to Lori's sale of her practice. He wondered how long that would take and whether she could really make her peace with it. They had yet to address just when the wedding would take place, or where, for that matter. It didn't matter to Caleb; he would be ready.

The wedding plans, even though they weren't happening yet, had caused Caleb to think again about the need to get a ring. The idea that they should shop together didn't appeal to him at all. This was his one chance to find and give the gift of a lifetime. He wanted to do it alone the more he thought about it. Lori was consumed with everything right now, and he had some time after she went back. He would take that time to find a ring. That's the way it should be.

Lonnie Rex snorted and caused Caleb to return his attention to the present. A quick glance at his watch told him that they had less than twenty minutes until Peter's arrival.

"Hey Lonnie," Caleb yelled. "Up and at 'em. Peter will be here soon."

Lonnie muttered, "Good. I'm here." Then he stretched and, opening both eyes, he started to enter consciousness. "Where have you been?"

"You know where I've been—at the farm with Lori. We've been getting it worked out."

"Getting what worked out?"

"We figured out what to do with the farm," said Caleb.

Lonnie got up and shuffled over to the rocking chair. He yawned and looked around for his cigarettes. Finding a crumpled pack under his chair, he retrieved them and turned his attention to Caleb.

"So, what are you going to do to the farm?"

"We decided! We're going to live there. Lori decided right away. She's going to sell her practice and move here. To the farm. With me."

"You still getting married?"

"Of course. What else?"

"Can I be your best man?"

"Absolutely. Who else would I have?"

"You make it sound like I got the job by default."

"You did. I mean, who else do I have as a very best friend?"

"Alright, I reckon I'll do it. Do I have to dress up?"

"Probably. Now wake up and get ready for Peter."

"I made some tea. Looked strong. I used ten of the big tea bags. Fix it however you want; I just want some more Dr. Pepper."

"I'll check it out. Ten tea bags are a bit much. I can water it down. I'll go get some."

"Don't water down the Dr. Pepper, you hear?" Lonnie yelled after Caleb.

Just as Caleb returned to the porch with a watered-down pitcher of iced tea and a big glass of Dr. Pepper, Peter pulled up in front. Caleb waved at him while Lonnie Rex shouted, "Go away!" and laughed. Peter knew better than to listen to Lonnie when he was in re-entry and proceeded to plop down onto the porch couch opposite the two of them.

"Hi, guys. Here I am. I've only got a bit less than an hour before I must report to the missus for dinner. What are we doing?" said Peter.

Caleb started right in. "In the first place, I promised you I would share everything with you this week. You have not seen the letter that Warren had me deliver to the mayor."

Caleb proceeded to tell Peter everything about what was in the letter to the mayor. When he finished, Peter exclaimed, "Money! There is money involved? And a lot of it, it appears. I thought this was only about the body, which is enough of a story, but the gift of this money to the city makes it even bigger. Why didn't you tell me before?"

"I wanted to allow the mayor a chance to take care of things without any interference. It was to be confidential, as per Warren's request. So, the mayor has had time, and we now know what he did with the time," explained Caleb.

"What did he do? Did he find the money? And the body?" asked Peter.

Caleb quickly summarized everything that he and Lonnie had learned in the last couple of days. He emphasized the evidence they had collected. As he related the story, he opened the box with the gun, the badge, and the affidavit, and showed them to Peter.

"Jeez, talk about a smoking gun! Pardon the pun. There's the proof. Dumar is trying to hide everything—the money and the body!" exclaimed Peter.

"That's just the beginning," said Caleb. He then proceeded to fully explain his meeting with the chief of police and how he was being investigated. He then told how he had set up a meeting for the next Tuesday to address the complaints.

Peter thought for a minute. "Uh, I don't understand. Why not just turn everything you have over to the chief. That evidence itself will trap Dumar and get you released from any real or imagined wrongdoing."

"That was my first inclination," said Caleb. "But here's the thing. We don't know just how deep the mayor is in on the whole deal. Even if Dumar is lying to the mayor, and if he believes Dumar, he still knows that he is a part owner and can be seen as colluding on the approvals. He might go along with a cover up to protect himself. And if he is guilty of more, then we think that he will certainly try to cover it up. He could back Dumar and get the chief to go along. Once we turn our evidence in, we lose some control."

"I don't know. You've still got the witnesses, the contractor, and the workers," Peter pointed out.

"That's true, but those workers could be easily intimidated, even disappear like before. And the contractor is a little guilty of going along with the disposal of the body. He might just clam up if the other witnesses disappear. He might cave to pressure. Then the chief might spin it any way the mayor and Dumar want it spun in order to keep his job or maybe even for financial consideration.

"Golly guys, I don't think that is likely. Surely the chief is not corrupt. That's just too much!" claimed Peter.

Lonnie Rex interjected, "Look, if we keep control of the evidence and produce it at once to all of them, they won't have a chance to spin it in confidence. They'll have to confront it together and in front of witnesses. There'll be no chance for them to alter the story. And if they are inclined to do the right thing anyway, then it will also work to give it to them all at once. Either way, it works. And it avoids the chance that they can still come after Caleb."

Caleb added, "That's right. And there is more to the plan. I asked for Henry Dawes to be in the meeting. I'm hoping he is straight. He seems that way. Everything comes out at once, the witnesses are there and untampered with, and finally…. Are you ready? You'll be there."

"Me? You think they will allow me? I represent the paper. I'm the press. They won't want me anywhere near the meeting," insisted Peter.

"I told the chief that I would bring all my information to the meeting, including any witnesses or others involved. He agreed. You are writing the story, but you are also part of the story. You can tell them how I came to you early and we did research to confirm the facts in Warren's letter to me. And you can tell them everything about what you found. It'll back up Warren's story and reinforce the truth."

Peter wasn't completely convinced but countered with, "Let's say they let me come to the meeting, and we give all the information to them, including the other witnesses. What do you think they will do?"

"Lock em' up! That's what," said Lonnie Rex.

"Wait a minute, Lonnie," cautioned Caleb. "Once we give everything over, then what they do is up to them. We know about Dumar, but we're not sure about the mayor. It could be that he's innocent of conspiring with Dumar and that he simply believed him. When he sees all the evidence, he will have to confront Dumar. That'll be interesting. And Peter will be there to see it all."

"Look, Caleb, the mayor is either completely guilty in the whole deal, or he is a little guilty of having a conflict of interest by investing and colluding. He should have stayed clear of the whole project. One way he is a criminal; the other way he is merely a typically corrupt politician," observed Peter.

Caleb looked at Peter. "You asked what I thought would happen. I think the question for me is what I want to happen. That's a great deal clearer to me. What I really want is for them to have followed Warren's instructions, honored Hollis's death, and done something appropriate with Warren's gift. That didn't happen, so I guess... wait a minute! Maybe it can still happen. We could give them a way to go back and do it right."

"How in the world are we going to do that? Dumar's already done the deed! And the mayor has already been compromised. Don't you want them punished?" asked Lonnie.

"I guess I want what I always wanted, and that is simple justice. If this thing had gone down correctly, there would have been some serious justice—for Hollis, for Warren, and maybe even for Vernon," admitted Caleb.

"Well, it's too late for that!"

"Maybe not, Lonnie. I'm going to have to think about it," Caleb stated.

Peter sat back and said, "Well, do you want me to write the story with all that we know? And if so, when do I print it?"

Caleb's head snapped up. "The story! That's where the real control is—not the meeting. We know the truth. We have the evidence. And we have the press in Peter," Caleb virtually shouted. "Yes, Peter, you can write the story. I want to help you because you are going to write two stories. The one we print will be decided after the meeting. So, hold it until then. I'll come by and show you what I have in mind."

"Two stories! What the hell are you talking about?" asked Lonnie Rex. "You're giving me a headache, and I don't even get 'em!"

"I'll tell you later when we all work it out together. I'm going to take Lori to the airport tomorrow, but let's meet on Thursday, okay Peter?"

"Sure. That's fine. Come by then. Show me what you want to do," said Peter.

A silence fell over the three.

"So how is Lori?" asked Peter. "It looked like you guys were having a good time."

"They're getting married!" said Lonnie Rex.

Caleb glared at Lonnie.

"Oops," mumbled Lonnie.

FIFTY-THREE

Caleb took Lori and Daniel to the airport on Wednesday morning. There was a reluctance to leave on both their parts, but it was tempered with an excitement to return and begin this new phase of their lives.

For Lori it was indeed a new life, and there was much to do. She had been thinking about the sale of her practice and how that could best be managed to bring the best price as well as ensure a smooth transition. She was aware that continued involvement in the clinic on her part might be required and stretch over as much as a year. She was confident that she could do what was required to make it happen. She was now anxious to begin a new life in Rogers with Caleb.

For Daniel, it was also a time of excitement. His concern over the coming enrollment in Berkeley had been dispensed with completely. He was thinking seriously about what he had learned about the University of Arkansas and its architectural school. He planned to return and go see the school as soon as possible. And the work on the farm project had entered a new dimension. Now his mother was his "client" in the project. That meant a bigger responsibility to find just the right approach and incorporate the things Lori wanted. Caleb was remarkably compliant and showed all the signs of supporting what was worked out between Daniel and Lori. Daniel nevertheless felt a strong desire to achieve something that Caleb would readily accept and appreciate.

Lori kissed Caleb goodbye at the entrance to the security check with a final farewell.

"I'll be back as soon as possible. There's a lot to do, and I can't get in too much of a hurry. It must play out, and I've got a lot to consider. But in my mind, it can't happen soon enough," Lori said.

"We've got a wedding to plan too, you know," bubbled Caleb.

"And on that, we will begin immediately. I'll call you, and we can talk. Love you!"

Caleb stood and watched them disappear through the check point. He experienced an aloneness that was unfamiliar to him, but it felt good.

Caleb returned to Sarah's house. He had every intent of relaxing for the rest of the day and giving some thought to all he had to do. He must focus on the upcoming meeting with the chief and figure out just how to handle that. A plan was being formed, but he had to turn it over in his mind until he was sure it would serve. It occurred to him that the best way to think would be to saddle up Cisco and go on a very long ride.

Sarah was not at home when Caleb returned, so his plan to take Cisco for a ride began immediately. That plan agreed with Cisco. He greeted Caleb with enthusiasm as the saddle was thrown onto his back. Caleb walked Cisco down across the field and went through the gate near the creek. He then had free riding for a long distance along the creek with many opportunities to explore other pastures. It wasn't as wide open as what he was used to in the west but would serve quite well.

The solitude of the ride brought a flood of realizations of what all had happened to him. This was a return to his home. He felt that. And more important, it was a reunion with a lost love. How could he be so fortunate?

As he dismounted and leaned against the base of a towering oak tree, he remembered a Kris Kristofferson tune that he had played many times:

"Why me Lord? What have I ever done, to deserve even one of the pleasures I've known? Tell me Lord, what did I ever do that was worth loving you or the kindness you've shown?"

The Lord had always guided him. He knew that. And now he had been guided by His gentle hand into these newfound blessings. Could it have happened sooner? He thought not. There was some living and waiting that was necessary for all the blessings to converge.

He gave a silent prayer: *"Thank you, Lord, for these many blessings that I am experiencing at this point in life. Help me as I continue along this path You have laid out for me, as I make decisions, and as I mold my life in further service of Your will. I have found a promised land, one with love and remembrance, one with hope and responsibility, and one with all the promise You have shown in Your words to us and in Your very presence within us. Thank You. Amen.*

Caleb became silent and inwardly focused. The gurgle of the stream, the wind in the leaves, and the solidarity of the oak to his back, spread a peace throughout his body. He savored the time in this very place.

Cisco, on the other hand, was anxious to resume the ride. He came closer to Caleb and drug the reins across his knees. A quick nod of the head and an energetic snort signaled his readiness for Caleb to mount up. The spell remained unbroken as Caleb quietly stroked Cisco's neck and swung up into the saddle. Without a word of encouragement being necessary, Cisco turned and moved down the bank to continue their amble along the stream.

Caleb could tell that Sarah had returned as he and Cisco returned from their ride. Her car was parked in the back by the kitchen porch. By the time he made it to the barn, Sarah had come out to greet them.

"Hey, you guys, where have you been?"

"Just took a good long ride to sort out the kinks and work up a sweat," answered Caleb.

"I went to the store to stock up. Did you get Lori and Daniel delivered? When will they be back?"

"Yeah, they got off just fine. I don't know when they will return. I mean Daniel should drive back in a few days. Lori will let me know about her. She's got a lot to do."

"Oh, I bet. You and Lori must plan a wedding. I'm brimming with thoughts about what we can do. Have you talked about when you want to do it or where you want to have it?"

"Nope."

"Do you want it to be big or just a few people? Anybody coming from the ranch? Do you know yet?"

"Nope."

"Well, when are you going to decide?"

"All in good time. I will defer to Lori on most everything. Whatever she wants."

"I bet Winnie is excited. Did you talk to her?"

"Nope. Not really. She said something about being pleased we were intelligent enough to listen to her."

"Are you going anywhere now? Are you staying for lunch?"

"I don't plan on going anywhere. I'm about done with going! I will be here for lunch and dinner and not go anywhere until maybe tomorrow morning."

"Good. I can fix us something to eat. I've got a lot of options. What sounds good?"

"Hot dogs."

"Hot dogs?"

"Yep, hot dogs."

"Oh, my! That does sound good. I think I've got everything if canned chili is good. Is that okay?" asked Sarah.

"Yep."

"Okay then. I can have it ready mighty quick. You want to eat soon? Or do you want to wait? Are you going to fix Cisco first?"

"I think I would like to eat in about three hours, Cisco will keep his saddle on all that time, and he likes hot dogs too, so fix him some—he'll eat at least ten, and he has already been 'fixed.'"

"Whaaat...?"

"I'm kidding you, Sister. I'll be up right away after I brush Cisco. I appreciate your efforts. I need to talk to you about something at lunch."

"What do you want to talk about? Is it..."

"At lunch, we'll talk about it. Be right up."

Caleb led Cisco into the barn to brush him and to enable Sarah to go fix the hot dogs. Caleb wasn't sure why hot dogs came to mind, but they sure sounded good.

After Caleb had deposited the last bit of hot dog in his mouth, he took a long pull on a glass of iced tea and sat back. The lunch was superb! Sarah had managed some potato salad and some classic chips. Caleb's only regret was that he hadn't invited Lonnie Rex to share in what must be exquisite cuisine for him.

"What did you want to talk about?" asked Sarah.

"What? Oh. Yeah. I decided to get Sarah a ring, and I want to shop for it on my own. I want to give it to her as soon as she comes back. I have no idea where to go and thought that you could tell me the best place to shop for a fine diamond ring."

"Do you know her ring size?"

"Nope."

"Well, call her and get it. You've got to have it to buy one. Or maybe Winnie would know."

"Yeah, I guess I can check with Winnie. But where should I go?" asked Caleb.

Sarah was uncommonly quiet for a moment. She looked intently at Caleb and said, "Caleb, I've waited a long time for this moment. I mean, a long time. Mother wanted you to have her wedding ring and band. I've had it for all these years, waiting for when you might need it, and I guess the time is right. It's yours if you want it!"

Caleb was quiet as he pondered another gift. "Wow! That would be great, Sarah, really great!"

Sarah stepped into her bedroom and returned bearing the wedding ring and band in the original box. She handed it to Caleb and watched as he opened it. The look on his face told the entire story.

"This means a lot to me. I had no idea!" admitted Caleb. "Do you think it will fit?"

"I think it might. And even if it doesn't, a jeweler can adjust it to fit properly."

"So, I'll give it to her and see if she likes it, then we can check the size. Is that right?" asked Caleb.

"Yes, I think so, and you can rest assured that she will like it. It's a beautiful ring. Mother never took it off. She was very proud of it. Dad brought it back from New York after he went there on some music jaunt. Mother couldn't believe how he had afforded it."

"I think Lori will like it because of the history alone. I'm anxious to give it to her."

"You can go to the jewelers and get a new box. This one is a little faded. A new box would set it off nicely."

"I don't think so. Look at the bottom. It says 'Tiffany & Co.' I rather think that she will like this one quite a lot!" said Caleb.

FIFTY-FOUR

Breakfast with Sarah on Thursday morning was a relaxed and pleasant affair. Caleb spoke again of how much the gift of the ring meant to him and how he knew that Lori would treasure it. Sarah sipped her coffee in a rare silence and with a pleased look on her face.

Returning to the present, Sarah considered Caleb. She got up from the table and freshened her coffee before saying, "Before you go out, tell me what's going on with the chief. I know you have the meeting set up, but what's going to happen?"

"I told you most of it the other day. Since then, I have given it some thought and met with Peter. I'm going to hold on to all our evidence until the meeting, and then I think I know a way to handle the entire situation—if it works."

"Are you sure that you will get released from the complaint?"

"Oh, I'm certain of that. It all comes down to what the other guys do. I'm just looking for justice. I'll tell you more after I've fully prepared. It'll take a couple of days."

"Do you want me to come to the meeting?"

"Absolutely. I'm going to bring everyone who knows anything about recent history. I'm going to talk to Nancy, and, of course, Lonnie Rex will be there. I just need to go and make arrangements for the contractor and his group to be there."

"What if they don't want to come? Or refuse to?"

"I don't think they will refuse after I explain a few things. If they don't come, then I'll let them know that the chief of police will be coming to interview them. It'll be better for all of them to get it over with all at once. Even if they refuse to come, my plan is unchanged. We have the evidence and the affidavit."

"But you still don't know the extent of the mayor's involvement. How will you find that out?"

"We may never know. It might come out at the meeting, or it might not. Truthfully, I don't care that much. My plan will work regardless of the level of his guilt."

"I don't get it. What can you do other than give the evidence over?"

"Legally, that's about all I can do. But I think I have an additional approach which may help justice be found beyond the legalities."

"Will you tell me everything before we go?"

"Maybe. Or there may be a little surprise. You might have to put a lid on your curiosity until the meeting."

"You do know how to punish me. This is almost unbearable."

"You'll be fine," promised Caleb. "Now I've got to go. I'll get lunch in town and see you tonight."

Caleb drove directly to Dennis Chiles's office at the construction yard. He greeted Sonia when he walked in and asked to talk to Dennis. Sonia let Dennis know that Caleb was here to see him and ushered him into Dennis's office.

Dennis looked up with a certain measure of concern. "What now?" he asked.

"There's been a few developments since we left here on Monday. I'm here to tell you about them and to ask for your assistance. I was summoned to the chief of police's office and informed that there was a complaint against me because of the attempt to find the money and the body at the site. It seems that Dumar is mad because the project was delayed by the digging, which, according to him, found nothing. And the mayor is upset by the cost of the effort. Dumar knows the truth of what he did and is trying to gain the offensive, I guess. The mayor is going along with the complaint," Caleb explained.

"We know that isn't the truth. We know what was found. You didn't do anything wrong. Didn't you turn over the evidence you found?"

"Not yet. The chief has set up a meeting next Tuesday to interview me about the affair. He will produce the complaints and I'm supposed to answer their questions. That's fine with me. I intend to do just that. I will be allowed to produce all the evidence I have in my defense. I intend to give the evidence at that meeting, and I also want to have witnesses available to back up the evidence. In that regard, I am requesting that you, Jersey, and the Montoya brothers be present to testify, if required."

"That means that I may have to tell everyone about moving the body," said Dennis.

"Yes, that will probably come out, but it is also the opportunity to explain Dumar's order to you to do that and put in perspective his motivation for demanding that you do so. He may not have known at that time that it was Hollis, but he certainly wanted to keep the project moving and avoid any further digging around where he had found the money. You are guilty of moving some old bones, which, as you assert, has happened before without consequence. There might be a minor fine, but no serious guilt since you didn't know the significance of the bones. This will give you the chance to state the facts. Your involvement will be seen as a minor issue, I believe. There should be no consequences for the Montoya brothers."

"I don't know. It all makes me a little uncomfortable."

"If we don't do it this way and I simply submit the evidence, then there will most likely be an investigation, which will bring you in and give Dumar a chance to blame you as he has done me. If that happens, it will most likely be more difficult for you. If you appear at the meeting, we can hit them with the whole story all at once and take control of the issue. That's the way I see it."

"I'm tired of Dumar and his shenanigans! He's always a problem. I don't want to give him a chance to blame me, cause that's exactly what he will do. If his lips are moving, he's lying!" proclaimed Dennis. "Alright. I agree to come. A good offense is the best defense, as you point out. If we come forth and explain it all, they can't do too much to me."

"That's right. I don't even think they will be concerned with you. Dumar and the mayor will be busy covering for themselves," said Caleb.

"Now, I understand about Dumar, but not the mayor. What has he done wrong?"

"Here's what. The mayor invested in the project, and without disclosing that involvement, he put pressure on the Historical Board to downgrade the status of the old station which allowed it to be torn down. It made the project have real value. So, he enriched himself through his influence as a public official without disclosing it. That's serious all alone. In addition, and we don't know this for sure, he may have known about the money and body before I gave him notification of their existence. If he already knew about the money and body since he is a partner of Dumar's, then he has gotten in deeper by helping to cover it up. It becomes the cover up of a real crime. The money is not Dumar's, and the body was evidence of a crime committed long ago. Dumar is guilty, and the mayor is either a little bit guilty or seriously guilty. Either way, he has some guilt."

"Wow! This is getting serious," observed Dennis. "You mean that the mayor is part owner in the project?"

"That's right. It's been confirmed."

"It's hard to believe. The mayor is a good guy. I think he has done a good job, and he's been helpful to me on many occasions."

"Well, for what it's worth, I personally do not believe the mayor is guilty of covering up Dumar's crime. I don't think he was in on the lie. The dead deputy was his uncle! He seemed genuinely moved when I showed him the information in the letter. I think Dumar lied in the beginning and continued the lie to the mayor. Now the mayor doesn't know what to do. He might think the information on the body and money is simply a hoax. It is rather fantastic and may be hard to believe. If that's the case, he might have decided to go along with the complaint and play innocent, hoping to avoid negative publicity."

Caleb continued, "When we show the actual evidence and make it clear that Dumar is the real culprit, I think we will find out just where the mayor stands. When the evidence of Dumar's crimes is revealed to everyone, including the mayor, I think he will react in a way that will make the depth of his guilt very clear. At least that's what I think."

Dennis looked chagrined. "This is a brain twister, isn't it?"

"Yep. But we'll soon know."

"Thanks, Caleb. We'll be there. What time is the meeting?"

"Tuesday afternoon. 2:00 p.m. in the afternoon. I'll call you and let you know where to meet. I may want the witnesses to gather elsewhere and be available to come in when called. I don't want Dumar to see the witnesses. I want him to feel free to continue with his complaint and not be aware of the existence of any evidence or testimony."

"You know, this could be fun. Let us know where to go. See you then."

FIFTY-FIVE

Caleb picked up Lonnie Rex, and the two of them went to Peter's office. On the way over, Caleb called Nancy and told her about the meeting the next Tuesday. He asked her to come to the meeting and bring any information she had, including any documents on the Historical Board approval of the declassification of the station along with what she had found on the mayor's being a partner in the venture. He also reminded her that she had been there when the trunk was opened and could speak to the truth of how all this originated. Nancy was only too happy to be involved.

At the close of their telephone conversation, Nancy reminded Caleb that she could bring up the fact that Dumar had searched the farm even before Caleb had arrived in town. That was an additional indication that Dumar had some interest in Warren's estate long before Caleb arrived. It reminded Caleb of Dumar's apparent knowledge that Warren had some money to give someone based on that conversation Warren mentioned in the letter. It all fit.

Peter was pleased to see them when they entered his office.

"I've been wondering what you have in mind since we talked. Now that you're here, please clear it up," said Peter.

"Sure," said Caleb. "I've been thinking. I have all the players in agreement to come to the meeting. Everybody's in. I want to keep them out of the meeting until I need them, and that way not let Dumar or the mayor know of the existence of any evidence or testimony. I especially want Dumar to think that he holds the cards and let him fully state his complaint. The mayor too. Whatever they have to say, I want to hear their story. Then I will respond by outlining the story from my point of view. First, I think that I will present the evidence we have and let the witnesses come in with support."

"The evidence is going to be hard to refute," Peter stated.

"Yes, I think so. As I said, the DA will be there, and he will hear it all for the first time. It will be hard for Dumar to spin it away. And it will be interesting to see the mayor's reaction. That might tell us right away just how involved he was. He won't see any way out of the facts, and if he was lied to by Dumar, then his reaction will be telling. At least that's what I think," said Caleb.

Peter asked, "So what's my role? Am I just there to get the story?"

"Two things. First, you can relate how we came to you and that you researched the story and found it to be historically accurate as far as you could tell. You looked up the history of Hollis's disappearance, and we saw how it all could fit. It will be clear from your statements that it all happened before I even delivered the letter to the mayor and supports the truth of how it all played out. Your testimony will demonstrate that it couldn't be a hoax," explained Caleb.

"And secondly," Caleb continued, "You will update the newspaper story that you have already prepared and have it on hand. But with a twist. I want you to write two stories. Both will be the same story up until the time when I gave the letter to the mayor. But after that there will be a different conclusion to each. I will outline the two versions for you and let you do it in your own way. But both will be ready for publication."

"How can I publish two stories?" asked Peter.

"I didn't say publish—I said write. You will go to print with the one that is the truth."

"How do we know which is the truth, if there are different versions?"

"You'll see. When I give you the two versions, it'll be clear. Trust me."

"Alright, I'll look at what you give me. I just don't see how we can tell a story accurately before it happens. We know the facts. They don't lie. We can print the story right now and Dunar will be boxed in. We can expose Dumar's lies and point to the mayor's guilt, all based on the truth. It would be quite a scoop and certainly clear you of any wrongdoing. Isn't that what you want? And don't you want these guys caught and punished?" asked Peter.

"I'm glad you asked that. Let me tell you again what I want. I want Warren's request to be followed. I want his admission of guilt and his donation to the city to happen, just like he outlined. I want justice to occur relative to the death of Hollis, the confession of Warren, and the gift to commemorate the real history. I want all of that to be achieved. I want to do what I can to see that it happens."

Continuing, Caleb said, "What I am not interested in is a big investigation with more lies and a bunch of attorneys spinning legal theories of this or that. I don't want Dumar to use the money he stole to defend himself and to slander any other people just to avoid punishment. I don't want to put the mayor in a situation in which he must choose to continue to spiral further down into a bigger lie. What I want is for the right thing to happen. Real simple."

"Well, you've got my attention. When will you bring me your two versions of the story?"

"Tomorrow. That'll give you time to do your own writeup."

"Make it as early as possible. I'm going away this weekend, and I don't want to wait 'till next Monday to pull it together."

"I'll work it up tonight. You want to meet me and Lonnie at Casper's Grill for breakfast? That's where we like to start our day."

"Perfect. I haven't had a grease fix in weeks!'

"You're in for a treat!" claimed Lonnie Rex.

FIFTY-SIX

Casper's Grille was humming on Friday morning.
Lonnie Rex had followed his usual routine and arrived much earlier than Caleb. When Caleb walked in at 7:45 a.m., he was carrying two manila envelopes.

Lonnie looked up and asked, "Them the two stories?"

"That they are. Worked them out last night. It's quite an interesting exercise to write a story that hasn't happened. I hope this works," said Caleb.

"How is it going to work?" asked Lonnie.

"Let's wait for Peter. We might as well go over this just one time."

"What do you want me to do?"

"When?"

"At the meeting. You want me there, right?"

"Yes. You know, or will know, everything I'm planning. I think I need you to stay out of the meeting and be with the witnesses. I can call you on the phone, and you can send them in as I request them," explained Caleb.

"Then I won't get to hear what's going on."

"Yes, you will. It's my plan to leave my phone on so you can hear everything. When the time comes, I'll just say send in so-and-so. You keep your phone on that mute thing, so no one can hear anything you or the witnesses say but you can hear me."

"Sounds like a plan—if I can hear. But the witnesses will be able to hear also. Is that going to work?"

"Sure. I want them to know what is going on. It's only Dumar and the mayor that I want to have in the dark about all the evidence until it is revealed one piece at a time. And the DA too, I guess."

The door opened, and Peter entered the restaurant. He looked around and finally spotted Lonnie Rex and Caleb in the back room. He stopped to say hello to a couple of men seated at a table in the front room before proceeding back.

"Morning, fellows. Have I missed anything?"

"You missed out on some daylight. Where have you been?" asked Lonnie Rex.

Glancing at his watch, Peter said, "Gee, it's only about 8:00. Was I supposed to be here earlier?"

"We been here since about six, wondering where you were."

"No, we haven't," protested Caleb. "Lonnie just thinks everybody should be up and at 'em real early. I just came in a few minutes ago."

"You can't intimidate me, Lonnie. I'm glad to be here, thank you very much, and I'm anxious to order some of the good stuff. At home, I usually get oatmeal or fruit."

"That's pitiful doin's for sure," stated Lonnie. "I wouldn't be able to maintain my physique or cherubic demeanor on that fare. Order some real food before you atrophy."

"I need to order too," said Caleb.

"Do we have to eat back here in the smoking section?" complained Peter.

"It's just us, and I won't smoke until after we leave, okay?" promised Lonnie.

"Alright, I guess." Peter looked the menu over and made his choice. Caleb joined him and once the waitress had taken their order, Peter looked at Caleb. "Did you write up what you want in the stories?"

"Got 'em right here. This envelope is marked 'Good Story' and this other one is 'Bad Story.' The good story is what will happen if they 'see the light' and go in the right direction. The bad story is what we will print if they stonewall or resist."

"So, you want me to add these endings to the story I already have drafted?" asked Peter.

"Yes. The one you drafted brings us up to the letters, or it will if you add the mayor's letter. You only learned about that yesterday. Put that in and then add the two endings."

"How are you going to handle these stories in the meeting? What do they get, a choice?" asked Peter.

"Yes, that's sort of it. On Monday, I'll come and look at what you have, and we can do a bit of a run-through of the meeting," explained Caleb.

"What's Lonnie Rex going to do?'

"He's going to be in charge of the witnesses."

"How many do you have?" asked Peter.

"Let's see... maybe six, I think."

Their food arrived, and it captured Peter's total attention. "Look at this! I must come here more often!"

"It's always a pleasure to see a fellow pilgrim come to his senses," observed Lonnie Rex.

Caleb started in on his food and said to Peter, "Thanks for coming and for doing this, Peter. Breakfast is on me."

"Okay, thanks. It just gets better and better," said Peter.

"What about me?" asked Lonnie.

"Of course, you too, Lonnie," agreed Caleb.

Lonnie nodded his thanks and asked, "Can I get some pie?"

FIFTY-SEVEN

Caleb arose on Saturday morning, looking forward to the day. He intended to spend the entire day at the farm working alongside Dickie and Estes. They would probably need some more direction and materials. He thought that with what he knew about the house plans, he could now give them directions that would be productive. Even without the final plans, he knew that Lori would be living with him, so he could now determine what to get rid of. He didn't need to keep anything not needed. If he wanted to stay out at the farm in the interim, he could always pull his trailer out there, and he and Cisco could get used to the place and do some exploring.

It was nice to finally have everything in place for the meeting with the chief and the rest. There wasn't anything else he could do, so he would leave that until Monday. Lonnie Rex had agreed to come out to the farm later in the day and help Caleb make a few decisions. Lonnie would probably not be much help, but it would be good to have him around and maybe do a little porch-sitting.

The only thing that was on his mind, other than the farm, was calling Lori to see how they were coming along. He wondered when Daniel would be back. Caleb opened his phone and dialed Lori's number.

After a few rings, Lori answered, "Hello."

"Lori, it's me. How's everything going?"

"Hi, honey. It's good, but it looks like I have a lot of work ahead of me. Imagining a move after so many years is making my head spin. And it's hard to know whether to do it piecemeal for now before I figure out the clinic or wait and do it all at once after it's settled. I think that I must stay here until the clinic is decided, so maybe the move will only occur then."

"That could take a while," said Caleb, hiding his disappointment.

"I know. I want to be there as soon as I can. I want to be a part of what you and Daniel will be doing."

"Well, you must do it right. Selling the clinic may take some time, but it's very important to get it worked out and get a good price."

"I've already talked to the others here, and there is a lot of interest on their part in putting together a buyout. That's what they really want. I need to give them the time to work it out, so I can't sell it out from under them, at least I don't want to. It would be easiest for me if they assumed control."

"That sounds like the right approach. Hope it works," said Caleb.

"I'm going to try to set it up so I can be here part-time while they get the deal put together. Then I could come out for a week here and there. No matter what, I will probably have to remain involved for up to a year, you know, until everything is smooth. I can't leave them in the lurch."

"When is Daniel coming back?" asked Caleb.

"He's getting it all together. I know that he can't wait to get back and start the final plans. He also wants to check out the university. He seems committed to the architecture thing. At this point, it looks like he will leave here next week, maybe mid-week."

"Whatever works. I'll be ready."

"We'll call and let you know. Then if I can, I'll fly back out the week after and stay for a week or a long weekend."

"Have you given the wedding any thought?" asked Caleb.

"What do you think? Of course, I've thought a lot about it. I want to have Gwen and her family there. They will have to work out leaving the ranch for a few days. That's always hard in ranch-ing—there's so much to take care of, as you certainly know. But she is excited and promises to be available for when we decide."

"I do know about ranching. Take their needs into consider-ation. We can be flexible."

Lori paused and then continued, "Caleb, I have been think-ing about having the wedding at Sarah's church. What do you think?"

"I can't think of a better place. I know it'll give Sarah a thrill," Caleb said while considering his pleasure at the thought.

"Good. Can you talk to her about it?" asked Lori.

"Absolutely! But, trust me, she will be very pleased. It will give her something to anticipate and plan. She might be a bit too anxious for her own good, but I would like to welcome her into the planning. Who do you want to have do the ceremony?"

"I don't have anyone. I think that it will be fine to have her preacher do the wedding. What do you think?"

"As long as we're hitched, I'm all in."

"I wondered about what to do for a reception. I don't know where would be good, but it occurred to me that Sarah's farm might be wonderful. It's so beautiful there. Would she be agree-able with that?"

"Lori, you're talking about nirvana for her. She will be on cloud nine. I can hear her now—What shall we serve? Dinner or afternoon? How many people? Shall I cook? Where do you want to have everyone sit? Do you want music? Who is coming...? It will go on and on. I'll be answering questions or trying to, on a full-time basis. I say we don't tell her until you come back for your next visit. Then you can be here and help make all the deci-sions and answer all the questions. But rest assured, she will be fine with it," explained Caleb.

"That's good. It'll give me a chance to think about who I want to have come. I don't think there will be many. Winnie of course, and any friends she might have, although I guess most of them have passed away. She's 88 years old, you know."

"Gee, she doesn't seem that old. She's so vibrant! But who-ever she wants."

"Yeah, this is big for her. A dream come true," said Lori.

"She's not the only one, you know," pronounced Caleb.

"I'm with you, honey. I'm with you. I can't believe this is happening. Every morning, I think I've awoken from a dream."

Both were silent for a moment and then Lori said, "I've got to go. We'll call and tell you when Daniel will arrive. Help him out with the university if he needs anything, okay?"

"Sure. I'll tell him which sororities have the best girls—or used to."

"I will leave that to your discretion. Gotta go. I love you."

"Okay, bye. I love you too."

FIFTY-EIGHT

Sarah had a mission on Sunday. Caleb had informed her of Lori's request to have the wedding ceremony at her church and have Pastor Wendell preside over the affair. Sarah could not wait to corner the preacher and break the good news. Caleb joined back in with the choir and band. They were happy to have him back. Having him sitting in the pew last week was unsettling to their sense of adherence to a standard practice. With Caleb's presence at the front of the church, the standard had been restored, and the music was complete with his violin once more in the mix.

This week, Pastor Wendell delivered the sermon. Sarah had not talked to him yet, so he didn't have any big announcement to make relative to Lori and Caleb getting married. That was just as well, thought Caleb. He would have to be there when Sarah asked Wendell to perform the ceremony. He could caution both about keeping it all quiet until he and Lori had settled on a date. Keeping it quiet was a lot to ask of Sarah, and Caleb was fully aware that it might be a lost cause and admitted that even he had told almost everyone he encountered. He reconciled himself to it being leaked and concluded that it really wouldn't matter.

After the service, Sarah waited around and told Pastor Wendell that she needed to talk to him. When he was finished saying his goodbyes, Sarah grabbed Caleb's arm and told him to come with her. They all met in the middle of the sanctuary where Sarah announced to Wendell that they had a favor to ask. She turned to Caleb and said, "Go ahead, Caleb. Ask him."

Caleb had been under the impression that Sarah wanted to be the one to ask, but he recovered nicely and said to him, "Pastor Wendell, Lori and I are getting married. She's the young lady I had with me last week."

"Well, I expect so. You couldn't have found a different one in a week now, could you?"

Caleb laughed and went on. "Lori and I have been friends, well more than friends, I guess, since high school. We finally got back together during our reunion, and it just happened very fast."

"Sounds to me like it happened rather slowly. How long has it been since you two were last together?"

"A good forty years—actually forty-one. She left here in our junior year. I haven't seen her since."

"Then, if you're sure, it sounds like it's about time!"

"Oh, we're sure. The thing is, we have decided to get married here in Rogers, and we were wondering if we could have you marry us here in the church?"

Pastor Wendell looked at Sarah then turned back to Caleb. "Is it all right with Sarah?"

Sarah interrupted. "Of course, it's alright. What are you thinking? I couldn't be happier!"

"Then I'll be happy to marry you. What church does she belong to?"

"She doesn't belong to any church. She liked it here."

"Is she a believer?" asked Pastor Wendell.

"She is sir. Yes, she is."

"Do you want me to do my premarital counseling?"

"Why, you can counsel us all you want. Maybe we overlooked something. That might be fun to sit down and have that talk. I think she would approve."

"Then, in that case, we can schedule something. It's for me to get to know you in Christ as much as it is to tell you anything. I would love the opportunity to get to know you and to welcome you into wedlock. Will you be joining the church?"

"We haven't even talked about that yet. I know I'm happy here, and I certainly expect she will be too, but we will talk and make that decision together," said Caleb.

"Sounds like you are off to the right start. When is the wedding?"

"We haven't decided yet. She must settle her work in Las Vegas first. She has a veterinary clinic there, and she needs to sell it. Somewhere in there, we will set a date for the wedding."

"I'll be ready when you are. The church is at your disposal. I'm looking forward to it," said Wendell.

Sarah finally let it all go. "This is so exciting! Having Caleb back, then having him getting married, then having him select the church—it's all so much! I couldn't ask for more. I'm so happy. Where will you have the reception, Caleb? Here at the church? What do you think?"

"Lori and I will talk, and you can join in with the decisions. I think you will be pleased with whatever we come up with. Let's wait 'till she's here, then decide, ok?"

"When's she coming back?" asked Sarah anxiously.

"A week or two. We can figure it out in good time."

"We could call her."

"But we won't. When she returns, you can cook us a gourmet meal, and we can sit around and plan 'till the earth looks flat.' Not until then," said Caleb.

"Oh, alright. It'll be fun. When's she coming back? Oh, I already asked that. Okay, never mind. Whenever you're ready. Will Winnie be involved?"

"She will be at the wedding. That's all I know now. Let's go, and I'll take you to lunch."

Caleb turned to Pastor Wendell and said, "Thank you so much. I'll let you know everything. See you next week."

As Caleb and Sarah walked out of the church, Sarah asked, "Do you want catfish? I don't like catfish. Where do you want to go?"

"It'll be a surprise," said Caleb.

"Where are we going?"

"Then it wouldn't be a surprise," said Caleb.

FIFTY-NINE

Monday promised to be a busy day. Caleb began with a nice ride on Cisco. He decided to skip breakfast with Lonnie, preferring to pick him up on his way over to see Peter. They could review the final copy of the stories and plan out the details of the next day.

Cisco was oblivious to the things that Caleb was involved in. All he required was to see him coming down to the barn for a ride. The grass was greener than anything Cisco had witnessed back on the ranch, and if a horse could be concerned about his weight, then Cisco should be very worried. He was certainly enjoying his new home, and if he had the continued attention of Caleb, then all was well.

Caleb brushed Cisco briskly, taking his time to demonstrate his continued care for his friend as he stroked his neck and told him about what was going on. He spoke about the farm and how Cisco was going to move to another farm replete with the same green fields and open space. Caleb knew that most people seriously doubted that a horse could understand what you told him, but he also knew that your tone and the way you talk to a horse tells a story, one without language but with plenty of communication. Cisco seemed to listen attentively as Caleb spoke. The movement of Cisco's ears was a tell-tale sign of his undivided attention.

There was no need to hurry their ride. Peter had agreed to meet for lunch at his office. He was going to have something brought in for them to eat. For a moment, Caleb's mind shifted to a question: How could Lonnie Rex eat lunch after the breakfast he woofed down each morning? It had been Caleb's practice to have a good breakfast, not unlike Lonnie does, but then not have another meal until dinner. That way he and all the cowboys could work uninterrupted for the entire day. They always managed to put some little snacks in their saddlebags, but that was it.

It was now past the middle of June, and summer was in full flower. The days were getting rather warm, but the real heat would be another month away. So different from the west. They had summer back on the ranch, of course, but it didn't really get hot until later, and then after a couple of warm spells, it began to move back toward fall. Such was the way in the high country. Caleb had to admit that the moisture in the air in Arkansas was a rather welcome change from the dryness of the prairies and mountains. To Caleb and Cisco, it felt good.

They rode for almost three hours, both getting a little sweaty and Caleb experiencing what he enjoyed most: being in the saddle. He thought there was almost no limit on how long he could continue an enjoyable ride. He knew that Cisco felt the same. As they finally rode up through the tall grass toward the barn, they both were a little disappointed that the ride was about to end. After Caleb unsaddled Cisco and allowed him his roll in the dirt, he brushed him thoroughly and turned him out to graze in the rich grass of the pasture.

Caleb took his time showering and changing clothes. He didn't want to smell like a horse when he joined Peter. He would let unique odors remain the domain of Lonnie Rex. That was unfair, thought Caleb. Lonnie didn't smell, but he looked like he should.

Sarah had gone into town, so Caleb was alone. He thought that she was probably spreading the word about the upcoming wedding, but then realized he was being unfair to Sarah also. She could stay calm for a while, if she could simply enjoy the expectations of what was to come. Caleb thought that he would talk with Sarah each day at length and include her in all their plans. He knew Lori would feel the same. This might just be as big an event for Sarah as it was for them.

When Caleb arrived at Lonnie Rex's house, he was not on the porch. Caleb went through the house looking for him. Lonnie was in his studio working on a painting. He had on some baggy sweats, puddling over some rubber shoes, and a tee shirt that had the following words on the front: "Sorry for being late, but I didn't want to come"

As Caleb stood in the doorway to the studio, Lonnie stepped back from his painting and lit a cigarette as he admired his progress. Without looking back, Lonnie asked Caleb, "You want to go fishing?"

"Uh… why do you ask that?"

"In order to find out if you want to go fishing," said Lonnie.

"Well, yeah, I would like to go fishing now that you mention it. Remember those whoppers we caught up on the San Juan?" asked Caleb.

"We didn't catch as many as we irritated. They were a little difficult to snag. I don't know whether I will ever get the hang of fly fishing. You were pretty good, but around here it is different. We can get some sloppy bait and work the rivers for some big catfish. What do you say?"

"When are we going?" asked Caleb.

"Once we get ready."

"Are you ready?" asked Caleb.

"Nope. But I will be soon. As soon as we quit fooling around with all your doin's, and as soon as I finish this painting, or get closer. Then I'll be ready," claimed Lonnie.

"Sounds perfect. Today we must get on with some of my 'doin's' as you say. Are you ready to go to Peter's?"

"Sure. Did I understand that he is providing lunch?"

"That's the story."

"Alright!" Lonnie stepped out of his sweats and left them in a puddle on the floor. Then he kicked his clogs off and headed upstairs in his underwear. "I'll be right back. Gotta find some clothes that are less restrictive."

Caleb was left with his imagination of just what that might be. He moved to the porch to wait. It was almost time for lunch, and he didn't want to keep Peter waiting. He was anxious to see what Peter had done with the stories. He didn't have to wait long. The screen door squeaked as Lonnie emerged from the house. He was dressed in blue jeans and a sport coat with no shoes. "You see my boots. I think I left them out here some-where," said Lonnie. "They're big."

"Look under the hammock," instructed Caleb.

"Bingo!" shouted Lonnie. "Let's go. I'll put 'em on in the truck. We don't want to keep Peter waiting."

When they arrived at Peter's office, he directed them into a con-ference room. The table was covered with a platter of sandwiches along with small servings of potato salad and some soft drinks. Peter told his secretary that Caleb would probably want iced tea and Lonnie drank Dr. Pepper, both of which she brought in. In front of three of the chairs there were two folders labeled "Good Story" and "Bad Story." Peter chose a seat and told them to help themselves to the food.

"There are the stories, labeled as you requested," said Peter.

Caleb opened the first of his folders and started to read.

Peter explained as Caleb read. "In each folder, there are two parts to the story. The first part is the same for both, and the sec-ond part is where they vary. I think that's what you wanted."

Lonnie Rex reached for a sandwich and, after unwrapping it, reached for a Dr. Pepper. Then he too began to read. While they read, Peter selected a sandwich and began to eat. It was quiet as they read. Caleb finished first and thought for a minute. "I think this is perfect. That's just what I had in mind."

When Lonnie finished reading, he said, "Now I think I get it, but how is it going to work?"

Caleb pointed out a simple truth. "We only have one strength. We—or more accurately, Peter—can write any story we want, as long as it is the truth and is corroborated. When one of these stories is printed, it will be the truth. Dumar and the mayor get to choose the story."

"This is going to be fun, isn't it?" asked Lonnie.

"Hopefully it works," said Caleb. "Now there is only one thing we must discuss. That is where are the witnesses going to gather? They should be out of sight but close to the police station. What do you think, Peter?"

"That should be easy. There is a muster room at the station. It won't be in use at that time of day, so they could wait in there. It's just down the hall. Sometimes it is used for press conferences. I'm sure they will let us use it," said Peter.

"That will work," said Caleb. Turning to Lonnie, he continued, "Lonnie, you will wait in there with the witnesses. With the phone line open, I will simply call out who to bring in when the time is right. Alright?"

"Sure. How long will we be in there?"

"I have no idea, but I can't imagine that it will take much more than an hour, two at the most. After the witnesses are done, they can go, or they can stay and see what happens if they want."

"Not a problem," said Lonnie Rex. "Peter, hand me some more potato salad, please."

"The only thing is—and this is important—Dumar and the mayor can't see the witnesses before. I want them to think that it is just their story to tell," said Caleb. "So that means that the witnesses have to come to the station right after we start the meeting."

"We can have them meet here. Then we can all walk over once the meeting starts. Maybe when you open the phone line, we'll know, and we can come over and go into the muster room," said Peter.

"That's good, but remember you will be with me in the meeting, Peter,"

"Oh, yeah, sure. Lonnie can bring them over."

"You got it, Lonnie?" asked Caleb.

"I'm your man, and I have it covered," declared Lonnie. "Is there any more Dr. Pepper?"

SIXTY

Caleb and Lonnie Rex waited at Peter's office at 1:00 p.m. on Tuesday. They expected everyone to arrive soon. As they waited, Caleb looked back over the stories and a few notes he had prepared. Lonnie Rex fell asleep in one of the conference room chairs while Peter gathered a few things to take with him to the meeting.

"You want me to say anything during the meeting?" asked Peter.

"Generally, no, but if there is a question you should address, then have at it."

At about 1:35 p.m., Nancy and Sarah arrived. They were shown into the conference room and exchanged greetings. Nancy shared the documents she had and what she could say at the meeting about the mayor's involvement. Sarah was unusually quiet, content to see how all this played out. Caleb had told her that she would only be called in if there were any questions on recent history.

Dennis Chiles arrived with Jersey and a nervous pair of Montoya brothers. They filed in and took seats at the table. Lonnie sat up and began to listen to Caleb's instructions. As Caleb told them all about the plans, Lonnie asked, "Caleb, if the Montoya brothers give any testimony, who is going to translate?"

"I guess I will. But that's a good question. Does anyone else speak Spanish?"

Peter said, "I know that there are some police officers that do. You could call on one of them if needed."

"If anyone objects to my translating, then I can call for one of them to come in. It might be a delay, but that's fine."

Dennis chimed in, "Actually, I speak some Spanish. I've had to learn since many of our workers are weak in English."

"I can't call you in with the Montoya brothers, so you won't be there when they speak. If you come in too soon, Dumar will suspect the depth of our evidence. I want to see his reaction to just the brothers. In fact, I will probably ask them to come in one at a time. You know, just slowly build the truth, following the chronology. But we'll see. There's no predicting how this will go," said Caleb.

Caleb looked at his watch and said, "It's time to go. Peter and I will go over and get started. When your phone rings, Lonnie, bring everyone over to the muster room."

Caleb picked up the box of evidence he had brought with him and left the room with Peter.

When Caleb entered the police station, the dispatcher was expecting them. She instructed them to proceed to the conference room and she would let everyone know that they had arrived. Peter stopped her and, after telling her some "more people" would be coming to join in the meeting, he asked if they could all wait in the muster room. She answered that it would be alright. The room was not in use, and they could wait in there.

Caleb and Peter entered the empty conference room. They noted that there were bottles of water set on the table and a court recording machine was set up in the corner. Caleb had not anticipated that the meeting would be recorded and wondered if it was always there. He welcomed the possibility that they would record it.

The chief of police walked in with Henry Dawes, the DA. Greetings were exchanged with them, and then the court reporter came in and took a seat at her recording device. She also carried a tape recorder. Caleb figured she would both type and record. This was becoming the real deal! After everyone was seated, the chief let them know that the proceedings would be recorded and asked for their approval.

Caleb spoke first, "That's fine with me. Okay with you, Peter?"

"Sure. Can the paper get a copy?"

"The recording is for our own investigative use. We don't plan on releasing it to the paper unless a compelling reason presents itself. This is only a preliminary meeting to question Mr. Atwood, and we want to be accurate."

The chief continued, "Mr. Dawes, our DA, is here at your request. Normally he would not attend a meeting like this before any investigation has been done, but I can see no harm coming from his being here. He will only listen and has not reviewed anything about the case, not until we develop it."

Turning to the court reporter, the chief said, "Okay, Cynthia, let's get started."

"For the record, I am Chief of Police Blaylock, along with Mr. Henry Dawes, the city district attorney. In attendance are Mr. Caleb Atwood and Peter Mason. Mr. Atwood, you are here at your own volition to hear potential complaints against you as lodged by a private citizen by the name of Dumar Ashton and by Mayor Bivens on behalf of the City of Rogers. Do you agree to these proceedings?"

"Yes sir, I do. But may I ask, where are Mr. Dumar and Mayor Bivens?"

"They will join us shortly once we get set up. First, you are hereby informed that after you have heard the complaints, you will be questioned. You are not compelled to give any information at this point, but it is our understanding that you wish to answer any questions that may arise. Is that true?"

"Yes, it is. And, in addition, I will submit any evidence I have to support my answers."

"That will be allowed, as we discussed. Do I understand that you may have some other people who might wish to speak or offer information?"

"Yes sir."

"Where are these persons?"

"I intend to call them as needed, if necessary, in the course of answering any questions which might be directed at me."

"Can they join us in a timely fashion?"

"Yes sir. It will only take a moment after I call them in," explained Caleb.

The chief turned to Peter. "Mr. Mason. Explain to me why you are here. It is not typically allowed to have the press in a meeting such as this."

Caleb interrupted, "If I may answer. Peter Mason has firsthand knowledge of events and activities which have led to this issue before us. He has performed research, at my request, in his role as editor of the paper and as the one who has access to the history of news reports from the past that have direct bearing on the actions I have taken."

"I see. So, you are not here as a reporter?" observed the chief.

"No sir," said Peter. "It's as Caleb has described."

"I'll allow it," said the chief as he turned to the DA. "Henry, you're here to observe, but have I left anything out?"

"No sir. This is just an informal meeting, but the way you are going is fine."

The chief pushed the button on the conference intercom and said, "Gentlemen, you can come in now. We are ready to get started."

Shortly the door opened, and Mayor Bivens came in first, followed by Dumar Ashton. Greetings were offered in a cordial manner as they took their seats on either side of the chief. Caleb noted the aggressive look that Dumar displayed as he took his seat. The mayor seemed complacent but interested.

Caleb looked at his lap and dialed Lonnie's number on his phone. It was on silent, and there was no sound at the connection. Lonnie had his phone on mute so no one in the meeting could hear anything. Caleb placed the phone on his notepad in front of him. The chief took no exception to the phone, except to instruct Caleb to please silence the device during the meeting. Caleb responded that he had already done so.

With a glance to Cynthia to assure himself that the recording was in progress, the chief turned to the mayor. "Mr. Mayor. Let's begin with your information first. It is my understanding that you were the first person in the city to be made aware of claims made concerning the property located on Second Street near the intersection with Walnut. Is that true?"

"Yes, Chief, it is."

"Would you tell us about those events and your actions taken subsequently?"

The mayor gathered himself and sat forward in his chair. He didn't look directly at Caleb but talked to the room in general. "On the afternoon of June third, Caleb Atwood came to my office to meet with me. He had requested the meeting, and it had been arranged. I had no idea what the meeting was to be about but agreed to meet with him at his request. After some initial pleasantries, Mr. Atwood produced two letters. He claimed that both letters had been left in a locked trunk for him to see when he arrived in Rogers. He claimed that was only a few days before he came to see me. One letter was open, and one was sealed. The sealed letter was addressed to me.

"He had me read the open one first. I have a copy here," Dale said as he handed out the letter. "This is a letter purportedly written by Warren Atwood to Caleb Atwood. You will see that it describes in some detail that Warren Atwood had killed my uncle, Hollis Bivens, back in 1944. I was stunned! The disappearance of Hollis is a very old mystery. He was never found, and here was a letter in which Warren Atwood admitted to the killing. In addition, and even more incredible, the letter states that Hollis is buried at the old station site. Only Warren and the past owner, Lippy Bendix, knew about the murder and the burial, according to the letter. It is claimed that they had kept the secret of the incident all these many years."

The mayor continued, "You can see that the letter went on to say some things about the fact that Warren was wealthy from overseas work and investments. It mentions how he had bought his farm and then signed the deed over to Caleb Atwood here. It also mentions that there is money being left over, which he intends to give to someone. But it didn't say who. Instead, it only mentioned that his instructions for the disbursement of the money were in the second letter—the one addressed to me."

The chief interrupted. "Mr. Mayor, tell us what you thought about the letter and also what Caleb, er... Mr. Atwood did while you read it."

"He just sat there and didn't say anything while I read it. He reiterated the claim that he had only opened this first letter a few days before when he opened the trunk. It's all there. What had I thought? Well, I was flabbergasted! This was a very old mystery that had affected my family in a big way. Having someone disappear without a trace is a big deal! I used to contemplate solving the mystery, and here was a claim as to what had happened. I was rather shaken up!"

"Okay, please proceed."

"Yes, well, the next thing I did was to open and read the second letter. That one was addressed to me. It was to be opened by me while Caleb witnessed. Here is a copy. In this letter, Warren Atwood repeats some of the stuff that was in the first letter. It goes on to admit to the killing and to describe how he wanted to give money to the city as a sort of restitution. Quite a lot of money—as you can see, he mentions $325,000. Warren wanted the money to be used to purchase and develop a park or some sort of memorial to Hollis. He also claimed that the money could be found, along with the body, on the old station site. He gives the specific location where each is buried, one above the other."

"What did you do then?" asked the chief.

"I wasn't sure what to do. I mean, I knew we had to investigate. I knew of the construction at the site and was thinking how important it was to check to see if the information in the letter was true. While I thought about it, Caleb told me that the newspaper had the story, or at least some of it. That worried me to think that the press was going to start printing stories before we could even investigate. But Caleb assured me that nothing would be printed or done until I had a chance to confirm the information. I think he referred to after their reunion, which would be about a week. He thought—well, we both thought—that it was urgent to check it out."

"And that is the way it was left?" asked the chief.

"Yes."

"What did you do next?"

"Dumar Ashton is the owner and developer of the project at the site. I called Dumar into the office and told him about the letters and the claims. I asked him if he had found anything. He was very angry about these assertions and stated that nothing had been found. However, I told him that we now had very specific information about the location, and he would have to assure me by doing some excavation in that exact spot to be positive."

"What was Mr. Ashton's response?"

"Uh, well, he thought that was uncalled for and reiterated that nothing had been found. He refused to investigate it further."

"Then what?" pushed the chief.

"I had to know. The city had to know. So, I directed Dumar to do the excavation, or the city would. I wanted him to shut down the work until we completed a search. I said I would have someone from the city there to check it out. In fact, I planned on being there. He objected but said that he would comply if directed to, but if nothing was found, he wanted full restitution for any costs incurred."

Continuing, the mayor said, "Dumar shut the project down, and the city workers went to the site and dug where it was all supposed to be. We dug deep, and all around the area. We found nothing. The city incurred all the costs of the dig, and that is why I joined in the complaint: to recover the cost at least. It seems that the information was all a hoax. I don't understand why, but I'm still left with the question of how all of this came about. That's all that I know, and that's why we are here."

The chief looked at the mayor for a moment and then asked, "Is there anything more?"

"No. Like I said, that's all I know."

The chief turned to Dumar. "Mr. Ashton, would you care to state your position in all of this?"

"Absolutely. It's like the mayor said. It's all some sort of a hoax. We have found nothing at all on that site. My job was shut down for two weeks and still is. The general contractor demobilized, and now I am left with a bunch of back-fill to do. At one spot, there might even be some damage to the slab that was already poured next to where the excavation was done. It's been expensive, and it has been wrong! I want full restitution from either the city or from Caleb Atwood."

"Now let me ask, did you see the letters?" asked the chief.

"Yes, the mayor showed them to me. But I didn't care. There was nothing there!"

"And you never dug up anything that would indicate any concern that there might be some truth to the letters?" questioned the chief.

"No! I already told you. I knew nothing. If the contractor dug anything up, that's on his shoulders. I know that sometimes stuff is found, but they just dispose of it. Certainly nothing like the letter claims was found. If I had found a bunch of money like the letter said, then happy days! But nothing was found. I think it is all a hoax, like I said, and like the mayor said. I want full restitution, and I personally believe that prosecution of Caleb At-wood is indicated for his role in perpetrating such a hoax on the city and ultimately on me."

"Anything else?" asked the Chief.

"Well, maybe. I've heard about a story being printed. If it is printed, then it will be potentially damaging to both the city and to me. It might make us look like we are hiding something. I don't want any negative publicity, and I'm sure the city doesn't. We need to set this thing right and stop any articles in the paper before they get printed," said Dumar as he looked at Peter.

The chief looked at the DA. "Henry, do you have anything to add?"

"No. I'm just here to listen."

"In that case, let's take a ten-minute break, and when we return, we will have Mr. Atwood answer these allegations and any questions which might come up."

With that pronouncement, Dumar and the mayor left the room, followed by the chief and the DA. Cynthia covered her machine and went out also. When they were gone, Caleb talked into his phone, "Lonnie. They're taking a break. Shut the door to the muster room and don't let anyone see the witnesses."

Lonnie couldn't talk back, so Caleb just hoped that it would work.

Peter said to Caleb, "They left out quite a bit, huh? Especially the mayor. He didn't mention being involved in the project or the approvals or any of the project history."

"Yeah, and Dumar left himself an escape route in case the information on the body comes up from the contractor. He can claim he knew nothing. I think he said that it would be on his shoulders, referring to the contractor. Pretty slick, don't you think."

"Perhaps, but it isn't going to work."

"No, it isn't," said Caleb.

SIXTY-ONE

Everyone returned from the break and took their seats. As Cynthia took her position and arranged to record, she signaled to the chief that she was ready. Anticipation hung in the air. Caleb repositioned his pad and phone in front of him while trying to appear calm. He was anything but. Even though he had thought this out many times, with his performance about to begin, he felt unsettled.

The chief re-opened the meeting. "Everybody ready to proceed?"

There was a murmur of consent from all.

"Cynthia, you can begin. Now, Mr. Atwood, you have heard the nature of the complaints against you. We want to determine the truth, and we must decide if there is any crime here. Would you like to take the time to explain your role in the affair, or would you prefer to answer direct questions?"

Caleb cleared his throat and responded, "Chief, the mayor and Mr. Ashton have told their story. At this point, I would like to tell mine."

"That is fine. You may proceed," directed the chief.

"Thank you. As I tell my story, I might need to ask some questions of my own. To fully make things clear. Will that be alright?"

The chief thought for a minute. "I don't see why not, but let's deal with that when it comes up. All we want is the truth, and we would like to get it as efficiently as possible. Please proceed."

Dumar interrupted, "Chief, I shouldn't have to answer any questions. I've told you everything I know. I don't even think that I should have to remain here. Investigating this is your job."

"That's true, Mr. Ashton, and the way I intend to investigate it is for you to be present as we do so. Is that understood?" asked the chief.

"Sure, I guess, but it doesn't seem necessary," Dumar said dismissively.

"It is necessary. Please proceed, Mr. Atwood."

Caleb began to tell his story. "First, let me cover a little history. Mostly to confirm some things. After my uncle Warren died, back in 2014, I received a registered letter he had prepared with instructions that it be delivered to me. I was still in Colorado at the time. The letter described how the deed to the farm had been transferred to me. It was mine free and clear. Warren said in the letter that he had taken care of everything. There were no debts or anything else to clear up. He did say that he left a locked trunk in the care of my sister, Sarah Westridge. He had delivered the key to the trunk to Nancy Matlock, a trusted family friend. I was told that I should get the key from Nancy and open the trunk when I came back. Neither Sarah nor Nancy knew of the contents, but they knew of Warren's instructions about it remaining unopened until my return. I came back to Rogers late last month. Both Sarah and Nancy are available to verify what I am saying.

"When I returned, we opened the trunk at Sarah's house. Sarah and Nancy were there at the opening. It contained many mementos that are of interest only to me and have no bearing on this issue. However, the trunk contained two letters, one addressed to me, and the one addressed to the mayor, both of which you have seen. When I opened the trunk, it was the first time I was aware of the existence of the letters. After reading the first letter, I was certainly curious as to whether the contents could be true. So, I attempted to learn a little history of the killing of Hollis Bivens. I wanted to know if it was probable or possible. It did occur to me that Warren may have become a little addled in old age and was dreaming something up. To satisfy my curiosity, I went to Peter Mason and asked him to do a little research. In short, he determined that the story could basically be true and that it aligned with the known facts from the time.

"I did not open the letter to the mayor. Warren had instructed that it was confidential and to be opened only by the mayor but with me present. After we had done our research to determine that it could all be true, I proceeded to make an appointment with the mayor, at which time I delivered the letter to him. I showed him the first letter, and then he opened the one to him. That's all as he said.

"After the meeting with the mayor, I told Peter to hold any story until we saw how it all came out. I suggested, as I had told the mayor, that no story should be printed until we heard back from the mayor. Peter wanted the whole story, of course, and he agreed to wait. I did not show Peter the mayor's confidential letter. I did exactly what I said to the mayor that I would do. I delivered the information as requested, and there was time for him to investigate. I waited until he called me back, as he had promised. However, I didn't hear back from the mayor. The first notice of any investigative results came from you, Chief, when you called me into your office. At that time, you informed me that there were these complaints. And that is why I agreed to this meeting, to hear and understand the complaints and hopefully to clear things up, which I now plan on doing."

Continuing, Caleb said, "During the week that the mayor had the letter, and prior to your call to me, I undertook a little research on my own. My friend, Lonnie Rex Stanhope, at my request, contacted the contractor on the station project to find out if anything had been found when they excavated. Lonnie was told that there were two digs, both done by a sub-contractor. The first dig was for borings to test the soil, and then the later one prior to construction. When Lonnie contacted the subcontractor, he was told that the borings did not find or dig anything up; they only took samples. But Lonnie was told that they did hit something solid in one location. It's called 'refusal,' I understand. They had to move their rig to another spot to continue the drilling. When they were finished with the work on the first dig, the subcontractor said that the owner of the project had approached him and asked to hire one of his workers for the weekend. He allowed it and said it was okay. That worker failed to show up for work the next Monday and has been missing ever since. The missing man is Onofre Montoya. He is the brother of Javier Montoya, who also works for the sub-contractor. Lonnie was told that they thought Javier knew where his brother was but that he seemed worried. They wanted Onofre to come back but didn't speak Spanish well enough to get to the bottom of it. I told Lonnie Rex that I spoke Spanish and would translate if it could help."

"Please bear with me," said Caleb to everyone listening. "I know this is involved, but it has bearing on the issue."

Caleb continued, "Lonnie Rex and I went to the sub-contractor's yard and met Jersey Stone, the foreman. We told him why we were there, and he allowed us to talk to Javier Montoya, the missing man's brother. We talked to Javier, and he told us that Onofre had left town immediately after working for some man. We asked if he knew where Onofre was, and he said that he was in Branson. He said that Onofre wanted to come back, but he was frightened of the man he had worked for on that one weekend. According to Javier, Onofre believed the man was, in his words, not a good man. However, Javier did not know who that man was. We had been told that the man was the owner of the project. We assumed it was Dumar Ashton, but we didn't know for sure."

"You're damn right you don't know for sure! Because it's all a complete lie! You don't expect us to believe some cock-eyed story made up by a damn Mexican! You're out of your mind. For all we know, you made all this up to cover your own wrongdoing!" exclaimed Dumar.

"Mr. Ashton! Please let him continue," instructed the chief.

"Sure, let him continue. Where's the Mexican? Eh, Caleb?" demanded Dumar.

Caleb looked at the chief. "Would you like to interview him now, or would you like me to finish the overall story? Onofre is here and ready to speak."

Dumar blanched at the news.

The chief thought for a moment and said, "If there's more to the story, let's hear it first."

Recovering, Dumar virtually yelled, "You gotta be kidding! Anyone can get some illegal immigrant Mexican to come in and tell a story. This is ridiculous!"

"Mr. Ashton, please let him finish. You had a turn, now it is his. Proceed, please."

Dumar crossed his arms and retreated into a sullen posture with hate filled eyes as he glared at everyone. Caleb stole a glance at the mayor who had an inquisitive but concerned look on his face.

"Let's see, where was I? Yes, Jersey Stone had us tell Javier that Onofre was welcome back and that there was plenty of work. We agreed to meet again with them as soon as Onofre came back. That turned out to be the next Monday. On that day, we went back to the sub-contractor's yard and talked to both Javier and Onofre. Jersey Stone was there when we talked. We learned from Onofre that he helped the "bad man," whom he then identified as Mr. Ashton, to dig up a steel box. The steel box was from the location where the rig had hit something. Working on the weekend after the initial borings were done, Onofre and Dumar Ashton completely unearthed the steel box, but Onofre was not shown what was inside.

"Once the box was out of the ground and loaded into Mr. Ashton's truck, Onofre said that Mr. Ashton gave him five thousand dollars. He said that he thought that the money came from the steel box. Then Mr. Ashton told Onofre that he could have the money, but he was to leave town, and if he ever saw him again, he would see that he was deported. According to Onofre,

Mr. Ashton spoke a little Spanish and used his phone to help with the words. That threat was the source of Onofre's fear. He went to Branson, Missouri, and worked there until recently."

"You can't believe any of this!" pleaded Dumar.

Caleb ignored Dumar and continued. "When we finished talking to Onofre, we were set to go, but Javier Montoya stopped us and told us that there was more to the story. Javier proceeded to tell us that a few weeks after Onofre had left town, they had returned to work at the site, and during the excavation for the foundations, they dug up a body. It was old and buried very deep."

"Oh, now it's really getting good!" remarked Dumar.

The chief turned to Dumar, "Mr. Ashton, I must demand that you refrain from comment as we hear this information. You will have a chance to respond. Go ahead, Caleb."

"Javier told us that the boss, Dennis Chiles, knew about the body and had him load the remains into the truck and that it would be disposed of. Javier said that Dennis and Mr. Ashton talked and argued. According to Javier, and confirmed later by Dennis Chiles, Ashton claimed that the body was not important and demanded that it be disposed of immediately. Ashton apparently made reference to it being a 'dead Indian' or such. They loaded it in the truck, and it was taken away. Javier did not know where they took it."

Unable to restrain himself, Dumar interrupted again, "Chief, I must object or at least point out that what we have here is a probable fabricated story from illegal immigrants and another story of a bunch of bones that are now gone. If it happened, which I doubt, then it is the contractor who disposed of the bones."

"Is there more, Caleb?" asked the chief. "Do you have any proof other than the stories?"

"Yes sir, I do."

"Then please proceed."

"Javier told us that he did not think it was just old bones. He thought it was important. When we asked why, he went to his truck and brought back these items." Caleb opened the box and laid on the table the tarnished sheriff's badge and the rusted 38 revolver. "Javier found the badge under the body and the gun was found next to it. We asked Javier why he had not shown these to anyone, and he said he was scared. He knew that Mr. Ashton was mad at the boss, and he was afraid that Mr. Ashton might do something to him, like he tried to do to Onofre.

"Javier also took a photograph of the body. It was on his phone. This is a copy of the photo," Caleb said as he laid out the photo for everyone to see. "Javier was also scared that he might lose his job, but Jersey Stone told us to tell him that would not happen. Javier also told us that Onofre knew nothing about the bones."

There was a stunned silence in the room as each person looked closely at the items that Caleb had produced. The mayor sat back in his chair and was clearly very angry. Caleb wasn't sure whether he was angry at Dumar or at being discovered. The chief examined the items and pronounced that they seemed to be genuine and indeed very old. The badge was certainly a deputy's badge and could be checked out easily. Dumar was now very silent.

Turning back to Caleb, the chief asked, "Is there more?"

"Yes. I have here an affidavit prepared by the people who attended the questioning of Javier and Onofre," said Caleb as he produced the document. "You will see that it outlines the facts revealed at the interview in some detail and the authenticity of the items recovered. It is signed by all in attendance."

"Caleb, why didn't you bring this stuff in immediately?" asked the chief.

"We only finished collecting all this late last Monday morning. It was my intent to bring it all to you after lunch that same day. However, that is when I learned that you had called looking for me. When I talked to you, you made it sound urgent. I hadn't heard from the mayor, and since the police were now involved, I began to suspect something was going on. I decided to get to know more before I turned in the evidence. When we set the meeting for today, I thought this would be the best time to reveal everything. Everyone would be here, and what we found could be revealed to everyone at the same time. In addition, I wanted to arrange to have the witnesses present. They are waiting in the muster room to be called in. They include my sister—Sarah Westridge—Nancy Matlock, Dennis Chiles, Onofre Montoya, Javier Montoya, and Lonnie Rex Stanhope who was present at almost every event."

Caleb paused and then stated, "Before we talk to the witnesses, there are a few more facts to relate to complete the story. If you would please take another look at the letter from Warren to me, you will see that he talks of an attorney who he consulted briefly about how to handle the money. The attorney was a man who had brought in his diesel truck for a rebuild. I know that Dumar Ashton is the man who went to Warren to have the truck rebuilt. That can be proven by a look at Warren's records, which I undertook to do. Here is a copy of the work order for a Dodge Power Wagon owned by Dumar Ashton and rebuilt by Warren. You will note the date. Dumar Ashton appears to be the man that Warren spoke with about the money, as outlined in the letter.

"After Warren's death and prior to my return to Rogers, over a year went by. I had Nancy Matlock look after the farm. She is a realtor and knowledgeable about property. She cared for it in my absence. During that time, Nancy's office received a request to tour the property. This was unusual since the property wasn't for sale. The request came from Dumar Ashton's office. It was reported to Nancy by the agent from his office who set up the tour, and that it was Dumar in person who toured the property. There is no suggestion that he did anything wrong by touring the farm, but it clearly indicates that he was aware of Warren's death and was looking into his estate. So, he knew there was money, but he didn't know where it was, and subsequently he visited the empty farm. We suspect that he was in search of the money, but we have no proof.

"Also, in regard to Warren's estate, Dumar Ashton became aware of Warren's lease on the property, then owned by Vernon Bendix. I spoke to Vernon and learned what had transpired. He currently lives in a retirement village near Springdale. He is also available if needed, but I decided not to inconvenience him by having him come down to the police station. He can be interviewed, if necessary, in his room. According to Vernon, Dumar negotiated a buyout of the station on the very same terms that were in place under the lease with Warren. That is, to have the option to buy the property for the same amount that Warren had negotiated but failed to act upon. There is nothing illegal in this transaction, but the amount paid would be substantially less than its market value if the historical restriction could be removed. As a matter of fact, Dumar applied to have the historical restriction lifted and was successful. Immediately after that, Dumar closed on the property.

"The events at the site unfolded once Dumar began construction activities. This was before the letters had been revealed. Dumar had no knowledge that the letters existed or that they contained the information that they did. It is our contention that he discovered the steel box of money, some $325,000 dollars, according to Warren. He knew what it was but didn't know Warren's intended recipient. He dug it up with the assistance of Onofre Montoya and then paid him off, or extorted him, to conceal the find. He kept the money. It is not his.

"Following the find of the money, the body was unearthed. Again, Dumar did not know about the letters at the time of the unearthing or about the location of the body, but he did direct the contractor to conceal the find, which is an infraction of requirements. Dennis Chiles grudgingly followed his directions and disposed of the body. It kept the project moving. We learned that the bones were disposed of at the landfill."

"Hollis Biven's remains are at the dump?" exclaimed the mayor.

"Yes, it appears so," answered Caleb.

Continuing, Caleb said, "What's very important to realize is that Dumar was shown the letters, as stated by the mayor, and from that point forward he was in full possession of all the important facts. He had the money that he knew didn't belong to him, he realized the importance of the body, and he should have immediately revealed all he knew and produced the money. He didn't, and that is where the cover-up began. That is also where the lie about my supposed hoax originated. That, I submit, is what has occurred."

The mayor leaned forward with his arms on the table and, looking at Dumar, said, "You bald-faced liar! You played me and the city!"

Dumar remained silent, refusing to even look at the mayor.

"Now hold on, Mr. Mayor," said the chief. "Caleb, are you done?"

"Not quite."

"There's more?" asked the chief.

"Yes, there is. It will only take a little more time. Can we take another break? I want to confer with the witnesses and present a little more information. If you don't mind."

"Yes, of course. Cynthia, are you getting all this?"

Cynthia nodded in the affirmative just as the chief announced, "Fifteen minutes everyone. Nobody leaves the station."

SIXTY-TWO

During the break, Caleb ignored everyone and went directly to the muster room. Everyone was waiting as instructed. It was clear that the Montoya brothers were nervous, so he reassured them in fluent Spanish that everything was going fine. They were safe from any difficulty and should be as relaxed as possible if they were called to speak. He thanked them again for all they were doing to ensure a fair and just outcome. Dennis seemed satisfied with the way things were going. He knew that Caleb had tried to create a soft landing for him, and it was appreciated.

Lonnie Rex said to Caleb, "You got 'em by the short hairs, huh, pard?"

"I'm not finished yet. Now I must figure out how to reveal what we know about the mayor. I still can't be sure of the depth of his involvement. I guess I'll just state my suspicions and see where it lands."

"Sounds like the only plan," said Lonnie. "Do you think they even want people to testify today? I'm thinking that the chief might be more comfortable talking to them alone."

"I'm beginning to think the same thing. Dumar now knows about all the evidence, so we don't need to intimidate him anymore. He knows what we say is true. If the chief goes it alone with the witnesses, it will only get worse for Dumar. Either way, I think Dumar is cooked."

Caleb turned to go back in. As he did so, he took a bottle of water from the muster room and noticed that Lonnie had a Dr. Pepper. "Where did you get that?" asked Caleb.

"I'm never too far from a Dr. Pepper. You know that," responded Lonnie. "But after today, it's going to take a lot more than Dr. Pepper to get me smoothed back out."

Caleb waved in understanding as he left the muster room. The conference room was full of everyone waiting when he returned. As Caleb took his seat, he thanked the chief for the break.

The chief confirmed everyone was in their seat and then turned to Caleb. "Let's continue. How much more do you have?"

"Only a little. Then you will have to decide whether you want to hear the witnesses now or later."

"At this point, I'm thinking later. We're getting a good picture of the events, all of which can be confirmed with witnesses as required. I may want to do that myself, as a part of my investigation as it unfolds. But please finish up," instructed the chief.

"Yes sir." Caleb paused and considered his approach. "There is no question in my mind about the role in all this that Dumar Ashton played. The evidence is available and very clear. However, there is another dimension to this story that I have some information on, but not all. It involves the mayor. I'm not here to make accusations, only observations. The old gas station was listed as a historical building for a very long time until recently. The removal of that classification allowed the building to be torn down and a new building built. As a result, the property went up in value significantly. The mayor played a role in gaining that approval from the Historical Board. It can be argued that it was good policy to make beneficial use of the property for the betterment of downtown. That I understand and would support. It can also be argued that the mayor intervened in a manner that benefited him financially. In that regard, I do have a question." Turning to the mayor, Caleb asked, "Mr. Mayor, do you have a financial interest in the project at the site of the old station?"

"Yes, I do. It is public information," responded the mayor.

"Thank you. Yes, it is public, but not very public. We had to do a bit of digging to find it out. And if you don't mind, could you tell us if that financial interest was disclosed to the Historical Board when you lobbied for the historical designation to be removed?"

"No, it was not, and didn't have to be because it had not occurred at the time. I only invested in the project later when I was approached by Mr. Ashton. It seemed a good investment, and so I made it at that time."

Turning to the chief, the mayor said, "I'm not sure I'm going to continue answering these questions. It has no relevance to the complaints against Mr. Atwood made by Dumar Ashton and joined by the city. In fact, I am hereby retracting my complaint against Caleb Atwood on behalf of the city. I am satisfied that he did not attempt to perpetrate any kind of a hoax. I think that he was acting in good faith from the very beginning."

Dumar emerged from his self-imposed silence. "You must be kidding! You're just going to cave in? Just like that? What about me? How do I get compensated for my trouble?"

The room became very quiet. Dumar sensed that he might have overstepped a bit.

It was the mayor who spoke first. In a very deliberate fashion, he said to all, "Dumar, the only trouble you are experiencing is of your own making. You lied to me when it served your purpose. You lied to all of us here. You continue to lie. Perhaps you can't even recognize the truth any longer. I tried to believe you, but never again. No matter how this turns out, I am not interested in pursuing Caleb Atwood for any wrongdoing." Continuing, the mayor said with genuine grief, "Because of your lies, my uncle is now buried in the damn dump!"

"I didn't do anything illegal, I only...."

"Shut up, Dumar," scolded the chief. "This is not the time nor the place to determine the level of your guilt. That will be decided at another time and only after a careful examination of all the evidence and a talk with the witnesses. You are hereby encouraged to remain silent. You know the drill, you're a damn attorney, unbelievably! Pardon me, Cynthia, strike that expletive."

The chief turned to Caleb, "Mr. Atwood, if you are done, I think we are finished here. I don't want any more questioning of the mayor or anyone else for that matter. The investigation that will ensue will be conducted by this department. We will require all your information and access to your witnesses. The decision on how to proceed will be up to the city and to the DA. I do not have the power to retract the complaint against you made by Mr. Ashton. That will be up to him. I suspect his decision in that regard might be strongly influenced by our findings. We will keep you informed on the progress of the investigation, and you can be assured that justice will be sought."

Caleb spoke once more to the room, "Chief, I would like to thank you for the way you have handled this matter. I did nothing wrong and only sought to carry out my uncle's last wishes for redemption and restitution by the actions he set in motion. In that regard, I have a strong desire to see those wishes still met. There are two ways for that to happen. One is for the wheels of justice to slowly churn through an investigation, legal claims, and counterclaims, along with large attorney fees, city expense and recriminations all on the way to some settlement that will occur long after this is forgotten. I'm quite sure there are some who might prefer this approach. I do not.

"There is also another way for justice to happen. That is for the proper events that should occur as a result of my uncle's wishes to simply happen. The city should announce the discovery of the body of Hollis Bivens, the confession of my uncle, and the gift to the city to memorialize as they so choose. That is as it should be. That my friend, is justice!"

"Well, I share your sentiments and the wisdom of your observations. That is up to the people involved, and I rather think that a thorough investigation is the only thing that will shake the snakes out of the trees. Too bad, but that's the way it is."

"Before you begin your investigation, I would like to tell everyone here what Peter Mason and myself are going to do."

The chief said, "Caleb, you can do what you want, but we have to—"

"Hear him out, Chief," interjected the mayor.

"Uh, well, okay. Go ahead Caleb; the mayor seems interested."

"Peter has written two articles for the paper. They have similar beginnings, but they each have a different ending. Remember it is the right of the paper to publish. To fulfill the press's obligation to the public, it must publish stories only after the veracity of those stories has been ascertained through due diligence and in the absence of any malice. What it prints needs to be the truth. Admittedly that may be a commodity that is in short supply in much of today's press, but not here. We want to print the truth, and Peter intends to.

"The question is, what is the truth relative to how Warren Atwood's dying request was handled? That truth has not occurred yet. As I alluded to before, there are two possible outcomes. These two stories represent each outcome. One of these stories will be published in Thursday's edition of the paper, without fail." Caleb produced copies of the articles to be published. "You will note that there are two stories, one labeled 'good story' and one labeled 'bad story'—I know, not very creative but okay for today's use," Caleb remarked lightheartedly. "Anyway, each story is identical through page seven. You will note that a full exposure of the facts surrounding the historical approvals, land purchase, investment by the mayor, and timeline is all included. After all, that is the truth that has already happened. Beginning on page eight, the stories diverge."

Now having their full attention, even that of Dumar, Caleb continued, "The 'good story' is there to see. Look it over starting with page eight. But to summarize, it tells how the mayor swung into action when he got the letters and immediately pursued the truth. In so doing, his business partner, Dumar Ashton revealed that the money and body were indeed uncovered in the exact place they were supposed to be. The money is now in the possession of the city. The mayor graciously accepts the money and pledges to consult with the city fathers as they determine a proper method of honoring Hollis Bivens's death. It tells how the mayor, being concerned about any hint of conflict of interest, pledges to divest himself from any interest in the project. He outlines how he had always felt that the site was too valuable to the downtown to not develop properly, and that was the basis for his support for the project. It also tells how Dumar Ashton, in keeping with his standing in the community as a developer of significant properties, pledges to personally guarantee and underwrite the full cost of care for Vernon Bendix as long as he should live. Dumar even remarks that it is the least that he could do since Vernon's selfless surrender of the property has helped this site to be developed in such a quality fashion.

"This will be the story going into the paper on Thursday, if and only if a press conference is held tomorrow, at which time the information in the article is specifically announced and made true. That includes the immediate surrender of the money to the city, the return of the mayor's investment, and the execution of a written contract for Vernon's care, guaranteed by Dumar Ashton or the LLC formed as the owner of the property. Once that happens, the residents of Rogers will all get the good news, and the mystery of the demise of Hollis Bivens will end. The charges against me will be retracted and no mention of them will occur in the paper. That is justice in my view and will make a most impressive article for all involved.

"In the event that such a resolution is not reached and there is no press conference to announce such events, then the other article will be published. Again, in summary, that article includes the full truth of what has transpired here today. All will be revealed. It includes the charges leveled against me, all the activities of Dumar Ashton as testified to by witnesses, the list of all the evidence along with pictures as submitted to the chief of police, and a lengthy summary of the financial investment in the project by the mayor. It will relate how all the evidence has been reported to and turned over to the police for a full in-depth investigation. The article pledges to closely follow the outcome of the investigation and report on all charges made against the players. At the time of the printing of that article, it will also be the truth, but the opportunity for the players to step up and get credit for doing the right thing will be passed.

"That is what we are going to do," pronounced Caleb.

There was a stunned silence around the room as they digested what Caleb promised. The chief looked at the DA and asked him, "Henry, do you have any questions or observations at this time?"

Henry Dawes broke into a slight smile and said, "No, Chief, I'm just here to observe. I will say, however, that charges to be considered would include theft, false claims made, extortion, collusion, threatening a private citizen, public corruption, and a few lesser charges, in no order of importance."

"Thank you, Henry. Anyone else have anything to add?"

"Well, I for one—"

"Shut up, Dumar!" said the mayor, echoing the chief's previous directive.

Looking at Caleb, the chief said, "You're a pretty smart fellow, aren't you Mr. Atwood? Well, don't get too smart. I'm rather smart myself."

"I think that wraps it up for today's meeting. Caleb, I'm sure you will be informed as to which way this is to go. Thank you for your work on this matter. It looks like it will save me a great deal of time, whichever way it goes," said the chief.

"And thank you, Chief, for handling this in such an unbiased fashion," said Caleb.

"Cynthia, wrap it up. I will need record copies tomorrow morning if you please," concluded the chief. As people got up to leave, the chief turned back to Caleb and asked, "Caleb, are you going to remain in Rogers permanently? This article, whatever one it is, will put the spotlight on you. Are you ready for that?"

"I guess so."

"What will you do here in your new home?"

"Right about now, I'm thinking of running for mayor."

The current mayor overheard the statement and the chief's parting remark to Caleb, "Well, you might make a good one at that. Best of luck to you."

SIXTY-THREE

The neck of the trailer slammed into place as Caleb backed his truck into the latching mechanism. He thought that he would take the trailer out to the farm to have a place to stay while he began to work out there. For now, Caleb thought that he would leave Cisco at Sarah's. He could bring him out when the fences were all ready and when he began to stay out there consistently. After all the activity of the last few days, Caleb wanted to have a nice place to stay far from the madding crowd, as they say. He would learn today which way the story about the station was going to go. Was there going to be an announcement by the mayor, or not? He hoped that it would turn out in the "good" way. Whichever way it went, it would be nice to be through with it and just be a spectator.

God has a way of opening doors as we walk with Him, Caleb thought. So many doors had been opened for him in such a short time, it was plumb difficult to walk through all of them. One at a time, he told himself. Now it was time to focus on the wedding and the farm, and he was anxious to do just that. The wedding held so many questions and details of such importance to all the people he cared for that he quickly realized that he should allow it all to play out in good time. Perhaps there was an argument that he should speak only when spoken to. He needed to let Lori and her anointed ones make all the decisions. He was glad to supply an answer to any direct question, assuming he understood the question. What was it about weddings that made them so potentially hazardous to the male participants? He tried to puzzle out how he could know any of this since he had never been married. Maybe God was warning him to be ready.

As he went back to thinking about the farm, it occurred to him that Daniel might want to stay out there while work was underway. The trailer had bunk beds, so it would be good for two if needed. That thought led to the realization that if he and Lori ever traveled with the trailer, the bunk beds would not serve, and that meant he would have to fix that, or he could get a new…. He realized he was doing it again. Trying to walk through too many doors at once. Back to the work at hand. He climbed in the cab and pulled away with the trailer in tow. Caleb wasn't aware of the concerned expression Cisco displayed as he watched the trailer pull away.

Caleb's thoughts turned back to the previous afternoon. After the meeting at the city, Caleb had taken all the "witnesses" to dinner. They went back out to Burl's Steakhouse. The group was certainly an interesting combination of folks. As diverse as they were, they had all enjoyed each other's company. The "comradery of witnesses," he reckoned, if there was such a thing. Caleb had been seated between the Montoya brothers and had learned that their English was not as bad as they let on. Sarah was in a sort of heaven with so many targets for her questions, and Nancy was clearly fascinated with the peculiar gathering. Even Dennis and Jersey fit right in and enjoyed everyone's company. Perhaps they were all just glad it was over. Caleb learned that Dennis was a respected contractor and that there was a possibility that he might be interested in doing the work at the farm. In addition, the Montoya brothers had a great deal of experience working horses back in Mexico. So funny how things interrelated. Lonnie Rex quietly enjoyed listening in on the conversations as he tipped back a few glasses of Redbreast Irish whisky. By the end of the evening, Lonnie was substantially placid.

Burl's Steakhouse reminded Caleb of Lori. He wished she had been here for the meeting, the dinner, and could be here for the work to be done at the farm. He had called her on the phone, and that would have to suffice for now. He learned that Daniel would be back late today and ready to meet on Thursday morning. Lori was rather quiet about her transition efforts but didn't indicate that there was any problem. She still hoped to fly back in a week or so. Caleb hadn't told her much about the meeting with the city because there was so much to tell her that saving it for an in-person talk would work much better.

Dickie and Estes were fast at work as Caleb arrived at the farm. He was amazed how steady these two were. Sarah sure steered him right on them. They were making great progress on cleaning everything up and demolishing what needed to go. There was now a full trailer of trash and debris to be taken to the dump. Caleb selected a good location for his trailer and backed it into position. After unhooking it and making sure it was level, he talked to Dickie and Estes, and they all agreed that the best thing to do was to have Caleb take the trash trailer to the dump. He hooked it up to his truck and pulled out of the farm. On his way to the dump, Caleb morbidly wondered if he would be dumping this stuff on top of Hollis but quickly let go of the thought.

After his trip to the dump, Caleb stopped by the store and purchased what he thought he would need in the trailer for comfortable living. By early afternoon, Caleb had completed most of his intended work at the farm and gotten the trailer set up for occupancy, his or Daniel's.

Caleb had heard nothing from Peter, so he thought a little trip into town might be in order.

It was 2:30 when he headed that way. His first stop was at Lonnie's house. When he didn't see Lonnie on the porch, he went in the house to search for him. Lonnie wasn't to be found in the house either. Caleb stepped back out onto the porch to wait. Just as he sat down, he realized that he could just call Peter to see if he had heard anything. His phone was in the truck where he had left it as he worked. As he approached the truck to retrieve the phone, he heard it ringing.

"Hello," said Caleb.

Peter's voice came through the phone. "Caleb, where have you been?"

"Out at the farm. I'm over at Lonnie's now, but he isn't here."

"Lonnie's over here at my office. I got hold of him, but you didn't answer."

Caleb realized that he must have missed the call while working. "I'm sorry, I didn't hear the phone. What's up?"

"You need to get over here. It was announced that the mayor is going to give a press release at 4:00 p.m. We can go over from here. This could be it."

"What's he going to say?" Caleb wondered aloud.

"I guess we'll find out, but what else could it be?"

"Alright, I'll come over. Hope it's what we think it is," said Caleb.

When Caleb arrived at Peter's office, he found Peter at his desk and Lonnie reclining on the sofa. It was about thirty minutes until the scheduled press release. Caleb shoved Lonnie's legs out of the way and sat down next to him.

"You mentioned a press release, didn't you? Isn't that some sort of printed handout or something?" asked Caleb.

"Yeah, you're right, but this one comes with a public announcement at city hall. There is a release, but first we will get to hear what he says in person."

"Do we have enough time to go to print with the story in the morning?" asked Caleb.

"Sure. It's all prepared—both stories. And there's enough time to tweak the one we print if there are any needed adjustments."

Lonnie interjected, "You guys hold it down, okay? I'm recovering from a good time."

Both Caleb and Peter stared at Lonnie Rex in respectful bewilderment.

When the time came, the three of them, along with a couple of the paper's staff, walked over to city hall. The conference room was set up for the mayor to speak, and the room was full of interested people. There were police officers there, the press, the DA along with some staff members, and a smattering of others. Chief of Police Blaylock was the last to walk in. Caleb noticed that Dumar was not in the room.

As everyone settled in, Mayor Bivens entered from the side door and went to the podium. He thanked everyone for coming on short notice and proceeded to announce that he had some good news along with a story of a very old mystery being solved. With that introduction, the mayor followed the script outlined by Caleb on the previous day. There was virtually no variation. The letters were released to the public, and the mayor told the story of what had apparently transpired back in 1944 when his uncle, Deputy Hollis Bivens, had disappeared. After receiving the letters, the mayor related how they had immediately undertaken a search for the money and the body as outlined in the letters.

The mayor told how they had worked together to find the remains of Hollis Bivens and the donated money for the memorial. The mayor singled out Dumar Ashton as being especially instrumental in finding and presenting the money and being very helpful in uncovering the remains of Hollis at the site. According to the mayor, Dumar was additionally magnanimous in his consideration for the longtime owner of the property, Vernon Bendix. With the recent history of the property sale and the increased value of the project, Dumar had pledged to cover the cost of Vernon's care in his declining years. It was a selfless and welcome gesture, as told by the mayor.

Additionally, the mayor told of his personal devotion to the redevelopment of the site, and how, because of that support, he had chosen to personally invest in the project. He told how, upon reflection, it could look improper for him to be financially involved because of his family's ties to the history discovered there. As a result, he announced that he had divested his financial interest in the property.

Finally, he pledged to work with the city leadership to determine the most fitting way to commemorate the death of Hollis Bivens and to fully acknowledge Warren Atwood's role in the unfortunate death of Hollis and his gift to the city in consideration of the responsibility he felt. The city would be announcing its plans for the memorial once they are finalized. The mayor also thanked Caleb Atwood for his handling of his uncle's last wishes and for his assistance to the city in all its efforts.

There were many questions from the audience in the room. The mayor answered all their questions without saying anything additional, a skill that the mayor had in common with most politicians. A lively discussion occurred when everyone had read the letters from Warren. The mayor handled all the questions well but turned the focus to the history of the mystery of the Hollis Bivens disappearance. It made for satisfying theater. When there were questions about why Dumar Ashton was not in attendance, the mayor simply said that Dumar wanted no credit and that he was just doing his civic duty. The entire conference took less than thirty minutes. The mayor then exited the room with a pledge to keep the public informed on the progress and with a wave to his constituents.

Lonnie Rex and Caleb did not return to Peter's office. Peter assured them that the story would go out in the morning edition. They got into Caleb's truck and went straight to Lonnie's porch. Lonnie Rex plopped down in the rocker and said to Caleb, "Well, he really put lipstick on the pig!"

"Who?" asked Caleb.

"Don't be dense! The mayor! He made Dumar out to be a real servant to the community! He's only a servant to his own greed. I think that we ought to go over and shoot Dumar!"

Caleb laughed. "I've seen you shoot. Dumar is safe."

"Don't you think it's just bloody wrong? Him getting off and smelling so good?"

Caleb thought for a minute. "Lonnie, my primary goal was to have Warren's wishes honored. If anything gets in the way of that, then I will feel that I have failed. A lengthy prosecution of Dumar would have prevented that from happening. This way it's done. Just like Warren wanted."

"I know what you are saying, and I agree, but it's a turd in the punch bowl as far as justice is concerned. You know it, and I know it!"

"I'm not so sure. Think a little about Dumar. All through high school, everybody called him 'Dumb Ash', because of his name and his demeanor. And it stuck. I can't help but think that we all helped cement his attitude. When we were in college together, he tried to be a different person, you know—sort of a new identity. But he always carried that baggage of disrespect we all heaped on him. I'm not proud of any part I played in that. I know that he is ultimately responsible for his actions, but I can't help thinking that a little positivity toward him might do more to straighten him out than prosecution ever could."

"I don't know, man. He's been that way for a long time."

"And if he is ever to get past it, it might take a long time. I remember this guy we had on the ranch. Everyone called him Possum. He wasn't too sharp, and all the hands gave him a hard time. He was the lowest of low on the totem pole. But I learned that once I gave him a chance to step up and do some real cowboying, he shaped up mighty quick. He was a good horseman, and it showed when he got the chance. Who knows? Maybe Dumar needs a chance. Of course, it might take some time."

"You're a dreamer, Caleb," pronounced Lonnie Rex.

"Yep," replied Caleb. "I've been called worse."

"No, my friend, you haven't," said Lonnie with profound respect. "But I still might shoot Dumar!"

"Stay calm, pard," Caleb said as he got up. "I'll see you at Casper's in the morning?"

"Yep. It'll be good to get everything back to normal. Bring money!"

SIXTY-FOUR

Thursday morning at Casper's Grill found Lonnie and Caleb back in their comfortable routine. Caleb had begun to think of the morning breakfasts as becoming a great start to every day henceforth. There is a delightful stability to having rituals, especially ones that are shared with a trusted friend.

Lonnie Rex pushed a copy of the morning paper across the table to Caleb. There on the front page was the story concerning the press conference and everything that was said. Peter had touched it up a little bit to include the mayor's spin on the story, but it was the story that Caleb had sought. He had read it many times and pushed it aside when he was satisfied with the result.

Lonnie shook his head and said, "Now it's in print. Dumar the community leader and doer of good deeds! It still sticks in my craw!"

"Just one more thing that you'll have to get used to. You can do it," claimed Caleb.

Lonnie fell silent and lit a cigarette. Caleb thought about the day. His only plan was to hook up with Daniel. Maybe a call a little later would serve. Daniel might just be sleeping in a little later than 6:30 a.m., he reasoned. Caleb was looking forward to seeing the plans that Daniel and Lori had come up with, and getting the project started. As it turned out, Caleb was surprised when Daniel called him. Caleb's phone rang loudly in the restaurant as he fished it from his pocket to answer. He had learned to carry the phone and not always leave it in the truck. He had missed too many calls.

Caleb answered, "Hello... Daniel?"

From the phone, "I'm back. Got in last night. Where are you?"

"We're at Casper's Grill. Lonnie and I. Come on over if you want."

"Uh, yeah, that'll work. Give me about a half hour."

"We're not going anywhere," pledged Caleb.

He hung up the phone and told Lonnie Rex, "Daniel's coming over."

"That's good. You know, I haven't met him yet," said Lonnie.

"You haven't? No, I guess not. Well, it's about time. He seems like a good young man. I'm liking him," said Caleb.

"That'll be handy since he's going to be your step-son," observed Lonnie Rex.

Caleb confronted that reality, perhaps for the first time. "Yeah, you're right. And so far, so good. Reckon I'll never have a son of my own, so maybe I will enjoy him. He might work out fine!"

"Looks like I'm not going to get any kids either, unless I find a Jaws Three that's a good bit younger," surmised Lonnie. "The more I think about it, the more I like that idea. Yeah, a young one! Maybe I've been looking in all the wrong places."

"Lonnie, you've been doing something wrong, that's for sure!" Caleb pronounced. "You've gone through two perfectly good candidates. The fault must lie with you. You better fix yourself before you subject another one to the rigors of being a Mrs. Stanhope."

"Ah, the voice of reason and compassion—it always depresses me. But I'll give it a try. The only thing is, I don't know what to fix," complained Lonnie.

"Seek and ye shall find!" promised Caleb.

After a few more cups of coffee enjoyed in relative silence, Caleb heard the jingle of the door as Daniel walked in. Searching the dining area, Daniel saw Caleb and came into the back room. Caleb rose and shook Daniel's hand.

"Daniel, meet Lonnie Rex Stanhope. You've heard a lot about him, and here he is."

Lonnie rose a couple of inches and grabbed Daniel's hand. "Welcome to the center of the universe. Right here is where big things get decided. Have a seat."

They all sat down, and Caleb asked, "Have you had breakfast?"

"Uh, no, not yet. Smells good in here. I'll order something," Daniel said as he searched for the waitress.

After he ordered, Daniel talked about his return drive from Las Vegas. It had taken him two long days with a stop in Tucumcari, New Mexico, to spend the night.

"That's a garden spot!" remarked Lonnie. "I spent one night there several years ago. Seemed like a week! It might be a good place to go if you only had a year to live—a year there would seem like a lifetime."

Ignoring Lonnie, Daniel proceeded to tell Caleb of his plans. "Caleb, can we wait on the drawings maybe until tomorrow? I contacted the University of Arkansas and found out all about the architectural curriculum. It sounds great, but it's late to be applying. They told me that if I could come in as soon as possible, I could have an interview and give them my records. With that, they will see if there is a spot for me for the fall. But I've got to hurry."

"Well, sure. The plans can wait. Get on down there and secure yourself a place. That's a lot more important," said Caleb. "Do you need me to come?"

"I guess not. I already told them about you and how I'm living here. I said that you would be a reference if needed. Today it'll be fine for me to go alone. Maybe later, if I get signed up, you can take me down and show me around."

"Okay, that'll work. Whatever you need. You can give them my address or Winnie's. Maybe you will get in-state tuition. You might, since your grades are good and all. They want students."

"I would like that, but it's not necessary. I've got the costs covered; I think. You know, it's a lot less expensive than Berkeley."

Lonnie Rex spoke up. "You betcha it's cheaper, and a whole lot better! You might become really goofy if you go to Berkeley. That place zaps people's brains!"

Daniel looked at Lonnie, and not knowing what to make of him, he simply said, "Yeah, I've heard. I never wanted to go there anyway."

Caleb asked, "What about your mom? She indicated that she was coming out next week. Is that still on?"

Daniel paused. "Uh, well, I'm not sure about that. She's been very busy at the clinic and all. I don't know when she'll come."

Caleb sensed that Daniel was holding back a bit but decided not to pursue it. He could call Lori on his own and get any update.

Returning to the issue of the plans and the farm, Caleb said, "Tomorrow is fine to start on the plans. We can wait even longer if the school situation requires more time. In the meantime, I have moved my trailer out to the farm. If you want, you can stay in it while the work goes on. Might be better than staying at Winnie's, but it's up to you. I'll probably stay out there some, but there's room for two."

"Gosh, that would be great. I think I would like that, especially when work starts. Will you have Cisco out there too?"

"Once the fencing is complete and the barn is stocked. Cisco can come out when the farm becomes my primary camp. He needs to be ridden and worked out several times a week."

"I would like to ride him too, if that's alright," explained Daniel.

"Absolutely! He likes to go as much as possible."

Daniel finished his breakfast and looked at his watch. "I've got to go to Fayetteville now. I have an early appointment."

As Daniel arose from the table, he reached in his pocket, but Caleb stopped him. "Breakfast is on us."

"Us! Oh nay nay, my friend. Breakfast is on you, remember? You're way behind," Lonnie claimed.

"Of course, Lonnie. Just as you say." Turning to Daniel, Caleb shook his hand. "Give me a call when you get back and let me know how it went and the schedule you want to follow. I'm ready for whatever."

"Thanks, Caleb. Glad to meet you, Lonnie Rex."

"I'm glad you got to meet me too."

As Daniel left the restaurant, Caleb stared at Lonnie.

"What?" asked Lonnie.

SIXTY-FIVE

After breakfast at Casper's, Caleb wasn't sure what to do with himself. Lonnie went home to paint, and there was no way he could help with that endeavor, so he decided to return to the farm and help Dickie and Estes in any way he could. He was mildly concerned about how Lori was coming along in her efforts to plan the move and the wedding. Daniel hadn't given him any news that was reassuring. In fact, Daniel seemed sort of deadpan about the whole deal. Caleb figured he would have to wonder a bit longer. It was still much too early to call Las Vegas. It would have to wait until a little later in the day.

Caleb's phone rang as he was driving. He pulled it out of his pocket and answered, "Hello."

It was Nancy on the line. "I just saw the paper. It all went down as you wanted. I thought the story was very good. Even old Vernon comes out with what you wanted for him. But Dumar escaped unscathed along with pats on the back! Quite a variation of his performance at the hearing!"

"Yeah, I know, but I'm satisfied. I just want it behind me," said Caleb.

Nancy's voice continued, "Caleb, I meant to ask you. The other day when you left the meeting, you said something about running for mayor. What was that all about?"

"Oh, it was nothing. I don't know, it just leaped to mind. Maybe seeing how the mayor behaved. It left me a little cold. I don't know," answered Caleb. "How did you know about that?"

"We heard it on your phone, remember? You didn't turn it off until a moment later."

"Oh, yeah. Well, it doesn't mean anything," insisted Caleb.

"I called Peter to congratulate him on the article in the paper, and he also asked me about the comment. He heard it because he was with you," said Nancy. "He wonders if you are serious about running."

"No. I mean why would I want to be mayor? I've never run for anything. I wouldn't get to first base. If you run for office and just tell the whole truth, you're doomed. I should have kept my mouth shut. Besides, who would vote for me?"

"Would you like me to give you a list?" asked Nancy.

"Now stop this! It was just a remark. Let it go."

"Peter is planning to publish a follow-up article, in more detail. He plans to tell more of your story."

"My story?" asked Caleb.

"Yes. You know, your history with Rogers, your dad and mom, your life out west, that sort of thing. Plus, cowboy stuff."

"Who's going to care about that?"

"You might be surprised. This story has captured people's attention. They're hooked. And according to Peter, the follow-up needs to be written while the interest is high."

"Maybe I can talk him out of it," Caleb speculated.

"Oh, let him have his head. He's earned it after all his work. It's a good story, and he won't print anything that might embarrass you, because there is nothing. It'll be fine."

"I just hope the running for mayor comment dies out."

"Okay, whatever you say, but you may have to confront your words," stated Nancy.

"I'll be ready, I guess. I'll talk to you later."

"Alright. Bye. See you later," said Nancy.

Caleb's phone rang almost the moment he hung up with Nancy. He had no way of knowing who it was because he had not entered any contacts in his phone. Every call was a blast from the unknown.

"Hello," said Caleb.

This time it was Dennis Chiles. "Caleb, I saw the article. I wanted to thank you again for how you handled it all. You gave me a soft landing. The city doesn't seem interested in me. I appreciate it."

"No problem, Dennis. Like I tell everyone, I'm just glad it's over."

"I also wanted to say that I would be interested in helping you out with the construction on your farm. I've got a good crew for residential and think we could do you a good job."

"Yes, I would like for you to look at it. We haven't finished the final plans yet. We only have some sketches, and the construction drawings are not done, but as soon as I'm ready, I'll give you a call," said Caleb.

"I will look forward to it, and you should know that we can prepare plans for permitting and construction. We do it in-house."

"Oh, really? Yeah, that sounds good. That might work. I'll call you as soon as I have something," promised Caleb.

"Okay, I'll wait to hear from you. And by the way, if you want to run for mayor, give me a call. Maybe I can support you. I've got a little stroke."

"Dennis, this is getting out of hand. It was only idle talk. I was just blithering.... Okay, look, if I decide to run, I'll let you know," said Caleb, thinking that it was the easiest way to escape the subject.

"I understand. I'll see you later," Dennis said and hung up.

By the time that Caleb almost made it to the farm, the phone had rung three more times. They were calls from people he hadn't met, but they had his number. Thankfully none of the callers had mentioned the running for mayor thing. They wanted to say they had read the paper and enjoyed the story. One man had reminisced about Warren and how he enjoyed him when he was working on trucks.

As Caleb turned onto the dirt lane leading to the farm, the phone rang yet again. Caleb sighed and answered one more time, "Hello."

"Caleb. This is the chief of police."

"Oh, hi, Chief. What can I do for you?"

"Well, now that all the drama and the story is behind us, we here at the station would like to talk to you."

"Who's we?" Caleb asked, fearing what he might hear.

"Just me on behalf of the police, and Henry Dawes, the DA. Not the mayor."

"And what is this about? I'm ready to have it all over with."

"I understand, but there are a few loose ends. Could you stop by?"

"No, I don't think so. I've about had my fill of that place. However, if you want to meet with me for lunch, that could work," said Caleb.

"Very well. We'll meet you out at the Landmark Steakhouse if that's okay. About 1:30 p.m. today if you can make it. Do you know where it is?"

Caleb resigned himself to one more appearance before the higher-ups, and commented, "Yes, that will do, and I can find it."

"Thank you very much. Oh, and lunch will be on us. See you then."

You betcha lunch will be on you, thought Caleb. "Okay, bye."

The first thing Caleb did was to put his phone back into the console of his truck. He had received enough calls for the day. There was still about three hours to get some work done before the lunch meeting, so he pulled up at the farm and decided to inspect the barn to see how much work there was to do so that he could bring Cisco out.

When the time came to return to town, Caleb told Dickie and Estes that he might not be back and asked if they needed anything else. He told them about what was needed in the barn for

Cisco and left a list of things they could do, along with another check. They suggested that he didn't need to do anything else for a while. Another trip to the dump the next day might be required, but otherwise they were good.

Caleb climbed into his truck and remembered his phone. In fact, he realized that this was a good time to give Lori a call. Before starting the truck, he dialed Lori's number. It rang several times and went to voice mail. He left a brief message that he was simply checking in and wanted to hear her voice. He said that she should call. As he hung up the phone, he hoped that none of the concern that he was starting to feel came over in his voice.

The Landmark Steakhouse was out in the new glittery part of Rogers. With all the growth in the area, they now had all the standard development of shops, big-box retail, and restaurants that inhabited cities across the country. It all looked the same and had the same traffic congestion. Caleb briefly reflected on why and how architects could manage to copy each other everywhere they went. He knew some of it was based on marketing of name brands, but signs used to do that while still allowing unique design to occur. It wasn't his concern, he told himself. However, it would give him a good discussion topic with Daniel.

Caleb arrived at the restaurant on time. When he entered the lobby, he could see the chief and the DA ensconced in a high back booth against the windows. He made his way over to them and sat down next to Henry Dawes. This way he could look at the chief directly.

"Thanks for coming, Caleb," said the chief.

"Good to see you," chimed in Henry.

"No problem. Good to see you guys. Never pass up a free lunch, huh?" quipped Caleb.

"We like this place. I usually get salmon. They do a good job," said the chief.

Caleb studied the menu. The waitress took their drink orders and promised to be right back. The chief opened the discussion with, "Caleb, let me get to the point. We have reviewed all the evidence you presented and checked it out. It all seems accurate and applicable. I don't think we feel the need to challenge anything you presented. And we understand your position on the whole deal. The press conference and the article fell into place just as you wanted."

"Okay, so what's up?" asked Caleb. "Is there a problem?"

Henry Dawes inserted, "No, no problem as such, but as DA—and I think the chief feels the same way—I am a little concerned that Dumar Ashton is being allowed to skate through this unscathed. We both feel that he should be held accountable for his actions. Right, Chief?"

"That's right. I mean, he stole the money and lied about it. He even brought a complaint against you that he knew was fraudulent. In addition, I even have concerns about the mayor's handling of the whole deal. Dale knew the drill from the get-go, I believe," claimed the chief.

"So, what are you going to do?" asked Caleb.

They were interrupted by the waitress taking their food orders. When she left, the conversation continued. The chief explained, "With the way things are now, it is difficult to take any action. It won't work to go after Dumar now that he has been allowed to change the outcome, and the mayor is even more difficult. We might be able to prove that he was in on the project from the beginning, but now he too has been allowed to frame the story in a way that suits him."

"I understand. So, I ask again, what are you proposing to do?"

"There is one way that we could proceed without interrupting the current direction," said Henry. "Dumar has not been allowed by anything that has transpired to avoid his responsibility for filing a fraudulent claim against you. He did that, it's on the record, and even if everything else is left in place, he should answer for that."

"However, for action to be taken, you would have to file a complaint against him for the fraudulent charge he made. Then we could investigate it and make recommendations, maybe file against him," interjected the chief.

"So, let me get this straight. You want me to file charges against Dumar for his filing false charges against me. That right?"

"That's the size of it. Don't you want him held accountable for his actions?" Henry said.

"Well, sure, but when you think about it, there are many ways he will be held accountable for his actions," stated Caleb.

"Not really. Only if we go after him," the chief pointed out. "That way, the law will be followed."

"Ah, the law!" said Caleb. "The law—that great institution through which justice is dispensed on the wicked, right? Let me ask you, does the law set things right, or does it just punish the people held responsible? Does the law mend the damage to the victims? Obviously, the only thing that the law can do is to exact a penalty on those who misbehaved. It doesn't change or amend the results of the bad behavior, does it? And it doesn't prevent the bad behavior going forward, does it? At least not very often. So, when the law is finished doling out its version of justice, we are left with angry and unrepentant bad guys who have only learned that it is them against the system. And on it goes."

Continuing, Caleb said, "Sure, it sort of pleases me to imagine Dumar being penalized for his actions. But it's not justice, it's retribution. That's what the law is: retribution, not justice. Justice is when all things damaged or hurt are set right, and when those who caused the damage are required to perform the corrective work and bear the cost involved in setting those things right. That's justice. In the process, those who caused the damage are required to confront that which caused them to do the damage, measure for measure. Dumar had to fork over the money, Dumar had to give up the mayor's investment in his project, and Dumar had to address and fix the unfair treatment of Vernon. That's the justice we all seek. As far as his complaint against me is concerned, there aren't any damages to me. He told a falsehood, I proved his complaint was false, and he suffered the loss of respect from those who know about the issue. I'm not damaged. If anything, my stature is strengthened. No, I won't press any charges."

"Well, that all sounds good, but what about when someone kills someone or does something that is not repairable?" questioned the chief.

"Then it gets tough, doesn't it? In those cases, law enforcement finds the guilty and requires them to surrender something very dear in lieu of replacing the irreplaceable. Maybe that is giving up their freedom, maybe it is paying large sums of money, or maybe both. Something considered equal to that which they took or destroyed. But ask yourself, if their early bad behavior had been met early on with a true form of justice, like I describe here, instead of punishing tradeoffs, would they have grown to commit irreparable crimes? I don't know, and this is all a little philosophical. The point is that in this case, there is no irreparable damage, and I won't press charges. Dumar skates, and we will see what he does in the future."

The waitress arrived with their food just as Caleb finished, and the table grew silent as the food was distributed.

"This looks good. I may have to come here more often," said Caleb.

"I told you so," the chief said before continuing thoughtfully, "I get your point, and I understand. No charges. We'll let it go and just hope old Dumar sees the error of his ways."

"There you go," said Caleb as he cut into his salmon.

"You know, you might make a good mayor after all," observed the chief.

"Oh, no! I beg you, please let that go," pleaded Caleb.

SIXTY-SIX

Late Thursday afternoon, Daniel called Caleb. When he called, Caleb was on another trip to the dump with trash from the farm. Daniel said that everything had gone very well at the university, and he was reasonably sure that he could be admitted to the architectural curriculum in the fall. He was excited about starting school and was anxious to have Caleb show him around campus. He needed to select housing options and schedule some tests for placement. It looked like a busy summer ahead getting ready for school.

Daniel suggested that they meet on Friday morning at 9:00 a.m. if that was agreeable to Caleb. Caleb thought that 10:00 a.m. would work a little better and would allow him time to have breakfast and give Cisco a workout, so they agreed that they would meet then and get started on the review of the plans. Caleb had still not heard from Lori but refrained from asking Daniel about it. He thought that he would probably hear from her later.

After returning to Sarah's at the end of the day, Caleb paid some attention to Cisco and then joined Sarah for a quiet dinner of bacon and tomato sandwiches and tossed salad. Caleb told Sarah all about his meeting with the chief of police and the DA. He explained what they wanted him to do and his answer.

Sarah listened to his account of the meeting and then said, "Well, I'm sort of in agreement with them. Dumar is getting out of everything. Is that really fair?"

"Fair? That's an interesting notion. Yeah, I think that it is 'fair' since everything is as it would be if Dumar had behaved from the beginning. I already explained that to them and now to you."

"Do you know anything more about the mayor? What did they say about him?"

"I don't know anything for sure. The chief did say that he suspected that the mayor was in it from the beginning, but he doesn't have anything, and I don't really care. It's not my job to police the guy. I guess the voters will decide," said Caleb.

"The good news is that it's over, huh?" asked Sarah.

"That's for sure."

"What's next on your busy agenda? When are you meeting with Daniel?" asked Sarah.

"At 10:00 a.m. tomorrow. I'll get some breakfast and work Cisco out and then go out to the farm. Daniel will meet me there. That's the plan."

"I'm preparing a late lunch here and… oops. I mean, if you want, I can fix a lunch."

"What do you mean, oops?" asked Caleb.

"Uh, well, uh, I just mean that it is up to you. Will you be finished by lunch?"

"Yeah, I guess. There'll be stuff to do, but lunch is good. Daniel and I can come back and eat here if you want to fix something," Caleb said disinterestedly.

"Okay. I'll do it. What time?"

"I don't know. Maybe about 1:30. I'll call if there is a holdup."

Caleb finished his sandwich and got up from the table. "I need to call Lori. I haven't spoken to her in a day or two. I want to see how she is coming. Daniel says she has been busy."

"Okay. I'll clean up."

Caleb went out to the front porch and dialed Lori on her cell phone. There were several rings, and then just when he was about to hang up, she answered. "Hello! Caleb?"

He sat up in the chair and responded, "There you are! I've been trying to get ahold of you. How is everything going?"

"I'm sorry for not calling sooner. It's been hectic. It's going slow, and I'm still at it."

"Do you know when you will be coming back?" asked Caleb.

"Uh, well, I'll see you when I can, I guess. How's Daniel doing?"

"I only saw him early this morning. He went to the university to be interviewed. He did call back late this afternoon and said it went well. He seems excited. Anyway, we're going to meet in the morning," explained Caleb. "Wish you could be here."

"Yeah, I know. Well, I hope it goes well and that you like the plans. We worked hard on them. You can look them over and then we can, um... talk," stammered Lori.

Caleb sensed that she was holding back but didn't want to press her. He was just glad to hear her voice.

Lori continued, "Listen, I've got to go. Bunches to do. I love you. I'll talk to you tomorrow, I promise," said Lori. "Bye."

"Okay, bye. I love you too..." he said into a dead receiver.

SIXTY-SEVEN

Friday finally arrived. Caleb would get to see the plans and begin thinking about their future home. He had dismissed Lori's dull responses on the phone the last evening as just a result of how tired she must be. He knew that it was a big transition for her, and there had to be a great many things on her mind. He was looking forward to fully digesting the plans and, as a result, would have something substantive to talk to her about. He was mildly regretting not including her in all that had happened in the last three days, but he had felt that it wouldn't be good to bother her with all of that.

His workout with Cisco and his breakfast with Lonnie Rex had transpired as planned. Lonnie had been interested in his meeting with the chief and the DA, but Caleb had explained one more time that it was over and that was that. Lonnie seemed to accept the finality of it and mercifully did not mention anything about Caleb's remark about running for mayor. At least Lonnie could not be fooled by his silly remark.

It was a few minutes after 10:00 a.m. when Caleb pulled into the farm. He noticed Daniel's car parked in front of the porch. Dickie and Estes were not working today. They had explained to Caleb how they had to help an elderly lady move into town. Those guys sure got around, he thought.

Daniel met him on the porch and began chattering immediately about his trip to the university. The architectural school had impressed him, and the displays of student work were certainly inspiring. He was virtually brimming with expectancy for a trip there in the fall. Caleb told him a few things about his time at the university and agreed again to go down for a tour.

The plans were spread out on a folding table in the middle of the living room. Daniel had brought some folding chairs and had even set up an easel with drawings attached. Caleb noticed that there were some pastries and a thermos of coffee on the table. This was certainly more than Caleb had expected. It was obvious that Daniel was highly motivated and intended to do this right.

Caleb started to leaf through the plans, but Daniel admonished him and indicated that he should sit down, have some coffee, and let the presentation begin. Caleb agreed as he grabbed a muffin and some coffee. Caleb was quite full of breakfast but wanted to display his appreciation for Daniel's efforts. He indicated for Daniel to begin.

"I am going to give you an overview of the entire project first. I'll briefly explain the layout and where everything goes, then we can come back and get into the details. Mom and I thought a lot about this and, well, I hope you like it," declared Daniel.

Caleb sipped his coffee and listened. Daniel began by describing a slightly new approach. He had planned for a new master bedroom wing and a guest bedroom wing like what they had talked about before, but the "music room" was no longer shown in the house. Instead, there was an addition between the house and the garage, which would be a large room Caleb could use as a combination office, studio, and music room. This allowed the small interior bedroom to be used as an office for Lori, and the master bedroom could have expanded closet space. The guest wing was like before, containing the bedroom and bath along with a new laundry room off the hall to the bedroom. Everything embraced a large screened-in porch to the rear. Daniel described a totally new layout for the kitchen, which would allow the addition of a small breakfast nook connecting to the front porch.

The barn and garage interior were also shown with all the necessary contents. As Daniel concluded his overview, he laid out copies of the plans on the table and said that it was now time for questions and discussion.

Caleb was quiet as he absorbed everything he had seen. He prefaced his remarks with, "Wow, this is very thorough! I'm not sure where to begin. Uh, tell me more about—"

Daniel interrupted. "Actually, a lot of this was mom's idea, and she should help explain it to you, so before we go on..." Daniel yelled, "Mom!"

Lori sprung out from the hallway and embraced Caleb from behind, surrounding him with her arms and burying her face in the crook of his neck.

"Surprise! You didn't think I would miss out on this did you?" asked Lori.

"Where did you...? How did you get here so fast? I talked to you last night." Caleb stood up and embraced her.

"I've been here since late Tuesday. I flew out while Daniel drove. I've got things to do too, you know," bubbled Lori.

"This is grand!" exclaimed Caleb. "I was getting a little nervous. You seemed sort of quiet and all."

"It's hard to keep a secret. I wanted to be with you and tell you how much I love you, but it had to wait. You had to get your stuff over with, and I had work to do," said Lori.

"You know about all that city stuff?" asked Caleb.

"Sure, well, most of it. You can fill me in whenever. It doesn't matter now. You're done, I'm here, I love you, and we have plans to make!" gushed Lori. "Now let's go over the drawings."

Lori and Caleb sat and faced the plans. Lori squeezed his hand and asked, "What do you think?"

Caleb pushed back from the table and looked at Lori and Daniel. He looked back at the plans, and said, "I don't have to think much about it. You guys worked it out, and I like it. I especially like the music room and studio idea, and that way you get an office too. The kitchen layout is quite unique but very functional. Just one thing: if there is room, could we have a real wood-burning cook stove over here next to the other stove? I used one for a long time and sort of like 'em."

"You know how to cook on a wood stove?" asked Lori. "For that matter, I didn't ever ask you if you even know how to cook. Do you?"

"Reckon you're in for a surprise," said Caleb.

"That could go either way, you know," chided Lori.

"Yep! It could," admitted Caleb. "I'm just so surprised you're here and so pleased, I don't know if I can make any more plans right now."

"Well, you're out of luck in that area. There is more coming."

Lori stood up and circled around behind Caleb. She hugged him from behind again and began, "I've got some more to tell you and to ask you what you think. Daniel, have a seat. Some of this you don't even know."

Coming back around to look at Caleb, Lori continued, "Okay. First thing. You know that veterinary clinic between here and Pea Ridge? The one that I thought looked so nice when we drove out?"

"Uh, yeah. The one on the right coming out?"

"That's the one. Well, I bought it!"

"You what?"

"I bought it, or more accurately, I have an agreement to buy it. On a lark, I contacted the owner and head vet last week. I just wanted to find more out about the vet situation around Rogers. He was very nice, and we talked for quite a while. Turns out, he wants to retire in a couple of years, but he has a good practice and no one coming up. Anyway, we corresponded, did the due diligence thing, and to make a complex story simple, he agreed to sell to me. He must stay at least two years and can stay longer if I agree, but I will own it outright after a one-year trial period. I will have to work here most of the time. What do you think?"

"What about your clinic in Las Vegas?" asked Caleb.

"I think that is worked out too. The others there have put together the necessary funding between themselves and the bank, and they want to go ahead with it. The great thing is that I would only have to work part-time for a few months, after which I could fall back to consulting. They're very experienced and think they can continue without difficulty. It dovetails nicely with my buying the one here. And to top it all off, the sale of the clinic in Las Vegas will more than cover the cost of the one here!"

"Wow! You have been busy!" said Caleb.

"So, what do you think?"

"You know, I just want you. And the you that I want is the one that is doing what she likes. It all sounds rather exceptional. I just can't believe it all fell into place so quickly."

"Good. I thought you would say exactly what you said," admitted Lori. "But there is an argument that all this has fallen into place, not as you say, very quickly, but very slowly! Forty years slow. Now it is finally here!" Lori said as she hugged him again.

Pushing back, Lori said, "Wait, there's more. This afternoon at 1:30, we are having lunch at Sarah's, and…"

"I know. Sarah and I talked about… wait a minute. Now I know what the 'oops' was about. You already talked to Sarah and planned it, didn't you?" asked Caleb.

"Well, not only lunch, but a bunch more. Sarah is picking up Winnie, so she will be there too. Lonnie Rex and Nancy will also join us. We have all afternoon to go over things and include the others in our plans. We'll do that after lunch. Be patient. But right now, let's walk from room to room with the plans and check it all out. Daniel, lead the way," Lori said as she grasped Caleb's arm. "We're burning daylight!"

Caleb shook his head and smiled as he and Lori followed Daniel.

"Oh, what's this about you running for mayor?" asked Lori.

SIXTY-EIGHT

Lunch at Sarah's was every bit the grand affair that she and Lori had planned. The table was set with Sarah's finest, and attention was applied to every detail. Caleb was bewildered trying to figure out how Sarah had gotten all this done without leaving any hint that he could pick up on. There was the "oops" comment, of course, but it simply registered as a part of Sarah's typical word storm. Caleb's surprise at all of this was total. Clearly, Sarah had gone to some length to organize the event.

Sarah had prepared a massive prime rib roast with all the fixings. There were mashed potatoes, green beans, collard greens, cream corn, and a large salad. Lonnie Rex was visibly moved by the spread before him, and Winnie was equally focused on what promised to be another memorable meal from Sarah's hand. As they all gathered at the table, Sarah offered grace:

"Dear Lord, we come before You today to give thanks for all that we experience. We welcome Your blessing on all of us gathered here today. Today is a time of great joy for each of us as a new phase of our lives has begun. Caleb and Lori have returned home to begin a new era in their lives, one where they will share the companionship that has so long been promised. In so doing, they unite all of us in a newly founded family of souls. We all share their happiness and look forward to their union of marriage. Help us to always attend to Your influence upon our lives, and to embrace it completely in everything we say and do. I thank You for this opportunity to provide all the support that I can give, and all of us here join in that very same sentiment. This is everyone's day, for the way in which it points forward to all that is to come as we continue our walk with You. Bless this time and this food for the betterment of our bodies. In the name of Jesus Christ, we pray."

As they all served their plates, there was a quiet and shared expectation of the meal and of the days to come. The conversation turned quickly to one of questions for Caleb and Lori. The details of how it all was going to happen had not been divulged by either. They wanted to know when the wedding was to take place, where it was to be held, who would marry them, how the farm plans were coming along, and much more. Finally, Caleb answered all their questions by simply stating that he and Lori would soon let everyone know their plans. For Caleb, it was Lori's show, and he would be happy to participate in any series of events that led to his union with Lori.

Lori concurred but added, "After this wonderful meal, Caleb and I will discuss a few things and then completely share all that we have planned. You do not have to wait much longer."

Winnie said, "Well, I'm sure that we all wish you the very best and all that, but I, for one, want to find out what's coming relatively soon. In case you haven't noticed, I ain't no spring chicken. I have waited for a long time to see you two together, and now that you have taken my advice, I say let's get it done!"

Caleb looked at Lori and, with a nod from her, said, "Okay, right after lunch, Lori and I will compare notes, exchange a few pleasantries, and let you all know what is about to happen. Now, if we can simply finish this wonderful meal, and everyone can be patient, you will soon know what we know."

"Sounds like some afternoon entertainment!" exclaimed Nancy.

Lonnie Rex added, "Let's not get in too big a rush. Could you pass the green beans please, and maybe a little more prime rib for me, Sarah, with some more of that horseradish aioli please. Oh, and what's for dessert?"

As Sarah fulfilled Lonnie's request, she said, "I thought that we could take our dessert out on the porch. Maybe we can wait, and have it when Caleb and Lori tell us more about their plans."

"And?" asked Lonnie.

"And what?" replied Sarah.

"What's for dessert?" insisted Lonnie.

"Oh, of course. Yes, I have prepared a wicked tiramisu cake. I think that you will like it, Lonnie Rex."

"You bet I will. You're a great cook Sarah. Now I can muddle forth in quiet anticipation," allowed Lonnie.

When all had finished eating, Caleb took Lori's hand and said, "Let's go check on Cisco. What do you say?"

"That could work," she replied.

Everyone moved out to the porch except for Nancy and Sarah, who stayed back to clear the dishes and lay out the dessert. Winnie moved toward her favorite chair while Lonnie assisted her into her seat. Daniel had been quiet during the dinner, and Lonnie asked him, "How did it go at the university?"

"The program looks very interesting. They have a very practical hands-on approach to design by immersing students in actual construction activities. That's what I like the most. It's not just theory or design, it's sort of on-the-job training. There's a program where we get to work on a construction site with participating contractors. It's rather unique. Not many schools have that in their program."

"When do you have to go, Daniel?" asked Winnie.

"In about two months. First, I must take a few tests for placement and then select my living arrangements. Caleb's going to go down with me and show me around. I'm excited."

"Are you still going to be able to work on Caleb's farm project?" asked Lonnie.

"Yes sir, I am. We want to get started right away. Caleb liked what I drew up, and since Mom helped me work it out, she's set to go. I think the thing that Caleb liked the most about the plans was the inclusion of a studio for him. He'll have a separate place for music and an office. He also liked the large screened in porch off the living room. It's big and looks out over the farm," explained Daniel.

"Is there a place for a hammock?" asked Lonnie.

"A hammock?"

"Don't tell me that there isn't a hammock! Don't you know how much Caleb likes a hammock?"

"Uh, no, he didn't mention it."

"You're being tested, son. You gotta find these things out if you want to be successful at design. Gotta have a hammock."

Daniel thought for a minute, then replied, "You know, I think that it is you who wants a hammock. Am I wrong?"

"Nope, you're not wrong. I guess you passed the test. Very perceptive! But do a hammock."

Winnie had nodded off during their exchange. Lonnie looked at her and considered joining her, but since there was no hammock, he decided to persevere. He didn't want to abandon Daniel. The silence that ensued was broken by the distant nickering of Cisco.

"Sounds like they told Cisco about what's going on. That horse will be the first to know everything," observed Lonnie.

"That's another thing. I'm going to ride Cisco lot. I love horses. Caleb said that if I wanted to get one, we could keep it at the farm. He said that Cisco would like a partner."

"Don't we all," mused Lonnie, fighting back sleep. "But be careful about them horses. Do you know the two things that frighten a horse the most?"

"Uh... no, what?"

"Things that move and things that don't!" Lonnie pronounced.

The door opened, and Caleb and Lori came out onto the porch followed by Sarah and Nancy. As they all gathered, Lori held out her hand to display the ring on her finger.

Sarah gasped, "Oh, it fits! It's beautiful!"

"I love it! Caleb told me all about it, and it is just perfect. It's a tiny bit loose, but we will have a jeweler fix that. I couldn't be happier! Thank you, Sarah, for holding on to this for so long. Its history is so important to me, and that makes it very special!"

Caleb was clearly pleased to present his new fiancé, now officially anointed. He motioned everyone to take their chair and said, "We have made our plans and will now share them with you. Lori, would you do the honors?" he asked as he hugged her closely.

Lori began, "There is so much to tell! First, the wedding. Caleb and I are to be married in Sarah's church. We talked to the pastor, and everything is set. He only needs the date. We have decided to be married on August 20. We will have a reception here at Sarah's. She has agreed and is looking forward to it. That gives us about two months to get it organized. It's going to be a casual wedding with as many friends in attendance as we work out. Daniel's sister, Gwen, and her husband will be here, and Caleb might ask some folks from the ranch in La Veta. Otherwise, it's people who live here. Lonnie Rex will stand up with Caleb, and Angela Dawes will stand up with me."

Looking at Lonnie, Lori said, "Lonnie, you will have to dress up some to even meet casual status!" she teased.

"That's fine. I've got two months to shop," allowed Lonnie Rex.

"We will start on the farm renovations as soon as possible. It won't be finished until quite a while after the wedding. While it is under construction, we plan to go on a long trip together. Caleb is going to take me out to the west and show me the places and faces from his history. That is very important to me—to see and touch his past. That might take a while, and when we come back, we will live in the trailer at the farm or maybe with Sarah, if she'll have us," Lori said as she winked at Sarah.

"Oh yes! Of course. This is so great!" exclaimed Sarah.

Caleb took up the story at that point. "Lori has entered into a contract to purchase the veterinary clinic in Pea Ridge. She has worked out a deal to take over from the current owner and allow him to phase out in the next two years. In addition, she has made the arrangements to sell her existing clinic in Las Vegas to the other vets there. She won't have to be there too much—only a few trips back during the first year. She's been very busy in the last couple of weeks, I should say!"

Looking at Daniel, Lori chimed back in, "Daniel will start at the university this fall and will have a new home right here with us. There is talk of him getting a horse so he and Caleb can ride together."

Lori looked over at Winnie. "And Winnie, we owe so much to you. You have kept me in your heart, you have always been there for us, and now you have played a big role in bringing Caleb and me together. Thank you."

"Just get on with it, dearie!" instructed Winnie.

Everyone applauded their satisfaction with the plans.

After the murmurs of joy subsided, Lonnie Rex asked, "Now can we have dessert?"

EPILOGUE

Caleb entered the Methodist Church and stopped to allow his eyes to adjust from the brightness of the spring day. It was Sunday, but he wasn't here for a church service. He had read an obituary in the paper describing how Vernon Bendix had passed away in his sleep at the rest home on the past Wednesday. It was announced that there would be a memorial service here, in the church of his choice, on this very afternoon. Caleb noticed that there were only a few in attendance. He made his way down the center aisle and took a seat in a pew about halfway back.

As Caleb waited for the service to start, he noticed the familiar figure of Dumar Ashton seated toward the front. It was the first time that Caleb had seen him since the events of the last summer. He knew that Dumar had pledged to provide the cost of Vernon's care until his passing but had not considered that he might have become involved in Vernon's life. Caleb wondered just what Dumar's presence signaled. He was curious to find out.

As the organ began to play, the minister rose to the lectern and presided over a very traditional service. The minister described how he had known Vernon for a long time and had visited him on occasion during his declining years. He told of his solitary history, as a member of the congregation, as a truck driver, and then as a respected local in the town. Vernon led a quiet life and attended church on a regular basis until he became too infirm to come to the services. There was no casket, only a picture of Vernon from healthier times. There were no eulogies or other events to distinguish the service, only the solemn atmosphere of such a traditional memorial.

At the conclusion of the service, Caleb waited and watched Dumar. Dumar continued to sit for a few moments before rising and walking up the aisle. When Dumar saw Caleb sitting there, he stopped and placed his hand on Caleb's shoulder. Caleb placed his hand over Dumar's and rose to follow him out of the church.

Back out in the sunshine, both men stepped into the shade of the large portico.

Dumar spoke first. "So, Caleb. How have you been?"

"I've been fine. Long time no see," said Caleb.

"I know that you and Lori got married. That's great. How's married life?"

"Well, in my case, there have been a few adjustments. Going from forty years of bachelorhood to marriage has been fascinating. It reinforces the fact that there is always another perspective on the world."

"Isn't that the truth!" Dumar admitted. "Tell Lori that I regret my words to her at that reunion. Tell her I'm very sorry if you don't mind."

"Oh, long forgotten, Dumar. Think nothing of it. How have you been?"

There was a pause. It was clear Dumar was not there for small talk.

Dumar looked at Caleb and began, "There's things you don't know about me. I want to tell you a little. My dad and I were very close in my younger years. He was a great companion. But he encountered some bad times and became a raging alcoholic. It strained our relationship—no, it destroyed our relationship. It all began when I entered high school. Those were difficult years for me. Then my mother died while I was in college, and my dad was all alone. But I was bitter and didn't attend to him at all in those later years. He died a few years after I graduated. I made no effort to reconcile with him as I held him responsible for the tough times. When he passed, I wasn't there for him. As time went on, and as I recalled all the good times that we had together back when he was sober, it began to haunt me because of the way I had totally neglected him. It was a big feeling of guilt that I pushed way down deep.

"Anyway, when I became obliged to provide for Vernon, at first, I just supplied some money and commitment as was required. I was just waiting for him to die and relieve me of my responsibility. Then, I began to visit him on occasion. He was very bright, you know, and I grew to enjoy our visits. He liked them because of the company, and I started to like them for the opportunity to make up for my neglect of my dad. I know it doesn't make any sense, but that's what happened. I can't say I loved him, but I certainly grew to enjoy the times I spent with him. Also, as time went on, I didn't resent for a minute having to provide for him. That made it real for me. He depended on me, and I came through. It helps me forgive myself for my failure with dad, at least a little, and it just felt good. Something inside stirred, and when I saw you today, I wanted you to know."

"I'm glad you told me, Dumar. And that something inside?"

"Yes?"

"Welcome it in, my friend. It will only grow."

www.ingramcontent.com/pod-product-compliance
Lightning Source LLC
Chambersburg PA
CBHW031932060726
47496CB00015BA/969